A NOBLE SIN

ALSO BY ANDREW BRIDGEMAN

FORTUNATE SON

A NOBLE SIN

AN EMMA NOBLE THRILLER

BY ANDREW BRIDGEMAN

M·P·P
www.MissionPointPress.com

Mission Point Press

Published by Mission Point Press
MissionPointPress.com
PO Box 700028
Plymouth, MI 48170

Cover design by Mark Swan
Book design by Sarah Meiers

ISBN: 978-1-965278-64-2 (hardcover)
ISBN: 978-1-965278-65-9 (softcover)

Library of Congress Control Number: 2025910042

Printed in the United States of America

For Jean and Jim

BOOK ONE

1

Three columns of blinking taillights stuttered up the highway. In the distance, thick plumes of sooty-black smoke billowed into the summer sky. Emma Noble squeezed the brakes and slid her fingers off the steering wheel, making a small prayer for movement. And if it couldn't be the cars ahead of her on I-95, she'd have settled for a breeze—anything to cut the stale, roasting heat inside her rental car with the limping A/C that blew engine-heated wind at six variable settings.

The accident was recent. First responders were just beginning to arrive, sirening down the breakdown lane. Traffic had choked, bumper to bumper—every vehicle hot-glued to the North Carolina asphalt. Emma shifted into park, then mopped her neck with a fistful of Burger King napkins.

Until ten minutes ago, the trip had been okay—even without air conditioning. She'd cruised out of Tallahassee early enough to miss traffic. For nine hours, her fingers slapped time against the wheel, grooving to the soundtrack of *Mamma Mia*. It had been a decent drive through the south—hair flying, elbow frying. But now, Emma was parked on steaming black tar, fanning herself with napkins—waving surrender to the North Carolina highway heat.

In front of her was a boxy pop-up trailer with hand-painted mushrooms dancing across the white fiberglass. The cluster of fungi had personality, waving at her with bulbous noses and goofy grins. She looked left at the dirt-grimed passenger door of a green eighteen-wheeler. Emma tilted the rearview mirror. Behind her was a sun-damaged red

Grand Caravan. In the passenger seat, a preteen girl was sobbing down the front of her blue T-shirt, her chest heaving for air.

Poor kid.

The bearded driver with male pattern baldness kept looking over at the girl, helpless. Either Dad wasn't good at consoling his kid or he'd given up trying. The guy wasn't enjoying his afternoon either, checking his mirrors and rolling his neck like a helpless bobblehead. It took a while before the kid composed herself—wiping down her tears with the heel of her palm. She passed a sippy cup into the backseat. Emma shook her head, realizing there was a toddler back there. Given the choice between drowning in perspiration or sitting in the comfort of a working AC with an infant and a sobbing ten-year-old, she'd choose heat stroke every time.

Tough luck, Dad.

Emma pinched the fabric of her shirt and brought it to her nose. Thanks to the glassy-eyed porter who'd brought the rental car around, the interior reeked of weed. The stench was baked into her clothes— something she would have to explain if she ever got out of this traffic jam and made it to DC. The FBI frowned on their people smelling like Willie Nelson's tour bus—even decorated agents like Emma Noble. She reached for her phone, scrolling through social media notifications. A text popped up from Uncle Gunny, her dad's best friend.

—Hey Squirt. What time is this thing tomorrow?

—Ceremony starts at 2 p.m.

Emma waited for the dots to turn to message.

—Okay Hero. Don't get a big head.

—Too late. It's practically Brobdingnagian.

—?

—One of Dad's words. You're welcome.

—Whatever. You in DC yet?

Emma hung her arm out the window, took a picture of the traffic jam, and pressed "send."

—Big words ain't getting you through that shit, Squirt.

Emma smiled and put the phone back in the cupholder. She was looking forward to seeing Gunny tomorrow. It would be good to catch up with him ... and a few of her Quantico classmates. But she wasn't thrilled about the reason everyone was coming to DC. The FBI was having a ceremony in her honor. Emma would have been happier

2

without the attention. She just wanted to get back home to her under-sized New York City apartment.

It had been an arduous two weeks on the road. Florida had been a bust—the informant a waste of time and resources. It was an expense-heavy trip with nothing to show for it. She decided to forego a costly flight, believing the long solitary drive would be a nice diversion. Now? Not so much.

Emma glanced back into the rearview. The bearded driver's demeanor had changed. He was more agitated now, running his hand through his thin hair. She watched him carefully. Something about the guy seemed off. Emma had a well-honed sixth sense, and for some reason, the guy in the van was making it hum. She focused on the girl in the passenger seat. The kid looked nervous. Maybe scared.

But Emma guessed the hum she was feeling was likely a bore-dom-induced mental mirage—her imagination spinning crimes and criminals. Emma watched the black smoke blooming in the distance. She was overheated. Probably dehydrated.

But that girl—the more Emma watched her, the more she couldn't shake the feeling that something was wrong. The kid leaned into the backseat, then turned to the driver. Whatever she'd said made him angry enough to jam a finger in her face. She flinched and retreated into the door—the waterworks starting up all over again.

Emma reminded herself that it wasn't a crime to be an asshole. Or to be a shitty dad. She'd been on the road for nine hours. She was stuck in traffic under a hot sun. *Chill, Emma.*

Through the side mirror, she caught sight of a state trooper zipping up the breakdown lane. Emma looked back. The beard saw him too. As the cop passed, the guy turned his head—down and away. The hum of her sixth sense became a siren. Emma's internal debate was a short one. She opened the car door and stepped onto the sizzling asphalt. She stretched her arms, then rolled her hips—oiling up her road-weary joints. Emma glanced back at the red Caravan and the miles of cars behind it. She had time. Nobody was going anywhere.

Emma walked in front of her rental car and stepped around the back of the mushroom pop-up toward the passenger door of the tow vehicle. The campers were heading to Lancaster, Pennsylvania. They seemed eager to chat. Emma was polite but shut the conversation down early. She kept a slow, casual pace as she passed her car, walking down the passenger side of the Caravan. Emma kept her head above the window, looking in as she passed. The girl's arm was dotted with red marks. In a day or two, they'd turn black and blue. She'd been grabbed. Forcibly. Emma glanced into the back window. There was a mess of baby clothes strewn around the booster seat. The naked infant was strapped in, his diaper hanging off his ankle. A shitshow.

Adrenaline leaked up Emma's spine. She stepped behind the van. North Carolina plates. She walked up the highway, ignoring the bearded driver, and onto the running board of the green eighteen-wheeler. She knocked on the window.

"You got a pen I can borrow?"

The ponytailed driver nodded and pulled down his visor. He leaned across the cab to hand it over. She scribbled a quick note and handed the Bic back to him.

"You know what's going on?" she asked.

"FedEx truck clipped a flail mower coming out of the breakdown lane. The two cars behind didn't have time to swerve. Big mess up there, and I don't care to see any of it until it's cleaned up. You know what I mean?"

"I do. Thanks."

Emma retraced her steps, revisiting the camper then walking down the kid's side of the Caravan. She put her face in the window next to the whimpering girl and waved. The beard glared, saying something to her under his breath. Emma knocked. And knocked once more before he lowered the window.

"Hey folks! What a mess, right?"

Beard nodded.

"What a day for my AC to die, you know?"

"Okay."

"Where you guys headed?"

"What do you need?" he said, impatiently.

"Some extra-strength deodorant," Emma smiled. "Trust me."

"Wha—?"

"Big wreck up ahead. Going to be a while before they untangle it." Emma lowered her elbow "Youch that's hot!" She rubbed her arm and winked at the girl. "Looks like you're having a tough day."

"She's fine," the guy said.

"So where'd you guys say you were headed again?"

He huffed. "The cold air is running out."

"How old are you, hon?"

"Nine."

"Nine! I would've guessed eleven," Emma said leaning in. She smiled at the driver. "Travel safe. And enjoy that AC, you lucky ducks."

The beard never saw her palm the gum wrapper with the hand-written note in front of the girl's face.

Emma returned to her car and opened the door with the bottom of her shirt. An oven mitt would have been better. She wiped her brow with the napkins then stared through the rearview, waiting to see what the kid would do. The girl seemed nervous, her chest rising and falling. She met Emma's eyes in the mirror.

The kid stole a glance at the driver then shoved a finger up her nose. *Shit.*

Emma ran her hands around her belt, making sure her ASP and cuffs were on her body. Her service weapon was in the glove box. It would stay there—no way she was going anywhere near those kids with a gun. She looked back at the Caravan. The girl had her index finger halfway up her nostril. From the look of it, she had no intention of taking it out any time soon.

Got the message, kid.

Emma's gum-wrapper note was quick and to the point—*I'm police. Pick your nose if you're in trouble.* The girl in the blue shirt was asking for help. She was bruised and frightened. And, if that finger got any farther up her schnoz, she was going to give herself brain damage.

But how much trust could you put in an emotional nine-year-old girl? Emma weighed her options. She wasn't eager to confront the guy. But she also wasn't the kind of cop to ignore a child's invitation. Emma opened her door and walked to the driver's side of the Caravan. She stood behind his window and knocked. The beard flicked his wrist with annoyance. Emma knocked again. Harder this time. He lowered it an inch.

"Get out of here."

"Roll your window down."

His face flushed. He lowered the window and stuck his head out.

"What the fuck do you want?"

With her left hand, Emma raised her FBI badge. Unseen, in her right hand, was her department-issued ASP—a steel baton that telescoped sixteen inches. When wielded by an expert, it packed a painful punch. And Emma Noble *was* an expert.

"I need you to step out of the car, sir."

She figured the guy would react in one of two ways. She was prepared for both. But instead, he did exactly what she asked him to do—violently. He pushed his weight into the door and knocked her backward, almost into the ass end of the eighteen-wheeler. Emma was over six feet tall. The beard was bigger and heavier. And pissed. She recovered her balance and lifted her badge again. "Sir, I need you to calm down. My name is Emma Noble. I'm an agent with the FBI."

"Fuck you. You're one of Theresa's friends, aren't you?"

"I need you down on your knees. Hands behind your head."

He roared something that Emma didn't hear and swung at her. The first punch came from his heels, a wild roundhouse that she easily parried. She jabbed the ASP into his neck and stepped back.

"You don't want to do this, sir."

He swung again—telegraphing the punch. Emma cracked the steel baton over his knuckles. He yelped, but kept coming. She ducked his next swing, wedging the ASP under his arm—locking his forearm in a suppression hold. The guy was a moose, but the combination of Emma's technique and the baton now made it impossible for him to move without breaking his arm.

"Down on the ground!"

Criminals with common sense knew when they were beaten. But criminals with common sense weren't such a common bunch. The idiot kept struggling. His forearm snapped under her baton. She winced and released the hold. It was an indiscretion born of compassion. But it was a mistake.

He charged forward, kicking her in the kneecap. Emma fell to the asphalt. The beard held his broken right arm against his chest while trying to stomp her with big-ass boots. Emma rolled away, spidering into a low, balanced crouch. She swung the steel into his ankle with as much whipping force as she could muster. The baton shattered the bony knob of his lower leg. Without a solid arm to brace his fall, the big tree landed hard—his face crashing into the scorching North Carolina tar.

Emma was on his back in an instant, cuffing his wrists. She was professional enough to ignore the congratulatory car horns erupting around her. In minutes, the guy was shackled in the back seat of a police cruiser.

"AMBER alert didn't go out yet," said the state trooper, handing back Emma's identification. "How'd you—?"

"Got lucky. Who is he?"

"Boyfriend. Apparently, Mom came to her senses and broke up with him. He didn't take it well. The guy's a piece of work—angry asshole. Decided he would hold the kids as leverage till she came back to him."

"Didn't think it through."

"Not sure thinking is his strong suit."

Emma spied the girl sitting on the back of a firetruck. She parted ways with the trooper and walked over.

"Hey, nose picker!"

The kid's face lit up in a toothy grin. Emma crouched to eye level. "You were very brave, you know that?"

"I'm supposed to look after my brother. That's my job."

"Well, you were fantastic. Your mom is on the way—she's going to be very proud of you. Want me to sit and wait till she's here?"

The girl nodded. She reached out, wrapping her small fingers around Emma's. They sat on the bumper, watching as the traffic unclogged. When the girl's mom arrived, the police vehicle didn't come to a complete stop before she jumped out and raced up the road to suffocate her kids in a tearful embrace. It was a satisfying mother-and-children reunion, but Emma wasn't sticking around. She waved goodbye to the girl, then turned, and made her way back to the rental.

Thunder rumbled in the distance. Emma clocked her head at the sound. Dark clouds were amassing in the north. She turned her face into the cooling breeze—welcoming it. But the approaching storm, flexing on the horizon, was far more threatening than Emma Noble understood.

And it was heading straight for everything she'd ever loved.

2

It was too late for night owls and an hour too early for bakers. Rythmic panting drowned out the hum of the hotel air conditioning—bursts of breathy grunts from the naked woman inside Room 210. The lights were off. Only the moon, casting a dim, grayish light illuminated her dark movements. Sweat pooled in the cups of her lower back. She bent her muscled arms, lowering herself again, her face contorted with satisfied fatigue.

It was Emma Noble's fourth set of push-ups. Thirty reps each.

It had been a long while since she'd been slapped awake by a nightmare. It might have been pre-ceremony nerves. Maybe it had to do with the kidnapper on the highway. Hard to tell. The night terrors didn't come often, but when they did, she knew how to deal with them. Five sets of push-ups and a shower. Emma stood, rolling her neck in a circle. She shook the burn from her arms. The moonglow guided her to the bathroom. She flipped the shower dial to its coldest setting and stepped in.

The high school psychologist had been interested in her nightmares. Emma refused to discuss them. Since then, she'd managed to stay clear of shrinks until last year's terrorist attack. The FBI mandated that she attend four sessions. The psychologist recommended more, telling Emma that the emotional scarring of her youth was significant and might be problematic for her long-term mental health. Without dedicated professional help, there was no telling how her pain would manifest. Emma thanked the woman for her concern and moved on. She had no desire to stroll through her memories with a stranger.

She'd earned her nightmares. They were personal—born from family tragedy. Emma was just seven when her older brother succumbed to the complications of the slow-growth cancer rooted in his spine.

She was a teenager when her mother died.

The nightmares began soon after.

Her father taught her what to do with them. Kill the fear by counting to one hundred. Kill the adrenaline with push-ups. Before becoming an academic, Sam Noble had served as an officer in the Marines and as an operative in the CIA. He'd been behind enemy lines. He'd lost friends. No doubt, he had his share of nightmares too.

Emma remembered his big hands on her shoulders after she woke up screaming one night in high school. *Don't hold the fear—let it pass. Outrun it. Outwork it. And when you're calm, find something to be grateful for. Fear is a waste of energy.*

In time, Emma had learned how to compartmentalize it. Box it up. File it away. After all, stoicism was pretty much a Noble family tradition.

She bent her head into the cold spray. What was she grateful for? Being alive for one. If things had gone differently last year, she'd be dead. The terrorist ambushing her in the middle of the night had smashed her face against the hood of a car, shattering her nose. He'd gotten his hand on her gun and almost killed her. Emma had fought like hell, managing to fire three rounds into his chest, dropping him dead in the grass. She'd made mistakes that night, and when it was over, she and her father dissected every second of the attack—breaking the action into small pieces. The only reason Emma was alive? She'd gotten lucky. And luck was a bad strategy.

She stood in front of the bathroom mirror and rubbed a towel over her nakedness. In the past year, she'd rededicated herself with an intensity to improve: an hour a day on the gun range—longer in the gym. She'd transformed her six-foot frame. Her legs were as thick as an Olympic skier's and her upper body was toned—sinewed and muscular. Emma squeezed a drop of white lotion into her palm and rubbed moisturizing circles under her eyes and across her sharp cheekbones. Inside her cosmetic bag was a picture taken last year after graduating from the academy. It captured the girlish, round-cheeked smile she'd inherited from her late mother. Now, after a year of fierce physical dedication, her face was more angular. Like her father's.

Emma waited for sunrise and scrolled through her cellphone,

opening a congratulatory text from the private cell of Kimberly Hancock. The vice president of the United States wished she could attend the ceremony today, but it would draw too much attention. It didn't surprise Emma to get an early morning text from the VP. She didn't seem to sleep much either.

Emma's actions last year had made her an unsung hero. She'd unraveled a plot to assassinate hundreds at the presidential inauguration. While most Americans would never know her name, now she had friends in high places—Kimberly Hancock in particular. Emma had saved her son's life, and as long as that woman had access to the Oval Office, exclusive doors were open to her.

Not that Emma Noble had any intention of walking through them.

• • •

The medal ceremony was held in the main auditorium of the J. Edgar Hoover Building, a room far too big for such an intimate crowd. Every footfall, every cough, echoed through the Bureau's empty cathedral. If the attack had been declassified, the event would have been held in the Rose Garden, officiated by the president of the United States. Emma didn't want that kind of wilting attention. But today wouldn't pass without some pomp. The director of the FBI was presiding. Director Fred O'Toole was a red-haired, freckled elf. His pink face gave the impression that he was in a constant state of aggravation—perpetually bubbling on a low boil. This morning, he appeared less annoyed, giving a highly redacted accounting of Emma Noble's actions the year before.

"They write books about the FBI. Movies. I'm told there's even action figures. For generations, the public has put their faith in us. They have put trust in our integrity. We must never forget how easy that trust can be lost. Emma Noble embodies everything the FBI stands for ..."

She stood next to him, her legs shoulder-width apart, her arms behind her back. But Emma was not feeling at ease. At least Director O'Toole wasn't long-winded. He wasn't the kind of guy that liked to hear himself talk. It would be over soon. Tomorrow, Emma would take the train to New York City and step back into the shadows—where she felt most at home.

She looked at her classmates from Quantico sitting shoulder to shoulder in the second row. Each of them wore a round pin on their lapel—the Chicago Cubs logo. Emma was a die-hard St. Louis Cardinals baseball fan. She stared at Roshelle Hess, knowing she was the instigator. They'd been roommates at Quantico—laughing, fighting and challenging each other through the pressure cooker that was the FBI Academy. Emma and Roshelle were the only two women to graduate from that class, and they were tight. Roshelle Hess smirked, adjusting the Cubs pin. From the stage, Emma casually swiped her eyebrow with her middle finger.

Uncle Gunny was in an aisle seat, back-straight and stiff. He was short, a former Marine with the biggest ears God ever slapped on a small head. But he didn't carry himself like a diminutive man—he walked chin high, embracing the cockiness of the self-made millionaire he'd become. He hadn't strayed far from his combative roots, building a security company from the ground up—wading deeper into the secretive, murky waters of spec ops and reconnaissance.

Emma flashed him a quick smile. He didn't return it—just squinted at her, as if desert sand were still swirling in his eyes. His lack of response didn't surprise her. As a kid, she'd wasted a lot of hours trying to get him to crack a smile. Gunny explained that he laughed on the inside. Emma was one of the few who understood that behind the bravado was a heart softer than pudding.

Retired Master Gunnery Sargeant Thomas Barnett was her dad's best friend. They'd served together in rough country. Suffered together. For decades, they were the tip of the spear, sent to dangerous places that required the best operators America had at its disposal. Uncle Gunny wasn't a blood relative, but he was family. And for Emma, after the death of her mother and brother, Gunny and her father, Sam Noble, were the only family she had.

Emma glanced at the bouquet of white tulips at the side of the stage. They were from her father. No text or call telling her he wasn't coming. Just the flowers.

Congrats, Emmaline.

It was a very Sam Noble kind of message. Like most of her father's communications, it required Emma to fill in the blanks—imagining the words a more emotionally available man would use. She'd spent most of her childhood filling in the empty space with the love he had trouble communicating. But she knew it was there. And that had always been enough.

Unlike Gunny, her father had made a clean break from his old life, trading desert camo for herringbone sports coats with elbow patches. Sam, an adjunct political science professor at St. Louis University, was teaching the summer session. Emma doubted it was his rigorous teaching schedule that kept him from attending. Her father hated ceremonies like this. He hadn't served to win medals or pats on the back, and he didn't think anyone else should. Award ceremonies weren't in his belief system and he wasn't the kind of guy to sit in someone else's church—even if the honoree was his daughter.

But he'd sent flowers. *Thanks, Dad.*

There was a smattering of applause. Director O'Toole swept his arm toward the podium, motioning Emma forward. Her throat went dry. It always did before public speaking. She popped a lozenge and looked down at the 3×5 cards in her hand.

Her remarks were brief. It was an easy crowd. She was done in under four minutes. Emma offered a half-smile and a nod to the applause and got the hell off the stage.

Roshelle Hess marched through the reception traffic toward Emma. She grabbed a deviled egg from a silver tray held by a food service employee. "Thanks," she said before turning her attention to Emma. "You ghosted me last night."

"Not my plan. Got caught in traffic."

"Hmm," Roshelle said, popping the hors d'oeuvre into her mouth, taking her time chewing as she looked Emma up and down. "How's it feel to be a hero?"

"How'd it feel being the only girl at the sausage fest last night? Did the boys behave themselves?"

"If you're asking if they've matured in the past year, the answer's no. And, to make matters worse, I got cornered by Jugs. The guy never shuts up. If you were there, you could have saved me."

Emma rolled her eyes. Her old roommate didn't need anyone to save her. She was a former point guard at Harvard. She joined the Bureau after a stint in the navy. Roshelle claimed to be the best profiler in the Bureau, and even though she meant it as a joke, Emma guessed she probably was.

Roshelle leaned in, lowering her voice. "Seriously, it was all fuckin' night. Jugs *never* stops talking. On and on. Jesus."

"*All* night?"

Roshelle's eyes were twinkling. "Don't judge, Noble."

Emma felt a hand on her elbow. It was Uncle Gunny, pulling her toward the door. When he got her away from the small crowd, he reached up and rubbed the ribbon around Emma's neck with his thumb and forefinger.

"So, what are you gonna do now, Squirt?"

"What do you mean what am I gonna do now? Go back to the city."

He slid his fingers down the fabric to the star shaped medal. He lifted it off her chest, getting the weight of it. "I don't know—time seems right to jump ship. What else can you do for the Bureau? Face it, Squirt, private sector's where the dough is." He released the medal. "I know a security firm in DC that might be interested in hiring you. I hear the CEO's not only brilliant, but very charming." He raised his eyebrows.

"Sorry Gunny. Not happening."

"Do me a favor. Think about it. My lawyers are grinding on me for a succession plan. I'll teach you what you need to know. You'd be good at it, Squirt. And you'll make boatloads. I promise."

"I like my job. Find someone else."

He shook his head. "I'll talk to Sam. He'll advise you that it's the right thing to do—"

"As I recall, he wouldn't work for you either."

Gunny huffed. "Where is he, anyway?"

"Making a point."

"Which is?"

"Medals are for posers."

"Sounds like Sam. Think about what I said. The door is open. You just gotta step through." The ex-Marine stood on his toes and gave Emma a kiss on the cheek. "I'm proud of you, Squirt. And … so is your dad."

• • •

Emma was too hungover for breakfast. She headed to the gym instead, intent on sweating out the two (three?) pitchers of skinny margaritas she and Roshelle had consumed on K Street the night before. But it was more than the headache that made her grumpy. For the second night in a row, a nightmare had ripped her from sleep.

The gym was busy and loud, clanging barbells and grunts echoing off the mirrored walls. Emma stepped on the treadmill and exhaled, concentrating on shortening her strides, fighting her natural long-legged loping form that made her a cross-country standout in high school. She increased the speed and upped the incline, planting quick, powerful strides that fell silently against the machine's rubber conveyor. She paid attention to her breathing: a shallow inhalation through her nose—a soft exhalation from her lips. Again, she increased the incline. By degrees she fell into a mental trance, her thoughts drifting beyond the Hoover Building's gym and her train schedule, pulling her back to the memory of another long run when she was fourteen. It was an unwelcome recollection. And it was vivid—running out of the Emergency Waiting Room at St. Mary's Hospital. Running away from the antiseptic smell and the bad-news doctor.

Emma increased the treadmill speed, reeling in the memory of that night—dashing full speed through the parking lot and up the bottle-littered embankment. Remembering how she hurdled the silver guardrail to race along the white line of Interstate 81. She recalled every detail: the sound her sneakers made against the asphalt, how the wind parted the bangs on her forehead, how her tears dried against her cheeks.

The state police found her on the road, somewhere between Mount Rock and Walnut Bottom—eight miles from the hospital. The next morning, Emma woke in her own bed with Sam Noble looking down at her, making her a promise:

"It's going to be okay, Emmaline. I got you."

The treadmill slowed. Forty-five minutes had elapsed in a blink. Emma inhaled, shaking off the memory. It had been a long time since she'd thought about that night. Why now? And what was with the nightmares? Slowly, the realization washed over her. Today's date. Her subconscious was, apparently, intent on reminding her that the anniversary of her mother's death was near. *Message received—you can stop now.*

The console beeped. It scrolled through her stats: calories burned, average speed. The numbers didn't matter to her. She wiped a towel across her face and neck, dabbed under her ponytail, and glanced at the gym clock. She was cutting it a little close to catch the train back to New York. She caught Roshelle smiling at her in the mirror's reflection.

"What?" Emma said, taking out her earbuds.

"Seriously? You didn't even notice, did you?"

"What are you talking about?"

"The snack running next to you? You didn't see him? He tried three times to talk to you. You ignored him—then kicked the treadmill up to Mach 5. The poor bastard tried keeping up for twenty minutes. I think he's throwing up in the locker room. You gotta get in the game, Noble."

"I don't slow down for *snacks*, Hess. I have standar—"

Emma cut her comments short noticing that the gym chatter had ceased. Roshelle noticed too. Emma followed her eyes. Associate Deputy Director William Monroe was in the doorway, standing stiff, his arms folded across his dark Brooks Brothers' suit—a perfect Windsor knot tucked under his prominent Adam's apple. He was staring at Emma.

"He doesn't look happy," Roshelle whispered.

"No. He doesn't."

Monroe curled his index finger, summoning Emma to join him in the hallway.

"Tough luck, Noble. Better you than me."

Not everyone in the FBI was enamored with Special Agent Emma Noble. As a consequence of her work flushing out a terrorist network last year, William Monroe had a lot to answer for. Investigators from three separate departments had sniffed through his life, making sure he was clean. After a six-month probe they concluded that William Monroe was not a terrorist, but his close association with a known traitor meant his career with the Bureau was coming to a close. In two months, he would move into a newly vacated leadership position in the Bureau of Land Management.

"Good morning, sir."

Monroe nodded grimly, "We need to talk."

Emma looked down at Monroe, trying to decipher the look on his face. He was being terminated because of her—that was enough to make her wary.

"What can I do for you?"

"Not here. We'll speak in my office."

Emma didn't glance at her watch—she didn't need to. She knew there wasn't time for chatting. Her train left in an hour and a half. She needed to be on it. And something in Monroe's eyes told her that he knew it too.

"First, I want you to go to the fourth floor. They're waiting for you."

"Fourth floor?"

"I need you to take a polygraph."

"A polygraph?"

"Don't give me that look, Agent Noble. Get up to four. Then come see me."

"Can I ask what this is about?"

"No." Monroe raised his eyebrows with a hint of smugness, "All I can say is, when I tell you, I don't think you're going to like it."

3

Emma was invited to sit in a metal chair in a small, windowless room with a large mirror on the back wall. It was an interrogation room—not a real interrogation room, but a mock room designed for training agents. However, the two-way mirror was real, and she suspected Monroe was sitting on the other side. She tapped her shoe against the floor, waiting for someone to come in and administer the test. This wasn't her first polygraph. She'd taken a few in the interview process, and one more last year. The FBI was enamored with the polygraph, and the men and women that interpreted the results wielded low-key power in the Bureau. Emma wasn't a fan. She also didn't like to be kept waiting when she had a train to catch. Her mood was beginning to curdle.

They were letting her stew. The FBI never rushed a polygraph. The innocent would find the delay annoying—the ones with something to hide would find it nearly impossible to control their anxiety. But this was neither one of these things. It was Monroe's goodbye present to her. A passive-aggressive stunt—putting her through a little administrative bullshit before he left the Bureau, hoping to drop her ego a peg or two.

Two agents came in without making eye contact. Men's Wearhouse must have had a sale. Same suit, different color ties—one red, one blue.

"Hey guys," she said. "I don't want to be a pain in the ass, but I've got a train to New York—anything I can do to help speed this along?"

They shook their heads in unison. Red Tie put a device on the table then backed into a corner of the room. Apparently, his job was to stare at her. Emma inhaled and accepted the clipboard from the other guy. She hovered the ballpoint pen over the paper as she read the boilerplate form, agreeing that she was taking the polygraph without force or coercion. The next paragraph had the teeth: the consequences of an agent lying on an FBI polygraph, which included, among other things, termination and potentially prison. Emma raised her eyes from the paper to the two-way mirror and signed.

Okay, Monroe. I'll play along.

Blue Tie strapped a thin belt across her stomach and another over her chest. He attached a black cuff over her bicep, and placed her finger into a wired harness. The three probes would monitor her respiration, blood pressure, and skin sensitivity. The guy wasn't in a rush to plug her in. When he finally sat in the chair beside her, he pulled a handkerchief from his back pocket and blew his nose—a longer than necessary process that concluded with some excessive nostril rubbing.

What was Monroe up to? Was he trying to trip her up on a polygraph? Catch her in a lie? It didn't make sense. Monroe knew that after last year's heroics, Emma had a full deck of Get-Out-Of-Jail-Free cards. Emma raised her chin toward the smoky mirror and smiled.

Blue Tie didn't look up when he asked her if she was ready to begin. Emma nodded.

"An auditory answer is required."

"You bet. Let's get rolling."

"State your name."

"Emmaline Barnett Noble."

"Please describe the weather when you came into the building this morning."

"Cloudy. Humid."

"Ten minus eight?"

"Math? You guys are making us do math now?" She glanced over at his humorless face. "Sorry. Two."

"Where were you born?"

"Hospital in California."

"Specifically?"

"Camp Pendleton Naval Hospital."

Blue Tie looked over at the guy in the corner. The real questions were coming now.

"Agent Noble, in the past twelve months have you conspired against the United States?"

Emma lifted her eyes toward the mirror. *Really, Monroe?*

"Of course not."

"In the past twelve months have you committed a crime?"

"A crime? Um, yeah. Quite a few actually."

The agent cocked his head. "Your answer is 'yes?' You've committed a crime in the past year?"

"Yup."

"Could you explain the nature of your criminality."

"No."

Emma watched the agents exchange looks.

"The admission of criminality will open an investigation into your conduct. You are aware of that?"

"No offense, guys, but my actions are still classified. If you need more detail, I suggest you interview the Director of the FBI—or the vice president of the United States. I'm not allowed to discuss it."

Red Tie coughed into his fist, a hint to move on.

"In the past six months, have you aided or abetted a criminal or a person suspected of criminal activity?"

"No."

"In the past six months, have you harbored a criminal or a person suspected of criminal activity?"

"No."

"Are you *currently* associating or aiding anyone that has committed a crime or suspected of criminal activity."

Emma sighed. "No. Come on guys. Seriously."

The questioner looked over at the agent in the corner who nodded back, and walked out of the room.

"Thank you for your time," said Blue Tie, untethering Emma from the polygraph.

"Sure thing."

"Please remain seated. Someone will be along shortly to see you out."

The door closed. Emma got out of her chair and walked over to the two-way mirror.

Enjoy the show, Monroe?

She looked at the clock in the room. They made her wait ten needless minutes before letting her out. Emma didn't take the elevator. Instead, she sprinted up three flights to Monroe's office. There was still an outside chance of catching her train if she could get out of his office in less than twelve minutes.

The assistant director stood behind his desk, his back to her, looking out the window with a cellphone pressed to his ear. He made a half turn and pointed her into a chair, then resumed his conversation. Emma slumped into the seat, looking at her watch.

Monroe kept a tidy office. Not a paper out of place. Not a picture out of level. A photograph of the president of the United States took top billing. Director O'Toole's official portrait was below it. There were precious few personal items. No wife. No kids. Emma almost felt sorry for the guy. Monroe had gotten himself within a hair's breadth of the FBI's top job. In the end, the political savvy that helped him rise up the ranks was offset by his penchant for shitting down the organizational chart. It had already been catching up to him before Emma's investigation revealed that Monroe's buddy was a very bad man. That had been the final straw.

Hello, Bureau of Land Management.

Emma bounced her knee up and down. Monroe was taking his time with the call. She listened to his half of the conversation—thirteen minutes of "uh-huhs" and a couple of "no's." Finally, Monroe said, "Whatever. Just get it done. I've got someone in my office."

Emma looked at her watch for the last time. She'd missed it.

Monroe lowered himself into his black executive chair. "Thank you for your patience, Agent Noble," he said with a smile. He looked down at his timepiece and made a face. "The day is flying by, isn't it? Sorry the polygraph took so long. How'd it go?"

She bit her lip, refusing to take the bait. "I'm confused about what's going on, sir."

William Monroe rubbed his hands together then laid them on the table, thumbs tapping against each other. "Your father wasn't at your medal ceremony yesterday, was he?"

Emma shrugged, smiling through her aggravation. "Guess he was busy. Why the polygraph?"

"If you were wondering, you passed."

"I wasn't."

"That's what everyone loves about you, Agent Noble. You're unflappable. Good for you." Monroe pressed a button on the console on his desk and leaned in. "Are they all seated?"

"*Yes, sir.*"

"Come with me."

Emma didn't move.

"It's not a suggestion, Special Agent."

Monroe opened the door to the director's private conference room. There was only one unoccupied seat at the table. Five men and three women. Emma looked around the room, trying to gauge the weather. No eye contact. No welcoming smiles. She looked back at Monroe, trying to figure out what he was up to. His face gave nothing away.

It had been a year since Emma was last in this room. She'd agonized for over an hour here, waiting to see if Director O'Toole would fire her for inadvertently helping a terrorist escape capture. He didn't. O'Toole let her off with a warning—it had something to do with her father. Some unspoken history between the director and Sam Noble.

Monroe walked past Emma to the unoccupied brown roller chair at the middle of the conference table and held the back of it, inviting her to sit.

"You know everyone, Agent Noble?"

She'd never seen any of them before, but based on age alone, she guessed it was a meeting of senior chiefs. "I don't believe so." She looked around the table. "I'm Special Agent Emma No—"

"They know who you are," said Monroe, walking away from the table to a chair in the back of the room. "Introduce yourselves, please."

The men and woman gave her nothing more than their name and section. They offered zero personal information and barely made eye contact. Emma had a better-than-average ability to read a room, and, looking around, she detected no warm fuzzies. Monroe raised his eyebrows and pursed his lips. He was smug as hell. Enjoying the moment.

"Can I ask what this meeting is—"

"The answer will unfold organically. Frank, can you *briefly* summarize the case?"

"Frank Byum, Chief, Cyber Division," the bald man said as a reminder to Emma as he picked up the red folder in front of him and stood behind his chair.

Emma straightened, glancing around the table at the grim faces. Byum smoothed his tie and gave her the kind of apologetic look people save for wakes and funerals. It was brief, but long enough for Emma to get an uneasy feeling in her gut.

Frank Byum picked the remote off the end of the table and coughed into his fist before speaking. The men and women around the table weren't watching him. All eyes were on Emma Noble. They already knew what Byum was going to say. The dog-and-pony show was strictly for her benefit. They were watching to see how Emma would react.

"For the past fourteen months, Cyber and CID have been collaborating on a joint operation: pursuing cryptocurrency theft with a special focus on ransomware payments. We've traced much of the activity to cartels and criminal organizations—it's an easy and profitable source of revenue for them. They're building out their infrastructure, recruiting hackers and others with exceptional computing skills. We think some have gone willingly. Most have not."

"Where are they operating from?" Emma asked, leaning forward.

"Wherever they want. They're difficult to track. We've developed a method to—"

Monroe grumbled, "Move it along, Frank."

Byum nodded. Emma suspected he had no more love for Monroe than she did.

"Six months ago, we caught a break, infiltrating a dark-web chat room that appeared to be a loose confederation of crypto pirates, or 'skimmers,' as they call themselves. We were monitoring the room."

Emma hoped her confusion wasn't apparent to the department chiefs staring at her. She didn't know anything about cryptocurrency or the dark web. Her specialty was criminal investigation. This case wasn't remotely in her wheelhouse.

"A month or two later, the chatter in the room changed. Something spooked them—we thought they might be onto us, but it was something else. They were being targeted. And they were scared."

The bald agent pointed the remote toward the screen at the front of the room. It brightened, displaying a photograph of a woman with a nose ring a few years older than Emma—early thirties.

"This is Maria Peterson. A software engineer. A few months ago, she was found dead in her Chula Vista apartment. Murdered." Agent Byum clicked the remote, showing a picture of the crime scene. "Shot three times. Twice in the chest. Once in the head." He clicked to a photograph of another woman with spikey red hair. "This is her roommate, Lilith Hart, a respected coder that, we believe, had a side-hustle as a criminal hacker. She's missing. Evidence suggests the killer took her."

"Can you go back to the murder scene, please?" said Emma.

She focused on the picture of Maria Peterson slumped in her chair. The two entrance wounds in the chest were large—probably a high-caliber pistol. The proximity of the holes told her the killer hadn't fired wildly. She leaned forward, noticing the gunpowder stippling on the woman's nose and cheek. The last bullet, the headshot, was fired at close range. The murderer had stepped closer and fired the final shot into her face. Whoever did this was a stone cold killer, and likely, a professional.

"Thank you."

Byum clicked ahead to the image of a well-tanned, twenty-something blond man in a Speedo, standing on a catamaran—a beer and a cigar in his hand.

"A few days after Ms. Peterson's murder, this man showed up in the Boston office. His name is Bryce Colliers. Calls himself Windjammer. He came in scared, telling us he thought someone was coming after him. We had two agents bring him down for an interview, but in the short walk down the hall he got cold feet. Decided he didn't want to speak to the FBI, after all. He was nervous. Evasive. Our agents followed up with Mr. Colliers at his home. Apparently, he was right—someone *was* coming after him. The houseboat where he lived was ransacked. His dog was shot. There's been no sign of Colliers since."

"What's the connection?"

"Like Ms. Hart, he was a coder. A little digging reveals they both attended the same hackers conference. Both won contests when they were there."

Monroe crossed his arms and cleared his throat.

"There have been others. I won't go into detail, but someone is taking skimmers." He pointed the remote at the screen. The polished image of an executive with salt and pepper hair appeared on the screen. "This is Ted Mortinson, a banker in upstate Ohio. He's been on our radar. We suspected he might be setting up phony business accounts—possibly laundering crypto through them. We didn't have enough to make anything stick, but one of our investigators noticed his online footprint was similar to those of Ms. Hart and Mr. Colliers. We wanted to get a closer look. Yesterday, we got permission to execute a search warrant and bring him in for questioning. This morning, when our team arrived at his house, an ambulance was in the drive. Mr. Mortinson was dead. Murdered in his study."

Byum clicked the remote, bringing up a photograph from the scene: the banker sprawled across his carpeted office. Two gunshot wounds to the chest. One in the forehead.

"Thank you, Frank," Monroe said, walking to the front of the room and taking the remote out of Byum's hands. "I'll take it from here. Agent Noble, what do you see? First impression."

Emma shrugged. "Without a ballistics report to confirm, it's only a guess … but by the look of it, the murderers were similar. Whoever did it is a pro." She looked at Monroe. "So, no witnesses to the killings or the kidnappings?"

"The murderer did a good job covering his tracks—until this morning. He had a little bad luck at Mortinson's home in Ohio. He literally ran into the cleaning woman on his way out the door. Fortunately for her, he kept running and didn't shoot her in the head."

"We get a description?"

"An excellent description. The woman's name is Margaret Banich. She's been very helpful, not only describing the man she saw, but recalling the out-of-state license plate on the killer's black truck."

"Let me guess … stolen vehicle."

"Wrong. Not stolen. Banich's description is a match for the owner."

"Then we got him," said Emma, wondering why it was necessary for her to be in this meeting. "Who is he?"

Monroe lifted his chin, staring at Emma while he clicked his index finger down on the remote. Filling the screen was the driver's license of a man in his mid-fifties—strong, angular cheekbones and a dimpled chin. Emma blinked at the familiar face.

Monroe laid his palms on the conference table.

"Where is Sam Noble? Where is your father?"

4

Emma stared at the photograph of her dad. She could feel the heat moving up her neck and into her cheeks.

"I asked you a direct question, Agent Noble. Where is your father? When were you last in contact with him?"

Emma focused on the screen, her heartbeats picking up pace.

"Agent Noble?" Monroe said impatiently.

Emma ignored him. She inhaled and looked around the table at the senior staff. "This is a joke, right?" The stone faces stared back at her. She clenched her fist, on the precipice of launching into a career-limiting tirade. Frank Byum spoke first.

"Agent Noble?" he said softly. "Take a breath. We don't have enough evidence to accuse him of anything. At this point, Sam Noble is a person of interest."

Emma nodded. She counted to ten before responding. "So," she inhaled deeply, "obviously, you've got the wrong guy. You're jumping to the wrong conclusion—a mistake has been made." She put her thumb in the air. "Sam Noble is a college professor." She raised her index finger. "Former Major in the Marine Special Forces." The next finger went up. "Bronze Star." And another. "Purple Heart. You want me to keep going?"

Monroe walked to the front and pointed at the photograph at the screen. "Agent Noble doesn't need to tell us who her father is. You've all studied his file and are fully aware of what he is capable of—and what he was trained to do."

"Really? Come on," Emma said to the room. "You've got the

wrong person. You're investigating a crypto-piracy ring—high-tech thieves with next-level computing skills. My father teaches political science and uses a flip phone. He's not your guy."

Monroe shrugged. "Fine. Give him a call. We'd like to hear what he has to say for himself."

"This is ridiculous," Emma said, pulling out her cellphone and dialing her father's number. The rings went unanswered. She waited for the sound of his gruff voice. Instead, a cellular recording told her "the number you've dialed is no longer in service." Emma glanced over at Byum and redialed. Same message.

"Sam Noble took the chip out of his phone yesterday," Monroe said. "Your father's on the run."

"My father doesn't run from anything."

"A man matching Sam Noble's description was identified *running* from the murder scene into a truck registered in his own name. He isn't using credit cards. He disabled his cellphone. Clearly, your father is on the run."

Emma exhaled slowly through her nose, dismissing the urge to jump over the table at Monroe. Byum was right. Losing her cool wasn't going to help. The cleaning woman made a mistake. She'd simply gotten it wrong and Monroe had jumped on the opportunity to give Emma some payback before packing up his office.

But the chiefs around the table had hundreds of agents at their disposal, maybe thousands. If *they* believed Sam Noble was guilty, they would be relentless. And even though an investigation would exonerate her father, they would destroy his reputation. When the FBI got it wrong, they ruined lives.

The metal latch on the conference room door popped. Director Fred O'Toole walked in. Emma glanced over at Monroe. He didn't look pleased to give up command. O'Toole looked at the photograph of Sam Noble on the screen. He stepped closer, studying it for a moment, then looked at Emma.

"You okay?"

"No." She glared at Monroe. "Not really."

The director nodded. "Bill? Can I have a word outside, please?"

O'Toole held the door open for Monroe. The leader of the FBI returned a few minutes later. Alone. He sat at the head of the conference table, his fingers laced together.

"So, how are we doing this?" he said to no one in particular.

The room looked at Emma, sending him their unspoken reply. The director nodded.

"Agent Noble, first, let me assure you this situation does nothing to tarnish your reputation with the Bureau. I meant everything I said yesterday. But … we need you to sit tight. Our team will get this thing sorted. Go back to New York. We'll keep you in the loop."

Emma's face flushed red. "I'm sorry, what?"

"I understand, you're upset, but—"

"With all due respect, sir, I'm not going to sit around while the FBI executes a manhunt on my father. If you need my badge, I'll hand it over, but when I leave this room, *I'm* going to find my dad. I *will* find Sam Noble. And then … I *will* bring him here," she said, pointing around the table, "so everyone here can apologize to him. In the meantime, I'll keep *you* in the loop." Emma hesitated. "Sir."

"Nobody wants your badge, Agent Noble," the director said softly, getting out of his chair and looking out the window to stare down on the Pennsylvania Avenue traffic. It took time for him to get through his decision tree. He pinched his nose, then turned to Emma.

"*You* want to find your father. *We* want to find your father. Here's how this is going to happen—and it's non-negotiable. First, I'm gluing an agent to you. They will be privy to every call you make—every text. You can choose your partner, but—"

"Roshelle Hess, sir."

"Let me finish. I will hold you both responsible. If you forget who you're working for—if you assist or abet Sam Noble in any way, I'll not only terminate you, I'll put you *both* in prison."

O'Toole raised his eyebrows. Emma nodded.

"Second, Sam Noble, is, at present, a person of interest. If at any point, the Bureau seeks his arrest, you are *immediately* off this case. No questions asked. Are we clear, Agent Noble?"

"Crystal, sir."

"Does anyone have a problem with this course of action? Frank?"

"No, sir."

O'Toole looked at Emma and shot his thumb at the door. "Okay. Get out of here. Go find your father."

5

Emma had time on her hands while Roshelle Hess was debriefed in Chief Byum's office. A cocktail of anger and anxiety fueled her as she moved through the J. Edgar Hoover Building. She jogged up stairwells and power walked the halls, her thoughts ricocheting like pinballs. She scarcely noticed an agent on the sixth floor smiling and saying "hello" as he passed. She sifted through her memory … when was the last time she'd spoken to her father? Two? Three weeks ago? Try as she might, she couldn't recall the conversation. Emma rounded a corner, barely missing a staffer. She was sure there hadn't been anything unusual about the call. Certainly nothing concerning. It had been a quick check-in. Neither Emma nor her father were verbose—their communication tended to run on thin fuel that sputtered out before getting too far down the conversational highway.

She was mad at herself for not asking more questions. For not being more curious. But nothing much seemed to be happening in her father's life. His days were spent lecturing. At night, he graded papers in front of the TV. Like most guys his age, he'd waded into still waters. He could be a helpful reference, a source of fatherly wisdom when she needed it, but his life was boring—steady, balanced, and unchanging.

Or that's what he'd led her to believe.

She sat down in the stairwell and pulled out her phone. It didn't take long to find the number for the Political Science Department at St. Louis University. Five rings. No answer. She looked at her watch—it was lunchtime in the Midwest. She left a message, then tried her father again. *No longer in service.*

She stood up and jogged down the stairwell, her hands never touching the metal rails. Two people kidnapped. Two more murdered. According to the cleaning woman, Sam Noble was at the scene of Mortinson's killing. In Ohio. Her father lived in St. Louis. Pretty damn unlikely that it was him. But there was no accounting for why his phone was off. That damned flip phone was Sam Noble's lifeline to Emma, and whenever she'd needed him, he was always on call. Last year, when all had seemed lost, her father and Gunny had answered her SOS. Without their help, the mission would have failed. Why would he go silent now?

The senior brass in the conference room believed Sam Noble was a killer. And they were right. But her father had retired from that line of work. More importantly, Mortinson hadn't been killed. He'd been murdered. There was a difference. Sam Noble lived by a code: he was a man that wouldn't hesitate to use lethal force in the defense of his family or his country. But murder? That was cowardly. And her father wasn't a coward. There was no world in which her dad, a political science professor, could have murdered Mortinson or kidnapped anyone.

If only he'd come to the medal ceremony. ...

Emma stopped halfway down the stairs. *The flowers.* He might not have been at the ceremony, but he'd sent flowers. Sam Noble hadn't walked into the Hoover Building to deliver them, but someone had. Someone took his order and his money. Emma beelined to the security suite on the second floor and sat next to a cop staring at a wall of monitors.

"I'm sorry, what are you asking?"

"Flower delivery. Yesterday morning. I need the name of the florist."

"Is this personal? Because I'm not—"

Emma pointed at the screen. "Probably delivered before 8 a.m."

It didn't take long for him to find the video of a woman walking through reception with a white bouquet and then leaving.

"Street view?" Emma asked, leaning closer as the recording showed her stepping toward a blue van idling across the street. "Zoom in, please."

Bloomtown: Alexandria's Premier Florist.

"Okay. Thanks. That's what I needed."

Emma's phone chirped. It was Roshelle Hess, finished with Byum's debrief.

"Where the hell are you, Noble?"

"Coming to you."

Emma hustled out of security, meeting Roshelle in the hallway outside Byum's office. The look on her face told Emma she hadn't enjoyed her visit. Neither spoke until they were out of sight of his office door.

"Jesus," Roshelle said, walking into the elevator.

"You know it's bullshit, right? No way in hell he did it."

"How you holding up?"

"Better now."

Roshelle pressed the button for the ground floor.

"What'd Byum say?" asked Emma.

"He told me about the kidnappings and the murder of Ted Mortinson. Also asked a lot of questions about you and me."

She tilted her head at Roshelle.

"He wanted to know why you volunteered me."

"What did you tell him?"

"I lied. Said we were friends."

They walked out of the Hoover Building, a pressing blanket of early afternoon humidity greeting them. Emma pointed to a bench where they could talk.

"What else?"

"He told me my assignment was to profile and track my friend's father who is suspected of murdering an Ohio man. Then, I think, he threatened me with prison. Not sure. Wasn't really paying attention."

"Hey, if everything goes to shit, we'll be roommates again. Like old times."

"Hating your sense of humor right now, Noble."

"In less than 24 hours we'll have it sorted. What'd they tell you about him?"

"Byum let me read the file on him. For an academic, your dad's a badass, huh?"

"What'd it say?"

"It was redacted as hell, but there were some interesting bits."

Emma looked at Roshelle. It wasn't always easy to decipher what was on her mind. She was an FBI profiler—a trained psychologist—and as much as she tried not to show it, Emma knew she was always watching and listening, shifting puzzle pieces around until she understood a person's mental jigsaw.

"Any idea where he might be?"

"No."

"Any plausible reason he would have for taking the chip out of his phone?"

Emma frowned. "No, but disabling his phone doesn't mean he murdered anyone. Does it?"

The question landed with more force than she'd intended.

"Hey, I'm on Team Noble. You know that, right?"

Emma exhaled. "Yup. Sorry."

"Byum wouldn't say it outright. But ... the brass believes Sam Noble killed Mortinson. I'm guessing that, if you weren't the FBI's prized pony, they'd have already sent his picture to every news outlet in the Midwest. I'm betting they give us a few days. Not much more."

"We won't need a few days."

Roshelle nodded. "Okay. What now?"

"Sam sent flowers to the ceremony yesterday."

"And?"

"Was just waiting on you, partner."

Emma pulled out her phone and dialed the flower shop. She paced in front of the park bench, questioning a woman in accounting at Bloomtown Florist. Emma put the phone in her pocket and looked up at the hazy sky, putting the pieces together.

"What'd they say?"

"He didn't send them."

"What? I thought—"

"They weren't from Sam Noble. Someone took pains to make it look like he did, though."

"That doesn't make sense."

"It does if you know Gunny Barnett."

"The short guy with the ears? He had something to do with it?"

"Probably."

Emma had Uncle Gunny's private number on speed dial. She held the phone in the palm of her hand so Roshelle could hear it on speaker. No answer. Her second call was to his corporate office.

"I need to speak to your boss. It's urgent. Tell him Emma Noble is on the line."

"I'm sorry, Mr. Barnett is in a meeting. May I take a message?"

"I wasn't clear. This is Special Agent Emma Noble with the Federal Bureau of Investigation. Put Mr. Barnett on the line. Immediately."

"Please hold."

Roshelle moved in closer.

"Squirt! You almost gave Mary a stroke—scared the shit out of her. I'm in a meeting with fourteen morons. Death by a thousand cuts. I'll call you tonight."

"Where is he?"

"Where is who?"

Emma raised her voice, "Don't do it, Gunny. Don't try to bullshit me. I know you sent the flowers. Where is he?"

"I don't know what you're talking about."

Emma put the phone closer to her mouth, "You know what's going on. I know you do. He's in world of shit. Tell me where he is."

"Sam?"

"Yeah. Sam."

"What kind of trouble?"

"The deep-shit kind. I need to find him. Now."

Gunny went silent.

"Did *he* tell you to send the flowers?"

His voice was softer than before.

"No. That was my idea."

"Why? Because you knew he wouldn't be at the ceremony, right?"

"Listen, Squirt. I just—"

"You *knew* he wasn't going to be there because you spoke to him. What's going on?"

Emma looked at Roshelle while she waited for Gunny to find his voice.

"Hey, it's your dad. Sam's got it under control. Don't worry—"

"He's wanted by the *FBI*. I need to be the one to find him."

"I, uh—"

"Spit it out, Gunny. What the hell is going on?"

"I don't know."

"I think you do. You spoke to him. Yes?"

"We talked."

"He told you he wasn't coming to DC?"

"Yes," Gunny said, his voice deflating.

"Why? What did he say?"

Emma waited through the long pause.

"I … um. You know I love you, but shit—I can't talk about this with you. It has to be Sam. I'm sorry, Squirt. I gave him my word."

"Goddammit, Gunny, this isn't a game!"

"Squirt, I gotta go."

The phone went dead in Emma's hand. It took all the control she could muster not to throw it out onto Pennsylvania Avenue.

"He knows," Roshelle said, looking at her. "Can we lean on him?"

Emma shook her head. "Gunny would never betray my father's trust. Never." She shoved the phone in her pocket and bit down on her lower lip. "I've known Gunny my entire life, and … I've never heard *that* in his voice."

"What?"

"Fear."

6

"Where do we start?" asked Roshelle.

"In Ohio. I want to talk to this cleaning woman who claims to have seen my father."

"Noble, you probably shouldn't go anywhere near that witness."

"Fine. *You* talk to her. But I'm going to be in the room."

They took a taxi to Reagan International. Emma's eyes were fixed to her computer screen, poring over her research on the cleaning woman. She glanced up at Roshelle.

"Hey."

"What?"

"I didn't thank you … for letting me rope you into this."

Roshelle shrugged. "Gets me a little closer to evening up the score, you know?"

Emma waved off the comment.

"So, tell me about your father. What's he like?"

Emma closed the laptop, wondering how to explain Sam Noble. People who knew him casually would say he was brilliant and quiet—often generous and kind. The men he served with would say he had a stubborn streak and, when properly riled, could explode with controlled fury. Emma had seen both sides. But knowing Sam Noble was tricky. He had a talent for keeping people at a distance, even Gunny. Even her.

"He's great."

"What makes him great?"

"I don't know. He just is. Get out of my head, Hess."

Roshelle smirked. "There's something in his file I don't get."

34

"What?"

"Your father was on the military fast track. A gung-ho, ooh-rah Marine. But he retires a month before his promotion to light colonel. Why? Who does that?"

Emma stuffed her laptop into a black computer bag. The problem with being friends with Roshelle Hess—the thing that made her good at her job—was that she had an instinct for finding the tender heart of an issue and stabbing at it until it broke open.

Emma let the question hang before answering. "Being a Marine was his life." She sighed and looked up at Roshelle. "He left because of me."

"Okay. . . ."

"My mom died. It was sudden. I had a hard time dealing with it. He resigned immediately."

"How old were you?"

"Fourteen."

"Shit."

Emma stared into Roshelle's eyes. "*That's* who Sam Noble is. A man who drops his life to catch his daughter when she's in freefall."

It was late when they landed in Cleveland. Emma suffered through a restless night in an uncomfortable hotel bed and, as usual, woke earlier than necessary. The night desk manager was easygoing about making coffee a few hours early. She waited in the lobby, her face buried in the laptop screen, looking up every now and again at the unenthusiastic parade of road-weary salespeople and tired travelers shuffling toward the buffet line.

Emma looked at her watch. An agent from the Cleveland Office was supposed to be coming to escort them to the murder scene in Windsor Hills. That didn't interest her as much as interviewing the cleaning woman. Yesterday, they took her statement but hadn't given her a photo lineup. The woman hadn't directly fingered her father. By this afternoon, Emma hoped to be flying back to DC with Sam Noble's reputation still intact.

Hess walked out of the elevator just as a diminutive, wiry agent in a gray suit came through the double doors—his FBI credentials on full display.

"You Emma Noble?" he asked.

"I'm Hess," Roshelle said, chin-bobbing at the chair in the corner. "That's her."

"Noble?" he said, waiting for confirmation. "Steven Buck, Cleveland Office. Apparently, I'm not to let you out of my sight. Welcome to Ohio."

"Lucky you," Emma grinned, shaking the short man's hand and sizing him up. He wasn't a rookie. Probably nearing retirement, he was short, fit, and impossibly thin. She guessed Steven Buck had been an athlete—not the conventional, college scholarship kind. He had the look of a free climber. The kind of guy that scrambled up sheer cliffs, a fingerhold from disaster.

She hopped in the passenger seat of his maroon SUV, a bit surprised that Agent Buck had gone to the trouble of wedging three coffees into the cupholders. He cracked the knuckles of his thin fingers and put the car in drive.

"We'll be there in forty-five minutes."

"You're up to speed with all this, Agent Buck?" asked Roshelle.

"Well, let's put it this way. I know who she is," he said, pointing his thumb at Emma, "and I was at the scene—saw firsthand what they *think* her father did. So, yeah, I know enough to understand that this might be about the most awkward assignment I've had the pleasure of—"

"Yup," Roshelle cut in. "You're up to speed."

"Glad you've made a friend, Hess," Emma said, buckling in. "You know I want to talk to the cleaning lady, right?"

Agent Buck nodded and merged onto Memorial Shoreway Drive. The clouds were dark in the east. Emma watched lightning flash behind Huntington Bank Field, momentarily illuminating the slate-gray waters of Lake Erie. It took twenty minutes for the sky to make good on its threat, unleashing a torrent of whipping white rain that nearly overwhelmed the wipers. Agent Buck didn't say much. He spent most of the trip muttering expletives under his breath until the storm finally spent itself and the sun pierced the billowy morning clouds.

The two-lane road into the town of Windsor Hills was riddled with potholes brimming with brown rainwater. Emma straightened in her seat as the SUV made a left into Pine Bluff Manors. They passed manicured green lawns in front of large, nearly identical homes. Three middle-aged power walkers with diamond earrings waved at the vehicle as it passed.

"Shit," Buck said, pulling up behind a tan sedan with government plates.

Emma waited for him to explain, but he had nothing to say.

The dead banker's house looked like the others in the neighborhood. The driveway was long, but the asphalt had been replaced with expensive paving stones. The grounds were landscaped with rose bushes and lilacs in fresh mulch. Emma walked halfway up the drive, then turned and went back to the curb, looking up and down the street. The cleaning woman had told the FBI that the truck squealed out of the driveway and up the street. Emma saw no evidence of tire marks.

Agent Buck coughed into his hand. Emma looked his way, noticing the woman who'd just exited the sedan. Judging by the way she carried herself, she outranked Steven Buck by a country mile.

"This is—"

The woman interrupted, "I'm Agent Shinsky. SAC in Cleveland. I've been debriefed by Chief Byum." She looked away and added a barely audible "Welcome to Ohio" under her breath.

Emma thanked her, wondering if the woman was going to offer her hand in greeting. She wasn't. She walked to the front of her car and leaned on the hood. The Special Agent in Charge from Cleveland was not at the crime scene to roll out a red carpet or to help with the investigation. Her presence was intended to send a clear message to Emma: the Bureau was giving her some leash but wanted to remind her she was on a choke collar.

It didn't matter. It would be over soon.

"Mortinson have family?" Emma asked, turning her attention to Buck.

"Wife. Lindsey. And a stepson, Henry."

"Were the wife and child in the house when it happened? Did they see anything?" asked Roshelle.

"We don't think so."

"You don't think so?" asked Emma, looking over at the SAC.

Shinsky folded her arms across her chest and waited for Agent Buck to answer.

"We don't have a statement from the wife. She's out of the country—at least that's what the neighbor said."

"Where?"

"We're trying to locate her."

"Trying?" asked Emma.

"She didn't use her passport."

Emma looked at him dumbfounded. "If she didn't use her passport, then she didn't leave the country. Right?"

"Let my office deal with Mr. Mortinson's widow. Your job, I believe, is to find our suspect," Shinsky cut in sharply.

"Person of interest," Emma corrected. She had more choice words she wanted to say, but sparring with Shinsky would only make things worse. She grabbed Buck's elbow and walked him into the lawn.

"You were here yesterday?"

He nodded.

"Was Mortinson pronounced dead at the scene or at the hospital?"

"Oh, there wasn't much doubt he was dead. The killer was very thorough ... no offense."

Emma bit her tongue.

"You want to go into the house?" Buck asked.

"Not just yet."

Emma stepped into the damp mulch, pushing aside the rain-soaked branches of a rose bush. She ignored the sting of the bush's thorn, wiped the spot of blood against her tan slacks, then crouched to look into the basement window. Emma stood and surveyed the property before stepping out of the landscaping and walking to the side of the house and down a small embankment. The cobblestone patio in the backyard was shaded by a broad-beamed cedar pergola and had everything required for entertaining: oversized grill, brick pizza oven, and neatly arranged, comfortable outdoor furniture. Emma stooped to look in the grass a few feet from the patio.

"What do you got?" asked Roshelle.

"Sawdust and cigarettes." Emma pointed at the ground, drawing an imaginary box. "Marlboro, Marlboro Lights, and Camel."

"So?"

"Contractors were working here. Maybe one of *them* killed Mortinson. And where's the wife? Out of the country? I mean, come on, Hess—*that* doesn't seem sketchy? We're not looking wide enough."

"Okay. But—"

"I know ... the cleaning woman. She got it wrong, Hess."

Emma turned and walked back to the front of the house, then up the brick steps to the front door, waiting for Agent Buck to fish the house keys from his pocket. He lifted the yellow tape to let her enter first. The entry had high ceilings with white millwork and a crystal teardrop chandelier. Emma guessed the antique tile floor had been imported. She followed it down the hallway, walking slowly. She stared at the wedding picture of Lindsey and Ted Mortinson. They looked happy.

But sometimes pictures lie.

The hallway led to a massive kitchen with French cabinets, blue marble countertops, and shiny copper cookware over the island. An expensive interior designer had gone to great lengths to decorate the home so visitors might believe the Mortinsons came from old money. Emma knew better. Ted Mortinson had money, but he hadn't had it for long.

"What kind of banker in Windsor Hills can afford this?"

Steven Buck nodded. "W-2 shows he made $135,000 last year."

"Wife?"

"Doesn't work outside the home."

Roshelle assented: "Definitely greasy."

Emma nodded.

"The study is back here. That's where we found him."

Emma walked through the office door, noticing a stain in the carpet beneath a mahogany-trimmed bay window. She closed her eyes, remembering the photograph from yesterday. Pictures never did a crime scene justice. Emma looked around at the walls: two diplomas, Chamber of Commerce certificate, a picture of Ted Mortinson with a Cleveland Cavaliers basketball player. She raised her eyebrows at the taxidermy over the desk. The deer was an underfed, six-point basket-rack in an expensive shoulder mount. Her dad found that kind of thing amusing—men who threw big bucks at scrawny bucks to prove they were outdoorsmen.

"Brass?" asked Roshelle.

The Cleveland agent shook his head. "No shell casings. The guy was a professional."

"Or *woman*," Emma said quickly.

"Like he said, the *guy* was a professional," Shinsky added, unnecessarily.

"What about latency? You check for prints on the victim?"

Buck nodded. "Came up with nothing."

Emma stared up at the dead deer, admitting to herself that whoever killed Mortinson knew what they were doing. Which meant that Emma's hope of pinning the murder on the wife or somebody working on the house was likely a Hail Mary.

"Can we speak to the woman now?"

"Margaret Banich," added Steven Buck.

"She know we're coming?"

He shook his head.

"Good. I want it to be a surprise."

They walked off the porch, ignoring the smattering of neighbors gawking across the street. Shinsky gave a curt handshake to Roshelle Hess and a dismissive nod to her Cleveland agent. Her work here was done. Shinsky opened the door of her sedan, looking Emma up and down. Whatever she was thinking about saying, she chose to keep to herself.

7

The faded entry sign to Fishman's Trailer Park featured a cartoon frog holding a bamboo fishing rod, a smiling minnow hooked on the line. The place was well past its prime. Most of the narrow homes in the neighborhood were built a few hundred miles away in Indiana—WIDE LOADS that were rolled across I-90, then planted at Fishman's. Most of the trailers were slumped on cracked concrete pads on yards with patchy grass—their vinyl siding, dirt-stained and sun-faded. Fishman's Trailer Park had probably been okay in its youth, but it was now a tired, emphysemic place.

"This one," Steven Buck said, pulling the SUV to a stop along the edge of the grass under the shade of a wide maple.

Margaret Banich's home was better cared for than the others. She'd strung plastic lights over the eaves and into the willow by the side of the house. Red and purple petunias grew inside a circle of white-painted garden stones in the middle of the lawn. A small, off-season Cleveland Browns flag fluttered by the wooden entry steps.

The rainstorm had done nothing to cool northern Ohio; the humidity had gotten worse. Despite the heat, Emma stood on the lawn and pulled her arms through her blue FBI windbreaker. She wanted the cleaning woman to know who the unexpected visitors were in her front yard. As planned, Agent Buck walked alone to the front door while Emma stood with Roshelle under the shade of the maple.

"She's just a witness," Roshelle said.

"I know."

41

"I know you know, but the look you're shooting at the front door is … a little aggressive."

"She—" Emma stopped herself and inhaled deeply.

The screen door opened. Emma got her first look at Margaret Banich. She was a woman out of balance with herself. Her upper half was imposing: a wide, jowly face sank into a thick, fleshy neck. She had a broad chest and a grand belly. But her substantial girth teetered above a thin waist and skinny legs that poked from baggy, white gym shorts. Standing on the steps in her tight gray T-shirt, Margaret Banich looked remarkably like the circular self-portraits the two-year-old in the apartment across the hall kept slipping under Emma's door.

Steven Buck nodded for them to join him.

"I'm sorry, the house is—if I'd known you were coming, I would have … please come in," she said nervously, opening the door for the agents.

Buck was first in. "Nice to see you again, Mrs. Banich."

"It's Peg," she said, swiping a sleeping yellow cat off the sofa. "I already told you everything I know. I didn't expect that you—"

"This is Agent Hess and her partner. Can we sit?"

Peg Banich nodded, clicking her thumbnail and index finger against each other.

"Let me get these papers off the cushion."

She apologized for the TV noise as she bent into the couch to fish the remote from under a cushion. She apologized for the humidity, the dishes on the kitchen table, then spent a minute getting the black fan in the corner to oscillate.

Roshelle raised her eyebrows at Emma.

"Why don't you sit there," Roshelle pointed at a kitchen chair. "We'll take the couch."

Emma was an observer. Buck and Hess were going to ask the questions. She leaned against the wall. Her shoulder bumped a framed photograph of Margaret Banich and her thin husband holding the yellow cat. They were all wearing Christmas sweaters—even the cat.

Roshelle put her elbows on her knees and clasped her hands together as Banich's face turned a fresh shade of pink. "Mrs. Banich, this is an important case for the Bureau. We need to make sure—" Roshelle stopped and studied the cleaning woman. "I'm sorry, but you seem *very* nervous."

The woman looked at the agents and shook her head.

"You want to get some water before we start?"

"No."

"Okay. Agent Buck tells me you own a cleaning service. Been doing that a long time?"

"Three years in November."

"And how long have the Mortinsons been clients?"

Peg Banich rubbed her nostril with the back of her thumb. "Two years. I do their place on Mondays. He texted to make sure I was still coming."

"Is it normal for him to confirm your appointment?" asked Steven Buck.

"Sometimes. But not from him. His wife usually schedules me."

Roshelle glanced at Emma then back to Banich, "Tell me about Mr. Mortinson."

"Well I know he is—*was*, very wealthy. And I know he was a banker at First Community down in Windsor Hills. But I never saw him in the lobby. He was an upstairs banker. My husband says that's where they put the smart ones with crappy personalities."

Agent Buck leaned forward. "Mr. Mortinson texted that he wanted the house cleaned—not his wife? When was the last time you spoke to Lindsey?"

Peg Banich unfolded her arms from across her chest and leaned back into her kitchen chair. "There were rumors she was leaving him. Then I heard she was on a long vacation. That's why I don't listen to the gossip—better to keep to my own knitting, you know? But it doesn't stop them from running their mouths. Rich and bored. That's what the women in that neighborhood are. I don't believe a thing they tell me."

"Do you know where Lindsey Mortinson is?" asked Roshelle.

Banich straightened in her chair, nodding like she'd just figured something out. "You think something's happened to Lindsey too, don't you? Or," she hesitated, "maybe you guys think she *hired* the guy that murdered him. The one I saw."

"Is she the kind of woman that would hire someone to kill her husband?"

Peg Banich looked up at the ceiling, then shrugged. "You never know what people are capable of."

A hint of amusement slid across Emma's face.

Steven Buck leaned forward. "Couldn't agree more. You just never know about people," he said, taking time to look at his notes. He glanced at Emma before speaking again. "I mean, you're a great example. You have an interesting history yourself, don't you, Mrs. Banich? Or should I call you Meg Brown or Melody Bouche?" Steven Buck looked over at Roshelle. "Am I missing one?"

"MaryAnne Bliss," she said, lifting her chin and staring at Peg Banich.

"Right. Bliss. That's the best one, I think."

Emma watched Peg Banich's face turn crimson. The cleaning woman stood up, then thought the better of it and sat back down at the kitchen table. "That was a long time ago. I, uh—"

"It really wasn't that long ago, was it?" said Roshelle. "They finally caught you down in Florida, and you spent almost five years in Raiford? I bet you know lots of murderers."

Banich reached back to the table for a dish towel and mopped her perspiration. "I'm straight. That life's behind me."

"What's behind you?" said Emma, finally joining the conversation.

"I don't steal anymore."

Roshelle raised her eyebrows.

"I'm not lying."

Steven Buck sighed, "An ex-con moves out of state, changes her name, and starts a business that gives her the keys to the finest homes in Windsor Hills. I don't know, but it doesn't look—"

"I didn't do anything—shit, *I called* the cops. Me. When I found Mr. Mortinson—I called! I'm not guilty of anything. I'm straight. I didn't steal from Mr. M. or his wife. But I could have. I could have cleaned them out if I'd wanted to. Him with all his watches. Her with—well, her stuff," she shook her head, "her stuff wasn't worth much."

"What stuff wasn't worth much?" asked Emma.

"She has cheap taste in jewelry. The only thing she kept in that little wooden trinket box on her dresser was some military ribbons, a couple of buttons, and a medal wrapped in tissue paper—nothin' valuable."

"So, you looked. But didn't touch? Is that what you want us to believe?" Roshelle asked.

"Yeah. I always look—but that's no crime. I married a good man. And I don't need trouble with the cops. Never," she shook her head. "I *never* took nothin' out of that house."

"Okay," said Roshelle.

"Check the 911. It was *me* that called the cops and waited for 'em."

Steven Buck nodded. "You did."

"So, you know I had nothin' to do with the killing, right?"

He shrugged. "I hope not, Peg. Because we're going to be listening carefully. If you didn't do anything, and you're truthful about what you saw, then you don't have anything to worry about. Fair?"

"I'm being truthful."

"Okay." He looked down at his notes. "You said when you arrived at the Mortinson house, there was a truck in the driveway?"

"Black one—parked at an angle. I couldn't get in. Had to park by the curb."

"By the curb?"

Peg Banich nodded. "That's a long walk with my kit. It was hot, and I was out of breath, dragging that Bissell in my left hand and my bucket in the right. Probably should have taken two trips."

Roshelle said: "You're at the front door. Is that when you confront the man?"

"Well, it's a heavy door. I have to wrestle with it cause it wants to slam quick, so you gotta lean into it, push it hard, then—quick—grab the bucket off the ground and stick your foot in before it swings closed. So, like I always do, I reach for my bucket, and when I come up, there's a man standing in my way. Scared the bejeekers out of me."

"Describe him," Buck said.

"6'5" maybe 6'6". A big boy and I was pressed up against him. Solid. All muscle."

Emma shifted her weight, trying to conceal her sudden-onset anxiety.

Agent Buck leaned closer. "What did you do?"

"Well, I know enough not to show a man you're scared of him, so I took a step forward and said, 'Coming through,' thinking he would back up. But he didn't move. I remember thinking something was wrong with the guy. He looked lost. And then he kind of came to. He pushed me out of the way. I hit my head on the door jamb and the cleaners and brushes scattered all over the floor. I watched him throw the truck into gear and he was gone. Just like that."

"Describe the truck."

"Like I said, it was heavy duty. Black."

"Make?"

"I'm not sure."

Roshelle held her pen over the notepad and raised her eyebrows at Margaret Banich. "You gave Agent Buck a license plate number when you spoke to him. Do you still remember it?"

Peg Banich nodded. She closed her eyes and slowly recited the numbers. Roshelle followed along in her black book. After the seventh digit she looked at Emma and nodded—the numbers matched her original statement.

"You said it all happened quickly, yes?" asked Agent Buck. "He slams into you and almost knocks you down, then he jumps in his truck and squeals out of the driveway. But … when this happened, you didn't know there was a dead man inside the house. Why'd you memorize the plate?"

Peg Banich pursed her lips and folded her arms back over her chest. "I'm an ex-con. A stranger runs out of an expensive house like that, I'm thinking he took something. Something goes missing, who they gonna blame first? The ex-con cleaning woman. So I concentrated on it. Self-preservation. That's why I remembered."

Roshelle leaned back in the cushion. "When you spoke to Agent Buck, you told him the truck had an out-of-state plate. You're sure?"

"Yes."

"And you're sure you remember what state it was from?"

"Missouri."

"You were concentrating on the plate numbers not the state. Maybe you got it wrong. Maybe it was Mississippi or Minnesota—Massachusetts even?"

Peg Banich shook her head. "Show Me."

"I'm sorry?"

"The license plate said, 'Show Me.' Missouri's the 'Show Me' State."

Emma exhaled and looked up at the ceiling. She had spent hours researching Banich's past. She'd been sure that when confronted, the ex-con would change her story. Not only was she sticking to it, Peg Banich seemed credible.

"When did you find the body?"

"Well, I clean upstairs first. Start in the bathrooms. Then the beds. Vacuum the hallways and down the stairs. Always save the kitchen for last. I cracked the door to Mr. Mortinson's study and pushed my Bissell in. My mind was somewhere else. I wasn't paying much attention. The vacuum hit something and started making this weird noise. I stepped inside to see my Bissell chewing on Mr. Mortinson's hairline. That's when I screamed and called the cops."

Roshelle unzipped her backpack and handed Peg Banich a three-ring binder. Inside were photographs, six on each page. Seven pages in total. Emma had compiled every photograph with care, and almost all of the pictures were of males in their fifties matching the general appearance of Sam Noble. Emma pressed her back into the wall—her breath locked in her lungs. Banich might have pegged her father's truck. But that didn't mean he was driving. It didn't mean she'd seen her father at the crime scene. All she had to do was point at anyone but Sam Noble.

Roshelle spoke. "I want you to look through these photographs. Take your time. Tell me if you see the man that came out of the house—the one that got into the black truck."

Emma stepped close enough to see the first page.

Peg Banich put her index finger under the face of a man in the upper left. She studied it for a few seconds, shook her head, grunted, and moved to the next. It took her two minutes to get through the first page. She flipped to the next and worked her way down, then stopped, her index finger running back and forth below the image of an ex-con with curly hair and puffy eyes.

Emma clenched her jaw. *Say it, Banich. Say that's who you saw.*

Instead, the woman grunted and flipped further into the binder. Sam Noble's picture was on the bottom right. Emma chewed on the skin inside her lower lip, watching as the witness shook her head and grunted through the first five pictures. She tapped her index finger below the photograph of Sam Noble. Leaning in closer.

"Yup. That's the guy. That's him," she said, pointing at the picture with visible relief.

Emma inhaled, trying to recalibrate.

"What else do you remember about him?" Roshelle asked.

"Like I said, he was a big guy. Could have played for the Browns."

Emma lowered her head, looking down at the shaggy brown carpet. There wasn't much doubt that Banich was telling the truth. People remembered meeting a man like Sam Noble. He was hard to forget.

Roshelle nodded. "What can you tell us about his emotional state? Did he seem angry? Or—"

"No. He seemed terrified."

Emma cocked her head. She doubted her father had ever been "terrified" a day in his life. He was the Iceman. What was it that could spook a man like her father?

Roshelle scribbled in her black book, then took the binder from the woman and dropped it into the backpack. Emma closed her eyes for a moment. When she blinked them open, Roshelle was looking at her.

"Anything else you'd like to ask, Agent?"

"Nope. All good."

• • •

Emma sat alone, her legs dangling off a weathered picnic table under a pavilion at the Windsor Hills Community Park. She was waiting for Steven Buck to end his call with Shinsky. Roshelle had gone somewhere to stretch her legs—a small but unnecessary gesture designed to give her partner a little space. Emma didn't want space. She wanted forward progress. And answers.

A mother and daughter walked from the parking lot across the soggy grass. The girl bolted from her mother's grasp, running toward the mulched playground. From a standstill, she jumped under the monkey bars, trying in vain to get a grip. Undeterred, she ran to the metal slide and up the ladder. Scooting to the edge, she shouted for her mother to watch the launch and then the splashdown as her butt slid through the pooled rainwater at the bottom of the slide.

Emma nibbled at the nail on her index finger. She looked down at her phone knowing there wouldn't be a message from her father, but hoping for it nonetheless. No part of her believed he had killed an innocent man. But what was he doing in Ohio? Why was he in the Mortinson house? Why had he gone dark?

She looked up at the laughter coming from the playground. The mother was pushing her daughter on the swing while the kid screamed to go higher. With every downbeat, the mom pushed hard against the girl's back, rocketing the kid skyward. Emma remembered being that age, on the swings of a military base playground—pumping her legs back and forth, trying to gain altitude—wanting to soar into the heavens. But by then, her mother had become overly cautious, consumed by worry. Instead of pushing Emma higher, she would catch her momentum, pulling her out of orbit.

Emma lowered her head, tucking back into her phone. There was a missed call from St. Louis University. She dialed, waiting to be directed to the head of the department. It wasn't a long conversation.

"You good?" Roshelle asked, sitting next to Emma.

"Yeah."

"Who were you talking to?"

"My father hasn't shown up for work—school hasn't heard from him in over a week."

Roshelle nodded, letting her silence speak for itself.

"I need to get out of here, Hess."

Steven Buck jogged from the SUV toward the small pavilion. "Shinsky needs me back in the office. Noble, she wants to know if you believed Banich."

Emma shrugged. Then relented. "Doesn't mean he murdered anyone." She got off the picnic table and started across the field toward the SUV. Steven Buck and Roshelle caught up quickly.

"Shinsky wants me to focus on tracking down the wife."

Emma opened the passenger door. "Buck, I want to know everything as soon as you get it. Is that a problem?"

"Shouldn't be."

"Something tells me the wife is the key to this. She knows what's going on." Emma clicked her seat belt and turned to the Cleveland agent. "We need wheels."

Roshelle Hess poked her head between the front seats. "Uh, where we going?"

"There's only one place I can think to look."

8

Emma acquainted herself with the interior of the no-frills, factory-fur-nished Bureau car, locating the windshield wipers and adjusting the mirrors. It was a newish Malibu sedan with low miles and coffee stains on the upholstery. She put the car in drive.

"Noble?"

"Yeah?"

"Any chance you're going to tell me where the hell we're going?"

"Southern Ohio."

"Why?"

"My family used go there when I was a kid to visit dad's brother, Lester. He was a bachelor. No kids. He died when I was twelve. It's my father's only connection to Ohio."

"The property passed to your dad?"

"Apparently. I called the county courthouse. Tax records show the ownership was transferred to him. He never told me—which doesn't surprise me. But whether he's there? I don't know—it's a long shot."

"Alright. Let's find out," Roshelle said, buckling in.

Emma attached her phone's playlist to the car's stereo system. The stuttering harmonies of "Take A Chance On Me" punctuated the silence.

"No! Come on, Noble."

"Driver chooses the music. You know the rules, Hess."

"ABBA? You're *still* listening to that shit?"

"Don't yuck my yum."

"And how many hours are you going to subject me to this shit, Dancing Queen?"

"Four hours. Enjoy," she said, turning up the volume.

Emma tapped her fingers against the wheel. The music was a fool-proof mood enhancer, transporting her to the kitchen dance parties that spontaneously broke out when an ABBA song played on the radio. Her mother would start a dance shuffle in front of the stove, never lifting her feet off the floor, her arms working like a locomotive. That was the invitation for Emma and her brother to join. Too young for dancing, Emma just hopped around, bouncing into her mother and brother. Just the three of them. Laughing. Swinging each other around. Before her brother's death, there had been a lot of joy in that kitchen.

"What do you remember about Lester's place?" asked Roshelle.

"Dumbass."

"Dumbass? Who's—"

"Our beagle."

"You named your dog Dumbass?"

"No. My dad did. When he brought it home from the breeder, its name was Boone. It was supposed to be his hunting dog and—he was very clear—it was *his* dog." Emma mimicked her father's deep voice, "'A hunting dog needs training, not coddling.' Dad was a maniac with the training—took it to special classes and workshops. Poor pup didn't have the disposition or the intelligence for hunting. My father gave up—he put Boone in my hands and said, 'See what *you* can do with Dumbass.'" We were buddies. We ran all over Lester's property: the woods, the clover fields—the dog followed me everywhere.

Roshelle reached for the volume control. Emma slapped her wrist.

"I'd be happy to drive."

"No chance," Emma grinned.

Roshelle muttered something to herself, then looked down at the navigation app on her phone. "We can go straight through and get in late. Or we can stop. What do you wanna do?"

"My father won't recognize this car. It's a bad idea to roll up on him in the dark, unannounced. We need him to know that it's his daughter in the driveway—not an ambush. Morning's safer."

Roshelle glanced over and raised her eyebrows, but said nothing.

Emma drove, setting the windshield wipers to intermittent and pointing the Malibu south. Roshelle was staring at her cellphone, every now and again scratching in her black notebook with a blue ballpoint pen. Emma appreciated the silence while it lasted. But she knew Roshelle was holding her water. The personal questions would be coming sooner or later. Hess was a patient shrink.

The Malibu motored down the rural two-lane highway through farm country, bisecting fields of high corn. Emma opened the window, smelling the post-rain sweetness coming from the fields. After her mother died, Sam and Emma moved to the Midwest, surrounded by black fertile soil. By late June, the corn was high enough to hide high school parties. Emma remembered walking into those fields, fifty rows deep, behind broad-shouldered boys with beer suitcases and giggling girls vying for their attention. While the freshman and sophomores chugged and wrestled in the dirt, Emma sipped, watching a certain lanky boy. Hoping he would show interest.

"You're quiet, Noble. What're you thinking about?"

"A kid from school."

"A boy?"

Emma nodded.

Roshelle turned and raised her eyebrows. "Spill it."

"My first crush. Michael. The corn reminded me."

"I'm all ears."

"That's beneath you, Hess."

"Whatever. You were saying—"

"I liked him, but I didn't tell anyone."

"That's it?"

"A bunch of us snuck into this farmer's field to drink, partying deep in the corn. Michael takes my hand and pulls me away from everyone. My heart was a stampede. I could barely keep my shit together."

"And?"

"He laid a blanket out between the rows. We sat. He gave me a beer."

"Okay."

"He was talking about baseball and school. Then he starts running his fingers up and down my arm. His touch was so light. I didn't hear anything he was saying. I was just nodding—concentrating on keeping my insides where they belonged."

"And?"

"He leaned in and kissed me."

"Your first?"

"Yup. Slipped me a little tongue, too."

"You little slut. How far d'you go?"

Emma inhaled. "He broke the kiss when Sam Noble burst through the stalks like a giant plow."

"No."

"Oh yeah. My dad lifted Michael off the ground—started poking him in the chest with his index finger. '*You think you're a man? Let's see what kind of man you are!*' All the kids raced over to see what was going on."

"Fuck."

"Michael literally pissed himself. Then my dad grabbed me by the bicep and pulled me through the stalks. I'm crying—the tassels are whipping across my face."

Roshelle ran her hand over her mouth. "Shit. Did you—"

"Did I fight back? I stood toe to toe with him in the garage. Believe me, Hess, I gave it to him. I screamed every curse word I knew—probably made up a few."

"What'd he say?"

"Nothing. He just walked away."

"That's it?"

"It was a quiet dinner. He cleared the dishes and washed them in the sink. I could see him looking at me through the reflection in the window. He said, and I remember it word for word: '*Emmaline, you don't understand what men are capable of. Even boys. You're right to defend yourself. And, if your mother was here, she'd probably be on your side. But men can be damn cruel. And, for sure, I know she'd agree with that. You don't need them. And while you're under my roof, I'm not going to let them get to you. That's just how it is.*'"

Roshelle shook her head.

"After that, high school wasn't so terrific."

• • •

A blue highway placard advertised a Love's Truck Stop, an Arby's, and a Days Inn. Emma took the exit. Roshelle entered the hotel room, threw her black knapsack on the floor, claimed a bed, and was asleep minutes after the room darkened. Sleep didn't come as easily for Emma. For hours, she stared up at the ceiling, listening to the rumbling gasp of jake brakes from the big rigs across the street powering down for the night.

They were on the road an hour before dawn. It was Roshelle's turn behind the wheel, driving down empty roads through small towns. Emma watched the morning glow brighten at the tree line. The landscape in this part of Ohio was thick with hardwoods and sprawling honeysuckle vines. She caught a glimpse of the Scioto River through a clearing in the woods before it vanished. A few minutes later, the road dipped toward the water, and for over a mile Emma watched the Scioto's movement through the window. The river was low on the bank. The water moved slower than she remembered. But this was a different location, not the section where she and her father fished. Downstream it got fiercer.

They passed two pickup trucks parked off the side of the road. Emma had good memories of those dark mornings in the back seat of her father's truck. The windshield was always fogged with dew and humidity. He would let her drink coffee. They'd park behind an old gas station, gather their vests and fly rods out of the truck bed, and walk almost a mile on the muddy shore of the Scioto in the early light of morning. Fly fishing was Sam Noble's church. It was the only time Emma felt that her father was truly at peace. He wouldn't bait for smallmouth. Trout were smarter. That was where the challenge lay, and with all things, Sam Noble wanted to be tested by the best.

Through the car window, Emma saw the rocks scattered in shallow water, knowing that under them were the midges, caddis, and stonefly that her father would have patterned his flies after. She sipped her coffee, turning her head around for one last look at the river before the road curved away.

"Trout are lazy. Don't look for them running with the current. They want to conserve their strength. They'll be resting behind rocks like those over there or where the water pools under that dead branch. Cast upstream. Let the line float into the foam. Take in the slack. Good. Another one just like that. That's it. ... You're a natural, Emmaline."

"You haven't said a word all morning."

"Sorry."

"Were you doing push-ups at 3 a.m.?"

"Couldn't sleep."

"You think he'll be there?"

Emma took a sip and shrugged.

Roshelle glanced over. "Do you *want* him to be there?"

Maybe. She wasn't sure. If Sam Noble had a good explanation for why he was in a dead man's house, then yes, she desperately wanted him to be there. But if he'd done something unspeakable—if he was guilty? Then no. Let him be long gone.

"Of course I want him to be there."

The map on Emma's phone showed they were within a mile of the property. She looked around, searching for familiar landmarks from her childhood, but the stretch of road wasn't ringing any particular bells.

"Make a right up here."

As the car slowed to make the turn, Roshelle pulled a hand off the wheel for an instant, then put it back. Emma understood the flinch. It was a law enforcement instinct, triggered by anxiety. Her partner was checking. Making sure her weapon was on her hip, where it was supposed to be. She corrected quickly, but the small movement told Emma what Roshelle Hess would hesitate to say to her face—she thought Sam Noble was a dangerous man. A threat.

The Malibu crunched through the gravel on the way up the drive to Lester's house. Sam Noble's black truck wasn't in view. The detached carport was empty. Emma exhaled, not sure if she was feeling relief or disappointment. Lester's brown house was wrapped in a ribbon of morning mist. She remembered it being bigger than it was.

Roshelle stopped halfway up the drive and put it in park. Emma told herself to focus—push away the memories that wanted to wash over her. Take nothing for granted. It was a lesson she'd learned the hard way last year when ambushed outside an abandoned country house. The mistake had almost killed her. And no matter how the memories of this property intruded, she'd focus on her job first.

"How you want to do this?" asked Roshelle, meeting her at the front bumper.

Emma looked around. The property extended for acres on either side of the patch of brown lawn that surrounded the house. She bent down, brushing her hand over the grass. Someone had mowed it recently. Her heart was thumping a little harder when she turned to Roshelle.

"You clear right. I'll take the carport side. Meet in back."

"Are you—"

Emma unholstered, answering her question before it was asked. Neither rushed. Their movements were deliberate and defensive, giving the house a wide berth as they moved around it. Roshelle waited, keeping her partner in view while Emma checked the detached car-port—a flat roof protecting a square of gravel bordered by railroad ties. Emma stepped under it. Two aluminum trash bins, two red jerry cans, six pints of brown motor oil, and a clump of greasy rags in the corner. At the back was a metalwork table where a few grimy, cobwebbed-covered hand tools rested on its surface. Four worn tires were stacked in the center of the carport. Leaning against them was a bright, silver breaker bar and a shiny torque wrench. There was no age on those tools—store-bought and out-of-the-box fresh. She lifted her head, looking to the other side of the lawn and nodded. Roshelle disappeared around the corner.

Emma saw the tire swing. It was still hanging off the old sycamore branch. Lester's voice was in her ear.

Careful, girl—them bees in there'll sting ya.

And they had.

Emma moved slowly around the belly of Lester's white, grass-stained propane tank. A few yards more and her foot grazed a rusted rebar stake. There would be another fifty feet away—the old horseshoe pit.

Jesus, Sammy, move her on back 'fore she gets her bell rung.

Emma tried to refocus, but she couldn't blink back the memories. To her left, by the tree line, she saw the wide stump where she'd rested the barrel of the .22 rifle she could barely lift—aiming at targets in the woods. She exhaled, remembering her father's breath in her ear and the scruff of his two-day beard against her cheek.

Pull the slack out of the trigger, Emmaline. Let your breath go flat. One Mississippi. Two Mississippi. Fire.

Roshelle was beside the wooden deck. It had weathered poorly. But even back then, it had always sagged a little. The Noble brothers spent a lot of their late afternoons sitting up there on cheap lawn chairs, their voices rising as the contents of the whiskey bottle lowered. That was about the time Emma's mother pulled her away. Standing there, looking up at the deck, she had a strong memory of her mother taking her hand and leading the retreat into the side yard and up the steps of Lester's Airstream where they would "camp" together.

Your father needs to let off a little steam, Emmy.

At night, Emma would strain to hear what grown men said when they thought they were alone. But all she ever heard was laughter, cursing, and intermittent gunfire.

Roshelle waited for Emma to go first up the rickety steps to the back deck. She twisted the knob, half-expecting the back door of the country house to be unlocked. It wasn't. Emma looked around the deck for the most likely place. It didn't take long. The key was under a terra cotta planter.

The kitchen was a mess. Dirty dishes crowded the counter: a red-splattered spaghetti plate, another with chicken bones, a bowl with the yellow, concrete residue of mac and cheese, the corpse of a wrinkled, half-eaten potato on the floor, seven dented beer cans, and an empty fifth of Wild Turkey in the sink.

Roshelle raised her eyebrows. Emma ignored her.

They cleared the upstairs master bedroom. The last room in the house. Roshelle holstered her service weapon and stood over the tangled sheets at the end of the unmade bed. She tugged on black fabric peeking from under the comforter, pulling out a huge cotton T-shirt.

Roshelle showed her the white tag: "XXL Tall."

Emma nodded. It was her father's. The shirt used to be his trademark. Before he became a professor, he wore black T-shirts like a superstition—tight across his chest and biceps, loose at the waist.

Roshelle Hess was outside, walking circles in the front yard, holding up her phone and trying to lock on to a cell tower so she could update Byum with the news that Sam Noble had been in southern Ohio.

Emma was studying the photographs she'd found on the coffee table in the family room. She was in two of them. The first was Emma's senior picture from college. She was wearing a white Celtic sweater, leaning against a boulder in front of the library. But it was the second photograph that she couldn't take her eyes off.

Mother and daughter.

It was the last picture taken of the two of them together. Her mother was behind Emma, arms wrapped tight around her daughter's teenage shoulders. They were both smiling.

But pictures sometimes lie.

The photograph held no bittersweet memory of the loving moment when the camera clicked. Emma's smile was fake.

"I don't want my picture taken. Leave me alone!"

A week later, her mom was dead. It was this photograph that had tortured Emma in the days, weeks, and months after the funeral. She could see the frailty in her mother's eyes. Her fingers were clenched so tightly, holding on to her daughter as if Emma was the only person who could keep her from drowning.

"You okay?"

The question startled her. She hadn't heard Roshelle come in.

"Of course. What's up?"

"What you got there?"

Emma put the photographs face-down on her lap. "What'd Byum say?"

"Couldn't get him. Spoke to Buck. Still no sign of Lindsey Mortinson. He's waiting on labwork on the husband—hoping he'll have something in the next 48 hours."

"What's taking so long?"

Roshelle shrugged, then pointed at the picture. "What'd you find?"

"Pictures."

"You're going to make me work for it? Okay: who's in the pictures, Noble?"

Emma flipped one over and held it up.

Roshelle's tone softened. "Your mom?"

Emma nodded, turned it over, and put it on the cushion next to her.

"Let me see," Roshelle said, extending her arm and waiting for Emma to pass it over. "She's beautiful. What was her name?"

"Candice. My dad called her 'Mole.'"

"Mole?"

"Her name was Candice."

"Why'd he call her Mole?"

"I don't know. My mom kept the house dark. It was a nonsense nickname—'*I see my little mole is still in her hole*'—then he'd open up the blinds and turn on the lights."

Roshelle lifted her eyes to Emma but didn't say the thing that was on her mind. She stared at the picture a while.

"Were you close with your mom?"

Emma shrugged. "I guess."

"This must have been taken shortly before—"

Emma nodded.

"You're just a kid here. It must have gutted you."

She avoided Roshelle's stare.

"You can't talk about it after all this time?"

"Let's just concentrate on finding my father."

"I get it."

"Get what?"

"I know you, Noble. You're freakishly good at your job—as driven as any person I've ever met. Something's gotta fuel it, right? You've buried all your unresolved shit in her grave, haven't you?"

Emma shifted uncomfortably in her seat.

"That's why you can't talk about it. The wound hasn't scarred over. It's still festering—because you're constantly picking at it, aren't you? Why? What happened?"

She felt her face flush. Director O'Toole had given Emma the opportunity to team up with anyone in the Bureau and she'd chosen the best profiler the FBI had. A friend who could see right through her.

"You take sugar with your tea?"

"Tea? Since when do you drink tea, Hess?"

"I saw some in the kitchen—not sure how old it is."

Roshelle blew into the brim of a white mug with an eagle riding an American flag. She had the photograph of Emma and her mother in her right hand.

"How'd she die?"

"Accident."

"What kind of accident?"

Emma shook off the question.

"Were you there?"

"No. Almost."

Roshelle pursed her lips. She wasn't going to give up.

"I was a counselor at a day camp. When I was dropped off at home, the ambulance was pulling out of our driveway. She died at the hospital."

"I asked if you were close with your mother. You said 'I guess.' So, it was complicated, right? Tell me about her."

"My mom was fine." Emma tilted her head. "Maybe a little smothering. I mean, I get it now, it's obvious—with what she went through with my brother's long illness and death. But back then ... I don't know, Hess. She kept pulling back on the reins—she wouldn't let me *be*. You know what I'm trying to say? She was scared of everything. I needed to get away. So, I pushed. I was an asshole."

"You were a teenager."

"I was a shit." Emma turned to stare out the window at Lester's dead lawn. "The last words I said to her were … unforgivable. When I said them, I didn't care; I just walked out of the house and slammed the front door. I never got the chance to apologize."

"I'm sorry," Roshelle whispered. "But, for Christ's sake, Noble, you need to talk this out with someone."

"I thought that's what I *was* doing."

"You know what I mean."

"My father was there for me after she died. I was spiraling—I was losing my shit. He made me believe it wasn't my fault. Hess, he's my fucking hero. And he isn't capable of—"

"Wait. *What* wasn't your fault?"

"That's not the point. He cared for me. And we got through it. Together. He sacrificed his military career for me. It was the hardest goddamn thing I've ever been through, and if it wasn't for—" Emma's lip buckled momentarily. She broke eye contact until regaining her footing. "I was lost. He was there for me."

Roshelle took a sip of tea, and made a face. "This tastes like sawdust." She glanced down at the picture of mother and daughter and cocked her head. "Wait. How old were you in this?"

"Fourteen."

"But you said Lester died when you were twelve. So. …."

"Sam brought it here. These photos used to be on his credenza in St. Louis."

"He brought them to Ohio? Why would he do that?"

"I've been asking myself the same question."

Roshelle got up and paced the floor. "Margaret Banich said your father looked terrified. He leaves St. Louis and takes a photograph of his daughter and his deceased wife?" She pointed at the other photographs on the cushion. "Show me those."

Emma held up her senior college photograph.

"What about that one?"

Emma shrugged and picked it up. "I've seen it before. He had it at the house." She turned it toward Roshelle. "Just a photo of a blurry geyser and some tourists."

"A picture with no meaning?"

Emma took one last look at the photograph before setting it on the coffee table. "So, are we done with tea? Cause we have work to do. I think my father's with Mr. Dolittle."

"Who?"

"It's a 'what' not a 'who.' Mr. Dolittle is my uncle's old Airstream. It's not here."

"It's been a long time. What makes you think it *would* still be here?"

"There were old trailer tires stacked in the carport with a shiny torque wrench next to them. Someone just put Mr. Dolittle back into service. And, yes, with a little luck, we can find it. It had a unique signature, red numbers on the front from an Airstream camping club. They should have a record of Lester's membership. If they do, we can get the numbers for a BOLO."

"Christ, why didn't you say something earlier?"

"And interrupt our tea?"

9

Emma walked the tree line of Lester's property, picking up brass casings from a high caliber rifle. The gun litter wasn't hard to find, still shiny from recent shooting. At first, the shell pattern confused Emma. But in the ensuing hours, she'd figured it out. Sam Noble had spent a lot of time out there blasting bullets into the woods. And it wasn't for sport. The spray of shells showed a man in movement, working multiple targets along the tree line and repeating the process from varying distances. Her dad had been practicing, gearing up for something. And the thought of what her father could do with an automatic weapon chilled Emma to the bone.

"They found it," Roshelle yelled from the deck.

Emma dropped the shell casings. "The Airstream?"

Roshelle nodded.

"Where?"

She pointed to the phone and turned her back on Emma.

"Where?" Emma repeated, running up the stairs to meet her on the deck.

"Don't approach, Officer. This is not—" she looked over at Emma apologetically, "—this is not a person you want to tangle with. Stay outside the entrance until agents arrive."

"How far?" asked Emma.

"Couple hours north. State Park on the Ohio/Pennsylvania line. A county cop found it. He takes his lunch in the park every day. Matched the Airstream numbers from the BOLO."

Emma nodded at the lucky break.

"It's on Shinsky's turf. Should we call her?"

Emma shook her head. "Let's call Byum. Hopefully, we can convince him to hold her back from moving on the Airstream until we get there."

The Malibu blistered north. The Cleveland team was waiting for them. Emma turned off the two-lane highway and rolled into a Wendy's across the street from the state park's entrance. It wasn't hard for her to spot Shinsky's plain-clothes agents. Two were parked in an AutoZone next door, their eyes glued to the asphalt road leading in and out of the campground. The other agents were sitting on the folded gate of a red pickup, wearing lime construction vests and sipping soda.

Emma backed the Malibu next to the truck. Steven Buck looked down at Emma from the passenger seat. By the look of it, he was in a sour mood. She knew why. Shinsky was in the driver's seat, chirping in his ear. He nodded to her and rolled down the window.

"We'll talk inside," he said, pointing at the restaurant.

Roshelle held the door for Shinsky who brushed past her without a thank you. Steven Buck grabbed Emma's arm, holding her back.

"Tread carefully, Noble."

"Shinsky?"

"She's pissed."

"Why?"

"It's her default mode. Do me a favor. For my sake, don't antagonize her, okay?"

"Of course, Buck. Anything for you."

"Thanks. Wait. Was that sarcasm?"

Emma smirked as she walked past him toward the restaurant.

Steve Buck laid the campground map on a table. "We've scouted the Airstream's position—confirmed it's the one we're looking for. The campground is laid out in a figure eight. This section, by the lake, is busier. Your father parked the Airstream here, in a remote area," Buck said, circling a site at the far corner of the map. "It's in the woods. There's no one else camping back there. We've got two agents in the vicinity, posing as campers, keeping an eye out. So far, it's been quiet. No sign of a black truck."

Shinsky took over, leaning in and pointing at the map. "We'll have a team come from here and here—cover the forest with agents positioning here, twenty-five yards apart. There's nowhere for him to go. On my mark, we'll converge on the Airstream from all sides."

Emma traded a look with Roshelle while Shinsky continued.

"Agent Noble, you and Agent Hess will remain here during the operation. Buck, ten minutes. Send the word out."

"I don't like it," Emma said.

"Agent Noble, you're here as a courtesy. You don't get a vote."

Emma looked over at Buck. "It's a bad plan."

"This isn't my first operation," Shinsky said, glaring at Emma. "Buck, confirm everyone's in position. We'll go on my mark."

Emma stared at Steven Buck. He studied her then glanced at Shinsky before speaking.

"What makes it a bad plan?"

"Agent Buck I won't toler—"

Emma interrupted Shinsky. "Because it's exactly what my father will be expecting. You've never approached a man with his experience and skill. This wasn't an arbitrary location. He purposely put himself in that site. If there's trouble, he'll know how to defend it. I promise, you don't want to corner a man like Sam Noble."

The SAC raised her chin. "Bullshit. Buck, do your job."

"What do you propose?" he said, softly.

"Let me go in. Alone." Emma looked up at Shinsky and softened her tone. "There's no reason to put your agents in harm's way. Hang back and let me bring him out. It's the safest way."

The Cleveland SAC looked at the map for a couple of beats before exhaling and nodding her head. "Fine. We do it Agent Noble's way, but my people will be in position no less than fifty yards away."

"Thank you." Emma said, rising from the booth and starting for the door.

Shinsky looked at Roshelle. "Where the hell is she going?"

"I think she's ready to talk to her father now."

"Dammit. Buck, get—"

"I'm on it," he said.

The black asphalt road wound around the lake. A man and a boy fished off the muddy shoreline. Emma walked past a smattering of pop-ups, trailers, and fifth wheels. It was a weekday. The campground wasn't busy. The asphalt turned to gravel and then to dirt as she walked into the most remote area of the park. She came up the path, catching

the glint of the silver Airstream tucked in the back of a wide site
guarded by trees and bushes. Emma approached cautiously. There was
no sign of her father's black truck, but his tire tracks were fossilized
in the dried mud.

Emma stepped around the hitch.

"Hello?"

The shades were drawn in the Airstream. She walked slowly,
keeping her back to the aluminum skin. She leaned her head around
Lester's old rig and got her first view of the campsite. The fire ring was
cold—only a charred log and a singed paper plate remained in the ashes.
A can of OFF! bug spray was in the mossy dirt under the picnic table.

"Dad?" she said, slapping the camper shell, "It's Emma." She
waited for a response. "Dad?" She hesitated before opening the door.
"It's Emma. Okay, I'm coming in." She put her fingers under the
metal latch and it clicked open. The solid door swung out and Emma
stepped in.

She froze, her mind refusing to believe what her eyes were seeing.
Oh, please. No.

Her eyes focused on the pink flip-flop dangling off the big toe
of the lifeless leg. A woman's leg. She was covered in dried blood,
sprawled across the blood-stained dinette.

Oh, Jesus.

Emma cleared a clump of hair from the woman's cold yellow face.
It was Ted Mortinson's wife, Lindsey. She recognized her from the
wedding picture in the hallway of the crime scene.

Agents were running toward the Airstream. Steven Buck yelled.

"Noble! You good?"

Emma stared at the defensive wounds on the woman's arms and
hands. She hadn't gone quietly. She'd put up a fight.

"Noble?"

Emma's breath was shallow, her lungs working overtime—desperately trying to keep it together.

"Yeah. Clear."

Roshelle Hess followed Buck through the door, swearing under
her breath. She and Emma locked eyes, trading an unspoken understanding that Sam Noble had graduated from "person of interest" to
"murder suspect."

Emma walked deeper into the Airstream, looking down at the twin beds in the back. Both beds had been slept in. Clothes and a backpack were tangled in the bedding. Emma reached out her hand.

"Noble!" Shinsky shouted. "Don't touch a fucking thing. Get away from my crime scene."

"I'm—"

Roshelle put a hand on Emma's shoulder. "She's right. Go outside. Clear your head. I'll find you."

On the way out, Emma looked down at Lindsey Mortinson's blood-stained body. She was having trouble coming up with a narrative that could exonerate her father. She silently submitted, walking past Shinsky and down the steps of the camper, past a dozen or more FBI agents huddled together, waiting for instructions.

Emma sat on a boulder by the edge of the lake, ignoring the activity behind her. She tried to puzzle out a scenario where her father could be innocent. Her imagination wasn't up to the task. Late afternoon turned into evening. Darkness fell. Emma stared at the reflection of red and blue police lights streaking across the black water. They weren't rushing to take the body away. A mobile forensics unit was at work, taking precedence over the ambulance idling down the road. The Ohio State Police had moved out the campers and closed the park.

Roshelle came over and sat next to her. "You okay?"

Emma blew a long exhale. She spoke softly, her words almost inaudible.

"This is so fucked up."

Roshelle rubbed her shoulder. "What do you need?"

"Answers. What's happening?"

Roshelle spoke quietly. "They found skin under Lindsey Mortinson's broken fingernails—they're doing a preliminary DNA analysis on it now. Won't be long."

Emma nodded. There was nothing more to be done or said. But Roshelle stayed, sharing Emma's silence.

A half hour later, Steven Buck interrupted the quiet, leaning down to Roshelle's ear, speaking softly. "Forensics came back with the DNA analysis on the skin under the victim's fingernails. Shinsky wants to speak with you."

"Thanks. I'll be right—"

Emma stood.

"Sorry, Emma. She just wants Hess."

Roshelle shook her head. "No. Noble's coming too."

Emma was in a private tailspin as she navigated the network of law enforcement to reach the Special Agent in Charge. Emma fought the pessimism bubbling inside her, willing herself to believe that the DNA analysis would exonerate her father. Shinsky's arms were folded across her chest. Her face glowed in the red taillights of the forensics van. A state cop was nodding at whatever she was demanding of him.

Shinsky dismissed the cop and turned toward the approaching agents. Her eyes locked on Emma's for a moment before she broke contact. In that split second, Emma saw it in her face. She had her answer. The skin under the victim's fingernails was Sam Noble's. Her father had attacked and killed a woman inside Lester's Airstream. And then, he left her to rot.

Sam Noble brutally murdered an unarmed woman.

Emma swallowed hard against the bile rising into her throat.

"I'm with you," whispered Roshelle.

Shinsky gave Steven Buck a long, exasperated look. He shrugged back. "She wanted to hear it for herself."

The SAC frowned before speaking—a little faster than usual. "Agent Noble, I spoke to leadership. You and Agent Hess are wanted in DC. I suggest you leave now."

"You have the DNA result?" asked Roshelle.

"I'm no longer free to share information on this case with Agent Noble. Does that answer your question?"

Emma took two backward steps, turned, and walked down the campground road and into the night. When she was out of view of the state police and EMTs and FBI agents, Emma ran out of the park, heading west down the two-lane highway. The evidence had snuffed out any hope of her father's innocence. For a while she was heartsick. Then the anger set in.

Lindsey Mortinson was a wife. And a mother. The image of the woman sprawled across the dinette was burned into her. It was his fault. Sam Noble killed her. Her insides rolled over. She gripped her knees, vomiting into a roadside gulch. She spat on the ground, then walked circles in the pavement, her hands on her hips, swearing at her father. There was nothing Emma could do for him. She walked down the road, her anger dissipating into hollow acceptance.

Why?

Who was this woman to you?
What reason could you have for killing Lindsey Mortinson?

• • •

Emergency lights no longer flickered in the park. With the exception of two vehicles, the Wendy's parking lot was empty. Roshelle Hess and Steven Buck waited for Emma on the tailgate of the red truck, a cheap Styrofoam cooler between them. He checked his watch.

"Should we—?"

Roshelle shook her head. "Give her time."

Buck dug his hand into the ice and pulled out a six-pack. He yanked a beer off the plastic ring and handed it to Roshelle. Neither said much for a while.

"To see that in the camper … to know her father did it. Jesus."

Roshelle nodded.

"Glad I'm not in your shoes. What the hell do you say?"

Roshelle ran her thumb across the can's aluminum rim. She was asking herself the same thing.

"At least you're here for her. You guys have history—Quantico classmates. That's not nothing."

"It's deeper than that, Buck. She's like a sister to me."

He nodded and took a sip.

"Without Emma, I wouldn't have made it out of the academy—I wouldn't be sitting here."

"Hess, I read your file. I'm sure you didn't have much of a problem with Quantico."

"You been creepin' on me, Buck?" Roshelle's smile faded. She looked down and fidgeted with her thumbnail. "I'm going to share something I don't usually talk about." She turned and looked over at the Cleveland agent. "Got it?"

Steven Buck put his beer down and nodded.

"Stuff doesn't come easy for me. I'm not the smartest one in the room. The resume might look good, but I've never had *natural* talent. What I have is an oversized fear of failure. Everything I've gotten is from working harder than everybody else—pushing myself. Sometimes, a little too hard, I guess." Roshelle lifted her chin and looked up at the night sky. "I should have known better. I mean, I've got a degree in psychology, right? All that pushing? It finally caught up with me at the academy. I learned, firsthand, what high stress and lack of sleep can do. My body had taken enough of my bullshit and sent my brain on vacation. It was bad. Temporary—thank god—but it was bad." Roshelle lowered her voice. "Emma was there for me, Buck. Got me help without compromising my future. She pulled me through it. She covered for me—Noble risked her career for me. I'd walk through fire for her, Buck. I would."

• • •

Emma took a deep breath. She exhaled slowly, clearing her head before stepping out of the darkness.

"Sorry to make you guys wait, I—"

Buck tossed her a beer.

"No worries," said Roshelle, hopping off the tailgate.

"How many beers you got in there, Buck?"

"Not enough to make a dent on a night like this."

"You okay?" asked Roshelle.

Emma nodded without looking her in the eye.

Buck guzzled the last of his beer then wiped his mouth with the back of his hand. He dropped the can into the cooler and closed the lid. "I need to get out of here. I don't know what to say, Noble." He pushed the tailgate up. "Maybe we can have a beer down the road—under better circumstances."

"Hold up," Emma said. "You can't go. Not yet. I need to see the file on the victim. Show me what you've got on Lindsey Mortinson."

Buck looked at Roshelle, then back to Emma. "You know I can't do that. Shinsky was clear. You're off the case—a civilian as far as the Bureau is concerned."

"It's a small favor."

"She's already up my ass, Noble. Don't put me in more—"

"Why?" Roshelle interrupted. "What are you looking for?"

"Answers. What's the connection between Lindsey Mortinson and Sam Noble? There's got to be one, right? Come on, Buck."

"Let's just wait it out," said Roshelle. "There's nothing we can do. The answers will come."

"Just an hour with it, Buck. It'll be our secret."

"Come on, Noble. Don't do this to me."

"I need this. Please."

"You understand why I can't, right? Help me out, Hess."

Roshelle looked at Emma, then shrugged, "I don't think Noble's going to let this go. You've got two choices, Buck—shoot her or show her the file."

"You're a big help." He shook his head, "It's on my laptop—I'm not letting anyone touch it."

Emma drained her beer and chucked it in the bed of the red pickup. "There's a Denny's about seven miles up the road. Read it to me over breakfast. I'm buying."

10

B esides an over-the-road trucker at the front counter, one line cook, and a disinterested red-haired waitress, the agents had the restaurant to themselves. It was after one o'clock in the morning. Steven Buck ordered steak and eggs. Emma and Roshelle chose coffee, black. After he'd scraped the yellow and run his rye toast through the meat juice, he hauled out his laptop and set it on his stained placemat.

"What do you want to know?"

"Everything."

"Of course you do," Buck said, putting his reading glasses on and scrolling down. "She was born Lindsey Orr in Buffalo, New York. December 13, 1977. High school. College. Single mom. Married Ted Mortinson ten years ago."

"You've got her employment history?" asked Roshelle.

"I got everything," he said, running his finger over the mouse pad. "She was a nurse. Gave it up when she married Mortinson."

Roshelle nodded. "Why work if you marry into money?"

"Dirty money," said Emma. "Tell me the places she lived."

"Looks like she lived in Cleveland for a decade or more. Before that she was in the military."

"Marines?" Emma asked urgently, hoping to find the connection to her father.

Buck shook his head, "Air Force."

"Banich said she found ribbons and a medal in her jewelry box," offered Roshelle. "Where was she stationed?"

"Germany."

"Damn," Emma said, rubbing her eyes. Lindsey had been Air Force. Sam was Marines. She'd been in Germany. Sam Noble was never stationed there.

"She went in as a Second Lieutenant in the Nursing Corp. Wiesbaden."

"Any of that helpful?" asked Roshelle.

"Not yet," said Emma, bouncing a spoon against her thigh. "There has to be a connection. Give me more."

"Born in Buffalo. Attended college in Rochester. Joins military. Leaves military. Single mom working her ass off until she meets Mortinson. Then she jumps on the gravy train."

"That's it?"

"They sent me her military records. Nothing interesting. She was honorably discharged after four years. No reserve call-up."

"Let me see," said Emma, pulling his laptop over to her side of the booth. "Okay, she left the Air Force a First Lieutenant after four years. Not exactly on a fast track." Emma scrolled through her assignments and reviews. "Her senior officers were good with her work, but there's no glowing remarks about her ability or leadership potential."

"That's what I mean. She's about as average as you get."

Emma read to herself, scrolling through page after page of military documents and finding nothing helpful. She was about to give the computer back when something caught her eye. Emma leaned in and pointed to the screen. "What's this?" she asked, turning the laptop toward Steven Buck.

"It's just a 'note to file.' Some paper pusher—filling out forms."

"Yeah, but look at the date. It's after she left the Air Force."

He nodded, "Not surprising. They keep the file active long after they're out of the reserve call-up window."

"What does it say? Let me see," asked Roshelle.

Roshelle studied the entry. "It's just some kind of reference number."

"Yeah, but look under it. It reads, 'Captain Jeremy Donnelly, Department of the Army, Judge Advocate General's Corps.'"

Steven Buck closed his computer. "If it was anything that mattered, there'd be supporting documentation. It's nothing," he said. "Noble, you're reaching for something that's not there."

"The Army must have thought something was there. They did an investigation. Lindsey Orr saw something shady or she was involved in it somehow. There *has* to be a reason for a JAG investigation. That's not reaching, Buck. And since *she's* not going to tell us what it was, I need to find out."

"All right, I'll bite," he said. "How you gonna do that?"

"Hess, is your brother-in-law still—?"

Roshelle waved her hands. "No. Not doing it, Noble. My sister and him are on the rocks. There's no way in hell I'm stepping into that mess."

"He's a JAG, right? Is he still stationed in California? It's a little after 11 p.m. there. Just a quick call. Have him pull up the reference number and see what it says. Simple."

"You weren't listening. I AM NOT calling that piece of shit—especially this late. And what the hell are you smiling at, Steven?"

"I don't think she's going to let this one go. You've got two choices, shoot her or make the call."

"Fuck you, funny man."

"It'll take him two minutes to look it up," said Emma.

Roshelle stared at her friend, then grumbled out of the booth with her phone. She came back to scribble down the file number and the name of the JAG officer.

"Say hi to your sis—"

"Noble, don't. Okay? Don't."

Roshelle Hess paced around the restaurant for a few minutes before plopping into an empty booth on the far side. When her forehead wasn't buried in her palm, her free hand was punching at the air. Twenty minutes later she returned, her face flushed with anger.

"Looks like that went well," said Buck.

Roshelle pointed an index finger in his face. "Do not poke the bear right now."

"What'd you find out?" asked Emma cautiously.

"Big fucking dead end. That smug bastard. I don't know why she doesn't just leave him. And she's pissed too. I woke her up and she had to get him from the other bedroom. Goddammit, Noble—"

"What'd he say?"

Roshelle took a long swig of ice water to calm herself before speaking.

"Nothing. There was no case. Whatever Captain Donnelly was

investigating went nowhere and wasn't important enough to make notes."

"That's it?"

"Yup. My asshole brother-in-law said Donnelly is no longer in the service and doesn't have a forwarding address. It's gone. He's gone. Nothing to see here."

"Where was Donnelly stationed?" asked Emma.

"Virginia. But he had to travel up to PA for this. Apparently, he looked around. Came home. Closed the file."

"Where in Pennsylvania?"

Roshelle looked down at the chicken scratch she'd made on the Denny's napkin.

"Carlisle. The Arm—"

"The Army War College," interrupted Emma. "Is there a date? Tell me there's a date."

"Got a year for you. It was sometime in 2007."

Emma blew a gust of air at the ceiling.

"What?" asked Roshelle.

"Sam Noble was stationed at the Army War College in 2007. We lived there before my mother died. It was his last post before retiring."

Buck asked, "I thought he was a Marine?"

"The Army War College has instructors from all branches," said Roshelle.

Buck tilted his head. "I don't get it. In 2007 Lindsey Orr was a civilian living in Ohio. What does she have to do with an investigation at an Army base in Pennsylvania? It doesn't add up."

"Exactly," Emma said, jumping out of the booth and grabbing the keys to the Malibu. "It doesn't add up. Yet. But it's no coincidence. Sam Noble and Lindsey Orr are connected. My father killed her. The answer to *why* he did it is in Carlisle, Pennsylvania." She looked at Roshelle. "Hess? Road trip?"

Roshelle winced. "We're wanted in DC. Remember?"

Emma raised her eyebrows.

"... And, if I know you, you're about to tell me that the Army War College is on the way, right?"

Emma nodded. "We're staying on the sidelines. Just a little diversion on our way to DC."

Roshelle didn't look convinced.

"I need this, Hess."

"Who's driving?" Roshelle narrowed her eyes.

"I am. You can sleep on the way."

"Okay. But I've got one condition."

"No. That's not the rule."

Roshelle folded her arms across her chest.

"Okay," Emma said quickly.

"Noble? I need to hear you say it."

"Fine. No ABBA."

"Alright then. Let's go."

11

Roshelle Hess was not a woman plagued by insomnia. She didn't snore. She clucked, fogging the passenger side-window with metronomic precision. Emma drove through the night, holding her phone against the steering wheel. The photograph she was staring at lit the darkness inside the Malibu. She'd taken it years ago at a backyard BBQ. Sam Noble was manning the grill. She'd snapped the picture at the perfect moment: he'd just snatched a falling bratwurst with his silver barbecue tongs—caught it in midair. His smile was childlike. Full of wonderment and joy. It had always been Emma's favorite picture of him.

Had been.

Looking at it now, she felt nothing. Emptiness. The laughing man in the chef's apron was a stranger to her. The Malibu's tires flapped against the highway's rumble strip. Emma caught the wheel and corrected the drift.

"We good?" said Roshelle, pulling her head out of the window and looking over with one eye open.

"Yup. All good," Emma said, throwing her phone into the backseat.

"Where are we?"

"Almost there. Twenty minutes."

"I was out," she yawned, sitting straight. "When was the last time you were in Carlisle?"

"Long time."

"You never went back after your mom died?"

Emma shook her head.

76

"So, what's the plan? Barge into an Army base, show them our badges, and demand to see all the documents relating to whatever this investigation was about?"

"Pretty much."

"You know, it's likely they don't have anything. Then what're we going to do?"

"Loving your pessimism right now, Hess."

Emma took the Carlisle exit off the PA Turnpike, driving past green, mowed lawns and massive sugar maples. She pulled into a Turkey Hill for a breakfast sandwich, coffee, and a bathroom. They sat on the hood of the Malibu, eating and biding their time until the base opened for business. It had been fourteen years since she'd been back, but it looked pretty much the same as she remembered.

Carlisle worked hard to present an image of intellectual quaintness: a historic town with tuck-pointed brick buildings, clean sidewalks, and blooming public spaces. But like most bucolic towns in America, problems with drugs and poverty sprouted in the cracks behind scenic Main Street. Carlisle was home to a semi-prestigious liberal arts college, an annual car show, and a hard-won designation as Tree City, USA. But for the military community, the Army War College was considered the pride of that corner of Pennsylvania. It was the Army's think tank, the place where the brightest officers studied to become generals.

A soldier stepped out of the guardhouse and looked into the Malibu. "Morning ma'am."

"I'm Agent Noble, this Agent Hess. We're from the FBI," she said, passing over their credentials.

"Who are you here to see?"

"Duty officer."

"You're here on FBI business, ma'am?"

Emma nodded.

"Please wait here."

She'd been through this particular gate hundreds of times with her father, watching soldiers salute Sam Noble. Back then, the family car barely slowed down. Not that she'd admit to it now, but when she was a teenager, she loved coming through the gate and watching men in uniform snapping to attention. A military base had been a good place to be Sam Noble's daughter—a giant Marine who'd earned the respect of the men and women he commanded. This morning, Emma *didn't* love sitting behind the gate in the Malibu sedan for fifteen minutes waiting for a young Army corporal. The soldier finally leaned into the window, returned their documents, and gave them directions to the base commander's designee, Captain Natalie Brown.

The captain was waiting behind her desk when they walked in. She was nearly as tall as Emma, her short, blonde ponytail pulled excruciatingly tight.

"Thank you, Captain. I'm hoping you can direct us to someone that can track down this investigation number."

The captain took the paper, paying more attention to Emma than to the information in her hand. "We're not used to the FBI showing up without an appointment. Why not go through channels?"

"We were in the neighborhood."

The captain nodded, unconvinced. "I see," she said, finally looking down at the note in Lindsey Orr's file.

"It's related to a veteran that was murdered."

Captain Brown nodded. "Please have a seat in the hall. Let me make some calls. Please leave your credentials with me."

Emma didn't sit. She paced while Roshelle watched her from an uncomfortable metal chair. The door opened forty minutes later.

"Please come in," said the captain. "I have Chief Byum on the line. He'd like to speak to you directly, Agent Noble."

Emma traded frowns with Roshelle and picked up the extension.

"Yes, sir," she said. "Thank you. It is a difficult time. ... No, SAC Shinsky did relay that message. But. ..." Emma clenched and unclenched her fist. "Yup. I understand. Yes, sir."

Captain Brown took the phone from Emma and placed it on her desk. "I'm sorry we couldn't be more help. Good luck. Travel safe back to DC."

"We're not leaving Carlisle. Not yet."

"If you'd like, I can have someone escort you off base."

"Not necessary."

"Then, I'll let you see yourselves out."

Captain Brown turned to face her computer screen. Emma got the message loud and clear. Roshelle was halfway out when Emma handed the captain a business card.

"My cellphone number's on it. Keep it on your desk—in case you want to get in touch."

"I don't think the ARMY will need to bother you, Agent." The captain took the card and tossed it on the desk. "But thank you. Good luck."

Roshelle had to jog to keep up with Emma's long strides toward the Malibu.

"What'd Byum say?"

"A Federal Grand Jury indicted my father for violent crimes in aid of racketeering."

"That didn't take long."

"Byum wants us in DC as soon as possible. He was very polite about it."

"Hand over the keys. You didn't sleep last night. I'll drive."

Emma ran her tongue under her bottom lip. "Not yet. I need to find out what Captain Donnelly was investigating. One more day. I need to dig into this."

"The army just took your shovel."

"We'll see about that. Give me a minute. I'll meet you at the car."

Emma walked away, scrolling through her cellphone directory for a number she never expected to call. Twenty minutes later, she returned to the Malibu wondering how much trouble she'd just caused for herself. But it didn't matter. Nothing mattered anymore. Not her father. Not the FBI. All she wanted to know was why he'd killed a woman in cold blood.

• • •

"You've been pushing that crepe around your plate for fifteen minutes," Roshelle said. "Don't like it?"

"It's fine."

The restaurant was Roshelle's choice. She didn't know it had history for Emma. The memory of the place washed over her. She'd sat at the very same table with her mother years ago. Before it became a creperie, it was a pizza joint within walking distance of their house. Emma looked out the window, recognizing the elm tree at the end of the road—her old bus stop. Down that street and to the left was where her nightmares lived.

"You okay?"

"Yup. I'm going to stretch my legs."

"You want company?"

"Nah. Thanks anyway."

Emma placed her fork on the plate, wiped her face with the napkin, and stepped out on the sidewalk.

When they were given orders for Carlisle, Sam Noble put in for off-base housing. It was rare for her mother to insist on anything, but she was forceful with him—if he was taking the job at the Army War College, she didn't want to live on base. After her death, Sam Noble tried to convince Emma that her mother would still be alive if they'd been living on base. It was a fiction, a device designed to lay her death on the steps of faulty architectural design.

Emma wanted nothing more than to believe her death was accidental. But she'd always known what had happened—what her mother had done. Emma and her father never talked about it. There was too much pain. Instead of talking, she exorcised her midnight demons with push-ups. So many push-ups.

She stood on the sidewalk, warmed by the pleasant Carlisle summer morning, the honey-sweet perfume of alyssum filling the air and the planters of blooming petunias lining the street. Emma noticed none of it. She inhaled, gathering her courage, and stepped off the curb, walking toward her oldest pain. She took the long way, passing college buildings and off-campus apartments, sneaking up on the three-story limestone house.

With her back against the wall, she slid down the brick building across the street from where she used to live. Emma sat cross-legged on the uneven cobbled sidewalk. She looked over at her childhood home. The front door was a different color. It used to be black. Now, it was blood red. But the rose bushes were still there, blooming under the bay window. Emma stared up at the dormer window in the center of the high roof.

"I hope they don't throw up in our roses again. I believe college boys are drawn to puking in our bushes."

Emmy smiled, "We could dump water on them from up here if they did!" She laughed and shoulder-bumped her mother.

"Careful, don't make me fall."

"Don't be a chicken."

"I can't believe your father lets you sit up here, Emmy."

"It's safe. Just stay on the sill and put your feet here. Everything's better way up here."

"Problems disappear?"

"Yup."

She nodded at her daughter and looked up at the moon, not saying anything for a long while.

"Mom?"

"Yeah, sweety?"

"I wish you were happier."

"Emmy, listen to me. Never make wishes for your parents. Save them for yourself, and someday, for your children. I'm plenty happy. We got each other, right?"

Emma closed her eyes. Today was the anniversary of their last conversation. She rubbed her hands against her thighs to keep them from shaking. That morning, Emma had thrown her anger like so many knives, aimed precisely at her mother's fragility—killing words from a puffed-up teen. Emma's eyes drifted up to the high dormer window. She imagined her mother there—sitting on the sill, drinking red wine from the bottle they'd found at the scene. Imagining what her eyes must have reflected in that moment. The pain. The sorrow. The helplessness that must have consumed her before she stood and. . . .

"Excuse me?"

Emma rubbed her eyes, then looked up at a woman standing over her. She was holding the leash of a ratty brown dog.

"Sorry." Emma said. "I didn't, uh, mean to block the—"

"You look familiar. I recognize you. You're the young girl that used to live in the house across the street. You are, aren't you?"

Emma froze.

"You probably don't remember meeting me. I knew your mother. She was lovely—such a shame. Maybe you remember me? After the funeral, I made a lasagna for you and your father. I put it right there on the front stoop. I rang the doorbell, but no one came out. Do you remember the lasagna? I was always curious if you got it. The dish wasn't there when I came back for it."

"I'm sorry. I, uh—don't remember."

"I was going to make another. Just in case. But that was my only baking dish. Don't worry about not returning it. I don't care." Her brown dog sniffed his ratty nose at something sticky on the sidewalk.

"Nutmeg. No!" she said, yanking it back. "He gets into so much crap, this dog. But I love him. So, where are you now?"

"Brooklyn," Emma said, glancing up at the dormer window.

"New York? We love the city. Saw Billy Joel at the Garden last year—such fun. You know, I think he just gets better with age. Don't you?"

"I'm sorry," Emma said getting to her feet. "I can't. Um, thanks for ... saying hello. And the lasagna."

"Oh, it's so nice—"

Emma turned and walked away from the woman and her ratty dog, not stopping until she reached her old bus stop where she leaned against the ancient elm, waiting for her stomach to unknot.

Roshelle was outside the creperie waving for her to hurry up the street.

"What?"

"You left your phone on the table. It was blowing up."

"Who?"

"See for yourself," Roshelle said, handing Emma the phone. "I think it's your favorite captain."

"That was fast." She found the missed call and dialed back. "Good afternoon, Captain. Mm-hm. I understand. You're just doing your job. ... Tomorrow morning is fine. What time?"

Roshelle cocked her head.

"A suite on base? Thank you. ... I look forward to meeting him too. Please thank the base commander. ... Yup. See you tomorrow."

"What the fuck was that?" asked Roshelle.

"I might have shaken the tree a little."

"A little? Who'd you call that could leapfrog the FBI and the Army?"

"I had a favor to spend. Now it's spent."

"That's serious juice, Noble."

"It's gonna bite me in the ass. I've pissed some people off."

"Did the captain tell you anything?"

"Just that she did a little digging into Donnelly's investigation—she needs the rest of the day to assemble everything."

"So there's more. Any hint on what's in there?"

"Nope. But the base commander wants to meet with me. Alone."

"Which probably means whatever he's got to tell you is either classified or it's personal—something to do with your father. What do you think?"

"I think I'm about to learn what secrets are buried in Carlisle."

12

Captain Natalie Brown was standing in the rain outside the base commander's office, waiting to escort Emma Noble. This time, there was no wait in reception. The captain knocked on the commander's door. It opened without delay.

The colonel was short and squat with bushy eyebrows and a wide nose. With a fake beard, he could have passed for an extra in the *Lord of The Rings*—mining mithril in Moria. He kept his arms by his sides—not at attention, but not necessarily at ease. Next to him, a sergeant first class was arranging a fruit tray and a steaming basket of scones.

"Colonel Anderson, this is Special Agent Emma Noble of the FBI," said the captain before retreating out of the commander's office with the sergeant.

The colonel waited until the door was closed before speaking.

"Did you have breakfast?"

"You shouldn't have gone to the trouble."

"Trouble? *This?* This was no trouble. Can't say the same for the rest of this matter though. Please, have a seat. You sure we can't get you anything. Coffee?"

"No, sir. Thanks."

Sitting behind his desk, the colonel looked more imposing. Unlike the bureaucrats in the FBI, the pictures on his wall showed him in the field with his soldiers, kneeling in desert camo under a Blackhawk helicopter.

"You're an unusual person, aren't you Agent Noble?"

"I've been called worse, Colonel."

"I don't doubt that." He let his smile linger, before frowning at the files on his desk. "Tell me why you came to my base yesterday. I have snippets, but I want your story. Unfiltered, please."

Emma cleared her throat. "My father killed an Air Force veteran. Her maiden name was Orr. Lindsey Orr. In her file was a reference to a 2007 investigation at the Army War College by a JAG officer named Captain Donnelly. My father was a Marine Major stationed here at the time of that investigation. I'm trying to understand why he killed the woman. What connection did he have to her?"

"Thank you for your candor, and I'm sorry—this must be a terribly difficult time."

"Getting through it, sir. Answers will help."

"I wouldn't be so sure," he said softly. Colonel Keith Anderson folded his thick fingers together. "The call you made yesterday made for an interesting afternoon for my staff and me. Took us a while to unpucker." He rubbed his nose. "I was on the eleventh green. Chipped up close for once—my short game's always been shit. I was putting for birdie. That's when they handed me the first phone. The putt was a gimme. I don't know how they do it in the other branches, but in the Army, we putt out. Never did get to finish the round. Never got that elusive birdie. You know who was on the phone. Don't you?"

"I'm not—"

"I had the vice president of the United States in my right ear. The Honorable Kimberly Hancock. Then, they handed me a second phone, so I could put the five-star in my left ear. We take those calls fairly serious around here. But I'm assuming you knew that when you pulled the fire alarm."

"I appreciate your help, Colonel."

"We'll see," he said with a deep exhale. "Where would you like to start?"

"Captain Donnelly. What was he investigating?"

Colonel Anderson opened the thick file on his desk.

"May I?" Emma asked, reaching out her hand.

"You may not. I'll try to answer your questions, Agent. But this stays on my desk."

"I understand. So, Captain Donnelly's investigation?"

The colonel held up the file while his hand fumbled on the desk for his reading glasses. "Donnelly was here to review. ..."

He put the file down on the desk and tugged on his thick brow. "You were saying?"

"The vice president had some good things to say about you, Agent Noble. I get the feeling you don't back down from a fight. In fact, from what I can tell, you probably seek them out. In the Army, we pick our battles wisely. If an action will be disadvantageous in the long run, we avoid it. In this matter," he said tapping the file, "I would advise caution. This hill you're trying to take—it might be a mistake."

"With all due respect, Colonel, a woman is dead. My father's skin was found under her fingernails. I'm looking for the truth. Sir, please tell me what Donnelly was investigating."

"Okay," he nodded, leaning back in his chair and adjusting his readers. "The JAG was looking into matters related to the suicide of Ms. Candice Noble, the wife of a Marine Special Forces Officer stationed at the Army War College."

It landed like a sucker punch.

"My mother's death? Why would Lindsey Orr be ..." Emma sat up straight. "Was she a suspect? Did she have something to do with—"

Colonel Anderson shook his head.

"I don't understand. Why was Donnelly interested in her?"

"Lindsey Orr was in Carlisle on the day Candice Noble committed suicide."

Emma couldn't sit. Her body was pulling her into movement. She paced along the back wall of the commander's office. "You're saying the woman my father killed ... she might have met with my mother just before she committed ... before she—?"

"That's what the file indicates."

"How did she know Candice Noble? What was she doing there?"

"Have a seat, Agent Noble."

"Did Lindsey Orr have something to do with my mother's death? Is that why my father killed her? Revenge?"

"There's more. Please. Sit down."

Emma relented but leaned forward, her palms planted on the edge of the armrest.

"Why did your father leave the Marines? What did he tell you? How much of this story do you know?"

"After my mother died, he sacrificed his career to take care of me. I was still a teenager."

"I see."

"Why'd you ask that?"

"It seems your father also had friends in high places. This case was treated rather unusually."

"Case? What do you mean?"

"From what I can tell, it was a negotiated settlement at a fairly high level."

"You're talking in circles, Colonel. What did Donnelly find?"

"Captain Donnelly didn't find anything. It was the Military Police that uncovered it."

"Uncovered what?"

Colonel Anderson stood up and opened the door to his office. "Sergeant, if you could wheel it in now. Thank you."

A small cart was rolled into the office, with a VHS player resting on the shelf below the television. Anderson nodded to his sergeant and the soldier disappeared as quickly as he'd come.

"I think this will answer some of your questions, Agent Noble."

The colonel dragged a chair next to Emma and pressed PLAY on the remote. She knew he was studying her, watching for her reactions. Emma ignored him. All she wanted was the answer to why Lindsey Orr was in Carlisle on the day of her mother's death—the answer to how she and Sam Noble were connected.

The screen flickered, then brightened, focusing on the image of a Coke can sitting on a tabletop. It was like the introductory scene in a bad student film. Emma looked over at the colonel.

He lifted his shoulders, "They get the hang of it later, but the audio is good."

"What is this?"

"It'll become apparent."

"We'll get started Lieutenant Orr, I'm Captain—"

"For the last time, it's Lindy. I want to know why you dragged us out of our hotel room in the middle of the night. I'm a civilian. You don't own me anymore."

"Lindy, I'm Captain Workman. This is Lieutenant Mayock."

"I want to know why I'm here—"

The statement was punctuated by the sound of her hand slapping the table. The Coke can shivered, then disappeared out of the frame, replaced by an unfocused image of the carpet.

"Lieutenant, can you—?"

"I see the problem, Captain."

The camera was re-aimed, and the woman slowly came into focus. Emma's stomach tightened. She recognized her face from the murder scene. The picture on the screen was of a woman only a few years older than Emma was now. She was young. And alive. Emma replayed the image of Lindy Orr sprawled over the dinette in the Airstream. There had been no hint that behind that bloody face was a beautiful woman.

"I apologize for the late hour, but given the circumstances—"

"What circumstances?"

"Please state your permanent residence."

"I asked, 'What circumstances?'"

"Lindy, we're just looking for some information. Your license says you live in Cleveland. Is that still current?"

Nod.

"Why did you come to Carlisle?"

"Captain, that's none of your business."

"Were you planning on staying long?"

"No," she said softly. *"I'm tired. Can you cut to the chase?"*

"A woman died late this afternoon. She had your name and number in her front pocket."

Emma watched Lindy Orr's face turn pale, her hand covering her mouth.

"Oh God."

"Did you visit Mrs. Noble's house this afternoon, Lindy?"

She closed her eyes.

"Lindy?"

She nodded. Her chest heaved.

"Were you close to the deceased?"

She shook her head. Emma could see that the woman was crumbling from the inside out.

"A neighbor says she saw you speaking to Ms. Noble about noon. That sound right? Lindy?"

She sniffled, working hard to maintain her composure.

"How did she—? What happened?"

"That's what we're trying to find out. Can you describe her state of mind this afternoon?"

Lindy put her hand to her mouth when she'd finished connecting the dots.

"No. Not that. Oh god. Please tell me that she didn't—"

"Didn't what?"

"Hurt herself."

"What did you talk about with Ms. Noble?"

"Did she—?"

"We aren't ruling it out."

"She did. Oh god."

"Lieutenant, can you get some tissues? Actually, let's take a break. The washroom is down the hall on the left. Lieutenant, could you escort her please?"

The video continued to run, focusing on Lindy Orr's empty chair. Emma ran her hand through her hair and took a deep breath.

"Colonel? It's Workman with a quick update on Major Noble's wife. We're taking a break. ... Looks like it. She wanted to know if she 'hurt herself.' Her words, sir. ... I understand the sensitivity. I'll call you back when we finish. ... Thank you, sir. I will."

The cognitive dissonance was overwhelming. It felt as if Emma was in two places at once. The memory of the night her mother died was seared into her—the apologetic doctor, racing out of the hospital, sprinting down the breakdown lane. This video of Lindy Orr had been recorded at the same time.

When she came back on the screen, Lindy's face was puffy and her eyes were red.

"Lindy, why did you go to the Noble home this afternoon?"

"I can't do this."

"Why were you there today?"

"Please. I just want to go."

"Had you ever met Candice Noble before this afternoon?"

"No."

"Was it your plan to speak to her today?"

She shook her head and looked away.

"No."

"But you did speak to her. What'd you talk about?"

"It doesn't matter."

"I think it does, Lindy. You said you never met Candice Noble

before today. How about her husband? Major Samuel Noble? Had you ever met him before?"

Lindy Orr stared ahead. Her face reddened. She crossed her arms over her chest.

"Yes."

"Yes? When?"

"Seven years ago."

"Where?"

"A hospital in Wiesbaden. I was a nurse. He was checking on the welfare of one of his injured soldiers."

"Did you meet on more than one occasion?"

"The soldier wasn't badly injured, but the Major came in every day."

"And how well did you get to know the Major?"

Lindy Orr shook her head, then balled her fingers into a fist.

"This is on him. The motherfucker," she said under her breath.

"I'm sorry. What was that?"

"This isn't on me. Goddamn him!"

Emma rocked in her chair, covering her mouth with both hands.

"I didn't want anything to do with him. I had a guy back home."

"You knew he was married?"

She nodded.

"You and Major Noble?"

Lindy Orr closed her eyes.

"Were you and Major Noble more than friends, ma'am?"

Her eyes flew open.

"Friend? He's never been anything close to a friend. He's just a guy that said what I needed to hear, then took off when he'd gotten what he wanted. She's dead because of him. Not me. It's his fault. I will not own that woman's death. Fuck your Major Noble. He can rot in hell."

Emma leaned back. "Can you pause it, Colonel?"

"Sure," he said, pressing the remote. He touched Emma lightly on the shoulder. "I think the rain's let up, Agent Noble. Why don't you get some air."

She nodded and walked out of the commander's office in a trance, unsure of where she was going. She followed a path along a tree-lined lawn, hands on her hips, trying to coax breath into her lungs. Lindy Orr's words were repeating in her head:

"She's dead because of him."
"Because of HIM."

13

Emma Noble walked aimlessly across the campus of the Army War College until she found herself in a familiar place. She leaned against a tree, staring at a building she used to visit regularly—Sam Noble's old office. Of all the places they'd been stationed, the Army War College had been her favorite. Her father was home every night. For the first time since she could remember, they were like other families. And she'd noticed a change in her mother too. She was less depressed. Carlisle had been good for them.

Three times a week, she'd lean on this tree and wait for him to finish work. They'd go to the on-base gym together. There were plenty who could have spotted for Sam Noble—standing over him while he bench-pressed more than his body weight—but he wanted Emma. The first five reps would come easy for him. The next three with labored breathing. But it was the last two that made her nervous. His face would turn beet red and his elbows would shake and his teeth would grind— Emma would hold her palms under the bar, praying he wouldn't falter.

Come on, Dad! You got this. Push!

Sam Noble would find a reserve, and when it was done, he'd wink at her and give her a high five. He'd take most of the weight off the bar and Emma would take her turn. She'd push with everything she had. She was Sam Noble's daughter, and she would find a way to go beyond her limits because that was how she earned his pride. And back then, that was all she ever wanted.

Emma closed her eyes. She never knew him.

The colonel was waiting in his office signing a stack of documents. The TV cart had been wheeled away.

"Have a seat, Agent Noble. Give me two minutes if you don't mind."

"I'd like to see what else is on that video."

Colonel Anderson scratched his forehead, then pulled on his eyebrows before looking up at Emma. He laid his pen on the desk and slid the papers off to the side.

"There wasn't much more to see. The captain turned off the camera when the nature of your father's relationship with Lindy Orr was established. A married, senior officer in a dalliance with—well, with anyone other than a spouse, creates a prickly situation. Especially in a circumstance like this one. I'm with you—I would have preferred they kept the video rolling, but I understand the instinct."

"Is there more?"

"I can read from JAG Officer Donnelly's report. I don't expect anyone ever intended it would see the light of day. I'll skip over the infidelity bit to his recommendations." Colonel Anderson put his readers on and scanned the document. "He advocated for a court-martial of Major Samuel Noble seeking loss of rank, punitive discharge, and loss of benefits." He laid the file on the desk and looked up at Emma. "You see the complication, right? A highly decorated *Marine* major has committed adultery with an *Air Force* officer and it becomes evident based on the discovery of an *Army* lawyer investigating the death of the major's wife's suicide. It was a little sticky."

"I'm guessing you're about to tell me that Sam Noble didn't retire from the military for the sake of his daughter."

The colonel rubbed his eyebrows and nodded. "So, his paperwork had already been approved. His promotion to colonel was rescinded. He was allowed to retire with full benefits. Keep his rank. Honorable discharge."

"Friends in high places."

"Yes, ma'am. It appears there was universal support for Sam Noble's immediate transfer into the Central Intelligence Agency. That's about all I have. What else can I help you with, Agent Noble?"

She got out of her chair and paced the back wall.

"Why was Lindy Orr in Carlisle? Were they still together?"

"No," he flipped through the file. "It appears it was a short affair."

"Then why does she show up on my mother's door six years later? It doesn't make sense."

Colonel Anderson exhaled and folded his hands over his desk.

Emma tilted her head. "What? She wanted to rekindle something?"

"No," he said, looking down.

"Colonel?"

"Apparently, Sam Noble wanted to meet his son."

"His *what?*"

"Lindy Orr brought her six-year-old son to Carlisle so Sam Noble could meet him."

"His son? *His* son?"

Colonel Anderson nodded and pulled on his bushy eyebrow. "You have a brother, Agent Noble. You didn't know?"

Emma stared at the carpet.

"Agent Noble?"

"No," she exhaled, looking up at the Colonel. "I didn't."

"You want to take a beat and—"

"No. I don't." Emma ran her tongue inside her mouth and looked up at the ceiling. "My father had an affair. Lindy Orr shows up on my mother's doorstep, and for whatever reason introduces her to Sam Noble's six-year-old son. That right? That's what you're telling me, Colonel?"

"Her testimony leads me to believe she didn't expect your mother to be home. Apparently, Mrs. Noble figured everything out on her own."

"Motherfucker."

Colonel Anderson nodded.

Emma held the back of the chair. Her mother had always been fragile—still grieving the loss of her own boy. And one day she is confronted with her husband's infidelity *and* his son with the woman he fucked. She'd lost her own son, was depressed, and then discovered this? Candice Noble hadn't had any fight left in her. A bottle of wine and a step off a ledge.

"Agent Noble?"

Emma looked up.

"I'm sorr—"

"Don't be," she said, righting herself and taking a deep breath. "I appreciate your assistance, Colonel. Thank you." She gave the commander a firm handshake. "Have a good day, sir."

Emma opened the door and jogged down the steps toward the Malibu. She kept her chin up as she passed the guard station and made a right out of the Army War College and drove a mile and a half down an old road, parking in a desolate area where she stared into the woods until tears spilled out of her and she made a fist—screaming and punching, over and over, until the plastic molding on the top of the dash cracked and she'd ripped the rearview mirror off its mooring.

14

Roshelle Hess sat on the hood of the Malibu, the heel of her boot tucked into the ridges of the grill, watching her partner pace back and forth along a patch of muddy grass along the roadside. Emma had recounted what she'd learned about Lindy Orr and Sam Noble with detachment, as if she were reading secondhand news from a teleprompter. But as the telling gained momentum, her stoic facade broke and her voice cracked. Then came a long silence when Emma bent into the roadside for a handful of stones that she fired, side-arm, into the woods. Roshelle was patient. She didn't speak until Emma had spent all her roadside rocks.

"I'm so sorry, Emma."

Emma nodded, staring out at the dense thicket of woods knotted with vines of perfumed honeysuckle. There was a part of her that wanted to step off the roadside, walk in, and never come out. But she wasn't like her mother. She was stronger than that. She could muscle it down. Emma kept her arms by her side, clenching and unclenching her fists. She inhaled deeply, then blew a clearing exhale. For a moment, she thought she'd gained control of her emotions—had mastered the pain. She stared at Roshelle.

And then, Emma's traitorous shoulders quaked, her eyes pooled, and her lip quivered. And her palms opened.

Roshelle caught her before she cracked, pulling her into a long embrace. "I got you," Roshelle whispered. "I got you."

Emma dropped her head and melted into her.

• • •

They sat on the hood of the car, talking about unimportant things—some time for Emma to distance herself from what her father had done. She leaned back on the palms of her hands and looked at Roshelle.

"I blamed *myself* for her death. He knew that. And the fucker let me—he let me absorb every ounce of guilt. The entire weight of it. He stepped back and let his teenage daughter heave it over her shoulder and carry it around with her for fourteen years. He had all that time to come clean but didn't have the balls."

Roshelle nodded, letting the silence linger in the air before speaking.

"You have a brother."

"Yup."

Roshelle raised her eyebrows.

"What do you want me to say?"

"I don't know."

"Why should I get my hopes up? Sam probably killed him too."

"He'd never hurt his own son. Just like he'd never hurt you."

Emma didn't want to hear it.

"I'm serious. Whatever your father became, it was a result of losing a son to cancer. Watching his boy suffer. Trying to hold the family together through his long illness. I'm guessing the Nobles were a functional, happy family while your brother was alive, right? After that, everything spiraled. Everything changed when he died. It had to."

Emma closed her eyes. She was in the backseat of the family car, buckled into blue upholstery.

It was cold outside. Late afternoon. The sky was dark with storming clouds—a dismal, heavy block of gray. Everyone that attended the graveside service had gone—they'd shaken out their black umbrellas by the side of their sedans and minivans and driven home. The family car was alone in the parking lot. Emmy listened to the sound of the freezing rain pattering off the roof and the whoosh of the heater blasting hot air into the backseat—hot enough to make her nose run. Mother was in the front seat, weeping through the rosary. "O my Jesus, forgive us our sins, save us from the fires of hell, lead all souls to Heaven, especially those in most need of Thy mercy." She repeated the prayers, pressing her shaking fingers into each wooden bead—a circular, unending plea to an unavailable God.

Emmy watched raindrops gather in the rubber at the top of the backseat window then slide down, keeping herself occupied by guessing which drop would win the race to the bottom. The heat and her mother's crying fogged the glass. With her small finger, she wrote her brother's initials in the corner of the window. Through the condensation, she could see her father kneeling in the mud of a fresh grave, his forehead leaning against a polished headstone. And Emmy Noble lifted her delicate finger to the glass and drew a heart around him.

"Your brother's death broke your parents open. Left a hole in each of them. And, Emma? Holes demand to be filled. With something. Anything. Your mother filled it with fear. She became more fragile and depressed. Sam Noble filled his with recklessness. He volunteered for dangerous missions. He cheated on his wife—slept around. He acted out. Psychologically speaking, it's predictable behavior."

"You're defending him?"

"Of course not. I'm just saying that Sam Noble has been broken for a long time. I'm sure your mother's death decimated him. And all that pain? He swallowed it. Because he couldn't let his daughter know it was his fault. He has to keep it secret—because Emma Noble is the last good thing in his life. And if she hates him then—"

"Fuck him."

"I'm telling you, he'd never hurt Henry Orr."

"He didn't have any problem murdering Lindy Mortinson. Or Ted Mortinson. Why'd *they* have to die? You're a profiler. Why did Sam Noble kill *them*?"

Roshelle Hess leaned forward, resting her thumbs against her forehead. "I've been struggling with it. Men like your father—they have a code. They protect the herd. It's how they self-identify. It's not out of the question that he could have had a breakdown and snapped, but there would have been signs—things you would have noticed."

"So, what then?"

"I thought, maybe, he was recruited by someone he trusted. Someone he respected that made him believe killing Ted Mortinson was moral—justified. But now? The connection between Sam Noble and Lindy Orr doesn't fit … it isn't what I was expecting."

"Kind of caught me off guard, too."

Roshelle leaned forward. "This starts with murders and kidnappings—all connected to some nebulous crypto-skimmer ring. But now? Knowing the significant relationship Sam Noble had with Ted Mortinson's wife? It looks more like—"

"A violent end to a love triangle."

"Yeah. But fourteen years later? It doesn't make sense."

Emma hopped off the hood. "Let's get out of here," she said, opening the driver's side door.

Roshelle picked the rearview mirror off the floorboard and tried in vain to reattach it.

"I think you killed it."

Emma yanked the mirror out of her hand and flung it through the window where it fell silently into the dense thicket on the other side of the road.

"Okay," whispered Roshelle. "Guess you're done looking backward then."

• • •

It was a two-hour trip to DC, a straight shot down country roads that wove through rolling green hillsides fertilized with the blood of Civil War dead. Her chest was heavy. She rolled down the window, wanting to feel the rush of cool wind against her face. But there was no wind—only oppressive humidity. For three miles, the Malibu crawled behind a black, horse-drawn carriage, clopping down the asphalt—a train of cars backed up behind its rickety wheels. Emma tried to ignore the churning in her stomach and the knot that seemed intent on wringing her out. She rolled her neck across each shoulder hoping it would alleviate the cramping muscles of her upper back.

"It's going to get worse, Noble. The night terrors, too."

"This car's not made for tall people—I'm stiff."

"Tick. Tock. Tick. ..."

"Jesus, you're a pain in the ass." Emma looked over at her partner and made a half-hearted grin.

The cellphone in the cupholder rang.

"It's Buck," Roshelle said, putting it on speaker.

Emma leaned toward the phone, "You find Henry Orr?"

"Good afternoon to you, too. What's going on? Why the sudden interest in *him*?"

Roshelle pulled the phone to her face, "Henry Orr is Noble's stepbrother."

"Wait."

"Yup."

"Shut up."

Emma interrupted, "Buck, I'd like to find the kid."

"Are you friggin' kidding me? He's your brother? That's the connection? The wife and Sam Noble were—?"

"Buck! Where is he?"

"No idea."

"I assume someone has been looking for him?" said Roshelle.

"Victim Services sent a chaplain to inform him of his parents' murder. He wasn't there."

Emma inhaled. "Wasn't *where*, Buck?"

"His dorm room at Indiana State. Apparently, he left."

"Jesus, it's the middle of summer. Of course he's not there."

"I don't know, Noble. He only has two addresses and he wasn't in Windsor Hills."

"Okay, so, what do we know about him?"

"Other than he's going to be a junior at Indiana State? Not much. Got a picture of him here. Pretty much all we have."

"Send it to me. I need you to find him. I want to tell him what happened to his parents. I owe him that."

Emma pulled to the side of the road, waiting for the image to load. When it did, she stared at the picture of the baby-faced kid with feathered hair parted in the middle. He was in a gray sports coat sitting in front of a mottled blue screen—probably a yearbook picture. Looking at him, Emma had no doubt that Henry Orr was her brother. She was staring at a younger version of her father. The ruddy complexion. The deep-set eyes and thin lips. Emma dropped the phone to her lap. After a moment she looked at it again, widening the image.

"Jesus."

"What is it?" asked Hess.

"I've seen him before."

"You've met Henry Orr?"

"No. Where are those pictures that were on my uncle's coffee table? There were three of them."

"My bag in the backseat. Why?"

"Let me see the one with the—the one with the geyser. There were some tourists in front."

Roshelle handed the picture to Emma.

"I knew it. See this kid? The one with the crutches? Tell me that's not Henry Orr."

"Looks like him."

"That picture was in my father's office. I asked him about it once and he took a long time to answer. Just told me that, if I ever go, I'd probably like to see Old Faithful."

"After what went down in Carlisle, maybe Lindy Orr wouldn't let him get close to Henry. If he wanted to see his son, Sam probably had to do it from a distance."

"*Old Faithful.* Jesus, it's almost funny."

Emma pulled the Malibu back on the road as Roshelle reached for her phone.

"I'll give Byum our ETA."

"No. Don't call him yet."

"Why?"

"There's one more spot I want to look—a hole Sam Noble might have crawled into. A hiding place. If he's there, I want to be the one who slaps the cuffs on him."

"Call it in. Let someone else do it. Your father is indicted in two murders. We'd be stepping over the line."

"They won't mind … as long as we bring him in."

Roshelle exhaled.

"Hess, he's probably not there. Besides, it's just outside DC. We're still on the way."

An hour later, the Malibu was in rural Maryland, managing potholes on a dusty stretch fifteen miles off the highway. Emma slowed. To her left was a green pasture where half a dozen Holsteins grazed in the shade of an American Elm. She was close. Two hundred yards later, she spun the wheel to the right, pulling into a small gravel parking lot in front of a weathered blue sign bolted to a tall chain-link fence.

Weaver's Storage.

"What is this place?" asked Roshelle.

Emma hopped out of the Malibu and walked to a low-slung, sun-faded trailer at the corner of the property. An ancient, dusty dial on a chipped plastic card in the window informed visitors that management would return in ten minutes. Emma tried the door. Locked. She cupped her hands on the window and looked in.

"You think he's hiding in *there*?"

"No."

"Noble, what are we doing?"

"This is a front. There's no business here."

"How do you know about this place?" asked Roshelle.

"It's Gunny's. He's wealthy and paranoid—and prepared for anything. It came in handy last year when we needed to hide a terrorist. You see the three storage buildings behind the fence? Each building has four orange garage doors. Twelve doors in all."

"Yeah."

"Middle building. Last door on the left. And so you know, Gunny's probably watching us."

Emma looked up at the camera perched over the fence and gave it the finger before entering her mother's birthdate into the black box by the gate. The red light blinked green and clicked. She grabbed the handle and swung the gate wide. Minutes later, Emma pulled up an orange garage door, standing in front of a mess of cardboard boxes, bikes, and junk.

"Noble, it's a storage shed. Nothing but crap in here."

Emma threw boxes to the side, making a path to the back of the garage. She waved Hess over and pointed to a steel handle in the floor. The keypad was behind a stained mattress leaning against the wall.

"Only Gunny, my father, and me know about this place." She entered the unlocking sequence, and the circular hatch unbolted. Emma lifted the handle and LED lights blinked down the circular staircase.

"Holy shit."

"Forty feet to the bottom. Come on."

Emma stepped cautiously, descending the steps—one hand on the rail and one resting atop her holstered Glock. "Sam Noble?" she shouted into the depths. "It's Emma. I'm coming down."

The bunker was cool, a constant fifty-five degrees. It smelled like gun grease. She stepped off the final metal stair onto the concrete floor. Roshelle was on her heels.

"Sam?" Emma yelled.

Her question echoed around the bunker. It looked the same as Emma remembered from last year: a small stainless steel table, two chairs, a refrigerator, microwave, and a stack of canned goods piled on a metal counter. Around her were three doors where Sam Noble might be hiding. Emma took the steel, blast door on the right, knowing it led to Gunny's weapons cache—a private arsenal of sniper rifles, grenades, claymores, and everything in between. *Something for everyone*—that's what Gunny had told her last year when the bunker had been a welcome resource in her fight against terrorists. Now, it served as a haunting reminder of Sam Noble's resources.

Emma listened to Roshelle's shouts. "Bathroom—clear. Computer Room—clear. He's not here."

Emma nodded and leaned against the concrete wall. She pinched her eyes.

"I'm out of bullets, Hess. I don't know how to find him."

Roshelle didn't say anything. Emma looked over at her. She was staring at the stainless-steel table. "Noble?" she pointed.

It was a small white card. Emma walked close enough to see the confident, cursive handwriting. A familiar script. *Emmaline.*

Adrenaline was pushing her heart around. She took a deep inhale and picked it up. She read the message from her father. And read it again. And again.

"Noble, what is it?"

"He wants to talk."

15

Emma didn't bother turning off the light in her hotel room. Going through the motions of pretending she'd sleep was pointless. She lay above the covers, staring up at the ceiling. She had memorized the short invitation from her father but couldn't help reading it off and on throughout the night. Sam Noble had known she was going to the bunker yesterday, and the implications of that had her mind spinning. In five hours, she would sit across from him and share a coffee. The note said he had some things he needed to explain.

Yeah. I guess you do.

At 3 a.m., Emma was showered and dressed. She sat on a worn cushion in her hotel room, the heel of her right foot tapping to the beat of her anxiety. By 5:15 a.m., she could sit no longer. Emma closed the door behind her, walked through the hotel lobby, and out on the street. The sun was barely above the horizon line, and the early morning was already hot and sticky with humidity. With the exception of a few dog walkers and some joggers, she had the streets of Alexandria to herself. Emma walked down Madison Street toward the Potomac to a small park on its banks. Her mind was a carnival carousel—in motion—going nowhere.

Emma sat on a bench for a while, watching the greenish-brown water lap against the decking of the short pier. She tilted her head into the morning sunlight, hoping its warmth might calm her. Emma was curious. And angry. The two emotions raced through her chest, running neck and neck.

At 6 a.m., two gray-haired women in summer dresses strolled along the path near Emma. They walked out on the wooden pier, their arms linked at the elbows, leaning in and speaking in whispers. She glanced left and saw a homeless woman rise from her nest of newspapers in a shady copse of maples to squat and piss against a tree before pushing her grocery cart of blankets and bags out of the park. Emma looked at her watch and tried to fill her lungs with summer air. It was almost time. She walked slowly out of Oronoco Bay Park and up Pendleton Street. For twenty minutes, she ambled through Old Town, walking the same square—two blocks up, two blocks over, two blocks down, two blocks over.

She kept her head glued to the sidewalk, stopping at the corner across the street from a small diner. Its name was painted in cursive on the window: *Rosie's Kitchen.* It was ten minutes before 7 a.m. She looked up and down the street before entering. A small bell tinkled above the door. A few disinterested heads raised, then lowered.

"You can sit at the counter," said a middle-aged man as he edged through tables with a tray of food.

Emma didn't want to sit at the counter.

"You want a table? That one by the window—give me a minute to run their check."

"Thanks."

Emma sat with her back to the wall under a framed poster of white-washed homes poised on cliffs above an aqua-blue sea. The menu felt heavy in her hands—seven pages for breakfast. A Greek diner. Sam Noble's favorite kind.

Emma sipped coffee, fully aware that caffeine would only amplify her anxiety. Her attention was drawn to a local know-it-all with a deep voice manspreading over a stool, ranting about politics to a couple that seemed unarmed for conflict.

"You want to order or are you waiting for someone?"

"Just coffee for now. Thanks," said Emma.

She looked out the window, watching the sidewalk—preparing herself for the sight of him. Her watch and the clock on the wall both confirmed that he was late. Almost a half hour late. A small group waited at the entrance, their eyes straying to her table, hoping she'd be leaving soon.

"Two scrambled, easy—no onion," the waiter yelled toward the kitchen.

The entrance bell tinkled. Emma swung her eyes to the door. It was him. He towered over the people waiting by the entrance. They gave him a wide berth as he made his way through the crowd. His chest and biceps rippled under his tight black T-shirt, but his normally clean-shaven face was whiskered. He looked tired. And why wouldn't he be? Being on the run for murder was exhausting business.

Their eyes met.

And, in the race between her curiosity and her anger, it was rage that won the day. She wasn't meeting her dad for breakfast. A killer was coming for coffee. The murderer of Ted Mortinson and Lindy Orr. The man who'd caused the death of her mother.

Her hand balled into a fist under the table.

"Emmaline," he said quietly, sitting down across from her. "Thanks. It's good to see you."

She lifted her chin. "I don't give a shit what you have to say. I just wanted you to hear it from me."

Sam Noble looked at his daughter.

"You're under arrest."

It happened at lightning speed. The manspreader had a weapon in Sam Noble's neck. The waiter screamed, "Hands on your head!" The agents posing as customers jumped out of their seats, Glocks pointed.

"Hands!"

He complied, never taking his eyes off Emma. They forced him to the ground and handcuffed his wrists. FBI cars appeared seemingly out of nowhere, blocking the street in front of Rosie's Kitchen. In seconds, more agents in blue windbreakers burst through the restaurant doors.

Emma bent down by her father's ear.

"You have the right to remain silent. Anything you say, can, and *will* be used against you in a court of law. You have the right to speak to an attorney, and to have an attorney present during questioning."

Her heart was racing. They lifted Sam Noble into a standing position. Emma spoke to the manspreader holding her father.

"Walk him up the steps of the courthouse real slow—bring him right through the front doors. I want the cameras to see him." Emma whispered in her father's ear, "You deserve everything that's coming your way. And I hope it's hell."

• • •

Sunlight poured through the restaurant window. Emma shielded her eyes, looking at the crowd forming behind the police barricade. Inside Rosie's, agents milled together, exchanging verbal backslaps—the post-game, locker room, high-adrenaline, after-action euphoria. Emma stared out the window for a while before gazing into the bottom of her coffee cup.

"Guy had no chance."

"Clockwork."

"You see Johnson blast out of the kitchen? Glizzy in one hand, whisk in the other? What were you making back there, Chef?"

Emma held the mug with two hands, staring into it, trying to keep her world from spinning off its axis. Her chest thundered. Someone patted her shoulder but was kind enough to keep moving past without speaking. She closed her eyes, willing her prefrontal cortex to spark the executive function—the self-control and adaptable thinking—that would distance her from the moment. Instead, it was her amygdala firing on all cylinders, replaying a Hallmark highlight reel of cherished father-daughter memories. Her traitorous inner eye conjuring every moment of love, playing it like a musical montage.

She tried to blink back the flood of tears behind her eyes. "Goddammit!"

It hadn't been her intent to yell it across Rosie's and force the heads of every agent in the place to dart in her direction. But it had worked: the slideshow behind her eyes had stopped.

It struck her how easy the takedown of Sam Noble had been. Late into the evening, she and a team of agents had explored every scenario they could imagine, trying to solve for the skills of the man they were bringing into custody. It was almost too easy. Emma replayed everything from when he entered the restaurant until he was pulled out the door. She examined the movie in her head in slow motion, frame by frame.

As soon as she saw him coming through the front door, she'd been consumed by adrenaline. But his eyes hadn't searched for her. He knew exactly where she was. Then he broke eye contact and looked around the restaurant, sweeping his vision clockwise, identifying every agent in the restaurant.

Sam Noble walked into the diner knowing exactly what was about to happen. He came knowing his daughter had betrayed him. Emma looked up at the ceiling. If he knew, then why did he come?

She pulled out the note, re-reading his words: *things I must tell you in person.* But it was too late for "things." Words couldn't cleanse the blood that he'd spilled. Words couldn't bring her mother back. Emma ripped up the note as Roshelle Hess pushed through the crowd of law enforcement by the door and sat where her father had.

"You okay?" she asked.

"Yup."

"How'd it go?"

Emma nodded. "Fine. Smooth. No problem."

"Did he say anything?"

"I wasn't in a listening mood."

"Then it's over," Roshelle said, looking around the restaurant. "How you holding up?"

Emma shrugged. "Fine."

Roshelle didn't seem convinced that her partner was "fine," but ignored the impulse to point it out. "I spoke to Byum."

"And?"

"He's pleased."

"So, we didn't damage our careers too badly then?"

"They're processing your father, then the interrogation will start. Byum wants you to meet him in the viewing room."

"Not interested. You hungry?" Emma said, passing the heavy menu across the table.

"It wasn't a request. He wants you there when they question your father."

Emma shook her head and grunted something under her breath. "You think he'll confess?"

Emma tugged at her ponytail. "He's already been indicted. There's more than enough evidence to convict. I honestly don't care what he does. It doesn't matter."

• • •

Sam Noble wore an orange jumpsuit. He sat alone in the interrogation room, a belly chain across his chest attached to handcuffs. Emma watched from the other side of the two-way mirror. Her father wasn't a narcissist, but for the full ten minutes that he was alone in the room, he stared at the mirror. Emma cleared her throat and folded her arms.

"I'm sorry, Agent Noble. This can't be easy," Frank Byum said, standing next to Emma. "Director O'Toole is pleased with your work on this. We all are."

"Thank you, sir."

"He's notified the SAC in New York: Three weeks. Paid time off. Go somewhere and clear your mind."

Byum stepped closer to the mirror as the FBI interrogators entered the room to speak with Sam Noble. Emma didn't recognize them, but she knew they wouldn't be rookies. Capturing someone that carried as many classified secrets as Sam Noble made this a high-profile case. The agents in the room would have been briefed about his military history and his counter-terrorism experience. They would be cautious, well aware that this was no ordinary criminal.

Emma stepped closer to the mirror, her shoulder next to Byum's.

"I'm Pilou. This is Agent Holt. Can we get you anything? Coffee? Water?"

Sam Noble didn't respond. His eyes never left the mirror in the back of the room.

"We're going to ask some questions. It's your right to have an attorney present. Do you want a lawyer?"

Sam Noble brought his silver-cuffed wrists to his face and scratched his forehead. Pilou asked again and got nothing from the prisoner. He made a show of looking through a file before asking his next question.

"You are Samuel L. Noble of St. Louis County in Missouri. Correct?"

Pilou waited, drumming his pencil. He glanced over at the two-way mirror. Agent Holt leaned forward.

"Mr. Noble, your DNA was found under the fingernails of the woman you killed in Ohio. You were identified at a murder scene—also in Ohio. A federal grand jury has indicted you for the kidnappings of Lilith Hart and Bryce Colliers, and the death of Maria Peterson. Based on the evidence before us, I can assure you, sir, you *will* be going away for a very long time."

The prisoner shifted his weight in his seat—his eyes never left the mirror. Emma watched her father. His face was stone. Impossible to read.

Pilou leaned in, "You can help yourself. Now's the time. The murder of Ted Mortinson. The kidnappings. We want to know who hired you. You give a little, you get a little. You don't have to die in prison, Mr. Noble."

Holt uncrossed his legs. He spoke gruffly. "You understand what my partner is saying? This is your chance. Who hired you?"

Emma bit the skin around her thumbnail. Her father stared at her through the two-way mirror. The agents were trying to turn the screws, but Sam Noble showed not the slightest concern about his predicament. She looked over at Byum.

"He's not going to talk."

"Let them do their job, Agent Noble."

"My father's stubborn. If he's decided not to speak, there's nothing they can say to make him change his mind. This is a waste of time. Anything else you need from me, Chief?"

Byum relented. "A three-week vacation is mandated, Agent Noble. Director's orders. He wants you to get some rest."

Emma opened the door and took the stairs two at a time until she landed in the lobby of the federal courthouse. Roshelle was waiting near the front doors, searching Emma's face for a clue to what happened.

"He didn't say anything."

"What now?"

"Apparently, I'm on vacation."

"I've got some days to burn. You want company?"

"Thanks. But I need some alone time."

"I get it."

Roshelle pulled Emma in for a hug. "Call me tomorrow and let me know how it's going. Okay?"

"You miss me already, don't you?"

"Not so much. By the way, Buck called. Needs to speak to you."

Roshelle turned and jogged down the courthouse steps. At the sidewalk, she waved, then disappeared around the corner. Emma moved behind a column and pulled out her phone.

"Hey Buck, you find Henry Orr?"

"I heard you brought in your old man this morning. How you—?"

"I'm fine. Did you find him?"

"No. But we're closer. Henry told his friends he was going to his girlfriend's parents' house in Maine for the summer. We've passed the information to Victim Services in New England."

"When you find him, let me know. I want to talk to him."

"You got it. I've got some more on him if you have time."

"All ears."

"Henry Orr has a bad wheel—birth defect. Bunch of surgeries, but still needs a cane to walk. Drags a leg. Doesn't seem to slow him down too much—nearly made All-State as a high school swimmer."

"Okay."

"He's smart—like crazy smart. Might be a bona fide genius. Computer whiz."

"Computers? Buck, his stepfather was connected—"

"Way ahead of you. I thought the same thing, especially when I heard Henry Orr attended a tech conference in Las Vegas—a convention where high profile hackers are known to congregate. You've got nothing to worry about. He was there legit—a university-sponsored trip with his professor and classmates. He looks like a good kid, Noble. No reason to suspect he knew what Mortinson was up to. Sit tight. We'll track him down. I'll put you in touch when we got him."

"Buck? This professor that took him to Vegas?"

"Wendy Oaks."

"I want her contact info."

"I got it somewhere. Why?"

"Just want to ease my mind that this skimming thing wasn't a family affair."

"Hold on," Buck said. "Yeah. Here. She spends the summer in a cabin in Northern Michigan. Lucky woman. You ever been up there, Noble? Beautiful place."

"Nope."

"All right, I just texted you her contact info. I'll let you know when we've got the kid."

Emma hung up and jogged down the courthouse stairs. She waited at the crosswalk for the light to change. She wanted to apologize for what Sam Noble had done to Henry Orr's family. It was unlikely that a sibling relationship born in such a hellish volcano of dysfunction had much of a chance, but she held out hope because she wanted to believe this story could have a happy ending—even if it was probably just a fantasy.

A car horn blasted a half block away. She turned her head to see a long, black Town Car parked against the curb. Next to the vehicle was a short man in a sharp suit with very large ears standing like an unhappy statue. Emma met Uncle Gunny's stare, and when the light changed, she turned her back on Sam Noble's best friend and walked away.

16

It was 2 a.m. With the exception of a two-person cleaning crew shuffling through Concourse C, dumping plastic trash bags into a yellow bin, no one else was in sight. Emma closed her laptop and, lacking the energy or care to unzip her bag, laid the computer next to her empty shoes on Gate 32's blue carpeting. The emotional rush that had kept her afloat for days without sleep had punctured. She was drowning in exhaustion.

Professor Wendy Oaks hadn't answered any of the calls Emma had made that afternoon. Nor had she returned any of the messages. There were two reasons she wanted to speak to the professor: one professional, the other personal. Yes, she wanted to confirm that Henry Orr had no connection to his stepfather's sordid dealings, but she was also curious about *him*. What kind of person was he?

Emma was on mandatory vacation. She could spend her time as she pleased. And the only thing she wanted to do was speak to Dr. Wendy Oaks. So, she booked a spontaneous vacation to Northern Michigan, reserving a yurt forty-five minutes' drive from the professor's cabin.

She'd missed her scheduled flight out of Dulles after getting mired in traffic on 267. The 10:33 she caught was on standby to Midway in Chicago. Wendy Oaks's remote home required three flights and a three-hour drive. If there were no delays or cancellations, Emma figured she'd be at the cabin tomorrow by late morning or early afternoon.

She'd done some background research on the professor. Wendy Oaks had been teaching at Indiana State for seven years and had tenure. Previously, she was at Northwestern for three, moving on when it

113

became apparent there would be no permanent offer coming her way. Professor Oaks had published two papers in the *Journal of Computer Science*: the first on complex multi-format media logic, the other on management systems featuring the intersection of fuzzy logic and artificial intelligence. Emma was grateful for those mind-numbing papers—they were the deep-sleep knockout punch she needed.

Emma's eyes were half open. She unleashed a long, open-mouthed yawn. The flight leaving Gate 32 wouldn't board for another five hours. If she could catch sleep now and doze on the next flight, she had a fair chance of feeling human by the time the plane hit the tarmac at Pellston Regional. Her eyes were so dry and tired that it hurt to blink. Emma stretched her long body across the short row of plastic seats, raising her knees to make her legs fit the space. She twisted her white earbuds into place. Her farewell song began with a flute solo joined by a pattering of percussion, and before ABBA could ask, *"Can you hear the drums, Fernando?"* the lights behind her eyes clicked off and she vanished in black-out sleep.

• • •

Emma threw her credit card on the counter of the rental agency. They pointed her toward a new car with less than two hundred miles on the odometer. This time, she checked to make sure the AC was functioning. It was. Emma called a few more times from the highway to give Wendy Oaks a heads-up that she was on the way. No answer. It was likely that the professor was out of town, but Emma didn't care. She could either try to track down Wendy Oaks or sit in a yurt thinking about her father's arrest.

With every mile closer to the woman's cabin, the roads got worse. She'd left pavement a while ago. The tires were kicking up mud, applying a thick patina to the undercarriage and sidewalls of the once-spotless rental car. She glanced at the bars on the phone—or lack of them. She was deep in the woods, in a cellular black hole. Interesting that a computer science professor would choose a technology wasteland for her summer home.

The dirt road forked. Emma went left, passing a yellow "Dead End" sign. Half a mile later the road turned into a wide walking path. The wheels sunk into wet, weedy grass. A hundred yards later, the rental had to ford a stony stream before beginning a final rattling ascent toward a rustic two-story cabin with a green metal roof. Emma parked behind a mud-caked, black Audi.

The weathered cedar-sided cabin sat in the middle of a two-acre clearing surrounded by tall pines. There were no electric lines coming to the property. The solar array in the side yard probably provided more than enough juice to manage her needs. A gray satellite dish and a green 500-gallon propane tank were on the other side of the clearing. The cabin was off-grid and self-sustaining. Emma gave Professor Oaks full credit for having the guts to live alone out here. It was far enough from civilization that surviving an emergency, even in summer, was unlikely. Emma glimpsed the ripples on the greenish-blue lake behind the cabin and understood the appeal.

"That's far enough," said a voice from the upstairs window. "You lost?"

Emma looked up at the open screen window on the second floor. She walked across the grass toward the cabin. "Professor Oaks?"

"I said stay put. I asked if you were lost."

"No, ma'am."

"I don't want whatever you're selling. Beat it."

"I'm Special Agent Emma Noble with the FBI. Not sure if you can see it from the window. I'm holding up my badge. I'm looking for some help with a case." Emma walked forward a few steps.

"The government gave you a badge. So what? You people think you can wander on private property and do whatever you like. Is that it?"

"I left messages. I'm trying to find one of your students. I'm worried he might be involved in something that could put him in danger—or jail. I'd like your help."

"Who's missing?"

"We're trying to locate one of your students that went to Las Vegas on the school trip last spring. May I come in?"

"Which student?"

"I'd prefer not to yell up to a second-story window. Can you come down to the door, please?"

"Hold your government badge to the doorbell. I want a look at it."

Emma walked up the rickety wooden steps and onto the gray porch in front of the open screen door.

"Can you see it, Professor?"

Emma waited for a response that didn't come. She cupped her hands to the screen door.

"Professor?"

"I saw the badge," said the voice *behind* her.

Emma jerked with surprise, wheeling around—her hand instinctively coming to her right hip. A woman in green coveralls was coming out of a garden shed hidden in the tree line. It was not the professor's wildly unkempt graying hair, or her vigorous gum-chewing that drew Emma's attention. It was the break-action double-barrel shotgun bent over her forearm.

"Professor Oaks?"

"Saw you coming three miles back."

For whatever reason, Emma had imagined the professor to be a liberal intellectual—a nature lover, foraging mushrooms in the woods of Michigan. She didn't expect to meet an anti-government paranoid toting a shotgun, but it had been a couple years since she'd graduated. Things change.

"I don't like sneaky people," the professor said. She walked slowly across the lawn, her rubber boots sucking through wet mud. Professor Oaks didn't meet Emma at the porch. The woman rooted herself on the grass, keeping her distance. It seemed to Emma that she was estimating how much time she needed to snap the hinge and pull the trigger before the FBI agent could reach her.

"I called. Many times. It wasn't my intent to sneak up."

"I don't pick up calls from unknown numbers. And I prefer to be left alone," said the professor, shifting her weight from one foot to the other. She held the shotgun with the confidence of a woman that knew her way around guns.

"Just a couple of questions. I'll be quick, I promise." Emma smiled, hoping it would warm the atmosphere. "Can we talk on the porch?"

Professor Oaks stared at Emma, grinding her gum with enough force to ripple the cheek muscles up her thin face. It took a while for her to comply. The professor clomped up the wooden stairs and laid the shotgun against the cedar shingles by the screened door. She pointed Emma into a black metal bench under the window and disappeared into the house.

Professor Oaks was an academic—a computer science professor spending her summer in a beautiful, isolated cabin. No doubt she had a top-notch noodle. But as Uncle Gunny often said, "*The smart ones? They're loonier than Hogan's goat.*" Emma didn't have the professional chops to diagnose the woman, but if the competing theories were the natural, well-placed caution of a woman living alone in the boonies or some kind of disabling paranoia, she was betting on the latter.

Professor Oaks returned with two floral Tervis mugs of steaming tea. She didn't hand one to Emma. Instead, she placed them both on a metal table beyond reach. She walked to the far side of the porch and skidded a wooden rocking chair across the planks until she got it up to the screen door, keeping herself within arm's reach of the shotgun. The professor crossed her arms over her chest and rocked a while, staring at the FBI agent and chewing her gum with vigor.

"Well?"

Emma leaned forward, putting her elbows on her knees.

"I have questions about Henry Orr. He is one of your students, right?"

Professor Oaks nodded. "He's missing?"

"That's probably not the right word, we're just having some trouble tracking him down."

"Smart young man."

"How smart?"

Wendy Oaks leaned back in her rocker to consider the question. "I don't suppose you have a computing background, Agent?"

Emma shook her head.

"Then my explanation wouldn't make much sense to you."

"Dumb it down."

"You work for the government. I don't know if I can *make* it dumb enough for you."

Emma couldn't help but smile. "I'll try to keep up."

"Computing has many languages and many rules. The best students have an above average talent to grasp the languages and follow the rules in order to find a creative solution to a problem. Henry Orr isn't like that. He has his own voice—his own language. He breaks the rules. I've never had a student whose mind is so balanced and functions at such a high level—logically and creatively. Both sides of the brain. He is, actually, fascinating. His intellectual curiosity is equally intense and he remembers everything he comes across. That dumb enough for you, Agent?"

Emma inhaled. The way it was going, it was doubtful that she and the professor were headed for a lasting friendship.

"How does that skill translate into the real world when he graduates? What lies ahead for someone like Henry?"

"He can do anything he wants."

Emma nodded. "Last spring you brought him to Las Vegas, to a tech convention. My understanding is that it draws a significant population in the hacker community. Why did you bring your students to that particular convention? It's certainly a long way from Indiana."

Wendy Oaks rolled her eyes. "You people. Hackers. My god. For your information, the department *requires* me to bring students to that convention so they can continue cashing checks from the Wenton Trust. It's the cheapest conference the school could find—not even that great."

"Okay," Emma nodded. "But we think it's possible that Henry Orr may have had someone in his orbit that was associated with cyber-crime. Did you see any sign that he could have gotten pulled into that?"

Wendy Oaks stopped chewing. Her eyes deadened.

"Henry Orr's going to be a junior when classes start up again. Already, he's got the top tech companies in the country competing with each other to make an offer. He could leave school now and make a killing. He doesn't need to do anything illegal. And, anyway, he's not that kind of kid. You people and your narratives. This is why no one trusts the FBI."

Emma sighed. She was looking forward to getting off this porch. The yurt was starting to look good—kind of. She was tired when she'd made the reservation. Maybe too tired. But as lousy as the professor's company was, the trip to her cabin had been worth it. Henry Orr was what Emma had been hoping he'd be—a good kid who, if he could get through the loss of his mother and stepfather, was headed for a bright future.

Emma clocked her head at the sound coming out from the woods. It was nothing—just a murder of crows bursting out of the trees—taking flight across the lawn toward the lake.

The only thing for Emma to do now was wait for Henry Orr to come back from New England. In the meantime, she'd try to figure out what to say to him when they met. Emma was pretty sure she'd never have the right words for that. As of now, she was on vacation, with more than enough time to wade through the many sins of her father. She'd mourn *his* loss differently than her mother's. It would undoubtedly be painful, but she was resolved not to sink into it. She didn't want to allow herself to get stuck in that mental mud. There were books to be read and naps to be taken. Lots of naps. And when she emerged from her vacation hibernation, she'd be ready for whatever would come next.

Emma leaned forward, offering her hand, thanking the professor for her time.

The next four seconds became a blur of instinct, action, and adrenaline as a blast of gunfire erupted from the treeline, splintering the cedar shingles near Emma's head. The professor froze. Emma did not. She leapt at Wendy Oaks, throwing herself with enough force to topple the professor—flipping her over the rocking chair toward the screen door. The next volley of gunfire blew across the porch like a hailstorm. The wood decking erupted with splintered shrapnel.

17

The professor's mud-caked rubber boots slipped under her as she attempted to right herself. It was an impotent scramble of elbows and knees until Emma drove her shoulder into the professor's rear end, launching Wendy Oaks through the screen of the front door. Emma followed close behind, swinging her foot and catching the corner of the interior oak door, slamming it shut before the next wave of bullets ripped into the cabin.

The men outside were yelling and firing a deafening barrage of gunfire. Emma tried to slow her mind. She needed to think clearly—and fast. All she knew was that, whoever was out there, they lacked discipline. It was a poorly coordinated attack. Professionals would have taken their time and ended both of them with two shots from a concealed position in the woods. Hell, as exposed as she and the professor had been, an amateur could have taken them out with ease. Somebody in the woods had wanted to be a hero and fired too early. But the fact that the small army coming at her was undisciplined offered little consolation.

Emma exhaled, fighting off a bonfire of inconsequential questions that didn't matter yet. Who were they? Why were they trying to kill Wendy Oaks? What the hell was going on? The answers would come later—if she lived. For now, it was about surviving and allowing her training and the rush of adrenaline to fuel her. She had a full tank of both.

Glock in hand, Emma belly-crawled across the red pine cabin floor toward the window to get a look at what was coming her way. Her head never got above the sill before her reconnaissance ended. The attackers concentrated fire on the first floor windows, exploding the knotty pine wall in the living room and sending Emma's head ducking into the baseboard.

Wendy Oaks remained where Emma had tackled her—a few feet from the door. Finally thawed from her frozen state, she was in motion, crawling on her knees toward the door—in the process of making a terminal decision—trying to snatch the shotgun on the porch.

"No!"

Emma pinned her down before she could turn the knob. Oaks didn't like that. She swung a fist. Noble deflected it easily. It might have been her cabin, but the professor was no longer in charge. Emma waved the barrel of her weapon toward the stairs.

"Up there! Now!"

Wendy Oaks didn't move. Emma pushed the professor toward the balusters.

"Get into a bathroom and lock the door."

Emma took a glancing inventory of the living room: leather couch, oval blue-braided country rug, stone fireplace, a hallway leading to the back of the cabin. She remembered the lake behind the house. Unless Wendy Oaks had a gassed-up powerboat idling for a quick getaway, running for it was a sucker's bet. She crawled to the other side of the living room and slid her back against the wall until she'd reached the corner of the hallway. Emma craned her head around to see if she could get an idea of the cabin's layout back there. Her head was ringing with the noise of war. She gave it a clearing shake, and the sound of gunfire vanished. It had stopped as suddenly as it had begun. *Why?*

Emma peeked her head around the corner to get a better view of the kitchen. She saw the fragile screen door at the back of the house knock against the frame before coming to rest. It wasn't the wind. There were men with guns already in the house. She scrambled back, throwing herself against the living room wall. Positioned where she was, two feet from the hallway, she could surprise the first person through the door and take them out easily. A fine strategy for one attacker. But multiple? It would leave her in the open. Her first shot would give away her location.

The cabin wasn't huge. It wouldn't take them long to clear the kitchen and whatever other rooms were back there. She looked at the leather couch across the room. Moving was a gamble, but Emma liked her odds better over there. She lay on her back, pushing her heels into the wood floors, scootching toward the sofa—her head up, the Glock aimed at the hallway. She rolled behind the couch and got herself into a semi-protected firing position.

Shit. She caught Wendy Oaks out of the corner of her eye. The professor was halfway down the stairs, a pistol in her hand. Emma waved her back up the stairs, but it was too late. The professor had stolen Emma's concentration from the hallway. She didn't see the man in the black shirt soon enough. He slipped into the living room, taking aim. Emma wheeled on him, firing two shots, but not before the intruder had pulled the trigger. Wendy Oaks staggered, lost her balance, and fell against the stair wall. Her eyes were wide open. She was alive—a black stain spreading across the thigh of her green coveralls.

Emma was ready for the next one. The heavyset guy came in sloppy, lowering his gun when he saw his comrade on the floor. She didn't hesitate, firing two killing rounds that sent him sliding down the wall, leaving a streak of blood down the knotty pine.

She stayed in cover, training her gun on the hallway. Helping the professor wasn't an option. Not yet. She waited—three long minutes of anxiety and controlled breathing.

The walkie-talkies from the belts of the corpses on the floor squawked.

"How we lookin' Danny O? You get the bitch?"

"Yo, Dan?"

"Couyon? Couyon?"

"This thing working?"

Their confusion bought Emma a little time. She ran for the stairs, grabbing Wendy Oaks and heaving her over her shoulder. The professor was dead weight, but she was still alive—groaning all the way to the top of the stairs. Emma laid her gently on her back in the upstairs hallway.

"Let me see," she said, ripping open the professor's pant leg.

Emma leaned into the wound and was greeted with a spray of pulsing red rain.

"Shit."

Wendy Oaks slapped her palm against wood floor. "I'm going to kill that motherfucker."

"Who? Who's out there?"

"Gardener, that motherfucker."

A wave of crippling pain rolled the professor's eyes back into her head.

"Stay still," Emma said, charging into the bathroom for towels and a wicker hamper she could use to elevate the leg. "Press the towel down hard. As hard as you can. Okay?"

The professor nodded.

The radio downstairs squawked again.

"Dan? Couyon?"

"Professor, who's Gardener? How many men?"

Oaks's face was turning milky white and waxy—she was going into shock. Emma took over, pressing her palm hard enough over the wound to elicit a back-lifting scream. A scream loud enough to be heard outside. The towel wasn't keeping up. The professor was bleeding out. Emma grabbed a pillow case from the bedroom and tightened it with the carabiner from her belt, locking it across Oak's thigh. It was all she could do for now. She leaned against the wall and put a fresh clip into her Glock. She ran her red-stained hands across her cheek, flipping away her hair. Emma felt panic rising in her chest.

Breathe. Slow your heart rate.

They were her father's words. Words from a few years ago. They'd been sitting at a bar and grill in the central west end. She'd just showed him her acceptance letter to the FBI. Sam Noble wouldn't give his blessing unless she agreed to train with him before attending the academy. He pushed his beer away and looked her in the eye.

"You need to learn how to be smooth. I'll teach you."

Emma smiled. *"Smooth? You? I invented smooth. I got all the moves."*

Sam Noble didn't think she was funny. He left the table and walked his beer to the other side of the bar, sitting on a stool with his back to her. Emma sat by herself a while before joining him.

"What do you mean, teach me to be smooth?"

"When your heart is beating out of your chest. When you can't get air in your lungs. You have to find balance. To be smooth is to live. To panic is to die, Emmaline."

She looked down at Wendy Oaks's face. Emma closed her eyes, concentrating on her breathing. Trying to remember everything her father had taught her.

Sam Noble had put her through her paces. Long mornings on the weapons course. Long afternoons in the weight room. He ratcheted up the pressure and the stress, demanding balance. *"Nec Temere, Nec Timide,"* he would yell when she was moving too fast or if she hesitated and moved slowly. He had a knack for worming into Emma's head, burrowing into her psyche. The training sucked. But, over time, he yelled less and spoke softer. One afternoon, seemingly out of the blue, he nodded and said, "You're ready."

Emma concentrated on the situation at hand—thinking through the threat.

It's not just about being smooth, Emmaline. You've got to be smart. Assets and Liabilities—you've got to think like an accountant.

Assets: three clips, 15 rounds each, and whatever Wendy Oaks had in her pistol. Liabilities: an unknown number of armed attackers, a middle-aged professor bleeding out, defense of unknown terrain with her back to a water body, no way to call for help. She stopped listing her debits—it wasn't helping her morale. She didn't need a green visor to know she was in the red. The men outside were regrouping for another attack. She didn't have much time.

To panic is to die.

18

Emma gently squeezed the professor's wrist. Her pulse was weak. If she didn't get medical attention soon, she was likely going to die. Wendy Oaks's paranoia was well-placed. She'd suspected someone might be coming for her someday, and with Emma's luck, that day happened to be the one when *she'd* strolled up to her property.

Emma looked down at the woman. The professor had a secret or two. Gun-toting militias don't make a habit of targeting antisocial computer science teachers from state schools in Indiana. But it didn't matter now. Emma's only job was to find a way out.

It'd been seven minutes without a shot fired. The radio squawks trying to contact Dead Dan and his friend Couyon continued. Emma checked her magazine cartridge again. Surely, whoever was leading the team out there had his thinking cap on, putting together a new plan. What would she do if she was in their position? There were really only two approaches: storm the cabin, or burn it down. The first was the most expedient, but had a greater potential for danger. Smart money was that, unless they were after something inside, they'd burn the house down. The cabin's location was far enough from civilization that the emergency response wouldn't arrive until after it had been reduced to a glowing pile of embers. She could picture them, drinking a beer on the lawn, waiting to pop anyone that stumbled off the porch with their hair on fire.

Emma looked down at the professor.

Her paranoia was well-placed.

Well-placed paranoia.

"Saw you coming three miles back."

Emma kicked herself for not putting it together sooner. Wendy Oaks had cameras—probably lots of them. And a speaker in the second-floor window.

Jesus, Emma.

She patted down the professor, searching for her phone. It was in the back pocket of her green coveralls. Emma rolled her onto her side; Wendy Oaks's eyes flew open in pain.

"It's okay, Professor. I'm going to get us out of here."

Emma tilted the phone toward her, assuming facial recognition would provide entry to her cell. It didn't. She leaned down.

"Professor, we don't have much time. I need you to open your phone."

Wendy Oaks's eyes were closed. Her head was drooping toward her shoulder. It was cruel, but there was no other choice. Emma whispered "sorry" before squeezing the professor's thigh.

"You motherfucker," the professor groaned thinly.

"Phone. Open it. The cameras are our only chance."

The professor licked her dry lips. Emma bent close to her ear as the woman exhaled a series of puffed breaths bearing symbols, letters, and numbers. The screen brightened and, before passing out, Oaks pointed to the app that connected the satellite dish, the cameras, and the speaker in the upstairs window.

"Thank you," Emma said, toweling the perspiration off the professor's waxy forehead.

The system was organized in folders: Interior, Lakeside, Front Perimeter, Road. Emma started with "Front Perimeter." The eight boxes on the screen were small—all live-streaming. She clicked the first. It was a wide shot of the cabin. A guy was jogging off the porch toward the woods. Fed up with the silence from their comrades inside, he'd been sent to peep in the window to see what happened. In seconds, he would be telling his boss that their buddies were dead. The ceasefire was about to end.

Emma looked at every perimeter screen. There were at least six men in the woods, all crouched in cover with automatic rifles pointing at the cabin. Two more were in the side yard behind the solar array. Another had taken up a position on the back corner of the cabin by the lake.

They'd done an adequate job of covering every exit. The professor's security system confirmed the situation was grim.

Emma pulled up "Interior," choosing the camera in the back by the kitchen. She half expected to see an attacker flipping open the propane burners and stove. They hadn't gotten to it yet. The next screen showed a laundry room and another door at the side of the house. The guy at the back of the cabin was covering both doors, waiting to drop anyone that exited. She toggled back to the perimeter cameras. The team in front was on the move, coming out of the woods in a line, their weapons trained on the cabin. Leading the way was a tall man in a black, skull-dripping Punisher T-shirt. He looked pissed. She double-checked the positioning of the guy lakeside. He hadn't moved. There wasn't a way out of Wendy Oaks's cabin without a firefight.

Emma bent her head closer, inspecting the image of the guy behind the cabin. There was something black behind him, tucked into the woods off the path. She widened the screen. Emma experienced her first flicker of optimism—it was a camo-painted ATV with beefy wheels. In order to reach it, either the guy had to move, or she'd have to take him out.

Upstairs speaker in the window.

Emma opened the audio app on Wendy Oaks's phone. She got to her feet, but in the process, she fumbled the phone, dropping it on Wendy Oaks's leg.

"Shit!" Emma yelled, her voice echoing out the second story window.

"Yeah, you *are* in the shit, lady," came the response from outside.

He wasn't wrong.

Emma yelled, "Wait!"

She saw the approaching army hesitate, lifting their weapons at the second-story window.

"Wait. Please!"

The tall man in the Punisher shirt raised his fist in the air. His men halted on the grass.

"It was Wendy Oaks! She killed your friends. I had nothing to do with it. I was just visiting. You don't want me. I'm so scared. Please don't hurt me."

"Tell the professor to come out. We'd like a word with her."

"She's been shot. There's so much blood."

"She alive?"

"Yes."

"Well, if you can't bring her to us, I guess we'll come to you."

"No! I have her gun. You stay where you are."

"You even know how to use it, Gumdrop?"

"Please. I just want to go home," Emma pleaded into Wendy Oaks's phone.

"We'll make a deal. You bring the professor down the stairs. Put her by the front door. You can run out the back. Free as can be."

"You won't hurt me?"

"I'm giving you six minutes. Starting now."

Emma closed the audio and took a deep breath. As expected, the guy lakeside moved closer to the cabin's back door. They weren't letting anyone out of that house alive. But he'd moved. He wasn't covering both doors now. And that's all Emma needed. But six minutes wasn't enough time. She bent down.

"Just leave me," said the professor.

"Nah. I need you alive. We got some talkin' to do."

Emma had the professor bite down on a towel, begging her not to make a sound. She nodded. Emma lifted her over her left shoulder, putting her in a fireman's carry.

"Five minutes. ... Hurry it along, Gumdrop."

Emma visualized her retreat: down the stairs, through the living room, down the hall, slip through the kitchen, leave through the side door, and scramble down the path to the ATV. If luck went her way, she wouldn't have to tangle with the gun by the back door.

Wendy Oaks was over her right shoulder, the Glock was in her left hand. Getting down the stairs required strength and balance. She stepped down with her right leg. The professor's weight shifted right. Emma lost her grip. She reached out to catch her. The gun tumbled down the stairs. She swore under her breath—a circus bear had more grace.

"Yo, Gumdrop! Three minutes."

At the bottom of the stairs, Emma was forced into a deep squat with the weight of the professor still on her shoulder. She retrieved the gun and power-lifted into a standing position, staggering to get her balance.

"One minute!"

The guy's watch was fast. There wasn't time—not while carrying Wendy Oaks. Leaving the professor wasn't an option. Emma had less than a minute to get across the living room, through the hallway, into the kitchen, and out the side door with a grown woman on her back. It was ludicrous to think she could manage it.

I'll teach you to be smooth, Emmaline.

She exhaled and moved. Not rashly. Not timidly. *Nec Temere. Nec Timide.* She was in balance, gliding through the living room and down the hall. The back of the house was trickier: she'd only seen it on camera, and if she made a sound, there was a killer by the back door waiting to pounce. Sweat beaded on Emma's forehead. Her right arm was going numb. She turned and backed through the kitchen, her weapon pointed at the door, just in case the guy came through. Passing through the kitchen, Emma was forced to rotate in the thin space by the laundry to avoid beaning the professor's head against the door frame.

"Coming in, Gumdrop!"

Time was up.

Emma heard the lakeside guy charge through the back door just as she stepped out the side door. There was no more thought of being smooth. Emma raced as fast as she could down the path toward the ATV.

The keys were in the ignition.

"Okay," Emma said, gently bowing Wendy Oaks off her shoulder and leaning her against the vehicle. "We're almost there. I'm going to put you—"

Somewhere along the way, the white towel had fallen out of the professor's mouth. Her eyes were open, but her complexion was no longer waxy white. She'd turned a sick shade of yellow and her lips were a bluish purple. Emma rested two fingers against the side of Wendy Oaks's neck. She was dead. Emma laid the professor's body across her lap and fired up the ATV. For the next five miles, she drove fast, looking over her shoulder most of the way.

Why had armed men come to kill Wendy Oaks? What secrets died on the professor's lips?

19

The smoky mirror behind the bar had a seam. A defective ripple. When Emma tilted her head left or right, it distorted her face. She was sure it wasn't a boozy mirage. Pretty sure. Hard to know. She'd been sitting on a barstool fashioned from auto parts for going on two hours. In that time, she'd learned the bartender with the swishy mustache specialized in two types of drinks for patrons who wanted to put their brains in park: a Detroit Dirty Martini and a Painkiller (for those needing to be sweet-talked out of sobriety). Her nose tingled. It was a boozy tickle—like a quartet of buzzing fireflies were dancing up the bridge of her nose. Bob Seger boomed through the speakers, and, while she didn't sing along, she was drunk enough to be thinking about it.

Emma looked at her reflection, moving her face side to side through the ripple. She positioned herself so the seam went through her nose, bisecting her face, dividing it into two distinctive halves. One side favored her, lighting her face with a soft, gentle glow. She wasn't staring at that half.

"How you doin' down there, Muffin?"

Emma put her Dirty Detroit on the bar and looked up at Mustache.

"Oh, honey," he said, flattening an eyebrow with his index finger, "It's too early in the day for angry drunk people. How about we turn that frown upside down?"

Emma Noble lifted her martini at him as more violin playing fireflies marched into her forehead. She looked back at the mirror, trying to find the ripple. It was just there. Where had it gone? She shifted in her seat. Then looked down to see if she was on the same stool.

Another sip. And another. Her enthusiasm for mirror ripples died. Emma lifted the coaster.

Gearheads—Detroit's Drag Capital

It wasn't her plan to stop here for a drink. She just came upon it as she walked aimlessly downtown. As good a choice as any for day drinking. Mustache had the good taste to close the blinds so the Tuesday morning sun didn't spoil the after-hours vibe. Gearheads was decorated with a vintage auto theme. Oil and gas globe lamps from long-extinct companies hung around the bar. Mr. Swirly Stache was adding ice to a silver tumbler under a Pure Oil lamp. But that's not the one Emma liked. It was the roaring cartoon lion that was her favorite. She squinted. Maybe it was a tiger.

Gilmore Blu-Green Gasoline.

It was a good name. Fun to say. Like a song.

"Gilmo-oore Bluuu-Gree-een Gas-oo-line."

"What's that, Honey?"

Emma waved him off and swiveled on her stool to see how many other party people were in the house. There was only one couple in the back, snogging in a booth. But that's not what she was looking at. The TV was playing local news footage from Wendy Oaks's cabin—ATF combing through the grass, putting shell casings in plastic bags. The crawl at the bottom of the screen: *Woman killed in attack. No suspects. If you have information call* ... She didn't need to see more. Emma swiveled, putting her face back in her Dirty Detroit. It was empty. She pointed toward the glass. Mr. Splisshystache nodded back.

Good man.

It had been a long day and night. The cabin was still standing when she'd gotten back to it after giving the local cops her statement. Wendy Oaks's mud-splattered black Audi was still in the drive. Of course, the amateur army was gone, and they'd taken Dead Dan and Couyon with them. The ATV had been reported stolen from Iowa two years ago. As impossible as it was to believe, other than shell casings and blood, the amateur attackers hadn't left much evidence in their wake.

Then there had been a long conversation with her SAC and Chief Byum that went on, ad nauseum, into the late evening. They seemed torn, not sure if her actions deserved punishment or accolades. Emma suffered through it, finally escaping and catching a flight through Grand

Rapids to Detroit. She took to the streets to clear her head. When that didn't work, she stepped into Gearheads.

Emma steadied herself, putting her palm against the bar. She closed her eyes.

"Gilmo-oore Bluuu-Gree-een Gas-oo-line. Gilmore. The Blu-Green-Gasoline. Blu and Green Gasoline. Roawwr."

"You doin' okay, Squirt?"

"Don't call me that," she said to the two bartenders with the identical mustaches.

She felt a hand on her shoulder. It was a short man with impossibly big ears—sitting on the barstool next to her.

"We need to talk."

• • •

An alarm screamed in her ear—a painfully loud chirping that pierced Emma's fitful REM sleep. She half-opened the lids of her bloodshot eyes, her brain slow to assess what was happening. As her vision cleared, she learned two things: 1) She was waking in a luxury suite. 2) Someone was pounding a spike into the back of her skull—a five-star, banging hangover.

Emma turned, barely lifting her head off the pillow, trying to find the source of the head-splitting noise. It was a miniature alarm on the bedside table. There were three ibuprofen and a plastic bottle of Gatorade next to it. For two minutes she fumbled with the blasted thing, trying to find a way for it to cease its barrage of chirping sirens. Emma rolled away. On the other side table was a tented marketing piece from the hotel—the MGM Grand Detroit. She couldn't afford a place like this.

Her memories of last night came slowly.

Check that, not last night. It was this morning. Hammered by lunchtime. Nice work, Emma.

She reached into her brain bag, grabbing for a clue to how she got here. Her memory was broken. There was the globe lamp—Gilmore Blu-Green Gasoline, the bartender with the handlebar mustache trying to poison her on Dirty Detroits, the wobbly stool, the buckling floorboards—then the spinning. The fucking spins.

She rubbed her palms across her face, sinking her fingers into her eyelids trying to stop the banging. Gunny? Was Gunny in Gearheads? What the hell was he doing there? Then she remembered him guiding her into an elevator. She looked at the tasteful wallpaper and white-painted millwork. A suite at the MGM Grand was right out of Uncle Gunny's first-class playbook. He was always looking for opportunities to throw down his AMEX Black.

The fingers in the eyelids weren't working. She picked her head off the pillow and reached for the ibuprofen and Gatorade. There was a handwritten note under the medicine.

Squirt—Dinner at 18:30. Meet in lobby.

P.S. You smell worse than Nebraska farm-wind. Shower.
New clothes are on the living room couch.

The suite's Bose Speaker displayed the time—5:45 pm. She had a notion to ignore the dinner invitation and sink deeper into the comfort of the soft pillows, but Uncle Gunny being in the same Detroit bar at the same time was no coincidence. He'd meant to find her—track her down.

We need to talk.

She had enough time to soak in the whirlpool and get her fill beneath the shower's massaging rain with its seven spray settings. The water and the medicine helped. Emma wrapped a long, soft towel over her nakedness and walked into the suite's living area. Two Nordstrom bags were on the tan couch. She emptied them—designer jeans and blouse in one, the other, a matching set of intimates that a woman with excellent taste must have selected for her.

Gunny was sitting in a lobby chair by a ficus tree. He was dressed casually. Sports coat over a blue Oxford with an over-the-cuff Rolex on display. Gunny uncrossed his black summer-wool pant leg, rising with the easy grace of someone half his age.

"I enjoyed the Foster Brooks impression this morning. How you feeling?"

"I don't know who that is. And I don't want to talk about it. And I'm not hungry."

"I see you got the duds."

Emma rubbed her eyes and inhaled. "Why are you here, Gunny? To scold me for arresting my father?"

"Let's not do this here," he said, giving her a one-sided hug.

He extended his short arm like a maître-d', pointing her toward the hotel's double doors. A black Town Car was waiting by the curb. Emma didn't wonder how much Gunny knew about Sam Noble's crimes. He moved in elite circles with people who owed him favors or were currying his. There was precious little information that stayed out of his grasp. Of course he knew what Sam Noble had done.

Uncle Gunny held the steakhouse restaurant's door for her. It was quaint and dimly lit. And empty. Only a solitary table in the center of the restaurant was dressed for dinner—a candle flickering on it broke the relative darkness of the place. Emma understood. Their conversation was meant to be private. So, in Uncle Gunny fashion, he'd bought out the entire steakhouse for the evening. She placed the cloth napkin on her lap then rested her forearms on the edge of the table.

"Did you help him? Because if I find out you did, you're going to jail too."

Gunny ignored the question, nodding toward the server who placed a silver bucket on a stand beside the table, a bottle of champagne inside. Emma didn't know anything about wine. What she did know, was that she had no use for alcohol. Ever. Again.

"There's a lot you don't know, Squirt."

"I know I put your buddy in a cell—where he belongs."

Gunny rubbed his nose. "He'd probably agree with you."

"I asked you a question. You knew, didn't you? You kept his secrets."

He shrugged and peeled back the cage guarding the cork.

Emma put her palm over her glass, "I'm not celebrating."

He poured a glass for himself, swished it counter-clockwise, then inhaled through his nose—taking a moment to appreciate it before speaking.

"He sent you a message. He wanted to speak with you. You didn't give him the chance, did you?"

"He's a murderer."

"He told me—I believe his exact words were, '*She'll have me in cuffs before I can sit down.*'"

134

"I let him sit."

"I lost the bet, then. *Not Squirt*, I said. But, as usual, your father was right. People want to believe love is unconditional. Apparently—"

"Really? I don't need this bullshit. We're done," she said pushing the chair back.

"You think Sam Noble is capable of *murdering* civilians?"

"Oh, I know a lot about what my father is capable of. Now."

"He made a mistake. Actually, he made quite a few. He asked for my advice. I gave it to him. He didn't take it. So, here we are."

"We're calling murders, kidnapping, adultery, and an illegitimate son that led to the suicide of my mother—we're calling those mistakes?"

"You're angry."

"Yeah. I'm fucking angry."

The water in her glass vibrated. Her phone was next to it. She turned it over. Steven Buck was calling. Between he and Gunny, it was an easy choice.

"I have to get this," she said, walking away from the table. "Yeah. What's up Buck?"

"Christ, I've been trying all day. Did you get my texts?"

"I was, um, indisposed. What's going on?"

"Henry Orr doesn't have a girlfriend in New England. He lied to his friends. We don't know where he is."

"What?"

"It gets worse. Forensics found hair samples in the Airstream. He was there."

Emma closed her eyes, letting the news sink in.

"Yesterday, they took your father out of his cell to interrogate him again. For all I know, they've still got him in there. They're searching the woods around the campground for the kid's body. Everyone's looking, Noble."

Emma lifted her eyes to Gunny. He was running his finger around the rim of his champagne glass, staring at her. The former Marine was a hard man to read. He rarely showed emotion—always calm, always above the noise. Like her father, he could be a cold, unemotional desert, but tonight he was giving something away. Emma could see it in his eyes.

"I'll call you later."

"Sorry to be the bearer, Noble."

Emma sat down, placing the phone by the water glass. She leaned forward, meeting Gunny's stare head-on.

"Where is Henry Orr? Is he alive?"

Gunny took a long, unchampagne-like sip, draining the contents of the fluted glass. He wiped his face with the thick, cloth napkin. "Sam should have been the one to tell you."

"Tell me what, goddammit?"

"What you need to do."

"What *I* need to do?"

"Your father predicted every move you've made this week, Squirt. You did everything he said you'd do."

"What on earth are you talking about?"

20

Sam Noble looked out the window, checking his watch for the third time in five minutes. The cleaning woman, Banich, was late for work. It was important to him that she showed up for work today. Because she was the first clue—and first clues were always the most important. He pulled a brown notebook from the front pocket of his cargo pants. He flipped through it, looking again at Ted Mortinson and the people in his life for something he'd missed—something he should have seen. He closed the notebook. It didn't matter now.

Sam looked out the window again. She should have been here by now.

The dented blue Buick rolled slowly down the street and pulled to the curb. The cleaning woman snuffed out her cigarette and blew smoke out the window before walking to the trunk to gather her supplies. She was an interesting woman with a varied history. He waited for the key to enter the front lock before swinging open the heavy wooden door. Peg Banich jumped back, half-launching an expletive before sucking it back into her mouth.

"Oh boy! You got me there, Mister," she said, tapping her palm over her chest.

"Can I give you a hand with that?" he said, leaning toward her bucket.

"No, thank you."

"You sure?"

"Like the lady says, never depend on the kindness of strangers," she said, pulling the vacuum over the threshold. "You know what

137

I'm—what was her name? You know the book? The trolley ... my head's not on straight this morning. The one that went crazy at the end of the story. She depended on strangers and look where it got her. You know what I'm talking about?"

Sam Noble nodded. "Streetcar Named Desire.*"*

"Tennessee Something-or-other. Can't remember. You like books? Or movies?"

"Both."

She pointed her thumb at her chest, "I'm strictly a reader. It's better in your imagination." Banich picked up her tray. "Hollywood always blows it. Read Steven King and you'll know what I'm talking about. They screwed up The Shining*—wasn't even close to the book. How hard is it? I mean, they have the story in their dumb little hands, how could they screw it up? But they sure do." She went back for the bucket by the door. "You a friend of Mr. Mortinson?"*

"No."

Peg Banich tilted her head, looking a little closer at Sam Noble.

"So you must be a contractor then—I saw your big truck. Mr. M didn't tell me you'd be here, but it don't matter to me as long as you clean up after yourself. I start upstairs and work my way down—finish in the kitchen. I'll try to stay out of your way."

"I'm not going to be here long, Peg."

She shot a look at him.

"Do I know you?"

"No."

"How'd you know my name?"

"I've been waiting for you."

"You know my name and you've been waiting for me*? You're giving me the willies, Mister."*

"Sorry. Not my intention."

"Why've you been waiting on me?"

"I need your help."

"But I don't know you."

"Put your things down. There's something I need to show you."

Peg Banich looked him up and down. "Mister," she said eyeing the front door, "this is Mr. & Mrs. M's house. Whatever you want, you need to talk to them. Not me. I'm leaving now."

"I can't talk to Mr. Mortinson. It's not possible."

"Have a good day, Mister. I'll come back later."

Peg Banich took a step toward the door, but that was as far as she could get before Sam Noble stopped her—pulling her gently into his shoulder.

"There's nothing to worry about, Peg."

"Why were you waiting for me? What do you want?"

"I won't answer the 'why,' but I'll tell you the 'what.' But first, I need to show you something."

"What is it?" she said, backing away.

"Mr. Mortinson."

"Mr. Mortinson?"

"He's down the hall. In the study."

Sam stood outside and nodded at Peg Banich with her hand on the knob to open the door. As he expected, she screamed when she saw her client lying in a pool of his own blood. Her hands flew to her mouth and she bolted out of the room. He caught her before she could run away. She swatted at his hands, recoiling from him.

"Shh. Relax."

"Oh Sweet Jesus!" she said, her eyes wide. *"You did this! Oh Sweet Jesus!"*

"Breathe, Peg."

"You killed him!"

Sam saw her fear turn into panic.

"I can't be here. Let me out."

"You need to call the police."

She shook her head violently, *"I can't be here. Oh, Sweet Jesus."*

"But you are here. The neighbors have seen your car. You know as well as I do that leaving now will make things much worse for you."

She stared at him.

"Make it worse for me?"

"An ex-con—a convicted felon—seen running away from a murder scene? That's not a good look for you."

Peg Banich took a step toward the front door.

"Think it through. You know it's going to be much worse if you leave."

Her neck turned crimson, the color inching north into her cheeks. Tears formed in her eyes.

"Who are you?"

"I'm not going to tell you that."

"You're going to kill me and make it look like I murdered Mr. Mortinson, aren't you? That's why you waited for me. You're going to kill me."

Sam Noble put his hands on his hips and sighed. "That's ridiculous. Come into the kitchen. We need to talk." He pointed at the glasses in the cupboard. "You need some water?"

"I'm not taking anything from you."

"That's a shame," Sam said, reaching into a compartment in his cargo pants. He pulled a wad of cash, hundred-dollar bills, tied with a red rubber band. "I was hoping I could give you a gift of appreciation—for the awkward situation I've put you in."

"You want to give me money?"

"It's all for you."

Sam watched her stare at the cash.

She wiped her face with the back of her hand. "I'm not going back to jail. And however much that is in your hands—it ain't worth prison. I'm serious. It ain't. I'm not going to cover for your murder."

"Good." Sam Noble nodded. "That's good."

"Good?"

"Look at my face, Peg. Could you pick me out of a book of photographs?"

She nodded.

"After I leave, you're going to call 911. And when the police come, you're going to be very upset about finding Mr. Mortinson's body. Tell them you saw me running out of the house when you got here. That's not so hard, is it?"

"Why would you want me—"

"The 'why' isn't important. Will you do that for me, Peg?"

Peg stared at the money. "That's all? Just call the police?"

"And tell them about me."

She looked up at him and then at the money in his hand.

"Tell the truth, but not the whole truth. Take the money, Peg."

"You killed a man and want to be found? Why not just turn yourself in?"

"That's not how this is going to work."

She relented and grabbed the wad of cash.

"You need to memorize my license plate."

Peg Banich put the money in her fanny pack. "Suit yourself. But I don't understand the game you're playing."

"It's no game."

It was done. Sam Noble had lashed himself to the mast. Whatever happened next ... whatever his fate, it was no longer in his hands. A higher power would absolve him or send him straight to hell. And he was at peace with either outcome.

21

G unny laid the napkin on the table. "I told him he was making the mistake of his life. You know what he told me? He said, 'I've already made the mistake of my life. It's all up to Emmaline.'"

"What's up to me?"

"His life. Your brother's. All of it. It's up to you."

"Up to me? What the hell is going on, Gunny? Where is Henry Orr?"

"Sam promised to protect them. He failed. They killed the mother and they took Henry. I don't know where he is—neither of us does."

"*They* killed the mother? You've got your facts upside down, Gunny. Sam Noble killed Lindy Orr. His skin was found under her fingernails. *That's* why he's in a prison cell."

Gunny rubbed his temples. "You don't know a damn thing, Squirt. Sam was trying to protect them. Lindy Orr called him out of the blue. Told him she was worried about their safety—her husband was mixed up with dangerous people. Sam put Lindy and Henry in his Airstream and started tracking her husband, trying to figure out what he was up to. He underestimated the danger. When he found her dead … when he saw they'd taken his son. He didn't take it—" Gunny coughed into his hand and took a sip from his water glass. "Sam called me. From the campground. He wasn't himself. I tried to talk him out of it, but there was no reasoning with him."

"I don't—"

"He's been drowning in guilt for more than a decade. You know the secret he's been keeping. I promise you, it's been killing him. He couldn't come clean because he thought he would lose you too.

I did everything I could—begged him to tell you when you were in high school. Even gave him the name of a good therapist who could help grease the skids. You deserved to know about your brother. Sam waited too long."

Gunny waited until the server had refilled his champagne and retreated. "Operationally, I don't know anyone with your father's courage. But with this thing—what he did to his family? All I can say is, shame is a motherfucker. It makes you do cowardly things."

"But his skin was—"

"Sam pulled her broken fingernails across his forearm."

Emma pushed her palms into the table. "Why the hell would he do that?"

"I asked him the very same thing." Gunny sighed. He looked up at the ornate millwork in the ceiling for a long while, trying to find the words. "Your father is brilliant. We both know that. He sees around corners better than anyone I've ever known. And he knows you, Squirt. He knew you'd rush to Ohio to clear his name. He knew you'd go to Lester's and see that the Airstream was gone. And he knew that, as the evidence mounted against him, you'd ask why. He wanted you to learn the truth on your own." Gunny rubbed the space between his eyebrows with his thumb. "He *wanted* you to be the one that brought him in—"

"You're saying," Emma held up her hand. "You're saying, Sam Noble framed himself?"

Gunny looked up at her. His eyes were tired. He nodded. "Yeah. That's what I'm saying."

Emma stared at Gunny, her head spinning. Framed *himself?* "You're telling me that his son ... that Henry Orr's life is in danger, and instead of searching for him—"

Gunny leaned forward and shook his head. "When he saw Lindy Orr's body in the Airstream and understood that they'd taken Henry, he flat out unspooled. The clarity of it hit him between the eyes. He'd lost everything that mattered to him. And it was his fault. He failed his wife. Failed his daughter. And now, he'd failed his son. He's—" Gunny shook his head, "Emma, your father's lost. He wasn't capable of mustering for the fight. So, he put it in your hands. All of it. Right now, you're better equipped to find Henry than he is. Check that. You're *better* than he is. And he knows it."

"Gunny—"

"Sam put himself in prison. For crimes against his wife. And his kids. And he was damn thorough about it. He walked in and double-bolted the cell door behind him." Gunny sighed and pushed his glass away, "Sam is broken. Your brother is the only person who knows what happened in that Airstream. The one person who can clear your father's name."

"*If* he's still alive."

BOOK TWO

Nine Days Earlier

22

The upside-down man blinked into the basement's dark night. He inhaled the dank smell of the place, the tinkering echo of engine grease, wood lacquer, and mildew. He was zip-tied into a chair at the bottom of the stairs. He'd been there a long time—long enough to now believe that this wasn't a waypoint but an entombment. He couldn't see the rusted pipe above his head, but he knew it was there—birthing bubbles of condensation that released out of the darkness. The last bomblet landed between his eyes. It lingered on the bridge of his nose a while before becoming a wet itch that trickled, patient and painstaking, under his lash, across his freckled cheek—finally dropping into the hollow of his inner ear.

By now, the upside-down man had lost his energy from straining against the zip ties that fastened his wrists and ankles to the chair. And he'd lost some hope too. But he would never surrender all hope. Giving up was the last measure of despair, and Henry Orr was not the kind of young man to forfeit himself with a whisper of helpless acceptance.

He was at the bottom of the stairs for a reason. It was his fault. He'd landed an improbably wild, suckering punch into the eye socket of his captor, a neanderthal named Mr. Rose. The man punched back, knocking the air out of Henry's lungs. Then, while Henry fought for air, the beast zip-tied him to a chair, opened the basement door, and kicked him in the ribs—launching him down the wooden stairs. Henry's skull broke the fall when it slammed against the concrete floor. He couldn't feel it with his hands, but he was sure a fist-sized knot was blossoming behind his ear. It wasn't his only pain. His wrists were cut and bleeding from hours of futile wriggling. His good leg, being at an altitude higher than his head, fired an endless barrage of pain missiles up his thighs, into his hips, and across the small of his back.

If that wasn't enough, an hour ago, Henry had lost his bladder. Maybe two hours ago. It was hard for him to judge time. And when his dam broke, the stream of his piss rushed up his chest and neck, then dripped off the back of his head where it pooled on the concrete floor. His brown Captain America T-shirt was damp with urine.

The pipe released another wet bomblet that landed under his bottom lip. Henry Orr screamed out with a voice too dry and too hoarse for yelling—swearing into the black night until he couldn't make another sound. A tear slid off his cheek and into the scraggle of his youthful sideburn, and, there in the dark, with time on his hands and a good and capable brain for thinking, he couldn't keep himself from being consumed by the one thought that debilitated him most. He'd been unable to save her, and no matter how he tried, he couldn't stop hearing his mother's screams.

• • •

He hadn't slept. Or he didn't think he had, but the basement had lightened without his noticing. Henry licked his cracked lips with his dry tongue. He could now see his nemesis above, the sweat-beaded copper pipe bracketed to the concrete ceiling. The basement was mostly empty save for an empty wooden bookcase, age-weary and bowed, propped against the wall with a half dozen mason jars on the floor next to it, the contents dark and unrecognizable. Henry blinked, aware that he wasn't alone. He had the company of a brown roach, slinking cautiously from the drain's weep hole. It had been a short staring contest before the roach charged—scurrying across the concrete floor and darting across Henry's neck on its journey toward an even darker place.

A few days ago, everything had been normal. He'd been playing *Call of Duty* in his room, minding his own business. Drinking a soda and munching on chips. Then his mother ran into his room, ripped off his headphones, and threw his game controller on the floor.

"Chill, Mom."

"We're leaving. Grab your things. Now. Don't argue."

Henry pressed for answers.

"Ted's not who we thought he was."

They didn't take her car. They got out of Windsor Hills on the backs of three separate Ubers, then waited in a grocery store parking lot for a stranger in a black truck to bring them to the campground. The muscle-bound fifty-something man didn't say much—just kept looking at Henry through the rearview mirror.

"Who was that guy?" he asked later.

"Someone came to help. That's all."

"That's it?"

"That's it."

His mother had slept across from Henry in the other twin bed of the Airstream. He was trying to remember the last thing she said to him. He spent a long time trying to remember, because last words were important. Or they should be. Henry decided it was probably just "goodnight." That must have been the last thing she'd said. But it hadn't been a good night. Far from it.

They were sleeping when the men came. Henry was thrown to the floor. His mother was dragged by her hair toward the back of the camper, screaming. He'd struggled to reach her. A knee slammed into his back and something sharp was jabbed into his neck. He couldn't move, but he was awake for a while. Long enough to hear her fighting for her life.

It ended with a whimper. Mr. Rose stood over her body, calling her a *fucking cunt*. Those were the words that ushered his mother into heaven.

• • •

Henry was upside down at the bottom of the stairs—he could've been in Brazil or Boston or Baton Rouge, or anywhere in between. But he was sure of two things: It was Ted's fault that his mother was dead, and if nobody came to rescue him, dehydration was going to kill him. It took three or four days to die from that. Still a long time to go, sitting upside down in death's waiting room.

School would be starting up again next month. The dorm's third floor would be loud the first couple of days—the laughter and shouts of friends echoing through the hallway. It wouldn't take people long to forget Henry Orr. He'd be a conversation starter for a week or two before his name would be lost on their tongues.

You hear what happened to Henry? Sucks man. Hey, you see Amy? She broke up with. ...

Henry enjoyed school. He'd been looking forward to finally being an upperclassman. He'd already picked his classes online. All that was left was the annual trip to Walmart with his mother to buy plastic tubs, notebooks, sheets, pillows—the works. It was unnecessary. The bookstore in Terre Haute had everything he needed, but she'd always insisted.

It's tradition, Henry—bad luck if we don't.

Since elementary school, when they lived in Cleveland, they'd been shuffling off for supplies together, followed by lunch at Cracker Barrel. They kept it up, every year—even after they moved into Ted's massive house in Windsor Hills.

Henry imagined himself pulling out of the driveway for school, waving goodbye to his mother. She would've been smiling, trying to keep it together, and in tears by the time his Subaru hit the expressway. On the way to Terre Haute, he'd have picked up a six-pack of Wee Mac with his fake I.D. to cool in the black mini fridge in his dorm room—banking them for a sunny, late September afternoon when the air was crisp and the sun was high and the smell of new-mowed campus grass wafted through his open window.

Henry winced at the pain firing up his good leg.

There would be no beer drinking on the sill of his window at Indiana State this fall. There would be no annual trip to Walmart. No sad-smile waves from the driveway.

His mother was dead inside a blood-soaked camper in Ohio.

And Henry Orr was somewhere else—at the bottom of the stairs, upside down.

Left to die.

23

Henry's hope was buoyed by the sound of gunfire in the distance. It was faint, but distinctive. Pop. Pop. Pop. It kept up through midmorning. Henry strained to hear. Maybe help was on its way. But the more he listened, the surer he became that the echo of gunfire was not the sound of rescue. The shots were coming from a fixed place. A firing range.

Sometime after that, Henry heard a different sound outside the basement walls. A car door slamming shut. And then he heard the creaking of someone walking on the floorboards above him. It didn't matter who was up there, even if it was Mr. Rose. Henry was prepared to exchange his current torture for a fresh episode of cruelty. He tried to shout for help, but his throat was too dry and too hoarse to produce more than a mediocre groan. Henry wriggled against his bindings, praying they wouldn't leave before finding him. He shouted again, this time managing to scrape out a gravel yell. Then another dry-shout. And another.

The basement door opened and a lightbulb brightened above.

"He's down here."

"What?"

"Down here."

The wooden steps creaked as the men descended.

"Christ. Pull him up."

"He smells like piss."

Someone behind him righted the kicked-over chair. The blood rushed to his head. Henry squeezed his eyes shut, holding his breath until the pain receded. When he blinked open, a man with piercing blue eyes was squinting at him—just inches from Henry's nose, his face as big as a moon.

"You're hurt?"

"Water."

"Dehydrated," said the voice behind Henry.

"Who brought him in? The new guy?"

"Yeah. Rose."

"How could he—?"

"It's not right, sir."

The blue-eyed man stood up. "He needs electrolytes. And a shower."

Henry tilted his neck, searching for the man.

"Please. Help me."

A knife cut through the plastic cords that fastened Henry's wrists to the chair. His arms dropped off the rests—too weak to fight gravity.

"He's got a hell of a knot back here," said the voice behind him.

"I was clear, wasn't I?"

"Yes, sir. You said unharmed."

"It's aggravating."

"Rose was out of line."

Henry swallowed hard. "Please."

"What's he saying?"

"Please. Please let me go."

The man with the blue eyes came around the front of the chair and looked down at Henry, studying him. He looked back at the other man. "I mean there's no point in doing this. Is Rose a moron?"

"Apparently."

"Please. I want to go."

"It's bullshit. Who the hell does he think he is?"

"Want me to talk to him?"

"No. We'll do it together. See what he says." He looked down at Henry's leg. "Can he walk?"

"I saw a cane upstairs."

"Bring him up. Put him in the kitchen. And watch his head."

Henry Orr was not a small man, but Mr. Hermann was bigger and had no trouble hoisting Henry over his shoulder and carrying him up the stairs into the farmhouse kitchen. He dumped Henry into a Windsor chair by a live-edge dining table made of reddish wood.

The man with the blue eyes entered soon after. He paced the kitchen in black sneakers, like he'd lost his keys—stopping, starting, changing directions. He ran his hands through his thick hair, then fixed his part and tucked a brown lock behind his ear. He shook his head.

"Who recommended Rose?"

Mr. Hermann shrugged. "Danny. They served—"

"He should know better."

"Yes, sir."

Mr. Hermann was a husky, muscled, rough-looking, no-nonsense guy in camo pants and a red Punisher T-shirt. Henry saw him for what he was: a thug with a gun holstered below his armpit and a long knife sheathed on his belt.

"I'll talk to Danny. It won't happen again."

"Fine," said the blue-eyed man opening the refrigerator door, bending for a purple sports drink. He looked over his shoulder at Henry. "I should introduce myself. Christian Gardener. I want you to call me Mr. Gardener." He held up a plastic bottle. "You want a glass or straight out of this?"

Henry cleared his throat. "You're not going to let me go, are you?"

"No. Sorry," he said, getting a glass out of the cabinet.

Henry downed the drink in one gulp. His captor refilled it. Henry stretched his fingers as far as he could then balled them into a fist before extending them out again. The feeling was coming back into his hands. His legs were a lost cause. The right was still electrified with a pain he prayed was temporary. The left leg was disfigured from birth. Even using a cane, his sneaker dragged on the ground when he limped.

Gardener looked down at Henry. "So, here we are."

Henry stared at the man.

"Still thirsty? I'll get you some more. But don't drink it so fast. Okay?"

"What do you want from me?" asked Henry.

"A lot. Maybe more than you can give. We'll see." He opened the refrigerator door and pulled out a hard-boiled egg. Gardener took his time peeling the shell over the sink. "You were hard to find. You and your mother just took off. How'd you know we were coming for you?" He took two bites, chewing slowly, staring at Henry. He looked over at Mr. Hermann, licked his fingers, and stepped closer. "Son, when I ask you a question, you can just go ahead and answer. How'd you know to run?"

"I didn't."

"Who helped you?"

"All I know is that you people killed my mother. That's it."

"Not a big fan of the tone," he said, looking over again at Mr. Hermann. "Did you hear it?"

"I heard it."

"You killed my mother you fucking coward!"

Mr. Gardener winced and shook his head. "Impulse control. That could be a problem. But it's curable." He turned his back on Henry and looked out the window. "I expected you to be something of a chess master, a savant with a mind working three moves ahead. Guess not. I mean, in a defenseless situation—not knowing the shot ... coming in hard with name-calling? I don't know, son." He looked at Mr. Hermann. "Right?"

"He might not be as smart as—"

"No, I *know* he's plenty smart. Just situationally impaired." He turned to Henry. "You should have held your water until you knew the shot. It's about moves and countermoves. If you find yourself fucked the way you are, son ... it's critical to know your opponent. You *don't* have a lot of good chess moves in front of you. Lashing out, calling me a fucking coward? That's not clever. It backs me into a corner—forces me to respond." Gardener hesitated, then tilted his head, staring at Henry a while. "Unless that's what you wanted. Did you want me to respond? Was it a calculated gamble to take the measure of *me*?" Gardener nodded. "Not sure that would have been my move, but it's an acceptable strategy for sure. All right, well, you've had your turn—called me a fucking coward in front of Mr. Hermann. Now, it's my move. How I respond gives you some insight into how I play the game." He walked to Mr. Hermann and touched him on the elbow. "Can you show the boy—so he fully gets the measure of me?"

"What'd you have in mind?"

"Remove his sandal."

Henry kicked his legs backward, but the Windsor chair was against the wall and he had no place to go. Mr. Hermann's hands were strong and Henry's good leg was too weak to kick.

"No. The other one. The twisted foot."

Hermann unsheathed his long knife. Henry jerked, but the man had a vise grip. The sharp blade nicked the skin between his toes. The big man looked up at Mr. Gardener.

"So, I'm going to teach you a lesson about impulse control. Mr. Hermann, the smallest toe, please."

The blade sank into Henry's flesh. The bone snapped like a celery stick. Lightning screamed up Henry's spine and out his mouth.

"If my math is correct, you can call me a *fucking coward* nine more times. Want to get anything else off your chest?"

Henry was shaking his head wildly, hyperventilating into the collar of his Captain America T-shirt.

"So, what did we learn? What's the takeaway?"

"I'm sorry," Henry said, wiping the tears off his chin.

"You learned that I'm likely to respond both unconventionally and disproportional to the offense. I'm just prone to having a short fuse, son. Goes back to childhood. Sometimes I can't control myself. But that, right there? That lesson? That wasn't *uncontrolled*. I haven't shown you that side of me. Let's hope you never have to see it." Gardener took a last bite of his hard-boiled egg and wiped his hands on his jeans. "I want to like you. I'm trying. So … now you know the shot—you see the chess board clearly. Right?"

Henry nodded.

"Good. So, I won that round. Let's clear the board and start again. You didn't introduce yourself. Do you want to be called Henry or something else? Any particular pronouns we should use?"

"Henry. My name is Henry Orr."

"Didn't take Ted's name, huh? Probably wise. Nice to be acquainted properly." Mr. Gardener threw a dish towel. "Put this over the wound. Stop up the bleeding."

Henry gingerly touched the stub of his toe. He took rapid, shallow breaths as he pressed down on the stump. The initial shock of the small amputation wore off, replaced by a searing pulse that radiated up his leg. He'd managed pain his entire life without pills. By the time he'd reached high school, he'd gained something of a mastery over it. Pain could sometimes be fuel. Henry closed his eyes, letting his tank fill with a mantra.

Escape or die trying.

Henry's cane leaned against the wall on the far side of the kitchen. He'd made it in high school shop class. It took weeks to turn the gnarly burl on the lathe, sand, then polish the oak. He'd slathered it with six coats of polyurethane. Enough to make it shine. Back then, Henry had been sure it would draw peoples' eyes away from his disfigurement. It hadn't.

Mr. Gardener bent down and pulled a black plastic box from underneath the cabinet and laid it delicately on the countertop. "Protein. That'll help. Let's get some bacon in you." He turned to Henry and pointed at the box. "Air fryer—flat out game changer. Crispy bacon without filling the kitchen with smoke. I'm making you breakfast, son. What do you say?"

"Thank you."

A boy in a San Diego Padres baseball hat wriggled past Mr. Hermann's knees and into the kitchen. A baseball glove dangled off his thin wrist, too big for his small hand. Mr. Gardener squatted down to eye level.

"Looks like you're ready for the game." He looked at his watch. "It doesn't start until ten after one. That's an hour from now. You want to hang here in the big house or go down the hill and see your aunt?"

The boy pointed at Mr. Gardener.

"All right. Wait in the living room. I'll be there in a minute. You sure you don't want to root for the Astros with me?"

The kid shook his head and frowned.

"All right, Beto. I get it."

The boy ran out of the kitchen.

"All right. Let's get back to it, Henry. Here's what's going to happen next. We'll fill your belly. Apply a little ice to your noggin. Wrap your foot. Let you get some shut-eye."

He placed three pills on the table in front of Henry.

"Take them. And because you're just getting the hang of this, I'll tell you what happens if you don't: Mr. Hermann will open your throat with his long knife and drop them down your gullet. Do you believe me, Henry?"

He nodded.

"Good. I'll make a chess player out of you yet." Mr. Gardener rinsed his hands under the sink then wiped them with a towel hanging off the stove. "Mr. Hermann will plate those for you." Gardener walked out of the kitchen. His voice echoed from down the hall.

"Welcome to the Farm, Henry."

24

Henry's eyes blinked open. The serenity of his drug-induced sleep peeled away. For a millisecond he thought it might have been a nightmare. Maybe she wasn't dead. Maybe.

The room he was awakening into was not his own—this wasn't Windsor Hills. The evidence of his unwanted reality pressed in on him—the throb of his missing toe, the lump on the back of his head, the pain in his wrists. It seemed impossible that his mother was murdered—that she was dead. They'd always been a team. She wasn't perfect—drank more than she should have, was quick to anger, and held a grudge longer than necessary. His mom was tough and proud. And she kept secrets. Important secrets. Henry had been patient. He always thought, in time, she'd wear down and tell him who his father was. She'd taken that one to her grave.

Henry looked around the bedroom. His clothes were folded on a rattan chair in the corner. He was naked. And smelled like soap.

"You awake in there?" A young woman put her face through the door. "It's time to get up," she said in a wispy, thin voice.

The door cracked open wider. She tried to enter but the boy he'd seen yesterday shot from behind her legs, running toward Henry. The woman grabbed him by his shoulders, pulling him back.

"I'm Lily."

She was older than Henry, but not by much. Her eyes had a kindness to them. The rest of her was an odd combination: red spikey hair, thick black eyebrows, a wide nose, and a pointed chin. She'd removed her ear gauges—her lobes dangled against her upper neck like wet fettucine. And while each of her features was not distinctly attractive, the sum of them was greater than the parts. Even as anxious and on guard as Henry was, he couldn't help but find her uniquely stunning.

"Mr. Gardener wants to speak with you."

"Where am I?" Henry said, pulling up the quilt as she approached.

"The Farm," she said, grabbing his freshly laundered clothes off the rattan chair.

"What do you people want with me?"

"Dude, I'm not the 'people.' I'm not doing shit to you. What I *want* is for you to put your clothes on and go see Mr. Gardener. Here," she said, dropping them on the bed. "They made me give you a sponge-bath. I bandaged your foot too."

"You're not one of them?"

Lily shook her head.

"Who are you? And, who is Gardener? What—"

"Save the questions—not while we're in the Main House."

Henry pulled his clean Captain America T-shirt over his head, then ran his hand through his mop of hair. He looked at the door. "I need my cane."

"Don't have it. You can lean on my shoulder."

Henry put his elbow on Lily's bony shoulder and hopped on his good foot toward the door. "How many people—?"

"Seriously, not here. Mr. Gardener's called all of us up here. That's never a good thing."

They entered the kitchen. There were four people already there, standing with their backs against the wall as if they were waiting to be given a cigarette and a blindfold. Lily directed Henry to sit at the table then joined the others. Minutes later, Gardener entered, the boy at his side. A step behind was Mr. Hermann. Gardener carried Henry's cane in his left hand, his palm resting on the lacquered, burled-wood head. He opened the refrigerator door and pulled out a can of Coke, handed it to the kid, then turned him around and gave him a gentle push out of the kitchen.

The people against the wall looked nervous. Apparently, they also knew the shot.

Mr. Gardener looked out the kitchen window, admiring the view. Henry glanced at Mr. Hermann. He was once again posted up in his watchful position under the door, scanning the room, his hand resting on the sheath of his long knife. Gardener inhaled deeply and turned to face the wall people.

"This is Henry," Gardener pointed. "I've met him. He's quiet—prone to being a bit impulsive, but I think we've taken care of that. You make your own decisions about him. Jury's still out." His voice softened. "Some of you might be irked about what happened with Ms. Barker. I liked her too. She just wasn't a team player." He looked up at the ceiling then back to the wall people. "I get it, morale is low. You'd like me to give you assurances. I'm sorry, I just can't. But I *will* give you some advice. Keep your nose to the grindstone. Things will shake out as God intends."

No one lifted their heads to look at Mr. Gardener.

"Lily, why don't you bring the gang into the living area. I'll have you fetched when we're done. Henry, please stay."

The kitchen emptied, each person shuffling away with their heads bowed. Mr. Gardener examined Henry's cane. He flipped it, attempting to catch the thin bottom end in midair. He fumbled it. The cane whacked against the refrigerator door. Gardener got a hand on it before it hit the floor. Gardener poured an orange juice for himself.

"You know, I heard a little gossip." He turned to Henry and raised his eyebrows. "Did you somehow manage to punch Rose in the face? That true?"

Henry nodded, clocking his head toward the sound of heavy feet coming down the hallway. Mr. Hermann moved aside, allowing Mr. Rose to enter the kitchen.

"Speak of the devil. The man himself. Have a seat right over here."

Under the Neanderthal's forehead was a swollen left eye—a greenish shade of yellow spreading across his wide nose. He sat down and folded his meaty forearms across his chest, smirking at Henry, an inferno behind his blackening eye.

"Thanks for coming all the way up here," Mr. Gardener said, flicking the cane from one hand into the other, then back again.

Rose yawned.

"Henry already admitted to injuring you. I'm having some trouble understanding how you managed to leave your face so well unattended that a crippled boy—no offense, Henry—could … well," he said waving his hand, "on second thought, never mind—it's neither here nor there. Job one this morning is just to clear the board—start again. Henry, I want you to look straight into Mr. Rose's horribly swollen black eye and apologize for hitting him."

He deserved far more than a black eye, but Henry had no interest in putting his hand in the hornet's nest. "I'm sorry I punched you, Mr. Rose."

Gardener flashed Henry a breezy smile. "Good. Simple."

He flipped the cane in the air. He stuck his hand out to grab it, but missed, banging it off the wood floor. "Dang it, Henry—the weighting's off. Your walking stick is unbalanced. The top of the thing is much too heavy." Gardener picked it off the floor.

"Mr. Rose? Anything you'd like to say to Henry after tying him to a chair, kicking him down the stairs, and abandoning him for eleven hours without water?"

"Not really," he said, his eyes never leaving Henry.

"Really? Nothing?"

"You didn't hire me to be a goddamned nanny. You told me to fetch the kid and take care of the mother. I did that. Now, can I get back to work?"

"That's disappointing. Well, if not to Henry, how about me, Mr. Rose? Would you like to apologize to me?"

"I didn't do nothing to you."

Mr. Gardener took a sip of his orange juice and looked over at Mr. Hermann lurking in the doorway behind Mr. Rose.

"How long have you been here? Two weeks? Apparently, our orientation program sucks. I'll tell you why you *might* consider it." He pointed at Henry, "This is *my* property. If your ego gets a little bruised rounding up my cattle, put ice on it. Never take *your* anger out on *my* animal. That, Mr. Rose, is why you might consider apologizing to me."

"I don't see it that way."

"Doesn't see it that way. Okay," Gardener shrugged. He flipped the cane and caught it cleanly. He looked down at it, massaging the burled-wood. He smiled and laid the cane on the table in front of Henry. "That was a close one, Mr. Rose."

"What was a close one?"

"I almost did it. Controlled my impulse, though didn't I, Henry?"

Rose narrowed his eyes. "What the fuck are you talking about?"

"You don't know how close I came to swinging Henry's heavy burled-wood walking stick right through your fucking head."

"Hitting *me*? What the fuck?"

"It was tempting."

"I don't need this shit."

"Mr. Hermann, is this salvageable? Am I being rash?"

"I don't think so."

"From what I hear, Danny felt sorry for you, Mr. Rose. But we have an overabundance of morons around here already." Gardener stepped back. "I'd do it myself, but firing people isn't my job. It's Mr. Hermann's."

The tall man didn't hesitate. His long knife was already unsheathed and clenched in his hand. Rose never saw him slip behind. Hermann slid the blade across Rose's neck, slicing through his windpipe. It was not a quick death. The neanderthal clawed at his throat, blood leaking between his fingers, his eyes wild with shock.

Henry looked away. Mr. Gardener was leaning on the kitchen counter, watching him die while he sipped orange juice. Rose succumbed, his face slumping into the live-edge wooden dining table.

"You want me to bring them back in?" asked Mr. Hermann.

Mr. Gardener nodded.

Henry refused to look at Rose, nor did he want to see the blood pooling on the table. Gardener stayed by the sink, sipping his orange juice. Henry didn't want to look at him either.

There was no collective gasp. Lily and the others walked across the kitchen floor, avoiding the blood as if they'd expected to see a murdered corpse at the table. They put their backs up against the wall. Mr. Gardener downed the rest of his orange juice then ripped a paper towel square off the holder to pat his mouth dry. He looked at the wall people.

"Any questions?"

They shook their heads and stared at the floor.

"All right, back to work. See them out, Mr. Hermann."

Lily gave Henry a cautious glance before leaving. Gardener waited for the room to clear. He tilted his head to look at the dead man's face.

"Rose was an asshole. It's just not my style to give people like that a pass, Henry. You can't build a winning team with 'em, you know?"

Henry didn't look him in the eye.

"Are you a social misfit, too?"

"What?"

"Misfits and morons." He looked toward the door and spoke softer. "That's what we have around here. It's impossible to have an intelligent conversation. I'm kind of stuck with it. I was looking forward to meeting you—hoping you were different." Mr. Gardener hesitated and put his fingers into the change pocket of his jeans. "What I'm saying is, I don't dislike you Henry. It's not personal. You know what I mean?"

"Okay," Henry said, leaning back from the blood-current streaming down the table.

"I hope it works out for you here." Mr. Gardener took a deep, clearing inhale. "You have questions—you want to know *why* you're here. Let me tell you. It's because … well, it's your father, Henry. Turned out he was untrustworthy—a man without honor. He broke the commandment. 'Thou shalt not steal.' Man, did he steal. We are not a wealthy organization. In fact, we've been living a little lean while your father was burning through our money. Did you know he was a thief?"

"He's not my father."

"Well, I'm not going to argue the semantics, but he kinda was, right? Not by blood, but you were family—went on vacations together and such." He pulled up a chair next to Henry. "Here's the thing. I've put myself in a little pickle with you. You see, I've made it plain to everyone: If you steal, I take your life—and your family's life. Believe me, Ted knew what he was risking. Just couldn't help himself, I guess." Gardener got up again and walked to the sink to wash his orange juice glass. "So, according to the rules, you should already be dead. But you're not. And believe me, people are watching. They're wondering: why's *that* kid still alive? That's what they're asking. You know why you're not dead yet?"

He walked across the kitchen floor and tapped his index finger on Henry's forehead. "Word on the street is that you've got some serious wattage up there. That's what they say, anyway. It intrigues me. I wanted to see for myself."

"I don't understand."

"I'm giving you an extraordinary opportunity. You've got a shot at living through this mess your father made for you. But you'll have to do something for me. I need you to pay off your father's debt. If you can manage it, things will go well. But, as I say, people are watching. My hands are tied. If you don't produce, I'll simply have to kill you, son. There it is. That's the hard truth of it."

Gardener stood up and patted Henry's shoulder.

"Two things you should know. The debt is enormous. And I'm just not in a position to be patient with this thing. But believe me, Henry, I *am* rooting for you."

25

Henry grabbed his cane and limped out of the kitchen and down the hallway toward Lily who was waiting for him by the door. She held it open for him and a warm breeze welcomed him onto the country porch, where weeping blossoms of fuschia, impatiens, and begonias draped from hanging baskets along the eaves. A row of sturdy Adirondack chairs stretched the length of the recently stained wood decking. The exterior of the Main House looked as if it was owned by a conscientious Connecticut grandmother. Henry limped past the window without looking in, knowing that all he'd see was Mr. Rose's throat-blood seeping into the cracks of the kitchen's floorboards.

The Main House stood on a hillock, giving Henry a good view of the property below. He'd seen corn out the kitchen window, but this wasn't the endless plain of fields he was expecting. It was a small patch contained in a six-acre clearing surrounded by forest. The woods were thick and diverse: beech, pine, and maple. The white tops of a birch in the distance had Henry wondering about a potential lake or river that way. But it was the tall pines he was most interested in. They wouldn't tell him where he was, but they might tell him where he *wasn't*. Henry had a good memory. Better than good. He remembered the flannel-shirted woman he'd seen on the nature show walking up a ridgeline. She too walked with a limp, planting a crooked stick into the earth as she moved. The woman had rested in front of a wide tree trunk, stroking her hand across the rough bark before looking into the camera.

"This beautiful tree has more to worry about than just the logger's chain saw. If the weevil has his way, we may soon be seeing less of

the Eastern White Pine's bluish-green tint on the horizon. The beetles threaten these pines from the Upper Midwest to New England, as far north as Newfoundland."

"You good?" asked Lily.

"Do you know where we are?"

"Everyone has a guess. But they're only guesses."

Lily flinched as gunfire erupted in the distance. Soon, the popping echoes of the volleys blended into the bangs of live fire. "I hate guns."

"How far away is the range?"

"Who knows. It's worse on the weekends. Nonstop."

Henry leaned on the porch railing, looking down at the red barn at the bottom of the slope. Nearby were a few small sheds dispersed across the rutted dirt and mowed grass. The age of the outbuildings suggested the property had been a working farm for at least seventy-five years.

One structure at the bottom of the hill stood in contrast to the sagging edifices around it. The coal-colored metal Morton building was new. Two satellite dishes were fixed to the roofline, and at the building's highest point, Henry saw a small balcony.

A drone zipped over the porch and out toward the cornfield. He watched it move in the sky. Then more appeared, at least six, circling the Main House and the buildings below. Lily looked up too but said nothing about the drones. She stepped down the porch stairs, taking the winding dirt path down the hill. Henry didn't immediately follow.

He watched two men with rifles slide open the barn door at the bottom of the hill. A yellow tractor rumbled out, coughing black exhaust as it chugged slowly across the flattened grass, its backhoe barely clearing the ground. It was heading toward a blue pickup truck parked near the cornfield. Three men with shovels waited there, leaning against the back bumper. From his position at the top of the hill, Henry could see down into the truck bed. There was a body under a red-stained bedsheet. Mr. Rose was down there, waiting patiently for the backhoe to open his personal portal to hell.

Four mounds of new soil were lumped nearby. No crosses. No headstones.

"How long have you been here?" asked Henry, limping down the steps to meet Lily.

"Three months—give or take."

Henry pointed to the small cemetery. "Are they—?"

"Friends? Yeah."

She turned her back on the men, the body, and the backhoe.

"Why'd they bring you here?" he asked.

"To satisfy Gardener's greed."

"How?"

"We all had one thing in common. We knew how to skim crypto."

"I don't understand," Henry said, looking down at the mounds. "Why'd he kill them if—?"

"Why does he keep killing his golden geese? Gardener is a lot of things. He can be charming. And there's no doubt, he's smart. But he's impatient and angry. And when his switch flips? You're in trouble. You saw what he did in the kitchen." Lily looked at him. "Seriously, you're lucky it was only your toe."

"How much is he making off you guys?"

"That's the problem. Not much. Almost as soon as we got here, it turned into a crypto winter. And our value to him dropped with the currency."

They walked down the dirt path toward the coal-colored building. Lily stopped every so often, giving time for Henry to catch up. He planted his cane and dragged his crooked leg over the hard-packed dirt. While she waited, Lily booted loose rocks down the hill. Some she kicked straight leg, others she attacked from the side, soccer style.

"Does it hurt?" she asked.

"The toe?"

"Sorry, I meant your foot. I shouldn't have asked."

"Doesn't bother me."

It was a lie, but he'd been telling that one since he could remember. Pity was harder to endure than the pain.

She pointed to a boulder by the side of the path. "Let's take a break."

Henry looked into the sky. There were seven drones in all. He followed each of them, watched their flight path, looking for a pattern in their aerial surveillance. Patterns were the key to understanding everything: stars, trees, people, computer code. Understand the pattern and you had the root of knowledge.

"Did you skim before you got here?"

"Nobody here's an angel, Henry. What's your story?"

"My stepfather stole from Gardener. So, Gardener killed him—then murdered my mother. I'm here to work off his debt."

"Stole from Gardener?" Lily said, raising her eyebrows. "Shit."
"I'm on a short leash."
"You got anybody else at home. Anyone to miss you?"
"Nobody."
Lily nodded and looked away. "Maybe that's better. Where you from, Henry?"
He told her. "You?"
"Originally from Eloy, Arizona—outside of Tucson. Not much there but a Circle K and a Food Town. I moved to Chula Vista after I graduated. Gardener's men broke in one night and killed my roommate. Brought me here. I have no doubt my little sister is out of her mind with worry. My parents—probably not so much."
A drone buzzed overhead. It dropped to eye level before ascending again. Henry followed it. This one had a mind of its own. Unlike the others, it didn't make lazy circles overhead. It didn't change elevation predictably.
"What's stopping anyone from walking into the trees and escaping?"
"There's a lot of people in those woods, Henry. Men with guns. That's how we lost Bear. He made up his mind to sneak out in the middle of the night and make a run for the woods. He promised me he'd bring help. Gardener's men had him in ten minutes. A half hour later, he had all of us lined up in our underwear to witness his execution."
Henry exhaled.
"And it's not just the drones or the men in the woods. Don't underestimate Mr. Hermann. He's scary too. Quiet. But he's a killer. Be careful, Henry. Keep your head down. Don't make waves. Follow the rules."
"Which are?
"Never leave the circle. Never go out after sunset."
"Circle?"
Lily pointed in the distance at a line painted in the grass in front of the coal-colored building.
"Never go outside that line. Ever. We can walk around the building or sit on the grass during the day. But never go outside the boundary. By the way, 125 laps around is a full mile."
"Not much of a jogger."
"Right," she said, sheepishly.
"Gardener said something about Ms. Barker. What—?"

"Elaine." Lily shook her head. "I don't want to talk about it. She didn't deserve what he did to her." Lily cleared her throat and brushed her eye with the back of her finger. "What're you gonna do?"

Down the hill, the tractor's curling backhoe had finished carving the crater. The black exhaust was now a bluish smog that carried into the corn stalks. Henry watched as the men heaved Mr. Rose's body into the chasm and went about the business of shoveling soil over his corpse.

What're you gonna do?

Escape or die trying.

26

"You ready?" Lily asked.

Henry pushed his cane into the dirt, lifting himself into a standing position.

"Careful. It's a little steep here."

Henry nodded and limped down the remainder of the path, following Lily across the dirt and grass toward the coal-colored building, getting a closer look at the yellow boundary line twenty-five feet from the exterior wall of the new two-story.

"The others are probably in the back. You want to meet them or go inside first?"

Henry shrugged.

"All right, come on then," Lily said, walking along the building's wall toward the back.

They were sitting in a circle on metal folding chairs, their faces bent in conversation. Only one got out of his seat to greet them. He was well-tanned with curly blonde hair and a four-day scrub of beard. He approached Lily and held her by the shoulders.

"You okay, Babe?" he said, pulling her into a rough kiss.

"Goddammit, Jammer."

"What?"

Lily turned her back on him and wiped the kiss off her mouth with the back of her hand.

"You're the guy that cold-cocked Rose?" he said, looking down at Henry's lame leg. "I'm Windjammer."

Henry looked at Lily's reddening face.

169

"I'm Francee … this is Ivan."

Francee was probably only in her mid-thirties, but her frail frame and stress-weary face made her seem far older. Ivan was a man hiding in plain sight: above his neck he wore a Ghillie suit of hair—his head a high helmet of black frizz and a wild, wooly beard camouflaging his face. His only visible feature was his wide nose and dark brown eyes.

Bingo was younger than Henry—maybe eighteen, small and pale with a thin, undergrown mustache.

Henry introduced himself. From what Lily had said, he was sure all of them were gifted with genius. But, with the exception of Jammer, they'd been stripped of their confidence. They were skittish and scared. Wall people.

Lily made some small talk. It was pleasant enough, but Henry was interested in getting answers to the questions swirling in his head.

"What do we know about Gardener?" he asked.

Bingo, Francee, and Ivan looked to Jammer. Apparently, he was their de facto leader. But Henry's eyes were on Lily, hoping she'd be the one to answer. The scruffy blonde stepped forward and pointed at Henry's foot.

"He took your toe, right?" said Jammer. "Killed the other asshole. What else could you possibly need to know?"

Henry nodded, registering his first impression. Jammer was an aggressive dick. Lily was kind, but passive. The others were so introverted he might never get a read on them. Henry had very specific questions he needed answered, but it was too early to place his trust in any of them. Gardener had taught Henry a valuable lesson about understanding the "shot." And Henry was a quick learner. The wall people were strangers.

But Lily. … It was hard not to trust her. He reminded himself to be careful.

"I'll show you inside. Ready?" she asked.

Henry limped along the yellow boundary line toward the front of the coal-colored building, his eyes not straying far from the nearby paint-chipped red barn. It was a tired, sagging relic of the previous century. The exterior boards were thin and rotting near the ground, but the barn had a new roof. It seemed a lazy fix. They should have shored up the building before repairing the lid. Which meant what? Gardener didn't care about the barn's long-term health, he just wanted whatever was inside to stay dry. And Henry doubted that it was for the aging yellow tractor. There were deep depressions and tire track grooves in front of the barn's door. Henry was curious, wondering if the outbuilding might be home for something more important than a grave-digging tractor.

Lily was at the entry door. "Henry?"

He watched the tractor rumbling from the makeshift cemetery toward the barn. There were two men aboard, their feet on the skid, holding on to the cage. The heavy machine stopped. The men jumped off, heading toward the doors. Henry thought, if he could get just a little closer, he could see what was inside the barn. He put his foot on the painted line and leaned forward on his cane. His view was limited—just some rusted farm equipment hanging from steel hooks on a graying wood-weathered wall and a spool of yellow straw on the floor. The tractor engine powered off inside the barn. The driver walked out, pointing to one of the men nearby.

"You got this, Couyon?" he said, tossing the padlock toward the heavyset man.

"You know it, Boss." The big man slid the barn door closed. Then, he looked over at the coal-colored building. "Hey there, Lily! How you doin'?" He waved, slapping the lock into the metal post.

"Just fine, Couyon."

Henry stepped a few inches over the line to make sure his eyes weren't deceiving him. The burly man had been more interested in saying hello than paying attention to what he was doing. He hadn't secured the other side of the door. The barn was unlocked—open for business.

"Henry!"

The drone came from behind, buzzing his head—within inches of his face. Henry ducked, almost falling over in the process. The metallic spider hovered in front of his nose.

"Come on," Lily said, holding the door open.

The workmanship inside the building was slipshod and amateurish: no quarter round where the walls met the concrete slab, gaps in the ceiling where the drywall met the black support beams, a thin coat of white contractor's paint that barely covered the taping. There were no recessed lights in the ceiling—LED tubes hung from silver chains. The only attempt at interior design were the framed prints on every wall. Motivational posters. Henry hobbled to one. It was a sculling boat—rowers, back-bent, gliding over the golden-orange waters of sunset. *Teamwork: Common people achieving Uncommon results.*

"This is our room," Lily said.

There were no windows. The artificial lighting was brighter here. Eleven workstations for five people. No cubicles. Each station in full view of everyone. No secrets. A gunmetal credenza ran the length of the back wall. A Keurig machine, K-Cups in a blue plastic bowl, seven boxes of Girl Scout Cookies, and a multitude of Slim Jim packs were positioned in a line across the white laminate top.

Henry examined the computer monitor closest to him. He bent under the desk to see the green and red blinking box below. Gardener hadn't pinched pennies on the hardware. It was state of the art. The best money could buy. He traced the bundle of black and gray wires across the floor where they disappeared into a white receiving plate in the wall. No doubt the cables snaked through the building, terminating in the rooftop satellite dishes he'd seen from the Main House.

"Which one is mine?" he asked.

"You're not in here. Gardener says you're supposed to work alone. You want a drink?" Lily asked, squatting into a small glass refrigerator on the side wall. She tossed him a purple sports drink. Henry stared at her. The question on his mind was, apparently, written all over his face.

"You're asking yourself why a house full of hackers hasn't figured out a way to call for help. You're wondering why any of us are still here."

Henry nodded.

"You'll see."

"I'll see what?"

"You can't outsmart the code. Don't even try. It's smarter than you are. It's intelligent—learning all the time."

"Gardener just figured out how to use an air fryer. Are you telling me he's a computer genius?"

Lily shook her head. She lowered her voice. "I don't think he knows shit. But he doesn't need to."

"I don't—"

"Someone else built the system. That's the genius you're looking for. And they built the network like a fortress—incredibly restrictive."

"Then how does he expect you to work?"

"I don't know how they managed to do it. We can run packet

sniffers. DHCP attacks. ARP and DNS poisoning. Spoofing. We can do it all, but it's like we're working from deep space—another planet. Everything is wiped. No messages in or out. No location information. I'm telling you, it's locked down—tight. And if you're thinking that maybe you can chip away at it without being seen—don't do it. The Architect comes in on Saturdays and reviews all our code from up the hill at the Main House. Don't mess with it, Henry."

"The Architect?"

"Every Saturday. Mr. Hermann walks in here and stands under that doorway and watches us while the Architect scours our work from the servers in the Main House. If he gets a phone call, someone's going to die. I'm not exaggerating."

Lily took a sip of her drink, inhaled, then closed her eyes before speaking. "Puddie and Mojo. They were good guys. Smart too. They teamed up—spent an entire week searching the system for weaknesses. They tried to exploit everything they could find. It took the Architect less than ten minutes to figure out what he and Mojo were up to. I was sitting next to Puddie when Mr. Hermann got the call. He didn't say a word. Just hung up his phone, walked past me, got behind Puddie and slit his throat. Mojo tried to run. He never made it out the door."

"Shit."

"Exactly. For a while, it was *Survivor* around here—someone's torch being extinguished every few weeks. We're pretty sure it's about to start up again. And Jammer thinks he's next."

"Why?"

"He's a smash-and-grab guy. There's no art to what he does. He hasn't produced much of anything in the past month. He's starting to take it out on everyone else—intimidating Ivan and the others, strong-arming them to share their skims with him."

"You're not *with* him?"

Lily shook her head. "What you need to understand is that Gardener is starting to turn the screws. No one is leaving here Henry. If we try to escape, we die. If we don't produce, we die. If we try to manipulate the system, we die. It was bad before. It's getting worse. It's going to be Hunger Games around here soon—Jammer, Francee, Ivan, and Bingo may be forced to start turning on each other to stay in Gardener's good graces."

"You don't trust Jammer?"

"I trust him least of all."

Henry heard the front door bang close. The wall people were coming back.

"Come on. I'll show you the rest of the place."

Lily walked ahead, then stopped, waiting for Henry to catch up.

"There's an exercise bike in that room and a couple of barbells. Kitchen is through that door—the fridge is stocked. No set meal time. Eat when you want. There's a tiny library that way—has a couple shelves of books and an old turntable if you want to listen to cowboy albums from the 1950s. Across the hall is the supply closet."

"Everything's analog?" Henry asked.

"Yup. Stone Age. No devices. No clocks. No phones. Nothing."

Access to the second floor came by way of a steel staircase. Henry put his weight on the railing and worked his way to the top. Most of the upstairs real estate was dedicated to one room, an open dorm with metal bunk beds along the wall, a small bureau of drawers on either side.

"The bath and shower are unisex. You're in the bunk below me— the one down at the end. Eventually, someone will put clothes in the drawers for you."

Henry pointed to a door off the sleep room. "What's in there?"

Lily made a fist and pushed her index finger in and out of the opening. "That's the Bounce House. Don't judge. Jammer threw an extra mattress in there for people to blow off steam."

"No guards in the house?"

"Nope. There's an old woman that comes in to clean. Besides that, they leave us alone."

"Cameras? Microphones?"

"Elaine was an expert. She looked everywhere. Told us it was clear and we believed her."

"Gardener trusts you?"

"No. There's just nowhere to go."

"It's a prison."

"Exactly."

Henry looked around the room for another door. "I saw a roof deck. How do I get up there?"

Lily pointed down the hall toward a narrow door. "There's a sketchy ladder in there that takes you up to the crow's nest."

"What's up there?"

"Not a lot. Couple of chairs. It's another place to chill—if you don't kill yourself climbing up. Nothing to see but trees and the Main House. Not a horrible place to catch a few rays, though, if you don't mind being dive-bombed by drones."

She led him back down the stairs to the kitchen. Lily pulled cold cuts and bread from the fridge.

"If I'm not with you guys, where's my station?" Henry asked.

"You're not going to like it."

"Why?"

Lily opened the mayonnaise jar and dipped a butter knife in—taking her time spreading it over the bread.

"Lily?"

She handed him the sandwich.

"Eat."

27

"Here," Lily said, opening the door to the restroom at the end of the hall.

A piece of plywood covered the hole where the toilet had been. A tiny desk was tucked against the wall—the monitor nearly as wide as the workspace. The hardware was the same as in the skimmers' room down the hall. Black cables ran through a punched hole in the ceiling.

"Give it a spin," she said.

Henry pressed his back against the wall to get around the desk. "Why'd he do this? There's more than enough room with you guys."

Lily shrugged. "He just told me this is where you'll be."

"To do what?"

"I have no idea, Henry."

Mr. Hermann materialized behind Lily.

"You can go now," he said, putting his hand on her back.

Lily winced at his touch. She dropped her shoulder, rolling away from him and walking down the hall.

"Mr. Gardener is on his way. He wants a word with you, Henry."

Henry sat behind his desk with a clear view of the hallway. It wasn't long before Mr. Gardener turned the corner. He was in no rush, walking with his fingers in the change pocket of his jeans. He looked around Henry's office.

"You don't have a poster. Mr. Hermann? See that Henry gets a poster."

"Yes, sir."

"So, here you are. First day of work. How're we feeling? Excited? Nervous?"

Henry shrugged.

"Remember son, answers always follow questions."

"I'm nervous."

"You meet everyone?"

"Yes."

"Social misfits. Every one of them. Except for Lily. What do you think of her?"

"She's fine."

"She explained the rules?"

"Yes."

"What did she say?"

"Stay inside the boundary line. No going out after dark."

"Not too complicated, right? I'm a simple man. Simple rules." Gardener turned his head around the room. "I thought it was bigger. Tight squeeze, isn't it?"

"Mr. Gardener, what do you want from me?"

"I told you. Pay off your father's debt."

"I mean, how?"

"Are you familiar with the term, 'Product as a Service?'"

"Yes."

"Explain it to me."

"Um, something—like an app or bundled product people pay monthly for instead of a one-time purchase."

"That's what I want. Something like that."

"Sorry? You want what?"

"Passive, ongoing income. Something recession-proof."

"I don't understand."

"That's how I think you should pay off what your father stole." Gardener looked around the bathroom office. "Design a program that my network of associates will pay for ... monthly. A subscription." Gardener put his face above the monitor, so close Henry could feel the heat of his onion breath. "It needs to be something unique. Something critical to their business. Something they can't live without. So far so good?"

It was not good so far, but Henry nodded anyway.

"The first rule of entrepreneurship is what? Solving a problem. Where is the customer's pain? Their fear? If you take it away, they'll pay whatever you ask. And, if they pay enough? Henry gets to stay

alive. How's that for incentive? Better than steak knives, right?"
Gardener took a step back and leaned against the wall. "So? What
question should you be asking me right now?"

Henry cleared his throat. "Who are your associates and what is
their pain?"

"Exactly. My friends don't think much of authority. Their convic-
tions do not conform with state and federal laws. Their pain is losing
money. Their fear is incarceration. You solve the problem. I sell the
solution."

"How?"

"I wouldn't dream of telling you how to do your work, son."

"Mr. Gardener, I'm just a college student. I don't know—"

"Stop," he said, putting his palm in the air. "You either can do it,
or you can't. Understand?"

Henry nodded.

"Today is Thursday. On Sunday, you'll pitch me your idea. I'll
decide then if we're going to work together ... or not. So, make it good.
You understand what's at stake, right? I don't have to spell it out?"

"I understand."

• • •

Henry turned off the light and hobbled across the sleep room toward
his bunk. Francee and Ivan and Jammer were in the kitchen. Bingo
and Lily were listening to albums. Henry was exhausted, still in pain,
and needed to think. Mr. Gardener didn't say it outright, but it was
implicit. The only way criminals could avoid incarceration was to
know if their operations were being infiltrated. Did he want Henry to
hack into law enforcement and give Gardener's friends a window into
their operations? If he could, he might stay alive. The problem was
that Henry had no idea how to accomplish it.

He stared into the darkness, his eyes adjusting to the glow of the
bluish nightlight on the other side of the room. There was something
etched in ballpoint pen on the wooden slat on the bunk above him.

Bear was here.

Henry traced his fingers across the dead man's epitaph. Bear was the
one who had run into the woods for help. Henry felt a strange kinship

to him. He must have looked up at the underside of Lily's bunk on his first night at the Farm too—probably thinking of how to escape.

Bear died because he ran. Puddie and Mojo tried to disable the system protocols. Elaine was not a "team player." Fear had kept the rest of them in line. But no one was leaving the Farm. All that the wall people had done for themselves by being compliant was to sign up for a slow death.

Henry wasn't going down like that.

Escape or die trying.

• • •

He was the first one awake. Henry swung his legs off the bunk and recoiled as blood rushed into the stump where his small toe had been. He pressed the pillow over his face, rocking until the searing subsided. He stopped three times on the way down the stairs, swearing under his breath at the radiating pain. He flicked on the light of his latrine office and was greeted by a framed poster of a man in a wheelchair, crossing a finish line.

The Only Disability In Life Is A Bad Attitude

The computer screen brightened. His practiced fingers flew across the keyboard, exploring the system's protocols and permissions. It didn't take him long to see that Lily was right. The Architect had built a wide highway. No traffic. No speed limit. But there was nothing to see in the periphery—nothing to tell him where he was, no way to message the outside world. It *was* like working from deep space.

Henry stared at the ceiling, thinking about what Gardener wanted from him. For the remainder of the morning and through late afternoon he walked the virtual perimeter of the FBI, ATF, and Homeland Security, looking for a way in. Not long ago, foreign operators wormed their way into what the government believed was an impenetrable system. They'd accomplished the feat through a seemingly benign third-party software that gathered data from the darkest, most classified corners of government. The feds had learned their lesson. They'd closed that tunnel and spent billions building a vigorous defense against hackers. Getting through it was impossible. There was no way Henry could do it. And in two days, Gardener would know it too.

28

Henry stared out the window of the coal-colored building, looking up the hill at the Main House.

"You okay?"

He turned. Lily was looking up at him with a worried look.

"Sure. Fine."

"You don't look fine."

Henry shrugged.

"Can I help?"

"Not unless you know how to break into the Department of Justice."

"What? You're kidding."

"If I can't figure it out by Sunday, he's going to—"

"Don't. Don't say it, Henry."

Lily reached for his elbow.

Henry removed it gently. "I need to get some air."

"You want company?"

"Nah. I … need some time alone."

Henry limped toward the door. It was sunny. No humidity. Under different circumstances, it could have been a perfect summer afternoon. He hobbled to the edge of the painted boundary line and sat in the grass. A drone dropped out of the sky and hovered near his head. He ignored it. Henry laid back, lacing his hands behind his head. He watched the white contrail of a jet streaking through the cloudless blue sky.

Escape or die trying.

It was a ridiculous notion. He was never escaping—not with his leg. He wasn't capable of running to freedom. And "die trying?" Death was aiming straight for him. It required no effort. The only way he was getting off the Farm was by rescue. And it was pretty damned unlikely that would happen by Sunday. Or anytime, for that matter. Henry rolled onto his elbow and looked at the mounds of fresh soil by the cornfield. He pictured one more grave: his own. Soon enough, the tractor would be firing up for him.

Henry saw a kid running down the hill from the Main House. He had a long stick in his hand. He brought it to his face and fired it like a pretend rifle. A man in a dirty, white tank top clutched his chest, screwing his face in faux agony. The little guy smiled. Then he shot a woman walking up the path carrying laundry. She grinned and faked a forward stumble. The kid ran past her toward Henry.

Beto. That's what Gardener had called him. The boy couldn't have been more than seven. He skidded to a stop in front of Henry. Beto stared, holding the skinny branch like a rifle. He pointed at Henry's left foot. Their eyes met. The boy pointed at his throat and shrugged.

"You can't talk?"

The boy shook his head.

"It makes us special, I guess."

Beto nodded and brought the stick to his cheek and aimed at Henry's face. The boy fired, jerking the stick with imaginary recoil—waiting for Henry to play dead. But the kid's game was a little too on the nose.

"Sorry Beto. I'd rather not die today."

The kid shrugged, waved, then ran into the woods.

Henry looked at the barn. He squinted. The door still wasn't properly padlocked. Henry had an insatiable curiousity. His mind required answers.

What's inside that barn?

Henry stared. And then a more dangerous question tugged at him.

Is there something in there I could use to save myself?

He lay back in the grass, staring up at the sky—reminding himself of the danger. It wasn't worth poking around. He'd be risking his life for nothing. Then again, at this point, did his life amount to much more than "nothing?"

The drones bunched together, hovering overhead, then zipped off in separate directions—two flew over the Main House. Another flew over the woods, so deep it became nothing more than a speck in the distance.

Do they fly at night?
Does Gardener have hidden cameras on the property? In the barn?
It wasn't worth the risk.

"What're you doin' out here?" asked Jammer, catching Henry by surprise.

The blond looked him up and down, staring too long at Henry's twisted foot before speaking.

Henry shrugged and made his way toward the door. Jammer stepped in front of him.

"Gardener didn't put you with us. What're you doing for him in that toilet?"

"I gotta get back to work."

"Is it a secret?" Jammer asked, walking in closer.

"I don't know. Maybe"

"You don't want to tell me? Why?"

Henry looked over his shoulder at the barn.

"You're not skimming, are you? It's something else, right?"

"Yeah. It's something else, Jammer."

Henry had a decent talent for reading people—at least that's what he thought, before meeting Mr. Gardener. If he'd read that situation better he might still have all his toes. But he had a pretty good idea about Jammer. The guy was a snake, and it didn't surprise Henry when he softened his approach.

"It's alright, man. I see you—putting on your brave face, trying not to let anyone see that you're shitting yourself with fear. Dude, it's obvious. You're alone and you're scared. Am I right?"

Henry said nothing.

"We all been there. Even me," he said. "I can help you."

"How?"

"I watch everything and everyone. I pay attention." Jammer looked around then lowered his voice. "There's things I know about this place—things I've learned. I can keep you alive, Henry." Jammer raised his eyebrows. "If ..."

"If what?"

"We make a deal. See, I'm bored with the crypto shit—I'm ready to move on. I need a new challenge—something worthy of my skills. I don't know what he's got you working on, but I can tell it's not going well. You need more talent on your team, Henry. I run circles around

Ivan and Bingo. And don't get me started on Francee. Lily talks a big game, but she can't hold a fuckin' candle to what I do."

"What are you saying, Jammer?"

"Tell Gardener you need my help. Get me on your project. You do that and I'll share all my secrets about this place. I'll keep you safe. How's that sound? It's a good deal. You need a friend—someone you can trust. I need a change of scenery. Anyway, you don't wanna be working in that shithole by yourself, right?"

Henry felt a little sorry for Jammer. Lily was right. The guy was scared. But Henry couldn't help him. He had his own problems.

"Right?" Jammer repeated.

Henry shrugged.

"So? You gonna ask him? Because this thing can go the other way too, Henry." Jammer bowed up. "I can make life miserable for you around here. Worse than it is now. Tell Gardener you need me on your team or—"

"Thanks for the offer," Henry said, interrupting the threat. "I'll think about it."

He turned his back on Jammer and limped into the coal-colored building. He wasn't physically intimidated by him, but that didn't mean the guy wasn't a problem. But he had bigger things to worry about. He needed more than just his wits. The thought of the barn came to him like an answer.

Was there something there that might help him escape?

Or something he could use to call for help?

He teased the idea of exploring the barn. To do it, all he'd need was the cover of night, a little good luck, and a lot of courage. And a light to guide him. Henry walked into the kitchen and opened all the cabinets and drawers. He got down on his hands and knees to search under the sink, hoping to find a flashlight.

There was a small supply closet across the hall. Henry entered, closing the door behind him. It was cramped and he had to step around a mop and a yellow tub to search the shelves. They were crowded with rolls of toilet paper, gallons of bleach, and old towels. No flashlight. A wicker basket was the only item on the top shelf. Henry balanced on the toes of his good foot and reached, pulling the basket toward him—catching it as it fell.

The closet door opened and Henry's heart jumped. He turned,

coming face to face with an ancient wrinkled woman with milky blue eyes.

"I uh—"

She pointed an arthritic finger at the mop and tub by Henry's feet.

"Yeah. Here you go," he said, wheeling the items toward her.

The old woman eyed the wicker basket in his hands. She scowled, then closed the door.

Henry looked down. Next to a spool of green thread was a red, white, and blue box. A matchbox. He slid it open. Seven matches. No telling how old they were. No telling if they'd light. But they were all he had.

That night, long after the others had fallen into REM sleep, Henry lay in his bunk—wide awake—losing courage with every passing minute. Venturing outside Gardener's painted circle in the middle of the night to search a dark barn with only seven wooden matches was foolish. A risk not worth taking.

There's a lot of people in those woods, Henry. Men with guns.

Henry stared at the epitaph of the dead man on the underside of Lily's bunk. Bear knew the risk when he slipped out of the bunk in the middle of the night. He'd found the courage to escape, and even though he'd failed, Henry saw the bravery in what he'd done.

Without rescue, he was dead. And, in a matter of time, probably everyone else around him was dead too. There was no future for him here. By this time next week, he'd be dead. There was nothing to lose, and that was the thing that pulled him out of his bunk and down the stairs in the middle of the night. He'd made a decision. Or at least half of one. He would investigate. Open the door and listen. Maybe stick his head out.

He turned the knob.

Click.

Henry froze, waiting for his heart to settle before opening the door. Carefully, he stuck his head out, tuning his ears to the sounds outside—listening for drones buzzing in the night or men in the treeline. He stayed in the doorway for five minutes—half in and half out.

There was no sound.

Henry stepped out, planting his right foot on the stoop. He craned his neck around the corner to see the barn. His heart sank. Two bright lights over the hay loft illuminated the entrance like spotlights. If there were men out there, they'd see him coming or going.

Nope. Too risky.

Henry leaned on his cane, readying for retreat. He blew a clearing gust from his lungs.

Fuck it.

Henry was incapable of running like an able-bodied man, but that didn't mean he couldn't move with decent speed. He made a herky jerky sprint toward the barn, pushing his cane and swinging his hip—dragging his foot across the bent grass. He wasted no time. Under the bright lights, Henry propped the cane under his arm and yanked on the door. It opened with a metallic rattle that echoed through the noiseless night. To Henry's ears, the sound was louder than a train whistle.

This is stupid.

Henry entered the blackness of the barn and pulled the door closed behind him. His heart was pounding. He couldn't see. Somewhere in front of him should be the spool of hay he'd seen the other day. He bent, groping in the dark until his fingers found it. That gave him his bearings. He remembered the tools he'd seen hanging from hooks. They would be to his right—ready to clang like an alarm bell if he knocked into them. Henry pulled the matchbox out of his pocket, willing his hands to stop shaking as he searched the nearly empty box for a wooden matchstick. He struck the ignition strip and flame erupted between his fingers.

The matchlight cast an eerie shadow across the interior of the barn. Henry turned, coming face to face with a fat spider dangling on a silken thread. He stepped back, knocking into a pitchfork—barely catching it before it fell. Henry moved to the left, holding the short match by his fingernails. He stepped around the tractor, finding a narrow path between rows of wooden crates. The flame flickered and died—putting him in darkness again.

"—you kidding? No way in hell. Notre Dame doesn't have the horses up front."

"Ten bucks."

Henry dropped onto the dirt floor.

"Straight up? Sure."

"Points."

"I'm not giving you points. You're full of shit anyway. You still owe me from—"

"Hey. Check it out."

"What?"

"It's not locked."

"Fucking Couyon."

"The guy's a hammerhead."

The barn door screeched open. A focused beam shot over Henry's head then swung around the interior of the barn before closing. He heard the unmistakable sound of a padlock clapping closed.

"What time you got?"

"Half past."

"Make it fifty on Notre Dame."

"You're a dumbass."

The voices drifted into the night.

Henry was on his hands and knees, rocking back and forth in the darkness, trying to jump-start his brain. He was locked in a barn with six matches and only two hours before daylight. Tomorrow was Saturday—the day Mr. Hermann would stand in the doorway while the Architect checked the code up in the Main House. If Henry couldn't find a way back into the coal-colored building before sunrise, the search for him would be a short one. He'd be dead by lunchtime.

He struck the match. The light flickered. He stayed on his knees, moving forward, trying to get to the side of the barn. He had to negotiate around a wall of wooden crates. His face took out three cobwebs on the way. The match was burning out. He held it over a wooden crate as it died.

Propiedad de Ejercito Mexicano

Henry had taken Latin for a couple years in high school then switched to German in college. Never Spanish. But he could make a guess—property of "something" in Mexico. Ejercito was the problem word.

He pushed against one of the heavy crates. It didn't budge. Henry had gambled that there was something in the barn that could save him. He'd lost that bet. And now he needed to get the hell back into his bunk. He crawled another twenty feet, running his hands along the barn boards as he went.

There was a small crack in a bottom board near the back of the barn. Henry ran his hand over the length of it in the dark before lighting another match. He lifted the flame, inspecting his prospects of escape. If he was going to squeeze through, he'd have to remove not one, but two boards. The match died. Henry kept the picture in his mind's eye. He gripped the cracked bottom board with two hands, wiggling it back and forth, hoping the nails would pop. They didn't. Henry shoved the bottom of his cane into the cavity and pulled up. The board split lengthwise—the snap of the break echoed across the Farm like a gunshot. Henry held his breath, praying the men were far enough not to hear.

He reached under the wall, running his hand over the grass outside. He was close. If he could pull off the next board, he'd have room to belly out. But this one was stubborn. It wasn't going without a fight. Henry burned two matches inspecting its weak points before finally wedging the cane under to pop the nails. It came free without a sound. Henry wasted no time getting his head and shoulders under the barn—pulling himself out. He was halfway to freedom. Then stopped.

Propiedad de Ejercito Mexicano

He wanted to know what was in those boxes and he had two matches to burn. Henry wormed back into the barn, feeling around for the closest crate. He didn't want to spend a match if he didn't have to. He sized up the wooden crate in the dark, letting his hands feel what his eyes couldn't see. He ran his palm across the sides. No latch. No lock. The crate was nailed shut. But there was a lip—just wide enough that, if he struck it with his palm, he might be able to pop the lid. It took a few whacks before Henry managed to squeak the lid off. He lit the next match. The flame brightened. He looked inside.

The crate wasn't giving Henry a way off the Farm. But it was giving him something. And he was sure he wanted nothing to do with its gift.

Packed tightly in the hay were rows of high explosives and grenades. *Shit.*

Henry moved the flame a safe distance away, his mind racing. He had no use for explosives. But there was something under the grenades: a black case. It was unlikely that anyone from Mexico would pack a communication device under high explosives, but Henry had one match and a couple minutes to find out.

He held the flame over the crate, carefully relocating the grenades to the other side. He pulled out the buried case and opened it. Resting on a pillow of foam was a black pistol, a full clip by its side. Henry stared until the match burned out.

He'd never pulled a trigger in his life. Never fired a gun—not even at a paper target. Having this weapon wouldn't help him escape or be rescued. All it could bring was trouble. Henry ran his hand through his hair. He couldn't use it for self-defense—there were too many men wandering around and not enough bullets. But he didn't have to go quietly when Gardener or Mr. Hermann came for him. Henry crawled out of the stale, dusty barn and into the fresh air—a loaded pistol gripped tightly in his right hand.

The rain started as a light drizzle. By the time Henry had hobbled back into the coal-colored building, it had become a proper storm.

29

Henry listened to the rain pattering off the metal roof. His heart was still racing. He hadn't slept. The gun was a problem. Specifically, where he should hide it. First, he'd tucked it in the PVC pipe under the plywood board in his latrine office. He second-guessed himself and put the gun behind the refrigerator. It stayed there only five minutes before he moved it again.

Thunder boomed outside. He looked up at the underside of Lily's bunk as rain banged steadily off the roof. Henry reached behind his head, feeling under his pillow for the gun's diamond-textured butt. He stayed in bed long after the others had shuffled into the bathroom and down the stairs. When he was sure he was alone, he took another look at the gun, double checking the safety and that he'd loaded the clip correctly. He lifted his mattress and stuffed it underneath.

Lily was in the kitchen. She smiled at Henry, but she was anxious. They all were. It was Saturday. Mr. Hermann was coming to lurk in the doorway, waiting for word from the Architect at the top of the hill.

"How'd you sleep, Henry?" Lily asked.

"Fine."

"You okay?"

"Yeah. Why?"

"I don't know. You just seem—"

"No, all good," Henry said.

He didn't like where he'd put the gun. The mattress. The pillow. He should have kept it in the pipe. He had half a mind to go upstairs and retrieve it. But tucking it in his waistband and walking through the building with Mr. Hermann on his way was a bad idea. Henry walked into his latrine office and looked down at the sheet of plywood. It was bowed. It wasn't the gun; it was the board. He definitely should have left it in there.

He squeezed past his desk into the metal chair and waited for his computer screen to brighten. His mind wasn't focused on the job at hand. He was thinking about the barn and the crates of explosives inside. Why would anyone need that much firepower? Gardener was either an arms dealer, a terrorist, or planning one hell of a fireworks display. He had no answers, and it didn't matter. Henry's barn adventure had not solved his problem. Mr. Gardener would soon decide his fate, and if he was going to stay alive, he needed to deliver. There was no other option. He needed a home run. If he could just gain some kind of entry into the Federal Bureau of Investigation, he might be able to string Gardener along.

Henry worked for hours, trying everything he knew. Every system in the FBI was walled off from the others. And segmented. It was like trying to complete a puzzle where every oddly shaped piece was hidden away in a separate, nearly impenetrable vault. Henry ran his hands through his hair, staring at the blinking cursor. The small office was suffocating. The gun under his mattress made him nervous. The FBI wasn't giving up its secrets. Gardener was going to kill him.

Breathe through it, Henry. Exhale the pain. Inhale the healing. Good. Again.

Henry put his palms on the desk. His mother's words brought him some relief. But not much. He wiggled the mouse and tapped a few keys, opening the "MAPS" application. As expected, there was no blue dot indicating his current location. But the app still worked. The Architect hadn't removed the functionality. Henry could still explore random highways and towns, magnifying down to street level. Playing around in MAPS did nothing to solve his problem with Gardener, but it gave his mind the diversion it needed.

Henry entered "Windsor Hills, Ohio" into the search engine and spent a few minutes "walking" the route from his house to the high school. He found the street in Cleveland where he used to live, and the recreation center across from the 7-Eleven where his mother used to take him when he was little. Henry searched for the campground on the Ohio/Pennsylvania line where she was murdered. All the while, his mind was thinking of another road—the one that had brought him to the Farm.

Ted's not who we thought he was.

You and your mother took off. You were hard to find.

Your brain's got serious wattage ... That's what they say, anyway.

You can't outsmart the code. It's intelligent—learning all the time.

Henry leaned back in his chair, letting his mind connect the dots. Someone had told Gardener that he was smart. That meant there was someone in his orbit that was responsible for him being taken to the Farm. Someone complicit in his mother's death. He closed his eyes, examining everyone in his life. After a few minutes he exhaled. There was someone. And the more he considered it, the more certain he became. There was only one person it could have been.

Ted Mortinson had an "old friend" at Indiana State; he liked the school and thought his stepson should go there after high school. Henry had no interest, but his mother encouraged him to visit. It would be a "bonding" trip with his stepdad. The Computer Science Department rolled out the red carpet for his admissions visit. Ted's friend was a professor, and she sold the program hard. There was an intensity about her—the way she talked, the way she listened. Even the way she chewed gum. School had always been easy for Henry, but the professor challenged him, asking hard, testing questions. He liked that. And he liked her. He committed to Indiana State that day.

It was what he'd hope it would be. The professor even invited Henry to join a small group of handpicked students for her "club." They met in her off-campus apartment. She had wine and, sometimes, made a crock-pot of chili or a casserole. They were a close-knit group. She'd talk about systems and codes and what she termed "reverse engineer-ing." Henry understood why she couldn't call it "hacking"—after all, it was a university.

The discussions were strictly theoretical—at first. But over the year it evolved. The students would gather around the professor's computer while she pointed out the online vulnerabilities of company websites. It would take her mere seconds to break the firewall. By the end of Henry's sophomore year, the club was hacking websites—nothing malicious, just taking a look around and leaving without a trace. Henry was good at it. Better than good.

At the convention in Vegas, the professor knocked on his hotel door and asked if he wanted a challenge. He agreed, always eager to impress her. She'd met someone in the bar who had lost his password. He needed something vital in his company's system by morning, and if he didn't get in, he would lose his job.

When Henry entered the hotel suite behind the professor, he had his doubts about the man in the terrycloth robe with the gold chain around his neck. He didn't seem particularly nervous about losing his job. It was sketchy, but Henry didn't protest. The man hung over Henry's shoulder all night, finally slapping him on the back when he got inside the network.

"I told you he was good," said the professor.

The guy wasn't discreet about opening the safe in his closet and handing her a wad of cash. A "thanks, kid" was Henry's reward.

His fingers flew over the keyboard as he watched the code scroll up on the screen. He studied every line of it. Every coder had a style— some element of design uniquely their own. A signature of sorts. If a person knew where to look, it could give them insight into the mind of the creator. It didn't take him long to see the familiarity between the professor and the Architect.

How's your summer, Henry?

He'd been bored inside the Airstream when he'd gotten the text from his college professor.

You got time for a puzzler?

Henry had downloaded the file. It wasn't particularly challenging. He remembered wondering why she bothered sending it to him in July. Now he understood. She'd sent him malware when he was in the Airstream. She'd embedded a tracker in the puzzle. Ted Mortinson's "old friend" was working with Gardener. And she was coming to the Main House today.

The front door banged open. Henry looked out. The wall people were marching to their stations under the watchful eye of Mr. Hermann. Henry limped down the hallway, past the doorway where the man in the Punisher shirt stood with his palm resting on the sheath of his long knife. He ascended the stairs. The sound of the summer storm outside intensified, echoing off the metal roof of the coal-colored building. Henry looked into the sleep room, confirming that his mattress was still undisturbed. He turned toward the narrow door at the end of the hallway that led to the crow's nest. Henry limped toward it.

Nothing to see except trees and the Main House. Not a horrible place to catch rays if you don't mind being dive-bombed by drones.
There would be no drones flying in this storm. Henry opened the door to a small room. Twenty feet above him, the ceiling hatch was leaking—a pool of rainwater collecting on the cement floor. Against the wall was an old-fashioned wooden ladder that someone had probably relocated from the barn. Water had run down the wall and dampened the lower rungs, making them slick and slippery. Other than exiting swimming pools, Henry had no experience climbing ladders.

A drip landed against his cheek. He looked up toward the hatch. Getting up there in wet conditions would have been a challenge for someone with two functioning legs. The ladder wasn't tall enough—it came a few feet short of the bolted hatch in the middle of the ceiling. Henry would need to climb up, and when he was at the top of the ladder, he would have to reach out, unbolt the latch, and pull himself through.

He leaned his cane against the wall and gripped the wet ladder, putting all his weight on his good foot while the other dangled in the air. He jumped to the first rung. Then reached up and jumped again. His hand slipped—he lost his balance, falling backward off the ladder. The back of his head crashed against the concrete floor. He lay there a while, trying to manage the wall of pain coursing through him. Another drop fell onto his eyebrow. Flipping onto his stomach, he crawled back to the ladder. He wasn't giving up.

Swimming had sculpted Henry's broad back and shoulders. From the waist up, he was a beefy, muscular athlete. The storm roared in his ears as he climbed higher. Halfway up, he rested, his left leg dangling off the ladder. He made the mistake of looking down at the concrete floor. Henry swallowed his fear and climbed higher.

The effort required to get through the hatch was becoming clear. There was only one way to get it done. He'd have to jump off the ladder, grab the wet bars near the opening, and pull himself through. All upper body. And if he *could* get up there, he wasn't entirely sure how he was going to get down safely. It was a risk, but it was worth it to know if his theory was correct. He needed to know if his professor was complicit in his mother's murder.

He reached out, unbolted the hatch, and threw open the door. The cold rain slapped his face. He rubbed his hands on his jeans. One shot.

No do-overs. Henry jumped for the bar, caught it, then grunted himself through the hatch and onto the wood decking of the crow's nest.

The rain thrashed him. It came in white sheets pouring out of a dark sky. He was drenched in seconds. Lightning sizzle-cracked above him. Henry stayed low, working his way to the corner of the crow's nest where two rain-soaked, folded canvas chairs rested against the balusters. Lightning flashed again, this time over the woods. He sat, keeping his head low, trying to focus on the house at the top of the hill. The cold wind whipped across the roofline. Henry blinked the rain out of his eyes, concentrating on the windows of the Main House. A shape would pass and he squinted through the sheets of rain trying to identify who it could be. It was impossible to get a read on anything going on in the house at the top of the hill.

Henry wiped his face with his T-shirt and folded the canvas chair. He took one last look up the hill on his way off the roof. The kitchen light turned off—he stopped. The porch door was opening. Gardener stepped out of the house, studying the skies with his hands on his hips. Henry watched him turn toward the door, inviting someone to join him.

The Architect, Dr. Wendy Oaks, walked out of the Main House and stood next to Gardener. She took a sip from a steaming mug, then sat in an Adirondack chair. She crossed her legs, smiling up at Gardener. It *was* true. His mentor. His professor. She had a hand in his mom's murder.

Henry no longer felt the cold. He was on fire, burning with rage.

Gardener and Oaks stayed on the porch for the better part of twenty minutes, talking and watching the storm. In the driving rain at the top of the coal-colored building, Henry watched. There was nothing he could do about the professor. Not yet anyway. If he couldn't give Gardener a viable money-making scheme, he was going to die. And then something flashed through Henry's mind. A beginning of something—just the spark of an idea. It was complicated. But, if he could pull it off, he might live long enough to find a way off the Farm. And with any luck, he could get his revenge on Professor Wendy Oaks.

30

Henry managed the rickety ladder out of the crow's nest. He grabbed his cane and hobbled out the narrow door, his wet shoes sloshing on the linoleum floor. The idea he'd gotten on the roof wasn't fully formed, but its potential consumed him. He turned into the sleep room—crashing into Jammer as he ran out. Henry shot a panicked glance toward his bunk, looking to see if it was disturbed. He couldn't be sure.

"You should watch where you're going," Jammer said, picking Henry's cane off the floor.

Henry squeezed out the bottom of his Captain America shirt.

"Why are you all wet? Were you up in the crow's nest? In a thunderstorm? Why were you sneaking around up there, Hank?"

"Don't call me Hank."

"You were on the roof. Why?"

"I'm not in the mood, Jammer. I'm cold. And I'm wet. And I need some dry clothes."

"Are you gonna ask him?"

"What are you talking about?"

"Gardener. You were going to get me on your project."

"I never promised that."

"So, you're not going to ask him?"

"No."

"You're a selfish fuck. You know that?"

"Jammer, I'm protecting you. There's nothing good about what I'm doing for Gardener. It's a dead end. And I mean that literally."

"Bullshit. I see how Gardener treats you—like you're better than the rest of us."

"It's not bullshit. But, believe what you want. I'm leaving."

Jammer scowled. "Maybe I'll tell Mr. Hermann that you were sneaking around the crow's nest in a thunderstorm. That might interest him."

Henry forced a smile. "We're on the same side. There's no need to threaten me, Jammer."

"I'm watching you. ...."

"Terrific," Henry said, limping into the sleep room.

Henry wriggled out of his wet shirt and opened the drawers of the bureau next to his bed, hoping for something dry. A red sweatshirt and a pair of rolled up socks were in the bottom drawer. Henry held the *Alabama* hoodie out in front of him. Bear's nickname clearly hadn't been ironic. The guy must have been huge. Henry put his arms through the sweatshirt and grabbed for the balled up socks. They had weight to them—heavier than they should have been. Henry glanced at the door before pulling the socks apart and reaching down the throat to discover the object hidden inside.

It was a silver watch, a quartz perpetual timepiece. The red second hand was still moving. He flipped it over.

Congratulations, Jonathon! Love, Dad.

Henry silently gave his thanks to Bear. It was a good gift—more than Henry could have wished for and better than anything he'd found in the barn. He lifted his mattress and placed it next to the loaded gun.

For what remained of the day and well into the night, Henry sat in front of his computer in his toilet office working. For nine hours straight, Henry refined his plan, his fingers a constant patter against the keyboard.

Lily put her head through the door.

"It's late."

Henry didn't look up.

"How's it coming?"

Henry blinked at her.

"You didn't have dinner, did you? I can make you a PB&J. It's kind of my specialty."

Henry shook his head then glanced at the monitor before speaking.

"The other day you said you didn't think Gardener knew much about coding. How sure are you?"

"I don't know. It's just a feeling. I wouldn't bet my life on it."

Wouldn't bet your life on it? Terrific.

"You want me to take a look at what you've got? See if I can help?"

"No thanks, Lily. I'm good."

It took four more hours before he was satisfied with his work. Henry leaned back, surveying the finished product. There wasn't much more he could do than hope.

He was gambling his life on a hunch.

Henry stared at the underside of Lily's bunk, second-guessing himself. What if it wasn't good enough? He thought about Mr. Hermann and his long knife. The asshole hadn't even flinched when he sliced the blade through Henry's toe—or across Rose's neck. If his gamble didn't pay off tomorrow, the knife would be at his throat too.

He felt the lump under his mattress. With all the men roaming the property, using the pistol would be a terminal decision. But if Mr. Hermann pulled his blade, Henry would pull his gun. He wasn't going down without a fight. He listened to the breathy snores around him. The sleep room was still. Silently, he lifted his mattress and tucked the gun in his shorts. In the dark, he limped down the stairs and into his latrine office to prepare.

• • •

The next morning, Lily met Henry in the sun-drenched kitchen with a smile and a cup of coffee.

"Morning! You get any sleep?"

She touched his forearm before pulling it back. It was intimate and slightly awkward, but Henry was glad for it.

"Not much."

They weren't alone. He glanced at the old cleaning woman in the corner. Her bony hands gripped a long mop, pushing it across the floor. She was thin and smelled like cigarette smoke—her face was sallow and wrinkled. She kept her head down, but Henry could tell she was paying attention. Lily carried on as if she wasn't there.

"But you've got something for Gardener, don't you?"

Henry crossed his fingers. Lily surprised him by giving him a good-luck kiss on the cheek and a quick hug. Over her shoulder, he saw the cleaning woman frown at him. Their eyes met for only an instant before she lowered her head and resumed mopping.

Henry was too nervous to finish his coffee. He hobbled to his small office and wedged himself behind the desk, his back against the wall, waiting and watching the hallway, imagining the moment Gardener would turn the corner. Henry was losing confidence in his plan. There were a lot of ways it could go wrong. He felt under his seat, confirming the gun was still there and the tape was secure. Henry tried to calm his breathing, but nothing worked. He stewed most of the morning, waiting for the men to come down from the Main House. He closed his eyes, visualizing how he'd reach for the gun—imagining the force required to pull the trigger and fire. If Hermann or Gardener came for him, he promised himself he wouldn't hesitate.

The men didn't arrive together. Mr. Hermann came in first, and without a word, he posted up next to Henry's desk. He was wearing a new skull-dripping shirt—a fitting uniform for a killer. A few minutes later, Gardener came around the corner. The wind had wrecked his hair. His black sneakers were caked in mud. The look on his face told Henry that Mr. Gardener was not having a good morning.

"Christ, can you move over?" he said to Hermann.

Gardener lifted his foot and turned his ankle, looking down at the glops of mud hanging off the heels of his black sneakers. He muttered something that Henry didn't catch. Gardener blew an exasperated exhale then combed his hand through his hair. Instinctively, Henry lowered his arm from the desk to the side of the metal chair.

"Alright. Here we are. Welcome to Shark Tank. Impress me."

Henry looked into Gardener's piercing blue eyes. Whatever remaining confidence he had in his plan melted away. His fingers gripped the seat, inches from the tape that held the gun.

"Did you think I came down here for a staring contest?"

Henry had practiced what he needed to say. Over and over. But now, the words weren't forming.

"I uh—"

"I'm listening."

"I uh—"

"I uh, suggest you stop stuttering. Pull yourself together, son."

"I tried everything. I couldn't, um—I couldn't get into the main servers. They're too secure."

Gardener frowned.

Henry's mouth was too dry to swallow.

"But—" Henry wiped a bead of sweat from his forehead.

"I don't want to discourage you, but Christ, Henry. So far? This is the worst pitch I've ever heard."

He turned his monitor around so Gardener could see it.

"I did find something."

Henry's heartbeats crashed against his chest. This was the moment. The gamble.

I wouldn't bet my life on it.

"I found a database in an adjacent system. The way the FBI were securing it, I knew it was important."

Henry looked into Gardener's blue eyes. He was paying attention.

"What database?"

"Informants."

"Informants? Confidential FBI informants?"

"Yes, sir. I need more time. It's a pretty big database."

"It has their names?"

"No. They're only identified by a numbered code. There's probably another file somewhere in the system that matches the number to a name. I just haven't found it yet."

Gardener frowned. "Not sure that's going to be very helpful."

Henry waited.

"So, that's it?"

"I think I can track them."

Gardener's eyes narrowed. "You know where they are?"

"Yes, sir."

"You can show me where every FBI informant in the country is?"

"Eventually."

"I want to see. Right now."

"Yes, sir." Henry's fingers flashed across the keyboard, opening the MAPs application. "See this red dot?"

"What am I looking at?"

"That's the last location of the informant. When they contact their FBI handler, the system logs the time of the call and their GPS coordinates."

Gardener put his hands behind his neck, not speaking for a few minutes. Henry waited for the man's mind to catch up to the solution.

"If we had the time of the calls and the location, we wouldn't necessarily need the name. Snitches could be sussed out pretty quick. That right, Henry?"

"Yes. I think so."

"So, this red dot. Who is this guy. Where is he?"

Henry entered the GPS coordinate for the red dot.

"Chicago."

"Chicago? That's pretty fucking vague."

Henry pointed at the screen.

"Yesterday, he or she contacted the FBI from the corner of Western Avenue and 111th Street at 2:12 in the afternoon. Eight days earlier, they called at 4:23 p.m. from California Avenue in Mundelein, Illinois."

"Show me more."

"It's time-consuming, sir. That's all I have right now. But I'll get quicker."

"I want all of it. The entire database. How long will it take?"

"I might be able to automate some of it, but it's going to take a while."

"I asked *how long?*"

"Three, maybe four months."

"What if I gave you Lily to help. How soon then?"

"That's not necessary. I can do it."

Gardener shook his head. "Nope. I'm putting her with you. It'll double the speed."

Shit.

"I don't need Lily. I'm sure she's more valuable doing—"

"I'm not asking for your opinion, Henry. You and Lily are now a team. Anything else?"

He didn't mean to bring Lily into this. She was going to hate him for it.

Gardener asked again. "Anything else you need?"

"Can I ask a favor?"

"You want a favor. From me? Okay, this'll be good. What do you need, Henry?"

"I'm a doodler."

"You're a what?"

"Geometric doodling—making shapes. It helps me think."

Gardener tilted his head and smirked.

"I just need a few colored pencils, some drawing paper, and a protractor."

"Jesus, you're a nerd," Gardener said with a smile. "You hear that, Mr. Hermann?"

"Yes, sir."

"Get Henry what he needs. Put Couyon on it—maybe he won't fuck it up. I need Lily and Henry working in private. Move their stations upstairs into the bunk room. Let the other misfits sleep downstairs by their computers."

Mr. Hermann nodded.

"This is a good start, son. You're as smart as they said you were and, congratulations, you've bought yourself a little time. But I need to see results. Soon."

Henry loosened his grip on the metal chair.

"If you can build this, I'll take care of you. And Lily."

Gardener turned and walked down the hall and around the corner. Henry covered his mouth, exhaling into his palm. Lily's hunch was right.

Gardener didn't know a thing about coding.

31

Mr. Hermann's men were in the sleep room, negotiating a desk around the corner. Henry watched from his mattress, moving his butt inches at a time until he could feel the gun lump under him. The men centered the desk in the middle of the room. Then they went back for Lily's, and later, the monitors and cables. Couyon's job was to take Francee, Ivan, Bingo, and Jammer's mattresses off their bunks and put them downstairs.

Lily came up and looked around at the new configuration.

"Hey," Henry said.

"What's going on? Mr. Hermann told me I'm supposed to work with you up here. Why?"

Henry hadn't been looking forward to this conversation.

"This isn't what I wanted, Lily. I didn't think he would bring you into this."

"Into what?"

He couldn't look her in the eye.

"Henry. Into what?"

He limped to his computer and fired it up.

"Take a look."

Lily sat in his chair, waiting for him to explain.

"I told Gardener I got into a secure FBI database and built a program to track FBI informants."

"Henry! You did it? Jesus, that's incredible."

He pointed to the screen. Lily opened the file with the FBI logo.

He watched her scroll through the code. She bent into the screen, tilted her head, then leaned back.

"Henry?"

"I'm sorry. I didn't—"

She waved him off and looked back at the screen.

"Shipping and receiving?"

"I didn't mean to involve you, Lily."

She opened the map and examined the code behind the red dot. She closed her eyes and inhaled. "You told him—what? That this was an FBI informant?"

Henry nodded.

"You hacked into a parcel service, mirrored the GPS tag, pasted an FBI logo in the corner, and had the balls to tell Gardener it was an FBI informant?"

He didn't look her in the eye.

"We're fucked, Henry. The Architect will find. ... When Gardener realizes. ... He's going to kill you, Henry." She exhaled. "Correction. He's going to kill *us*."

Lily got out of the chair, turned her back on Henry, and walked to the corner of the room.

"I'm sorry. I didn't have anything for Gardener—he would've killed me. I had to make something up."

She nodded but her face didn't soften. She shook her head, walked back to the computer and sat down to recheck the code. Two minutes later, her fingers dropped off the keyboard.

"There's nothing we can do to hide this. The Architect is going to see it right away. You knew that, didn't you? You knew if you saved your life today, you'd still be dead in a week?"

Henry nodded and looked down at the floor.

"So? That's it?"

"I'm working on a way out."

"A way out? There's no way out."

Henry nodded. "You're right. I don't think there's a way to escape the Farm. But that's not what I'm trying to do. I want to call for help. Get us rescued."

Lily stared at Henry then shook her head. "Did you even look at the system? How are you going to call for help? The Architect closed every loop. No messages in or out. Come on, face it—in a week it's over."

"We can't send an SOS, but we *can* send attack commands."

Lily crossed her arms. "I'm not following."

"The Architect built a system to give us an unimpeded ability to attack secure systems, right? So, if we bombarded the FBI, Homeland, ATF—every law enforcement site we can think of—even though it won't penetrate their systems, it would get their attention."

"Yeah, but—"

"But instead of blasting them with malware, we embed our GPS coordinates inside the assault. If we hit enough targets, they'll be smart enough to make the connection and come looking for us."

"Our coordinates?"

"Right."

"Well, that would be brilliant if we knew where we were Henry. Face it, we're as good as—" she stopped when one of Hermann's men put his head through the doorway.

"Hi, Lily."

"Hey, Couyon."

He walked into the room holding a plastic grocery bag.

"I have some things for your friend."

"His name's Henry. This is Couyon," Lily said, walking over and taking the bag out of the big man's hand.

"Okay. Nice to see you again, Lily."

"You too, Couyon. Take care."

She looked inside the bag, but said nothing until she heard the outside door bang shut.

"Crayons? Paper?"

Henry limped to her.

"There should be—"

"A protractor?"

Henry nodded and took the bag.

"What's all this for?"

"It's going to tell us where we are."

"Crayons?"

"No, the protractor. And the watch I found in Bear's sock."

"Slow down. What are you talking about?"

"We need our GPS location. I can use the watch to get longitude—find solar noon and subtract it from Greenwich Mean Time. I'll make an inclinometer with the protractor. That'll tell us our latitude."

"You're serious?"

"Yeah. It's how sailors found their location in the middle of the ocean."

"How do you know this?"

"I don't know, I was just curious. Watched a couple of YouTube videos. It's pretty easy. We just need a sunny day and a clear night."

"YouTube?"

Henry nodded.

"So, *if* you can actually get our GPS coordinates—" she paced the room. "And *if* the Feds managed to see it, they'd have to mount up and rescue us before next Saturday. I don't know, Henry. We'd have to send a massive attack—a blitzkrieg—for them to notice."

Lily walked quickly across the room and sat down at her computer. She didn't speak for the next ten minutes, her face inches away from the screen. Finally, she spun in her seat and faced him.

"Okay. ... If you can get our location, I can send an attack program they won't miss."

• • •

Henry lay on his mattress and replayed the movie—Gardener in his office, swallowing the big lie. He'd taken a huge risk and bought a little time for himself. But sitting there in the dark, it wasn't victory he was feeling—an elephant was sitting on his chest. This morning, he'd meant to burn his own boat on the shore. But now Lily's fate was tied to his. What if the FBI didn't recognize the message in a bottle? What would happen if they brushed aside the benign attack without investigating its contents? There were a lot of reasons it wouldn't work, and lying in his bunk, his mind had little difficulty making a list of them.

By the end of the week, they'd be rescued. Or dead.

Above him, Lily's arm dropped over the side of her bunk like an invitation. She wiggled her fingers. Henry reached up and clasped her soft hand. And for a long while, they held each other with nothing, not even a whisper, spoken between them.

32

L ily and Henry sat across from each other in the sleep room, each stationed at their computers, working in near silence. He dug Bear's watch out of his pocket. They still had some time.

"You sure this is gonna be accurate?" asked Lily.

"Yup. With luck, it'll be pretty close—within a half mile. Longitude is north to south, from pole to pole. We just have to subtract our solar time from GMT. There are 15 degrees in an hour so—"

"But you'd have to know our time zone."

"We're in Central."

"Central? How can you be sure of that?"

"Eastern white pines only grow in the eastern portion of North America. That puts us in Central or Eastern."

"Then why are you so sure we're in Central and not Eastern?"

"Gardener told the little kid that the Astros and Padres game started at ten after one. That's a Midwest time slot. Which means we're in Central."

Lily shook her head and smiled.

"Okay, genius. I'm going down for coffee. Want anything?"

"No, I'm good."

Fabricating a map of informants from a parcel website was easy. Constructing an assault code big enough to get the attention of law enforcement was time-consuming and difficult—an intense, complex assemblage of piecemeal construction. Henry looked at the watch in his pocket. The longitude calculation was trickiest because they had to get it right the first time or wait until noon the next day. Henry would have preferred to take readings over the course of a few days. But they didn't have that luxury. The sooner they sent their coordinates, the better their chances of being rescued.

Lily put a coffee on Henry's workstation.

"Thanks."

"Shit is hitting the fan down there."

Henry looked up. "What?"

"A huge crypto exchange just went offline. It folded. They're freaking out."

"Why?"

"It's the only one we had access to. It either went bankrupt or the Feds shut it down. There's nothing to skim."

"Does Gardener know?"

"He will. It's probably all over the news."

"Can't they find another?"

"It took Ivan and Bingo weeks to find the key to that one. Gardener was already losing interest in crypto. They're pretty sure he's going to shut down the skimming operation. You know what that means?"

He did. It meant that the wall people were running out of time too.

"Stay clear of Jammer. He's bad-mouthing you. Says all of this is your fault. I tried to talk to him, but he's pissed."

Henry nodded and looked at Bear's watch. "We should get up there."

Lily held the ladder for Henry as he climbed into the crow's nest. She followed. The conditions were perfect for a reading. Blue sky. No clouds in sight. Henry placed the ceiling tile he'd taken from the second-floor bathroom on a level spot on the deck. He repurposed the nail from his motivational poster and stuck it into the center of the tile. A drone rose over the roofline. Lily rolled her sleeves up to her shoulder and leaned against the short railing, tilting her head into the sky while Henry blocked the tile from its view. He turned, taking a moment to admire Lily with the sun on her face. She was beautiful.

It was nearly noon. They had a small window to get their reading, but the drone was stubbornly hovering over the crow's nest. Precious minutes were slipping by.

"What the hell?" Henry said, trying not to move his lips.

"I don't know. Why isn't it moving on?"

He looked at her with the sun on her face. Then back at the drone.

"Lily, go back down."

"What?"

"The drone isn't watching us. It's watching you. I think the pilot likes you."

"Shut up."

"I'm serious."

"What about the reading?"

"Call up the time from below."

Lily retreated down the hatch and the drone zipped away.

"What do you have?" Henry said, leaning his head toward the hatch.

"Five of. We still okay?"

"We'll know soon enough. Call out the time every thirty seconds. I'll make a dot on the tile where the shadow hits. Solar noon will be the closest dot to the nail."

"Three. Two. One. 11:56."

"11:56 + 30. Now."

"11:57. And, now."

Her last reading was 12:08 + 30.

"Okay. We're good. I got it."

It was as good a reading as they could have hoped for. The next step was finding latitude. In front of him was the protractor, scotch tape, a silver washer, the green thread he'd found in the supply closet, and a red straw from the kitchen. Weather permitting, tonight they'd have their GPS coordinates. Henry picked up the straw and brought it to his eye, looking through it like a tiny telescope. They worked in silence, ignoring the shouting downstairs.

Jammer was taking his anger out on somebody.

To make the inclinometer was child's play. Literally. The YouTube video Henry had learned it from was for children. The challenge wasn't in the construction, it was in getting an accurate reading. A mistake of one degree could put his coordinates off by 60 miles. But unlike finding solar noon, he could keep taking readings all night.

Two hours after sunset, Lily opened the narrow door at the end of the hall, holding it open for Henry to limp in.

"Are you sure the drones don't fly at night?"

"Reasonably sure, yeah."

Henry pulled himself into the crow's nest and inhaled the fragrance of the summer night. He surveyed the starry night, then put his head down through the hatch.

"Clear skies," he whispered down.

"Thank god."

While he took latitude readings, Lily would be putting the finishing touches on the malware that would bombard federal law enforcement with their GPS coordinates. In a few hours, they'd send it. Thanks to Lily, it was going to draw attention. She was a hacking assassin.

There was nothing to dim the stars. No clouds. No moon. No light pollution. Henry wasn't sure he'd ever seen the night sky as glorious as it was that night. The Milky Way. Orion's Belt. The Big Dipper. Polaris. It was as bright as he'd ever seen it. He needed to sight the star through the red straw taped to the protractor. A weighted string would slide to the horizon angle and give him the degree of latitude. He leaned up against the waist-high railing and looked down the barrel of the straw into the universe of stars. He had the north star in his sights when he heard Lily coming up the ladder. Henry didn't take his eye from the star.

"Everything good?" he asked without turning.

There was no response.

"Lily?"

He lowered the inclinometer and saw Jammer pulling himself into the crow's nest.

"What the fuck are you doing up here?"

"Keep your voice down," whispered Henry.

"Don't tell me to keep my voice down. I've got nothing to lose, do I?"

"Shh. I'm trying to help all—"

"Bullshit. You only care about yourself. And Lily."

Jammer snatched the inclinometer out of Henry's hands.

"Give that back. Seriously. Jammer, we need that."

"Who's we? You and Lily? Gardener's little pets?"

"You don't understand—"

"Understand? I'm downstairs drowning while you're in the Bounce House with Lily. I don't care how you do it—talk to Gardener and get me up there with you guys."

"That's not going to happen. Just trust me—"

"Trust you? Fuck that. Get me up there."

Jammer was handling the inclinometer too roughly, bending the straw and protractor against his thigh.

"Jammer, please. Give it back."

"Get me on your project."

"Seriously, Jammer—" Henry said, reaching to take back the inclinometer.

Jammer pulled it away.

"Talk to Gardener."

"I can't talk to Gardener. Please—"

"Then fuck you!" Jammer said, snapping the inclinometer and throwing it over the rail.

Henry bolted toward him. "No!"

It was an accident. Henry never meant to push him. Jammer lost his balance. One second he was standing by the short rail. And the next, he was gone—screaming all the way down.

"No. Oh god."

Henry gripped the rail, looking into the darkness—praying that Jammer was okay. Then he heard the spine-snapping thud from below.

"No. No. No."

A whistle cut through the quiet of the night. And then another. The chorus of whistles came from every direction. In seconds, flashlight beams were waving through the woods. Men were running. Up the hill, a light turned on in the Main House. Henry limped to the hatch and, as quickly as he could, lowered himself down the ladder, closing the narrow door behind him.

He hobbled down the hallway.

The whistles were getting closer.

"What's that sound?" Lily said, looking up from her computer.

"I didn't mean to—"

"Henry? What's wrong?"

"They're coming!"

A door slammed downstairs. Men were running through the first-floor halls. Seconds after Lily turned off the lights and jumped into the top bunk, the door opened and the light flicked on again.

"Who's there?" Lily said, feigning grogginess.

She let her feet drop over the side of the bunk and sat up. Couyon was in the doorway, holding a gun.

"Hey, Lily."

"What's going on?" she asked.

"When the whistle blows we go to our stations. This is where I'm supposed to go."

Lily swung herself off the bunk and onto the floor.

"I thought I heard something. Don't shoot. Okay?"

"Liiily. You know I'd *never* hurt you. I just got to wait here until Mr. Hermann gives the all-clear." Couyon looked over at Henry. "I guess he's a good sleeper, huh?"

"And a snorer," she said. "Hey, Henry. Something's going on."

His heart raced uncontrollably. Jammer was dead—because of him. His head was spinning with guilt.

"Henry."

He held his breath and lowered the bedsheet.

"Why are you sweating?" asked Couyon.

Lily answered. "He gets night sweats. He's damaged goods, like all of us."

"Hm." Couyon looked at Henry.

"Snores a lot. Sweats a lot. Might as well marry him, right?" she smiled.

The big man looked at her with wide eyes. "I'm a snorer too, Lily."

Henry closed his eyes, practicing his mother's breathing exercises. *In with the good. Out with the bad.*

It took twenty minutes before Mr. Hermann walked into the sleep room and ordered Henry out of his bunk.

"What's going on?" Lily asked.

"There's a dead man in the grass."

She looked at Henry. "What?"

Mr. Hermann rested his palm against his long knife.

"Who?" Lily asked.

"Windjammer."

"Oh my God. What happened?"

"By the looks of it, he jumped off the roof. Maybe he fell. Hard to know."

Lily looked at Henry, then back to Mr. Hermann. "He *jumped* off the roof?"

Gardener's henchman reached into his back pocket. He pulled out a piece of the plastic protractor, the bent red straw still taped to it. "We found this near his body. Look familiar?"

Henry stared at the dripping skull on Mr. Hermann's shirt. His heart was banging in his chest. He looked over his shoulder at the mattress. Could he reach the gun before the long knife was plunged into him? Not likely. Hermann was waiting for an answer, but no words were forming in Henry's head.

"Couyon, did you give this to Henry yesterday?"

"Yes."

"Then I'll ask again. What's it doing next to a dead man?"

Henry felt faint.

"I—uh."

"Jammer must have been the one who took it," said Lily. "Henry was looking for it this afternoon. He thought someone stole it." She looked at her bunkmate.

Henry managed a nod. But before he could put his hand out for the instrument, Hermann pocketed it.

"Jammer was a piece of shit. No one's going to miss him. Let's go, Couyon."

"Bye, Lily."

"Couyon—don't be an asshole," Hermann said, pulling him out. Lily closed the sleep room door. "Henry?"

"I didn't mean to."

"Why? Why would you?"

"He came up there—he was threatening us. I tried to tell him. He took it away from me. I just reacted. Lily, I swear it was an accident."

"You killed him."

Henry closed his eyes and nodded. Jammer was dead. Their plan was dead. And soon, they'd be dead too.

It was early morning. Henry and Lily stood side by side in the wet grass behind the coal-colored building. Francee and Ivan and Bingo were there too, staring at the spot where Jammer's body had landed.

"Someone should say something."

No one took the initiative. They just stared. Henry was debilitated by shame. Jammer was an asshole, but he didn't deserve to die. And he'd failed Lily too. There would be no SOS message. No one was coming to save them. Next Saturday, Wendy Oaks would see what Henry had done and deliver their death sentence. He looked over at Lily. Her face was pale.

"I'm sorry. I—"

A sound in the distance interrupted his apology: the coughing bellow of a tractor starting up in the barn. The residents of the coal-colored building walked to the front to see its slow progress across the lawn. They watched the backhoe slice into the earth a few feet from where Mr. Rose was buried. It pulled up brown dirt and large stones, tossing them aside as it gorged deeper. The hole grew wider and wider. Too wide. It didn't take Henry long to understand. He turned to Lily. She said nothing, but her eyes told him she knew it too. This was not a hole for Jammer. The tractor was digging a mass grave.

Lily reached out her arms. Francee and Ivan and Bingo closed ranks. They stood together, their feet wet with the morning dew in front of the coal-colored building, watching the heaving and jerking of the tractor's backhoe as its blue smoke drifted across the grass and over their future resting place.

33

Henry looked at Lily sitting in front of her computer, staring at a blank screen.

"It's my fault."

"Stop apologizing. It's not helping."

"Your code was brilliant. It would have worked. They'd have rescued us. I know it."

Lily didn't respond.

"I'm sorry."

"Goddammit, Henry. Stop. Okay? I can't. ..." She walked out of the sleep room and down the stairs to be with the others.

He sat on his bunk, feet on the floor, his hands pulling through his hair. He tried to clear his mind, tried to think of some other way to save Lily and the others. But, mentally, he was empty. Wrung out. No one knew where they were. They couldn't call for help. They couldn't run. And judging by the huge, gaping grave, it wouldn't be days, but hours, before Gardener started dropping Ivan and Francee and Bingo in.

He and Lily would live until Saturday. It would take Professor Oaks two minutes to see through their grand lie about an informant database. Henry guessed that by midday, they'd be dead too. It was a foregone conclusion—nothing to be done.

Henry balled his fists, grabbed his cane, and stood.

Fuck it.

He lifted the mattress, flipped the safety off the pistol, and tucked the gun in his waistband. Henry's anger fueled his movement. He limped down the stairs, opened the door, and stepped into the sun. He ignored Lily and the others—hobbling past them toward the painted boundary line.

"Henry?" Lily called.

He stared up the hill at the Main House.

"Henry. Come back," she said.

A drone zipped across the sky and dropped in front of his face.

"Henry?"

He stepped across the boundary circle with his right foot. He dragged the left to join it. The drone buzzed near his face. He ignored it. Step. Drag. Across the lawn.

"Christ, Henry. What are you doing?"

With every aching step his anger grew. Six more drones shot away from their locations and flung themselves at Henry. They hovered in front of him. He could feel the wind of their blades against his face. He swung his cane, catching one of the rotors. It crashed into the path, spinning in circles—kicking up dirt before righting itself and taking flight overhead. Henry limped forward. Farther up the path.

Ahead of him, at the top of the hill, walking slowly down the path in his skull T-shirt was Mr. Hermann—his long knife slapping against his thigh. Henry limped toward him, tightening his grip on his burled-wood cane. The drones swarmed around his head, taking turns darting at him and then lifting away. A propeller clipped his ear. Henry brought his hand up and saw blood on his fingers. The mechanical spiders taunted him, hovering in his face, buzzing at him, then backing off. They were everywhere. Henry stopped his progress and waved his hand to keep them away. He looked up the hill. Mr. Hermann was getting closer. He looked pissed.

Henry reached behind his back and lifted his shirt, gripping the gun's frame.

A drone hovered inches from his eyes. He was about to swing the gun out of his waistband, but he hesitated. His eyes widened. He released his grip on the gun and brought his hands to rest on top of his burled-wood cane. Instead of waving them away, Henry willed the drones to come closer. And they did. He watched them and his mind began to work. The idea didn't come instantly. But it came.

"What the fuck do you think you're doing, Henry? You know the rules."

"I want to speak to Mr. Gardener."

Mr. Hermann pulled the long knife out of his leather sheath, the blade glinting in the sunlight.

"That's all," Henry said. "I just wanted to ask him something."

"I'll say this once. And I'll say it slow. Turn around or—"

"But—"

"I'll take your fingers first, then your—"

Henry interrupted, "Tell him I can finish his project this week."

Mr. Hermann lifted his chin. "How?"

"I'm getting closer." Henry glanced over at the huge mound of dirt left from the tractor. "I need Francee, Ivan, and Bingo. With their help, I can finish this week. And tell Mr. Gardener that if he kills them, he should murder me too. Cause if they die? I'm going on strike. He's not getting shit from me."

Mr. Hermann pricked his finger on the blade of his long knife and showed Henry the spot of blood.

"Still sharp. Got a lot of cutting left in it. Are you sure that's what you want me to tell the boss?"

Henry nodded.

"Your funeral, Gumdrop."

Henry hobbled as quickly as he could back down the path toward the coal-colored building.

"What the hell were you thinking?" Lily shouted.

"Come with me."

"Seriously," she said, drawing close to him, "I thought he was going to kill you."

"Almost did. Might still. But come with me."

"Why? What's up with you?"

"I think I've got it. Come upstairs."

Lily was over his shoulder as he punched keys.

"Okay. Here we go."

"What are you doing?"

"Looking for a 2.5 Ghz signal."

"Why?"

"The answer was right in front of us the whole time, Lily."

"Henry. Stop. Talk to me."

He turned. "The drones."

"What about them?"

"There's seven of them."

"I know."

"They each have cameras. They're connected wirelessly to some-one on the ground, right? They send images by radio waves. And each drone has to be on a separate frequency to avoid interference. You've seen them, they fly very high and very far. They have to sacrifice con-nectivity speed for distance. Which means they can't be on the same signal as our network. They have to be on a lower band."

"2.5 Ghz. Not the Architect's 5 Ghz?"

"Exactly. They're not behind her firewall."

"Henry. If we can hack the drones, we—"

"Can do anything we want. The one that clipped my ear—I recog-nized it. They sell them at Best Buy. It's not encrypted. We can mirror the signal, we can take the controls, and more importantly we can—"

Lily put her hand out to stop him. "We can pull whatever images are stored on the drone's SD card. We right click and—"

"We've got our *exact* GPS coordinate."

She hugged his neck. "You're brilliant."

Henry turned back to the screen. He pulled up the PC settings and pointed. "I missed it. Didn't even think to look."

"The signal was there the whole time?"

"Like I said, not so brilliant."

It didn't take long for Henry to lock on to a drone. He dropped his index finger on the return key, launching the packet sniffer. He held his breath. Lily was by his side. She wasn't breathing either.

"Why isn't it loading?" she asked. "It should be loading."

Henry stared at the screen, biting his finger. The white progress bar on the screen wasn't moving.

"There!"

The bar began back-filling in blue—marching to the right. The packet sniffer had found the drone's mini-SD card, sending video and image data to Henry's computer.

"Want a birds-eye view of the Farm?"

Lily nodded. "Show me."

Henry opened the video file. The camera was lifting off. Higher and higher above the trees. Soaring across the sky. And then it hovered a while and Henry could finally see what surrounded the Farm.

"Shit," he said. "Look at that."

The Farm was like a wheel. The Main House was at the center, tents and encampments surrounding it like spokes. No wonder Bear had been found so quickly. There was literally nowhere he could've run without being caught.

The drone hovered over the coal-colored building then zipped deep into the woods, focusing on a dozen tents and some old RVs, all draped in camouflage. Men and women, some with slung rifles, walked through the camp near smoldering fire pits. There were even children down there, chasing each other with sticks.

"What the hell?" Lily said under her breath.

The camera made a pass over the gun range. It was farther away than it sounded. The range was shaded by a pergola, with ten pickup trucks parked nearby. In the distance, paper targets hung from what looked like wooden posts stuck in grassy mounds.

"I want to know where we are," Lily said.

Henry pulled up the images on the SD card. He searched the thumbnail files for a picture of the coal-colored building. He right-clicked the image data. And there it was. No solar noon or inclinometer required. The image gave them their exact GPS coordinate.

He pulled up a map and entered the data. "We're somewhere in Michigan."

"Zoom out."

They bent their heads to the screen. Henry stared at the blue pin on the map, studying the roads, rivers, and access points. The next town was more than ten miles from them.

Lily murmured, "We're in the middle of nowhere."

"But they'll find us. How long before we can execute our SOS?"

"It'll take a little time to enter our coordinates into the payload. An hour at most."

While she got to work, Henry leaned on his cane and closed his eyes, rocking back and forth. The GPS coordinates would bring the authorities. Eventually.

"You've got that look. What are you thinking?" Lily asked.

"Every Saturday? That's what you said, right?"

"What?"

"The Architect comes every Saturday?"

"Yeah."

"Always on a Saturday? Never another day?"

"What are you—"

"Think. This is important. Has the Architect ever shown up on a day other than Saturday?"

"Why?"

"Lily."

"No. It's only been on Saturdays."

"Good."

"Why?" she asked, as they both turned their heads at the sound of a door slamming downstairs.

"Henry? Come down here!" came the voice from below.

"Fuck, it's Gardener."

Henry limped to his computer. "You have to buy me some time, Lily."

"What—?"

"Please."

Lily raced down the stairs. Henry pulled up the map of Gardener's fake FBI informants. His fingers flashed across the keyboard, racing to manually enter the data. He could hear footsteps on the stairs. Coming closer. He hit RETURN just as Gardener came into the room with Mr. Hermann.

"I called for you. Why didn't you come down?"

"I think my toe is infected."

"Didn't stop you from trying to climb the hill to confront me. Did it?" Gardener inhaled deeply, catching his breath. "Mr. Hermann said you were kind of an asshole."

"I'm sorr—"

"And 'strike'? Is that the word you used? Strike?"

"I was upset."

"The Farm is not going union, son."

"I'm sorry."

"Do you think you're irreplaceable?"

Henry shook his head.

"Explain."

"I was upset about Jammer. And then I saw the grave, and I thought—"

"Thought what? That I was finished with the skimmers?"

"They're worried."

"They should be."

"I need—what I mean to say is, *we* need them. We can finish so much faster."

"You told Mr. Hermann a week. Is that true?"

"I think so."

"How far are you now?"

"About 50% of the way."

Gardener crossed his arms. "I want to see."

"I think we've found all the FBI informants east of the Mississippi."

"Already?"

"Yes. I took the time to make the map interactive—user friendly. It could use some more tweaking—"

"What do you mean by interactive?"

"All your client needs to do is enter a zip code or a county. It'll show you if there's been FBI activity." Henry cleared his throat, hoping his voice would keep steady. "You want to try it out?"

"I just type it into this box at the top?"

"Yes."

Gardener looked at Mr. Hermann.

"Henry, go over there. Sit on your bunk. Give me a little privacy."

"Yes sir," he said, his heartbeats pounding against his chest.

Gardener motioned Mr. Hermann to his side.

"What county is Caesar in?"

The man in the black Punisher shirt whispered in Gardener's ear. The blue-eyed man delivered a series of one-fingered staccato punches to the keyboard.

"Look at this."

"Ouch," said Mr. Hermann.

"He's going to be pissed. They're crawling up his ass." Gardener smiled at Henry. "Mr. Caesar is about to make me a rich man."

"Yes, sir," Henry said, standing up.

"Did I say you could come over here? Stay put."

Gardener typed in new information. He tilted his head at the computer. He muttered something. Cleared the information and retyped.

"Motherfucker."

Mr. Hermann looked over his shoulder. "There's a red pin."

"I see the pin for Christ's sake."

Gardener was fidgeting. He looked at Henry.

"When you showed me the guy the other day—the guy in Chicago.

You said it showed where he called from last, and where he'd called the day before. Does this have history?"

"Yes, I can show you," Henry said, trying to stand.

"Stay the fuck where I told you. Tell me. How do I find the history?"

"Well, we built it in a way that's accessible in a number of—"

"Henry!"

"Click on the red location pin. It'll show the date, and time of the informant's contact with the FBI."

Gardener clicked. Stared at the time stamps.

"You see this?" he said to Mr. Hermann.

"I see it."

Henry waited for the moment of collective realization. It came quickly.

Gardener's face turned a dark shade of crimson. He slapped the table.

"That fucking cunt!"

Henry watched the satisfying eruption.

Payback's a bitch, Professor.

34

Mr. Gardener stared at the monitor, then jumped out of his seat and did a lap around the room, then back to the monitor, and up again. Henry could almost see his mental machinery kicking into a higher gear. The man cycled from anger to disbelief to acceptance, then back to anger. The wheel finally stopped and he stood in the middle of the room. He put his fingers in his front pockets and looked at the floor. Gradually, his color returned to normal.

Mr. Hermann, who'd had the good sense not to interrupt him while in motion, stepped closer to his boss and whispered in his ear. Gardener looked up at him. Then turned to Henry.

"You know about this?"

"Know about what, sir?"

Gardener got into Henry's face, looking into his eyes as if the truth was written in small font across his pupils. Henry didn't blink. He kept his poker face while his insides roiled. Finally, Gardener exhaled and shook his head. He walked back to the monitor and looked at the screen.

"It appears," he said, blowing a gust out of his mouth, "that your program caught a shark swimming in our pool."

Gardener looked at Mr. Hermann.

Henry kept silent.

"What do we do, Boss?"

"Let me ask you, Mr. Hermann—what would her dear, old dad have done?"

Hermann raised his eyebrows.

"It wouldn't have mattered who it was. Agree?"

"That's right, sir." Mr. Hermann looked over Gardener's shoulder at the computer screen. "How'd they get to her?"

"The question is *when* they got to her." Gardener pointed at the history markers on the screen. "Four weeks."

"Is that good?"

"Good? Jesus, Hermann. No. Nothing about this is good. It means," Gardener took a moment to put the puzzle pieces together, "the FBI was probably already sniffing around Mortinson. Maybe she was sloppy, left some crumbs for them."

"She knows everything."

"No. She knows *some* things. And if I know our little shark, she's making big promises to the FBI, but passing information slowly—trying to weasel her way into full immunity."

"What do we do?"

"Well, first, the FBI is going to lose their witness."

"Me and Danny can go today."

"Wait. I want Joneser's crew with you. And tell him to bring Slicker and Matches this time. I don't care how many pieces. I don't care how far you have to spread her around. The FBI never finds her. Understand?"

"Me and Danny can do it ourselves."

"Goddammit." Gardener turned on him, "What'd I say? Do it like I said, and do it tomorrow."

Henry inhaled. He'd reset the clock. With Wendy Oaks gone, they didn't have to worry about being discovered on Saturday. Lily only needed an hour to send the SOS. They had the luxury of time. He looked at Gardener and Mr. Hermann, imagining them in handcuffs, or better yet, dead for resisting. Oaks, Gardener, and Hermann. They were going to pay for killing his mother. And Bear. Puddie and Mojo. And Elaine. For the first time since coming to the Farm, Henry felt the tight strappings over his chest release their grip.

Gardener closed his eyes, flapping his thumb and index finger against his blue jeans.

Mr. Hermann said it softly, but Henry heard it.

"Are we evacuating?"

Gardener walked along the row of empty beds. He scrambled up to the top bunk and sat, swinging his legs back and forth. "Of course not. We're not going anywhere. We circle the wagons. Bring everyone in.

Everyone in from the camps. Everyone outside the gates—bring 'em in. And I want their families. Kids too. The kids are important. Got it?"

"What do I tell them?"

"Tell them, 'the wolf is in the wire.'" Gardener wiggled off the bunk and hopped back on the floor. "Tell them the fight has come to us."

"You believe that?"

"Just tell them. I want 'em on edge."

Mr. Gardener pulled a thumb drive from his pocket and plugged it into the USB port of Henry's computer. It was obvious what he was doing—making a copy of the bogus program. "When this is done loading, I want it all shut down. Rip the goddamn satellites off the roof. Dump the computers outside the barn. Anything she's touched, anything she's worked on—I want it powered off and disposed of."

"What do I do about the—"

"Get everyone out of the building." He looked at Henry. "That means you. Get out of here."

Henry limped across the room, watching as Mr. Hermann ripped the cord of Lily's computer out of the wall. The green and red lights under her desk went dark. And the beautiful feeling that had blossomed inside Henry just moments before, died on the vine. His actions had killed their hope of getting out alive. There would be no SOS. No rescue.

Too clever by half.

• • •

Henry sat cross-legged on the grass watching as the Farm's open acreage cluttered with men in pickups unloading gear. A caravan of worn and faded RVs drove out of the woods to park in formation on the grass. The small army included children helping their mothers and fathers pound tent stakes into the ground.

Couyon was on the lawn, standing guard. He looked nervous, his eyes darting from Lily to the gaping hole near the cornfield and back to Lily. He closed his eyes. Whatever he was working out, he'd come to a decision. The big man ran his fingers down the chain on his neck. He pulled a silver medallion out of his shirt collar. He rubbed it with his thumb and forefinger. Couyon lifted it off his neck and poured the chain into his fist.

"Lily?" he whispered, bending next to her.

"Yeah, Couyon."

"I want you to have this," he said, extending his big hand. "It's for protection. It works. I promise."

Lily glanced at Henry before smiling at Couyon. "That's yours. I can't take it, but thank you."

He stole a glance toward the cornfield. "I want you to have it."

"Are you sure?"

"Yes. Please put it on, Lily."

"Well, thank you. I'll wear it right now. That's very sweet, Couyon."

He gave her a smile that bubbled over with relief, then walked back to the other guards.

The first of the rooftop satellites was unbolted from the roof. Henry watched it fall to the ground, snapping in half in the same place where Jammer had landed. Minutes later the second crashed to earth. Men, women, and teenagers were making trips in and out of the coal-colored building carrying computer monitors and servers, piling them on the dirt next to the barn. The tractor was working in the cemetery, digging up bones. Nearby, men with bandanas over their faces carried logs and sticks into a pile, pouring accelerant over them. Henry knew what was happening. Gardener was pulling out the evidentiary roots. The remains of Elaine, Bear, and the others were to be set ablaze.

A line of black trucks was pulling up to the open barn. A guy they called Sarge ran urgently from vehicle to vehicle, shouting to his men, pointing at which crates they should take out of the barn.

Henry didn't want to see any of it. He looked down at a patch of green grass. He pulled a single blade, running his smooth finger over its rough skin. He brushed his hand back and forth, sweeping the warm summer grass. He shut out the noise and the activity. Lily placed her palm over his hand, stopping it. She gave it a gentle squeeze.

In late afternoon, when they were readmitted into the coal-colored building, Lily helped the others bring their mattresses back up to the sleep room. Henry didn't sleep that night. He doubted the others did either. In the morning, one by one, he watched them sift out of the room and down the stairs.

The walking dead.

Henry chose to stay in bed, lying on his mattress all morning. Awake. Eyes open.

Bear was here.

He got out of bed and limped to the other side of the room, return-ing with a black ballpoint pen to carve his own epitaph into the soft wood above.

Henry was here too.

Lily stuck her head in the doorway.

"Something's happened. You gotta see."

Henry grabbed for his cane and followed her to the narrow door at the end of the hall and up the ladder into the crow's nest. The Farm looked like a small town. More RVs. More trucks. More people. In the distance, white smoke rose from the still-hot embers of yesterday's bonfire. He followed Lily's eyes to a parade of black trucks, four of them, creeping across the field. People half-jogged from the outskirts of the encampment toward the trucks, learning what was happening from others as they approached. Women wiped tears from their eyes and held their children close. The fit young men and the old beer-bel-lied men stood together at attention, saluting the bodies in the back of the pickup.

"Oh no," Lily said, instinctively reaching for the protection medal-lion around her neck.

Henry recognized one of the two men in the back of the hearse-truck. It was Couyon, his heavy, blood-soaked corpse being rolled across the Farm.

Gardener was standing at the top of the hill in a leather vest and white shirt, a bible in his left hand, saluting the procession with his right. Behind him, the American flag was flying at half-mast. The assemblage looked up every now and again at the man at the top of the hill. Mr. Hermann got out of the backseat of the last vehicle and walked up the path. They spoke together. Gardener reached into his pocket and pulled out his phone. The call lasted ten minutes, and when it ended, Henry was almost sure he saw the man raise his head and grin toward the crow's nest.

The funeral ceremony that afternoon took place without chairs. Everyone listened to Mr. Gardener as he stood on a steel tool box, eulogizing his fallen soldiers. Neither Henry nor Lily could hear what he was saying, but whatever it was, he was working hard to pull on their every heartstring. His hands were opening and closing, punctuating the air with the grace of a southern preacher. He cried with them. Sang with them. Finally, Gardener pointed at the flag at the top of the hill, then stood in silence, bowing his head for a few minutes. He ended his remarks with his fist pounding into his palm, then sweeping his arm across everyone in attendance. They left the service with grim faces, walking across the grass back to their tents and RVs.

Lily and Henry stayed in the crow's nest. They watched the sun set below the tree line, holding hands as the sky burned red and orange, then faded to purple. Stars blinked on in the night sky, and campfires crackled below—more than a half dozen, burning inside stone circles, men and women sitting around them on camp chairs, their somber faces glowing in the firelight.

"How long do we have?" Henry asked.

Lily inhaled and looked up at the stars. "Which one is Polaris?"

He pointed.

She put her head on his shoulder. "It was a good idea, Henry. It really was."

35

It was nearly noon the next day when Henry limped across the painted boundary line, past campers cooking over Coleman stoves, past the eyes of staring children, and past the trucks where rifles leaned against the quarter panel. Mr. Hermann walked behind while Henry made his way up the dirt path to the Main House. When he got there, Mr. Gardener was on the covered porch in front of a grill. Over his blue button-down shirt he wore an apron—*Kitchen Bitch*.

"How do you like your steak, Henry?"

"What?"

"So you know, I refuse to cook it past medium-rare. Any more and it's un-American. How you want it?"

Henry shrugged.

"I prefer rare plus. Sometimes, Pittsburgh-style. You ever had it that way? No?"

Gardener lifted the lid of the grill, ducking his head away from the white billowing smoke. There were two tomahawk ribeyes on the sizzling grates. Mr. Hermann, wearing a black armband across his bicep, walked to the end of the porch and trained a thousand-yard stare on a rose bush below him.

Gardener snapped the metal tongs twice, like jaws, before pulling the meat off the grill and onto a white platter. He brushed his hands across his chest, then untied his apron and draped it across the porch railing. With two hands, he brought the platter up to his nose and inhaled.

"Mmm-mm. Son, anyone ever teach you about steak? The secret is to keep it simple. Don't listen to all those backyard-show-off-chefs on the TV. They make a mess of it with their seasoned salt, A1, garlic—rubbing their meat with this or that. Steak is perfect. God made it on the eighth day—and saw that it was good. Just salt and pepper. That's all. And this piece here?" he pointed the metal tong at a square section of yellow fat. "This is the land scallop—to be eaten and savored." Gardener's smile faded. "You look pale. Are you well, Henry?"

He nodded.

"Protein'll do you some good. Come into the house where we can talk in private," Gardener said, lifting the platter. "Get the door, son? Thank you. The other secret is patience. Rest it for ten minutes so the blood-juice can settle and not run out all over your good plates."

Henry followed him, thinking of Mr. Rose's blood-juice spilling across the dining table.

"Sit. Make yourself comfortable."

He did as he was told. Gardener pulled out a chair and leaned close.

"You have any idea what's going on?"

"No."

"You saw the funeral service? Mr. Hermann ran into some difficulty. We lost two men—the Farm is mourning their loss. Mr. Hermann especially."

Gardener got up and walked to the white platter, forking the steaks onto blue dinner plates. He opened the cutlery drawer and pulled two steak knives. Gardener looked at Henry, then returned a knife back to the drawer and cut one of the steaks into cubes.

"I'm fascinated by irony," he said, bringing the plates to the table. "Here you go." Gardener cut a large square off his ribeye and popped it into his mouth. "Don't just look at it. Eat," he said, pointing at Henry's steak with his knife.

He waited for Henry to lift his fork.

"Good, right? Anyway. I was talking about irony. The shark, the one Mr. Hermann and his men visited yesterday. Well, she was the one that insisted you were worth keeping alive—because of your genius. I wasn't interested in making an exception out of you. But the shark was persistent. Do you know who the shark was, son? You must be curious. This is going to blow your mind. It was your professor. Dr. Wendy Oaks. Surprised? Of course you are."

Gardener took another bite and stared at Henry while he chewed.

"So, the irony is that you—the person she saved from death—ended up being the one that discovered she was an FBI informant, which led to her demise. I mean, that's crazy, right?"

Henry nodded.

"You're wondering what happened," Gardener said, holding a finger in the air while he finished his chew. "Someone was at the professor's cabin when they got there. A woman. If Mr. Hermann had run the plates on the car and realized it was rented to an FBI agent, he might have approached the situation with more caution—"

"I'm sorry. What?"

"Exactly. We caught the professor in flagrante delicto with an agent of the Federal Bureau of Investigation. Yes. I see it in your eyes. You're as shocked as I was."

"What? What happened?"

"Nothing went to plan. The agent killed two of ours. Praise god, we did manage to kill the professor, but the agent escaped. You know what this means, Henry?"

It meant the FBI was on the case. It meant that there was hope.

"It means that not only does your program work, it's fucking verified. The story is all over the news. My colleagues? Well, they're not dismissing us now, are they? You can't imagine the phone calls I'm getting."

"What about the FBI?"

"Now you're thinking like a chess player. Good. The heat is on. Too hot for you to continue working on the Farm. I'm auctioning you and the software off to the highest bidder. I've sent all of them a copy of your program so they can do their due diligence. But I'm not giving them long. The secret to a successful bid process is fairness and speed. We can't give them too much time—can't let their competitive flames wane. A quick deadline makes for a hot market. And, to ensure fairness, I've closed the auction site. I will entertain no conversations or questions until it opens."

Henry put his fork down. "How long did you give them?"

"You're not eating your meal."

"When?"

"Tomorrow. One o'clock. I can't say how long the bidding's going to last. But it's a fair bet that your father's debt will be repaid in full. And if it's not, I'll forgive the difference. The bitch of it is, I was looking forward to hanging out with you, but what can we do?"

"What about Lily and the others?"

"I made mention of them. It looks like none of them are interested in the team. Just you. You're the star, Henry. The primo uomo." Gardener smiled and pointed his fork toward Henry's plate. "Now, I've made something special for dessert, so eat up."

Henry walked into the kitchen in the coal-colored building with a plate wrapped in foil. "Help yourself," he said, putting the plate on the counter.

Lily tugged at his bicep. "What happened?"

He told her.

"Wait. The FBI was *really* there?"

"That's who killed Couyon and the other guy."

Lily covered her mouth with her palm, trying to work out the coincidence. "You think they know we're here? They're coming?"

"They'll be too late. Gardener downloaded my bogus program and sent it out for auction. When it starts tomorrow afternoon, he's going to find out it's a shipping and receiving manifest. He'll go apeshit. There'll be no mercy. Not to me. Not to any of us."

"Tomorrow afternoon?"

"At one o'clock tomorrow, he's coming to kill us."

BOOK THREE

36

Emma Noble stared at Gunny, her head spinning—Sam Noble *wanted* her to arrest him. To put him away for life. He'd framed himself for two murders in the hope that Emma would follow the evidence back to his crime against her mother. Instead of searching for his kidnapped son, Sam Noble, a combat veteran who'd never backed down from a fight in his life, had broken. Wilted.

Gunny reached for his water glass. He spoke softly. "Henry Orr is the only person who knows what happened in that Airstream. The only person who can clear your father's name. Sam is broken. His son can put him back together."

Emma shook her head. "It's been how many days? Nine? Nine days, since he was taken, Gunny. Nine days of me chasing my tail. Nine days on Sam Noble's scavenger hunt. Goddammit!"

"I know," he sighed.

Emma stared at him.

"We weren't sitting on our hands, Squirt."

"Okay. Where is he?"

Gunny looked away.

The server approached the table cautiously. "Your guest is here Mr. Barnett."

Gunny nodded. "Fine."

The server in the white coat lifted a dining chair from a dark corner and placed it at their table. He silently set another place with glasses and silverware, preparing the table for another guest.

Emma stared. "More surprises? Now what?"

Gunny shifted in his seat, propping his elbow against the top of the chair and looking toward the restaurant's front entrance.

"Who—"

Emma's question was answered when Roshelle Hess walked around the corner. Gunny stood and pulled the chair out for her.

"I got it," Roshelle said.

"Hess?"

"He called me. Told me everything. I got on the first plane out."

Gunny grabbed the champagne bottle and tilted it over Roshelle's fluted glass. She covered the stemware with her palm, refusing the offer.

"I'm here to help. Where are we?"

"I'm glad you're here—and, to answer your question, apparently, we're nowhere."

"I wouldn't say nowhere," Gunny said, pulling a thick envelope from the inside pocket of his suit coat. He pulled three photographs and laid them on the table. "Sam took these after he put Lindy and Henry Orr in the Airstream. He went back to Windsor Hills to surveil Ted Mortinson—to find out what he could." Gunny turned the photographs toward Emma. "At that time, we thought Lindy Orr was exaggerating the danger."

"Hmm."

"I know, Squirt. It looked like a domestic situation. Had we known …" his voice trailed off.

Emma looked at the first photograph. It was a wide shot of the Mortinson estate. A white utility van was parked in the driveway. Ted Mortinson was at the front door, speaking to a tall guy in blue coveralls on the stoop. The second image was the same, but enhanced. It focused on Mortinson and the man he was speaking to. The last was a blown up, grainy photo of only the man in blue coveralls.

"According to Sam, the two of them spoke on the stoop for about five minutes. Mortinson seemed nervous. Then they went into the house. I ran the plates on the van for your father. They were expired. Not registered to that vehicle. It raised suspicion, but not alarms. Sam had been watching the house for a few nights. By then, he knew Mortinson's bedtime routine: porch lights flicked on at 9 p.m., master bedroom light extinguished soon after, then he'd see the television light flickering behind the shade."

Emma nodded.

"Sam watched the house for a while, then when out to get some grub. He came back around 10 p.m. The van was gone. No porch lights. No television flicker. Your father walked around the house and saw Mortinson's car was still in the garage."

Gunny took a sip of water.

"He watched the house for another couple hours. Sam and I spoke. I told him not to go in. Of course, he did the opposite. He found Ted Mortinson in the study, dead. That's when we both understood the danger that Lindy Orr and her son were in. Sam hightailed it back to the campground. By the time he got there, Henry was gone and Lindy Orr's body was cold."

Emma stared at the picture, then looked up at Uncle Gunny. "You think this guy killed Lindy and took Henry?"

He shook his head. "The timeline doesn't fit."

"Two killers?" asked Roshelle.

"Looks like it."

Emma took the enlarged photograph of the man in coveralls off the white linen tablecloth and studied it. "Did you find out who he is?"

"Yeah. His name is Everett Hermann. Ex-Army infantry. Big dude. Dishonorably discharged. Should have been sent to prison for torturing Afghani civilians near Chahar Dehi but managed to skirt it somehow. He grew up in the upper Midwest. My security team thinks he still has ties to there, but that's as far as we got with him. He's been flying under the radar for the past few years."

Emma frowned. "That's it?"

"Like I said, under the radar a long time."

She frowned and passed the photographs to Roshelle. "Nine days? And this is it?"

"We can see if the Bureau has anything on him," Roshelle said with an encouraging shoulder shrug. "Maybe—"

Gunny leaned forward. "That's all we had *until yesterday*, anyway."

"What do you mean?" said Emma.

"We were at a dead end until your firefight at the professor's cabin. How'd you know to look into her?"

"I wasn't looking. Believe me. I just happened into it."

"Noble is a shit magnet," said Roshelle.

Emma smirked, "Right?"

Gunny laid his palms on the table. "Nah, it's not magnetism. They both have it. Sam and Squirt. It's instinct. A sixth sense. Whatever you want to call it. That's what led you to Wendy Oaks's cabin. Brought you to the right place at the right time."

"And almost got me killed."

"What did you know about her before you went out there?" he asked.

"Did a quick background check. No priors. Computer professor. That's it. Nothing to see. Why? What'd you learn?"

"Well, while you were drinking your breakfast, we did a deep dive on Wendy Oaks."

Roshelle and Emma looked at each other.

"And?" they asked in unison.

"Oaks is her married name. It was a brief union. She got married and divorced in grad school but kept his name. Her given name is Gwendolin Masterson. Grew up in Michigan. Homeschooled. Her father was Colonel James Masterson, deceased."

"Should we know him?" Emma asked.

"Colonel Masterson was former Air Force. Over time, he got disenchanted with the direction our country was headed. This is back in the eighties. He assembled his own little army of antisocial, anti-government dipshits that wanted to freeze their asses off in the Michigan woods. They called themselves the Michigan Liberty Rangers. Gwendolin Masterson, aka Wendy Oaks, grew up there."

Emma nodded. "When I met her she didn't seem to have a very high opinion of the FBI or the government."

Uncle Gunny pulled another photograph out of the envelope and laid it in front of Emma. "This is the colonel."

"He looks like hell. When was this taken?"

"We think a few months before he died. Cancer."

"And who is this? Who's the guy next to him?"

"We're pretty sure this is Christian Gardener."

"Wait. Gardener?" Emma looked at the picture. "His last name is Gardener?"

"Does that mean something to you?" asked Roshelle.

"I dragged Wendy Oaks up the stairs after she was shot. She was bleeding out and said, 'Gardener, that motherfucker.'"

They sat silently while the server made his way behind each of them, filling up water glasses.

"In addition to our award-winning selection of dry-aged steaks, we have a seared sea bass with artichoke and a butternut squash puree—"

Gunny shook his head. "Ask the chef to bag it for us. We'll take it to go."

"As you wish, Mr. Barnett," he said, giving Gunny a quick bow and making a retreat from the table.

Emma inhaled, "Okay. From the beginning. The FBI suspects Ted Mortinson for money laundering. He pisses somebody off. And gets executed by—what's the guy in the coveralls' name again?"

"Everett Hermann."

"Right. Hermann—who might have ties to this Liberty Ranger group in Michigan. But they don't stop with Mortinson. They kill his wife, Lindy. And kidnap his stepson, Henry, who is supposedly a talented computer science major at Indiana State. And then we have Colonel Masterson—Wendy Oaks's father—the leader of the Michigan Liberty Rangers. Which leads us to this guy." Emma pointed at the photograph. "Christian Gardener, an associate of Masterson and the very person Wendy Oaks accused of attacking us. Oh, and Wendy Oaks was Henry Orr's professor, which is why I went to her in the first place. Did I miss anything?"

Gunny shook his head.

"Gardener is the key. We find this guy," she tapped on the photograph, "we find Henry Orr."

Gunny left to fetch the Town Car. Emma rubbed her forehead and looked over at Roshelle.

"How you holding up?"

"You got the story on what my father did?"

Roshelle nodded.

"How fucked up is that?"

"Very." Roshelle sighed. "And, then again, it isn't. He swallowed a lot of shame, Emma. It's poison. The system doesn't digest it, you know?"

Emma shrugged.

"What's the deal with him," Roshelle asked, flicking a thumb toward Gunny standing outside the restaurant window.

"What'd you mean?"

"Poor guy got himself right in the middle of this thing with you and your dad."

"Not a poor guy. He picked his side a long time ago."

Gunny inserted his gold hotel key into the silver panel of the MGM Grand's private elevator and pressed the red button. Roshelle saw they were headed for the penthouse and raised her eyebrows at Emma.

"Gunny's got more money than sense."

"I'm right here, Squirt. I can hear you."

He held the elevator door open for the agents, then walked down the hall toward the mahogany entrance at the end. Instead of inserting his key, he knocked.

"My analysts have a tendency to get jumpy if I burst in," he said.

Four of Gunny's people populated the penthouse, all staring at laptop computers: two on the powder blue couch, one on the white sofa by the window, and another on her belly, working on the vanilla-colored wool carpet. Gunny made quick introductions, then got down to business.

"Christian Gardener is our man. We need everything we can find on him. Huddle up."

While he conferred with the analysts, Roshelle and Emma walked to the corner of the palatial suite.

"I don't know if I said it earlier, but thanks for coming."

"Believe me, Noble, I've seen some dysfunctional shit in my life, but *your* family? Jesus, Mary, and Joseph."

"No argument here."

They sat together at a high table and Roshelle opened her laptop. "Michigan Liberty Rangers. You ever heard of them?"

Emma shook her head.

"If they're a threat, you'd think the Bureau would have something on them, right?"

"You'd think."

The FBI file was substantial. It dated back to the mid-1990s. The ATF had issued an arrest warrant for Masterson and a few others for firearm violations. Those warrants were never served. From what Emma could see, there had been good police work over the decades. But no arrests. Ever. Roshelle noticed the same thing.

"Why?"

Gunny had the answer. "The colonel had good timing."

"What do you mean?"

"It was before you were born. The US Marshals, ATF, and FBI

learned some pretty hard lessons about serving warrants on armed compounds. They tried it in Idaho at Ruby Ridge. It was bad. What happened the following year outside of Waco, Texas, was a disaster. The ATF tried to serve an arrest warrant against the leaders of a group called the Branch Davidians. They didn't surrender. The siege lasted almost three months, and when it ended, four ATF agents and eighty-two people inside the compound were killed—including two pregnant mothers and twenty-five children. The political and public fallout was massive. Law enforcement got a little squeamish about driving into armed compounds with arrest warrants after that. Nowadays, when those groups think they're in danger, their first play is to bring the women and children close."

"They use kids as human shields?"

Gunny nodded to Hess. "It's effective. Law enforcement stays out, hoping they can get the ringleaders alone. It's a cat-and-mouse game that allows men like Colonel Masterson to die of old age and illness in their homes instead of behind bars."

"The Liberty Rangers. Do we know their current location?" Emma asked.

Gunny rocked his head. "General idea. We don't know how many. Don't know how well-armed."

Roshelle Hess turned to Emma, "The Bureau's Michigan field office is a few blocks away from the hotel. In the morning, while you guys are drilling down on the location, I can try for a search warrant."

Emma shook her head. "And how's that conversation going to go, Hess? They've already arrested the man they think killed Mortinson and Lindy Orr. Sam Noble is their number one suspect for Henry's kidnapping. Even if they believed you, they won't have the stomach to serve a warrant. And if, somehow, you managed to get them to consider it, it'd be weeks or months before they acted on it. Henry doesn't have that kind of time."

"What do you suggest?"

Emma stared at her shoes, then looked over to Uncle Gunny. He nodded.

"What?" asked Roshelle.

"Hess, you should go back to Miami. We got this."

"What are you talking about?"

"Whatever happens, it's going to be without approval. It *will* kill your career. I've asked a lot of you. This is too much. Go home."

"What are you going to do?"

"Don't know yet."

"Well, the two of *you* aren't going to be blasting your way into an armed camp. Right?"

Emma and Gunny looked at each other.

"Noble? Right?"

Emma looked away.

"Because, obviously, that would be suicide. You both know that. Tell me you know that."

"We'll figure out a way," said Gunny.

"Go home, Hess."

Roshelle puffed her cheeks and looked each of them in the eye. She shook her head and paced the suite. Emma touched her on the shoulder.

"When this is behind us, I'll fly down to South Beach. We'll party—drink some rum." Emma smiled.

"Fuck that, Noble."

"You're saying 'no' to rum. That's not like you."

"I'm not leaving."

"Hess—"

"You didn't think twice about *your* career when you helped me at Quantico."

"This is different and you know it. This isn't your fight."

"I'm staying—conversation's over." Roshelle looked at Gunny. "What happens now?"

The former Marine looked at Emma.

"I need to make some calls. Get some sleep. We'll talk in the morning."

"You're going to regret this, Hess."

"Probably," she said, turning her back on Emma. "But I can't let you and Scrooge McDuck have all the fun, can I?"

37

Henry Orr blinked open his eyes. He looked down at Lily's thin arm lying over his chest, her naked body spooning into his back. He thought it was nice to share his last awakening with her. By dusk, he'd be dead. Henry brushed Lily's skin with his fingertips. Gardener would kill her too. And the rest of them. At one o'clock, Gardener would discover that Henry had played him—and that would, no doubt, send him into a killing rage.

He felt her breath in his ear. He closed his eyes, thinking about last night when she'd reached for his hand in the kitchen, led him upstairs, opened the door to the Bounce House, and kissed him down to the mattress. The night had been lustful and tearful—conversational and sentimental—and ultimately, mournful before they fell into sleep. Henry felt her fingers lightly trace the hairs on his chest and down to his nipple.

She kissed his ear. "I'm glad for last night."

"Me too."

"It feels like waking up on the last day of vacation. When you have to go to the airport and leave."

"Vacation?" he whispered.

"Life. The hourglass's magic sand is running out."

Henry didn't know what to say. He held her hand and squeezed.

"I don't think I'm scared of death," she said. "But, I'm scared of dying. Is that silly?"

"No."

"Ever since they executed Bear, I lost hope about getting out alive." She hesitated. "It's not fair. There were things I wanted to do."

"Like what?"

Lily stroked the side of his face, brushing hair off his brow.

"No. Tell me yours."

"I don't know."

Lily propped herself on an elbow and looked at him.

"One thing. What would it be?"

Henry closed his eyes. "It would have been nice to know my father—have had a cup of coffee with him, at least."

"What would you ask him, if you could?"

"I honestly don't know. I think I'd just want to know where I come from."

Henry stared up at the ceiling, then turned his head.

"What about you? What's your one thing?"

"More than anything?"

"Yeah."

Lily didn't speak for a while. A tear dropped out of her eye and fell against his forearm.

"When I was little, I'd sit on my meemaw's thigh and rock with her on our old porch in Eloy, listening to her songs and her stories. She was a big woman. Really big. With the most beautiful gray hair. Her laugh was the best—loud and cackling. Meemaw was the wisest person I ever knew."

Lily sighed and put her hand inside Henry's.

"No one's ever held me like she did. No one's ever made me feel safer. I wanted to be like that—like she was. I've always wanted to sit on a country porch, rocking a little one on my lap. I would've sung to her and combed the knots out of her hair. And when she got scared, I would have held her close and told her it was going to be okay. And she'd have believed me."

Lily lowered her head, resting it against Henry's shoulder. She wiped her eye.

"That's my one thing. To be someone's safest place on earth— where they always knew they were loved. To be the light for a child."

38

Emma walked out of the bedroom. Gunny was staring out the window in the living room of the MGM Grand's penthouse, watching the Detroit sunrise. She'd known Gunny all her life. She remembered him when he was in uniform, just scraping by financially, and she'd witnessed the success of the security company that launched him into the highest tax bracket.

Emma knew he hadn't slept, but it was more than that. Time had screwed Gunny's shoulders closer together, pulling his upper back into a slight hunch. His once T-shirt-stretching iron biceps that she'd swung from as a child had shrunk by half. The crepe skin on his forearms had circles of discoloration that would soon sour into brown age spots. He was still fit. Still strong. But standing there by the window, he no longer seemed the pint-sized steamroller of old. Gunny's armor was showing its rust. It shouldn't have surprised her—he'd turned sixty last year. But it did. Uncle Gunny, and her father, were movie characters—part Eastwood, Willis, and Cruise. But better. They were the real thing. Gunny and Sam Noble were too strong, too cantankerous, and too tough—too big to fail.

Emma thought back to Gunny's words the night before.

Right now, you're better equipped to find Henry than he is. Check that. You're better than he is. And he knows it.

"Mornin'," Emma said.

Gunny turned.

"Get some sleep, Squirt?"

"Not really. Had a couple of things on my mind."

Roshelle Hess came out of the master bedroom buckling her holster strap and looking around the room at the analysts.

"Coffee left?"

"Get it while it's hot, *Princess*."

She looked at Emma. "Tell me he didn't just—"

Emma shrugged, "He dances on the line. Ignore him."

"Well, tell him he dances like shit—and *that* line? We moved it."

Gunny made a sour face, but his eyes twinkled as he rubbed the lobe of his giant ear. Emma took a bite of puffed pastry from the wired basket on the sideboard.

"Where are we?" she said through chews.

"We've been learning what we can about Christian Gardener."

"What's his deal?" asked Roshelle.

Gunny pulled up a recent picture of Gardener. Emma looked closer, comparing it to the other photograph with Colonel Masterson. The former Marine took a sip of coffee before speaking.

"He grew up in Connecticut. His mother came from money—a blue blood. Gardener's father was a successful entrepreneur. He grew up in a rich, liberal family with country club memberships. Christian Gardener gets accepted to Yale. He's expelled his sophomore year for beating the shit out of a fraternity brother. A year later, he was booked on a drug offense in Massachusetts. His daddy got the charges dropped. Sends him back to college—this time, Michigan State. Gardener was in ROTC for a hot minute before being dismissed for a personality disorder. Apparently, the man has a very bad temper."

Emma nodded. "So, we can assume he met Masterson around that time."

"We found a former Liberty Ranger. Now lives in Central Illinois. He left with his wife and kids less than a year ago."

"You got someone to speak to you?" said Roshelle with raised eyebrows.

"Sure. Why not? I have a pleasing way about me. People delight in telling me their stories and secrets. It's all about charm, Princ—"

"How much did it cost?" asked Emma.

"A two-bedroom in Peoria."

Roshelle shook her head. "Was it worth it?"

"Yup."

Emma nodded. "What's his story?"

"Our guy, his wife, and their two kids roughed it out in a pop-up trailer in the woods, damn near freezing to death in winter while Gardener lived at the top of the hill in a fine old house. The Rangers are a diverse group: military pensioners, the unemployed, the disenchanted. The one thing they have in common? The rules don't apply to them. They have their own laws—their own code. And they don't appreciate the government or anyone else telling them what to do."

"Sounds charming," said Roshelle.

"Apparently not. Their membership has fallen considerably since Masterson's death."

"Why?" asked Emma.

"Masterson was charasmatic and committed. He was respected by the community. Masterson chose Gardener as his number two. The guy dies. Gardener takes over. Everything's fine for a while, but it's not too long before people start seeing through him: his greed, his unnecessary cruelty. A lot of the old guard, the ones that had the means, left the Rangers. The people that stayed either had nowhere else to go, or believed Gardener's bullshit about making them rich."

Roshelle nodded. "Okay."

"But they're not anemic. Thanks to Gardener, the Michigan Liberty Rangers now attract ex-cons and bad actors. The guy I talked to didn't trust Gardener. Said he's only in it for the power. He's paranoid and often goes off half-cocked. He's dangerous. Nobody tangles with him."

Roshelle looked at the picture.

Gunny took another sip of his coffee. "He's got a security team to keep the discipline. Everett Hermann and his men are behind Gardener every step of the way, and they're ruthless."

"How are they funded?"

"Not surprisingly, Gardener's parents disinherited him. But he'll try anything to make a buck—thinks of himself as an entrepreneur like his father. Since Masterson's death, the Liberty Rangers have dabbled in a lot of illegal shit, and most of it has failed—our guy thinks Gardener has financial problems and is getting desperate. He'll lose more followers if he can't produce."

Emma walked over to the window. "But none of this explains why he took Henry Orr. He hasn't asked for ransom. Why? Why take *him*?"

Gunny nodded. "Neither Sam nor I could figure out why anyone would want to kidnap him. Now it's more clear. Our new Peoria homeowner told me that, before he left, he was working on a crew constructing a new building. He *thought* Gardener's plan was to move them out of their tents and RVs. He thought he was building a barracks to take 'em out of the cold."

"It wasn't?"

"No. Satellite dishes were installed on the roof. Thick power and computer cables were wired through the walls. That's when he figured out it wasn't a barracks. It was Gardener's new money-making scheme."

Roshelle raised her eyebrows. "Skimming crypto?"

Emma nodded. "The kidnappings. The murders. Now, it makes sense. Gardener's using Henry."

"I assume we know where this place is now?" Roshelle asked.

Gunny nodded, unfolding a map on the dining table.

"Grandpa's old school," Roshelle smirked.

"He's old *everything*," Emma chirped.

Gunny gave her a sour look, then made a circle on the map with a red marker. "They call it 'the Farm.' It's about twenty miles south of Wendy Oaks's cabin."

Emma leaned in.

"He's there, Gunny."

"He's not alone. There are still over a hundred souls on the Farm, not including women and children. And according to the guy we spoke to, most of them are armed. This won't be an easy extraction. And we can't go in with guns blazing—too many kids. Too many families."

Roshelle shook her head. "Noble, we need more agents."

"Nope," Emma disagreed. "We can't wait. The Bureau's a non-starter, Hess. I'm not risking Henry's life waiting weeks or months for the suits and senators to make political calculations."

"I can make the odds a little better," Gunny said.

"How?"

"I've already called a friend—specializes in wet work."

"Mercenaries?" Emma asked.

"He's lending me a team. Fifteen of the best men he has."

"Let me get this straight: you want a 'no guns blazing' approach, and yet you went out and hired mercenaries?" asked Roshelle. "And how does fifteen improve our odds?"

Gunny gave her the stop sign. "They're just a diversionary force. They'll fake an incursion—make lots of noise, blow tons of smoke.

Their job is to draw out the Rangers so we can slip in behind and rescue Henry Orr."

"How soon?"

"Tomorrow. They're assembling out of San Diego. We expect them by noon." Gunny pointed at the map. "We're going to bivouac here. It's three klicks from the Farm. We'll learn what we can while we wait for the California team—fine-tune it when they get here. Best course of action is to wait for tomorrow night. Hit them in the dark while they're sleeping."

Roshelle looked at Emma.

"You think this'll work?"

"It has to."

Gunny poured another coffee. He looked at his watch.

"We're wheels up in an hour. We'll get there first—do some recon before the team comes tomorrow."

Hess tilted her head. "Grandpa's got a private jet?"

"That's in DC," Gunny said, closing the laptop. "We'll take the chopper."

Roshelle shot a look at Emma. "Of course we will."

39

Henry watched a ladybug crawl up his forearm. He and Lily hadn't moved all morning. Her naked body was still snuggled into him.

She put her lips against his earlobe and whispered, "Let's stay here. In bed. It's a good place to die." She kissed his sideburns. "What do you think?"

The ladybug spread its wings and flew off his arm, landing on the fluorescent light above his head.

"Henry? Did you hear what—"

"I need to show you something."

"What?"

"Come on." He got off the mattress and limped out of the bounce house and into the sleep room. "A couple of nights ago I snuck into the barn."

"You did what?"

Henry lifted his mattress.

"You have a *gun*?"

"The barn is full of weapons and high explosives."

"When? When did you do this, Henry?"

"Last week."

"All this time you've—?"

"Yeah."

"What are you going to do with that?"

"I don't know."

Lily stared at the displaced mattress. "I don't like guns."

"I know."

They turned toward the sound of the door slamming downstairs.
"Hey, Henry! You're wanted up at the Main House. You here?"
It was Mr. Hermann running up the stairs.

"Yeah," Henry said, quickly lowering the mattress and pulling Lily down on the bunk with him.

She pulled the blanket up to cover most of her nakedness.

Mr. Hermann poked his head into the sleep room, his eyes widening.
"Oh, shit. Sorry."

"What's going on?" Henry asked.

"Mr. Gardener needs you. Wants you with him for the celebration. We'll have a little beer and bourbon. A little barbecue. You're making us rich today." Mr. Hermann gave Henry an out-of-practice smile. "Meet you downstairs," he said, his head disappearing out of the doorway.

Lily cupped Henry's face with her palms. He took hold of her wrists and lowered them to her lap.

"When I'm gone, take the gun. Get everyone up in the crow's nest. Pull the ladder up behind you. Close the hatch."

"Henry, when Gardener finds out that—"

He interrupted her with a kiss, then stroked her spikey red hair.

"I want to change my answer," he whispered.

"What?"

"My one thing? It would've been you, Lily."

40

An unlit Marlboro Light dangled out of Jean Saucier's mouth as she tugged at the black Hefty trash bag, pulling it down the steps of her RV and onto the grass by the side of her rusted station wagon. It was the last of her grandson's clothes. Couyon had no use for them now. She sat on the bag, taking its breath away, then tied the red drawstrings tight. Her back was crooked, but she stood tall to see who was coming out of the coal-colored building on the other side of the clearing. Jean took out a cigarette, brought her bony knuckles to her mouth, and spun the lighter's steel wheel, watching as the limping man left with Dick Hermann's boy.

On the grass behind the RV, her generator sputtered and died. She sighed and walked away from the bag of Couyon's clothes to check on it. Out of fuel. The old woman lifted the red plastic jug next to it. It was light. She swished the remainder and dumped the gas into the generator. She pulled the handle and it revved to life. It would be dead again soon.

Jean Saucier stepped into the RV and took the keys of her Oldsmobile off the hook. The gas station was ten miles away. In thirty years, that was as far from the Farm as she'd ever gotten. They'd been there since the early days. Her husband, Willy, had served with Colonel Masterson—said he'd follow the man anywhere. And he had. Jean didn't have much say in the matter when her husband picked up and left Louisiana for Michigan. She hadn't seen the point in moving away from their parish and family—and into the cold. But she loved her man and sat in the passenger seat of their new Oldsmobile station wagon as Willy towed their two-tone Prowler north through six states.

The Farm was better back then. During the day, the men played with guns. At night they played guitars on the porch of Masterson's house at the top of the hill. She had friends. They weren't southerners, but they were strong and sturdy women of faith. They were all long gone by now. Some died. Others left after Colonel Masterson passed.

Cancer took Willy. He died on the brown sofa, right there in the Prowler. Their daughter died not long after. Jean Saucier lacked the imagination to go anywhere else, and for ten years it had been just the two of them. Couyon and her. He'd always been a good boy—slow sometimes, but to her mind, a good heart was more preferable than a good brain.

Couyon deserved better.

Jean Saucier creaked open the door to her old station wagon and got behind the wheel. She blinked her milky blue eyes at the coal-colored building and blew a trail of cigarette smoke out her nose. She'd spent a lot of time in that building. No more, she decided. No more yellow tub. No more mop. No more Christian Gardener. No more.

The station wagon rolled forward. She applied the brakes, gripping the steering wheel as her head bent into an urgent coughing spell. They were productive hacks. Jean rolled down the window and spit toward Christian Gardener's house at the top of the hill. The man said he would protect Couyon—said he would look after him.

Gardener was a liar.

And Jean Saucier was alone in the world.

41

Henry limped up the porch steps of the Main House, looking down the hill and across the field at the coal-colored building. They were there. All of them. In the crow's nest. He felt his chest tightening, the air in his lungs locking up.

"Come on, Henry."

He took a last look at Lily in the distance, then turned. Mr. Hermann was holding the door, the palm of his free hand atop the leather sheath of his long knife. There was music playing inside the Main House. It was loud, the bass reverberating down the hall. Henry didn't know the band, but he recognized the song. His mother turned it up every time it came on the oldies station—"The Boys Are Back In Town."

Henry turned the corner. Gardener was on his knees in the living room, playing air guitar with Beto. He dropped his hands, got up, and turned down the volume on the stereo.

"How's the man of the hour?"

Henry looked out the window, wondering if he could see the crow's nest from where he stood. He couldn't.

"Jesus, Henry. Why are you such a sad sack? Lighten up. Can I get you something? Beer?"

"I'm not thirsty."

"Take a good look Mr. Hermann. This is what passes for a college student these days." He smiled and lifted a near-empty whiskey glass to his lips. "In my day, we knew how to party. How about a soda? Maybe, you and Beto can drink together."

"Okay."

"Beto, get Henry a Coke from the kitchen."

Gardener looked at his watch. "Auction opens in a half hour, Henry. Come over here. Sit on the couch with me. Mr. Hermann, help yourself to whatever you want."

"Thanks, Boss."

Gardener leaned back into the couch cushions and swished his glass. He emptied it, sat up, and replenished his glass with three fingers of bourbon.

"You don't drink, Henry?"

"Sometimes. I guess."

"If you drink *sometimes*, why won't you drink with me? You don't like me, Henry?"

"Just not thirsty for alcohol right now."

Gardener glanced at Mr. Hermann. "How about this," he said, pulling a clean whiskey glass off the table and pouring a dash into it. "How about we make a toast to your mother. Here you go."

Henry looked into the bottom of the glass.

"What was her name, Henry?"

"Lindy."

"Okay. Mr. Hermann, you're in on this too," he said, raising his glass. "To Lindy Orr. And to Danny and Couyon, and our friends that have gone before us—too soon. May they walk forever in heavenly light until we are reunited—always loved, never forgotten."

Mr. Hermann blinked hard and opened his throat, draining his glass. Henry took a sip.

Gardener smiled and nodded. He downed the entirety of his drink. He wiped his mouth with his forearm. "Okay, that's it for me—need my wits about me for the auction." He looked at his watch. "Twenty minutes. That's when everything changes for us, Henry."

Henry nodded and accepted the Coke from Beto. He popped the top and swished the whiskey out of his mouth.

• • •

Emma Noble's first ride in a helicopter had been the previous year, in an Army Blackhawk, riding with a special forces team to find the man responsible for what was nearly the most devastating terrorist attack in the country's history. Gunny's Bell 500 with the cream-colored interior was more comfortable. From the passenger seat, he pulled the microphone close.

"This is our pilot, Mike Folger. Former Special Forces."

Roshelle and Emma shook hands with the man up front. The pilot consulted a laminated checklist—flipping switches and pressing buttons. Emma looked at Roshelle. She was fidgety, tightening her seat belt straps—her head on a swivel, looking from window to window. The blades rotated slowly, making one complete turn, then another. The thwacks of the blades were like heartbeats, growing faster and faster until they became a whir of sound and wind.

Emma raised the microphone to her lips.

"We got an in-flight movie, Gunny?"

"Sorry, Squirt. But I'll see that you get a juice box and some fruit roll-ups when we land."

"You remember, huh?" Emma chuckled.

Gunny turned. "Yeah, Squirt. I do."

It was fleeting, but she saw it. Uncle Gunny finally smiled.

The Bell 500 wobbled off the ground, rising above the nearby hangars. The nose lowered and the chopper accelerated away from the Detroit skyline. Emma looked down at the snaking asphalt highways. It wasn't long before the interstates gave way to narrower roads that vanished in and out of the cover of dense woods. It was a quiet ride, each person wading through their own thoughts. Emma's mind was on Henry Orr, the brother she never knew.

They soared over a clear blue lake as round as a wheel. Cottages littered the waterline. Docks protruded from the banks like broken spokes. A single-masted sailboat tacked against the wind. A Jet Ski gained on it from behind and turned sharply, kissing the boat with spray.

Her brother had been in the Airstream—he'd seen his own mother killed. He had no one left. Which meant, if he was still alive, it would make sense for Emma to step up—and step in. She looked down at the lake and the sailboat and the Jet Ski. What would she say when she met him? How was that going to go?

Hi, Henry. I'm your sister. Your real father couldn't be here. He's in prison for murder because he's a guilt-ridden coward who framed himself for a crime he didn't commit to avoid telling his daughter the truth. You met my mother once—sorry, but seeing you caused her to jump off a roof and kill herself. But don't worry, it had nothing to do with you. By the way, my name's Emma. Nice to meet you, Bro.

The helicopter descended gradually. The pilot hovered over a clearing—a field just off a dirt road. Emma looked down at the swirling wind-circle of brown grass. Two vehicles were waiting nearby: a desert-colored Humvee and a maroon SUV. Emma turned to Roshelle and pointed at the ground.

"Is that...?"

"I told Buck what was happening. He insisted."

"Why didn't you—?"

"I knew you wouldn't like it."

Emma jogged, ducking under the rotating helicopter blades toward the SUV. Steven Buck opened the driver's side door and met her by the hood.

"Morning, Noble," he shouted.

"Buck?"

"I needed to burn some vacation days."

"Why would you—?"

"You need help."

Emma shook her head, "Shinsky won't be pleased."

"No," he yelled back, grinning. "Probably not."

The helicopter noise ceased.

Gunny tucked his helmet under his arm and walked over to the Humvee to shake hands with a muscled man in desert camo.

"Squirt, come over here. Bring Princess and the skinny FNG."

Buck looked at Emma for the translation.

"Fucking New Guy," she said with a shrug. "Gunny, his name is Agent Steven Buck—he's one of the good guys."

"Fine. Welcome to the goat-fuck."

Buck grinned. Gunny and his employee pulled a large, metal box from the back of the Humvee and laid it on the ground.

"What is that?" asked Roshelle.

"State-of-the-art drone. Bluebird. You don't even want to know the price of this baby. She'll do our recon—tell us what we need to know."

"They won't spot it?"

The man in camo took the question. "No. Not at the altitude *she* flies."

"All right. Get her in the air." Gunny looked at his watch. "It's almost thirteen-hundred now. Get the tents up. Sleeping bags are in the backseat of the Humvee. I'll do a weapons walk-thru when we're staked in. Our guests from San Diego won't be here for another 24 hours. Plenty of time."

42

Mr. Hermann refilled his whiskey glass for the second time, chasing it with beer. Gardener got off the couch and pulled a wooden box off the shelf. On his way back to the coffee table, he winced in pretend pain as Beto sliced his leg off with a plastic lightsaber.

"Cigar, Henry?"

"No thanks."

"Everett?"

Mr. Hermann accepted a stubby cigar, punched the bottom, and fired the top, puffing white smoke toward the hallway.

Gardener took his time selecting a stick, his fingers dancing across the brown wrappers. He chose a wide gauged, non-banded cigar from the humidor. He put it under his nose, savoring the smell. Henry watched, expecting to hear another lesson on the art of manliness. But it wasn't coming. This was just for Gardener. A meditative, private ritual. He inspected the cap and the foot before snapping down the cutter's guillotine. Gardener lit a cedar spill as thin as paper and toasted the cigar before inhaling, flaming the foot into a red glow. He laid the phone on the coffee table and leaned back in the cushions. Waiting.

The grandfather clock in the hall chimed once. Gardener sat up, staring at the phone, waiting for fish to jump on his line. Henry's heart thumped.

Mr. Hermann sat down in a chair next to Gardener. Both men stared at the phone.

"Sit down, Henry. You're making me nervous."

"Sorry. I'd like to stand if—"

259

"I don't give a shit. Sit. Stand. Whatever." Gardener said, looking at his watch.

Henry stared at the phone on the table. It was going to ring. And when it did, Henry was going to die. He exhaled and gripped his burled-wood cane. A memory surfaced—a small, unimportant recollection that had no business emerging at a time like this: an afternoon when he'd run out of gas on the highway. And another: a doughy Christmas ornament he'd made in kindergarten. Getting a second-place medal at a swim relay. If this was his life flashing before him, it had been a pretty damn inconsequential one.

The three men waited, staring at the coffee table.

One minute after one: the phone was silent.

Six minutes after one: Gardener laid his cigar in the ashtray.

Eleven minutes after one: Gardener stood.

Fifteen minutes after one: Gardener paced the room, ignoring the plastic lightsaber swats from the pint-sized Jedi.

Twenty minutes after one: "What the fuck is going on?"

"Maybe they thought Pacific Time?" offered Mr. Hermann.

"No. That doesn't make sense. I don't understand. They were interested—all of them."

Mr. Hermann drained the last of his beer. "Be right back. I'm taking a piss."

Gardener walked over to the couch and sat on the edge of the cushion. He picked up the phone. Henry watched Gardener dial, his chest spasming with adrenaline.

"Yeah, it's Christian Gardener, let me speak to Caesar ... hey man, auction's open—waiting on your bid. ... What?... What do you mean? Of course, I'm serious. ... No, it's not a fucking joke. ... You're full of shit, Caesar. ..." Gardener rolled his neck toward Henry. "Wait, say that again?... Your guy says what?... But ... uh, huh. ..." Gardener's eyes were burning through Henry. "Well fuck you too, Caesar."

Christian Gardener balled his fists, then inhaled. He put his palms together like a prayer. He breathed out. With two hands, he laid the phone on the coffee table. "Now Henry, I'm going to kill you," he said, getting off the couch.

Henry put his weight on his good foot, reared back, and swung the burled-wood cane into Gardener's face. His eyes rolled up in his head and a wide gash opened across his forehead. Christian Gardener, his arms by his side, fell headfirst into the hardwood floor. Beto dropped his lightsaber and ran to him. A toilet flushed down the hall.

Henry limped toward the door as fast as he could, his leg dragging behind. He stumbled off the farmer's porch, righted himself, and hobbled toward the path that led to the coal-colored building. His body jerked with unsteady momentum. Henry's mind wasn't working—it was instinct. *Get down the hill. Get to Lily.*

He limped past the yellow tractor. Past the cornfield with the gaping hole. Henry raised his head. Lily was in the crow's nest, her hands covering her mouth.

Henry was halfway down the hill when he heard the first whistle coming from the Main House. In seconds, they became a chorus of sirens from every corner of the Farm. Henry lost control of his lurching pace—his right foot caught against something. He fell hard, his face landing in the dirt. Sand and pebbles caked his lips and chin. He planted his cane in the dirt and heaved himself up, resuming his wild limp down the hill.

Men were running at him across the grass.

In front of him, the door of the coal-colored building opened, and Lily stepped out on the stoop. She was wiping tears off her face with her left hand. In her right, hanging limply at her side, was Henry's gun.

He couldn't breathe, but he was making progress. He was almost at the yellow boundary line when Lily raised the gun. Henry saw her look at the men racing across the field from all directions. Lily and Henry locked eyes. She wilted, shaking her head in apology—dropping the weapon on the grass.

Two men streaking across the field tackled Henry, knocking the wind out of him. They punched him in the face, then lifted him into a standing position. One of them balled his fist and swung into Henry's stomach, doubling him over. Blood leaked out of his mouth. He raised his head.

They had Lily on the ground. They were kicking her.

43

Jean Saucier had completed her errand. She was on the dirt road back to the Farm. She turned the wheel, rounding past the red barn. She slammed her foot on the brake, narrowly missing three men who were running out of the woods. She put the car in park and turned off the engine. Everett Hermann's men were being rough with someone. It took a moment to see that it was the kid with the bad foot. And Couyon's friend—the girl—they were manhandling her too, dragging them both toward her station wagon.

Jean Saucier flinched when their faces bounced off the hood of her rusted-out Oldsmobile. The men were pushing their faces against the engine cover while they zip-tied their hands behind their back. The woman's name was Lily. That was her grandson's friend. Her face was red and wet with tears. Couyon had liked her—said she was "nice."

A man jerked her by the hair, exposing her neck.

And dangling there, swinging in front of Jean Saucier's eyes, was Couyon's silver medallion. And the sight of it—on Lily's neck—the meaning of it took her breath away.

• • •

Emma Noble, Roshelle Hess, Steven Buck, and retired Gunnery Sargent Thomas Barnett huddled around a folding table inside a green tent. They were waiting for the monitor to display video from the drone.

"I thought you said this thing was 'state of the art.'"

Gunny grumbled.

"Sometimes it takes a minute to synch," said the operator. "Before it snagged, I got a clear frame if you want to see it."

Gunny nodded. "Pull it up."

Emma studied the image. She pointed her finger at the screen. "So, that's got to be Gardener's house." Her finger trailed down. "Here. Your guy said it was the newest building, right? That's it. That's where they're holding them."

Buck leaned in. "There's something on the roof."

"Zoom in," ordered Gunny.

"Three people," said Hess.

Emma leaned in. "Any of them Henry?"

Gunny shook his head. "Nope. I see Olive Oyl. Jerry Garcia. And a kid—might be Gilligan."

"We need eyes, Gunny."

He nodded. "I know. Be patient. Bluebird's got this."

• • •

Jean Saucier watched the men yank the couple off the hood of her car. The young man's cane was gone. They had to drag him across the painted line toward the new building. The men propped them up against the gray metal siding and waited on the grass, turning their heads intermittently toward the Main House.

Jean stayed in her car, staring at the silver medallion glinting off the neck of Couyon's friend. He should never have given away his protection medal. It was his treasure. But it was his to give. His sacrifice to make.

She followed the eyes of the men toward the Main House. Christian Gardener was walking down the hill, his fingers in the change pocket of his jeans. Everett Hermann stepped next to him, holding out a towel. Gardener refused it. A river of blood ran down the man's face, branching into angry red streams that poured across his neck. His shirt was streaked and splattered.

There were nearly sixty men on the grass. They parted in the middle for Gardener. He looked at the man and the woman standing against the wall with their hands zip-tied behind their backs. Gardener wiped the blood out of his eye and reached toward the hip of the man beside him—pulling the long knife out of his leather sheath.

263

The old woman looked at the medallion dangling off Lily's neck. *It was his to give away. His sacrifice to make.*

Jean Saucier grabbed her smokes from the cupholder and exited the vehicle. She walked behind her Oldsmobile and opened the back hatch of the station wagon, pulling out the plastic jug she'd filled at the gasoline station ten miles up the road. She walked to the old barn, set the red jug on the dirt, and reached into her pocket for a jangle of keys. The old woman had to push hard to open the door wide enough for her thin body to squeak by. Jean lifted the red jug and stepped inside. She walked the length of the barn, sloshing gasoline over the tops of the wooden crates. When the jug was empty, she set it on the ground, and walked over to the spiral hay bale. The old woman slapped the cigarette box against her thigh and pulled out her last Marlboro Light.

She spun the steel wheel of her lighter and bent her head toward the flame.

Her sacrifice was not for the girl. It was for Couyon.

She inhaled deeply and let the smoke drift out of her nose. Willy would be waiting for her on the other side. Her daughter too. And, of course, sweet Couyon.

Jean Saucier closed her eyes and flicked the cigarette off her index finger.

44

Emma Noble walked out of the green tent, looking in the direction of the Farm. She was close, just three klicks from her brother, but it felt like he was an ocean away. She bent down to get a sports drink out of the Yeti cooler.

The blast rocked her.

She looked up at a fireball rising into the sky. White smoke. Black smoke. It spiraled in a fury.

"What the—"

First Buck, then Hess, then Gunny ran out of the tent, looking at the explosion in the distance.

"Goddammit!" said Gunny, pushing his way back into the tent. "Show me what's happening!"

Time seemed to drag, but it was only a matter of seconds before Bluebird had the video. Emma focused on the screen. The old red barn was gone. In its place was a firestorm. The grass was littered with blast shrapnel—and bodies. The newer building was still standing, but fire was licking up the eaves. Three people ran out of the coal-colored building.

"Focus!" screamed Emma.

The video zoomed on two men, one young, one bearded. A woman ran off the stoop, a step behind. She knelt by someone on the ground and helped her up. Whoever she was aiding had their hands tied behind their back. The men lifted someone off the ground and dragged him toward the building. His hands were tied too.

"That's Henry!"

A few bodies on the grass began to stir.

"We've got to move!"

• • •

Henry was having trouble with his eyes. They weren't focusing. He knew he was inside the building but his head was on fire. Lily was looking down at him, her hand stroking his head. Henry rolled his neck, trying to blink the fog away. Ivan and Bingo and Francee were barricading the door with anything they could find: desks, chairs, credenzas.

He found Lily's eyes. "What happened?"

"Shhh."

• • •

"What's the play?" Roshelle asked, checking the weapon on her hip and looking at Emma for the answer.

Gunny was waiting for orders too. Emma ran her hand across her forehead, trying to coax out a rapid-fire strategy.

"Show me the roof!"

The flames along the roofline of the coal-colored building were slow to catch. The roof deck was intact.

"We get airborne now," she said, pointing at the pilot. "Drop me and Hess in the tree line, here—or as close as you can get. Put Gunny and Buck on the deck. We're extracting prisoners from the top. Hess and I will work our way toward the building and draw fire away from you. That work, Gunny?"

He nodded, handing out automatic weapons and ammo.

"We've got comms. We'll figure it out on the fly. Everyone extricates off the roof—Henry Orr and the prisoners first, then Hess, Buck, Gunny and me. In that order. We good?"

They nodded.

Emma spun her index finger in the air. "Let's roll!"

• • •

Ivan and Lily dragged Henry against the back wall behind the barricade.

Lily bent down next to him. "How are you, Henry?"

He pointed to his ear and shrugged.

"Listen!" shouted Bingo.

Their heads lifted toward the ceiling.

"What is it?"

Lily jumped up. "Helicopter! Get up, Henry!"

"What?" he asked.

"Helicopter!" she shouted in his ear. She pulled on his arm.

He waved her off. "Go! Get up there. Make sure they see you."

Lily didn't move.

"Please, Lily. Hurry. It's okay. I'm fine here."

The four of them scrambled up the stairs. Henry pinched his eyes and leaned his head against the back wall. His head was fuzzy with white noise. He exhaled, wincing at the pain shooting through his left leg.

• • •

The Bell 500 was crowded with agents and weapons. Folger hovered the chopper over a dry river bed. He pointed down.

"This is as close as I can get you."

Emma gave him the thumbs-up and opened the door, planting her feet on the helicopter's skid rail. She leaned forward. The whirring blades were sweeping the dry riverbed clear of loose sand. Exiting required a five-foot drop and roll. Then she and Roshelle would hoof it through the woods three or four hundred yards to find a firing position to cover the roof extraction.

Emma hopped off the skid. She landed hard then rolled into a crouching stance under the whirring blades. She squinted, holding her forearm against her mouth as the dust swirled around her. She'd bitten her lip on the landing. Emma spit a rope of blood onto the ground.

Gunny's bird rose, and when it was above the trees, the nose dipped and it shot forward toward the coal-colored building at the center of the Farm. Emma brushed hair out of her eyes and turned to see if Roshelle was ready. She wasn't. She was still on the ground, her eyes squeezed tight, rocking back and forth, her hands gingerly holding her ankle.

"Shit. Hess," Emma said, slinging her weapon over her shoulder and rushing to her partner's side. She took a quick glance at the sky. The chopper was almost out of sight.

"It twisted under me. I felt it go. Noble, I'm sor—"

"What can I do for you?"

Roshelle dropped her chin and shook her head in disgust. "Nothing." she slapped her hand on the dirt. "So stupid."

"You sure?"

She nodded, then pulled extra clips from her belt, holding them out for Emma who stuffed them in her cargo pockets.

"Gunny, Hess got injured in the jump," she said, touching the earbud. "She's going to hang here awhile. We'll pick her up on our way out of town."

"Copy that. Hang tough, Princess. Watch your six. Over."

"Roger."

Emma squeezed Roshelle's shoulder.

"Get out of here, Noble."

Emma followed the winding path of the dry riverbed into the woods until it ended in a dense, green thicket. She forced her way through, holding the rifle in two hands and swinging the butt end to clear a path for herself as the branches and stickers cut stripes across her face. She couldn't see the helicopter, but she could hear it—she was getting closer. The thicket thinned into a clearing. Emma moved slowly under the canopy of tall pines, her rifle in ready position, ensuring the encampment she'd come upon was abandoned. She kept a wide berth, moving past the wooden latrine shed and the cold campfire pit and the blue awning tied to a maple tree that was snapping in the breeze. She sprinted toward the tree line.

Small arms fire from the other side of the building pinged against the helicopter's aluminum hull. Emma couldn't get a bead on anyone. The chopper was rocking and wobbling over the roof. Steven Buck was sitting in the doorway, his feet on the skids, reaching out to a person on the roof. Gunny was already on the rooftop deck, helping a woman up. A bullet cracked the windshield. The copter lost its balance and jerked, almost knocking Buck into the air. Despite the bullets and the danger, former special forces pilot Mike Folger lowered the bird toward the deck.

They were in trouble. She needed to draw fire away from them—engage the guns firing from the front of the building. But rushing across the field wasn't promising. Dozens of men, women, and children were in her path. At the moment, they were occupied, triaging the wounded from the barn explosion. But Emma saw the weapons leaning against pickup trucks. It was likely that every RV she'd pass had an arsenal inside. Running across the field would be suicide. The only way was the long way—a time-consuming run through the woods, taking the outside route that would bring her up on their flank. There, she could fire from a protected position. The question was, could she get there in time to help Gunny and Buck. She pressed her comms bud.

"Hang in there, guys. I'm on my way. Over."

"Bad idea, Squirt," Gunny said from his position on the roof deck. "There's a functioning force of twenty on the grass out front. More coming across the field."

"You concentrate on getting those people off the roof. I'm two minutes out."

"Squirt, listen—"

Emma clicked off her comms, inhaled, and focused on the line she would take through the woods. She would cut the corner, popping into the clearing for a few seconds. It was a calculated gamble—they weren't looking for her. Emma sprinted through the trees, cut into open field, and then back into the woods, moving along the outer edge of the clearing. She was too far away to do much good. Emma bolted out of the trees, throwing her back against a blue pickup truck near a cornfield. The barn explosion had decimated the Liberty Rangers; there were more bodies on the ground than men standing to fire at the chopper. Despite the bullets pinging off the hull, Folger held the skids steady against the balcony's wooden rail.

She clicked on her comms. "I'm in position. Looking good, Gunny."

Buck had one hand gripping the chopper door, the other pulling a man off the deck and reeling him in. A shot pinged into the aluminum above Buck's head. Emma whipped around the truck's quarter panel, laying down a burst of gunfire that sent clumps of dirt and grass spraying near the feet of the men firing at the chopper. She ducked back as their return volley blistered around her. Emma looked up. Buck had two prisoners in the bird. Three more to go. The best she could hope for was to keep the attention on her so Gunny and Buck could do their thing. Emma got to a knee and swung her weapon around the corner of the truck, firing twice and falling back. Again, they returned fire. With Roshelle's extra clips, she could play this game for a while.

Emma laid down a strafe of bullets then rocked back to peek at the roof. Steven Buck was a man without fear. He was dangling off the skid rail, pulling the third of Gardener's prisoners off the balcony and into the chopper. It was a woman with spikey red hair, something dangling from her neck.

There were two sounds that caught Emma's attention almost simultaneously. One was a diesel engine firing up. The second was more immediate. Footfalls. Someone running past her. She peeked around the bumper. A tall man in a black T-shirt with a melting skull face was running with something bulky and heavy. A big green tube.

Everett Hermann with an RPG.

Emma lifted her rifle, but was sent ducking around the corner as a barrage of bullets sprayed near her. *Shit!*

She pressed her comms, screaming, "RPG, RPG!" as she sprang from behind cover. She heard the hollow THWOOP of the missile launch—saw flame exit the back of the weapon as she held the trigger down. She blew Everett Hermann away with a burst of killing rounds. He vanished from sight, tumbling into a giant tomb next to the cornfield.

The helicopter jumped higher and jerked hard to the left, trying to dodge the RPG. Steven Buck and the woman didn't have a chance. The quick counter-maneuver flipped them out of the chopper. Buck's chest slammed against the rail of the rooftop balcony.

Emma couldn't see where the red-haired woman landed.

Folger was quick, but the RPG was faster. The missile exploded into the tail. The chopper immediately began to spin out of control, zipping over the roof, spewing contrails of black smoke.

"Get out!" Emma yelled into her comms.

"I got it," said Folger. "I got this."

For a split second, she believed him. The chopper stabilized, black smoke pluming from the back section. Then she saw an explosion of fire blasting through the back seats. The chopper spiraled over the coal-colored building in free fall.

"I got this. I got this."

The helicopter was veering from the sky in her direction. Emma had to move fast. She bolted, racing past the melee of men on the grass and running for cover at the side of the coal-colored building. She put her back up against the wall, watching Gunny's Bell 500 spin out of control. Folger's confident voice was in her ear. "I got this. I got this. Igotthis. Igotth—"

Emma blocked her face with her forearm as the chopper skidded headfirst into the field, blasting whirling dirt. She winced at the metallic screech of the helicopter's blades bending and snapping off, whipping away at high speed. The fiery explosion wiped out any hope that Folger or the two prisoners had survived.

With her back pressed against the building, Emma closed her eyes for a moment. She'd lost track of the diesel engine, but now she heard it clearly. It was getting closer. She peered around the corner to see a yellow tractor crashing through the building.

• • •

Henry was on the floor, leaning against the wall in front of the barricade. He couldn't hear the tractor outside, but he could feel the vibrations—something was coming. Henry pressed his palms against the wall, trying to get to his feet. It was too late. The tractor crashed through, buckling the metal wall in front of him like a soda can. The swinging bucket widened the hole, jerking violently from side to side and exploding the barricade behind the door. In the seconds before everything crashed around him, Henry saw Gardener's bloody face behind the wheel, speeding forward like a maniacal sea captain. The storm of debris—metal, wood, drywall—surged toward Henry, drowning him beneath the rubble.

How long he was unconscious, he didn't know. When he came to, he was covered under a pile of ceiling tiles and broken drywall panels. His eyes were crusted over and his mouth and lips were filled with the coppery taste of his own blood. He lay motionless, listening to the tractor idling by him. And then he heard Gardener.

"Where the fuck are you, Henry?" he said in a sing-song voice as he fired bullets indiscriminately around the room. "Don't hide. Come down and take your medicine. Don't make me come up there!"

From under the broken panel of drywall, Henry could see Gardener's foot.

"Okay, Fucker. I'm coming up then!"

Gardener sprayed another burst as he took two steps toward the stairs. His foot was within arm's reach. Henry didn't hesitate. He wrapped his hand around the killer's ankle and yanked with all his might. As Gardener fought for his balance, Henry put weight on his good foot and burst out of the debris, tackling him into the blast litter.

He put all his might behind the punch, pummeling the man in his blood-soaked face. Gardener released his hold on his rifle to block the next punch. Henry hit him again, mashing his nose. He swung again, but Gardener managed to wriggle free, quicker than Henry expected. He slid down a corner of drywall, falling toward the rifle. He had a hold of the stock and, in an instant, his finger was on the trigger, wheeling the muzzle across his body.

Henry saw a silver glint by his thigh—a length of heavy pipe, broken and sharp. He lifted it with both hands, whipped it up over his head, and before the leader of the Liberty Rangers could pull the trigger, Henry Orr drove a stake through Christian Gardener's heart.

• • •

Emma sprinted around the building and leaped into the tractor-sized hole. She stuck the heel of her hand into her eye, wiping out the dry-wall dust. She got to her feet and scanned the debris inside the gray building: pink insulation, broken furniture, shattered wood beams, twisted metal. The first floor was destroyed. Outside, she could hear the moans of the injured. She crouched low and sneaked a look out of the gaping hole. Steady black smoke was drifting across the grass over the men writhing in pain, their families rushing to their side to give first aid. For the moment, the Liberty Rangers seemed to have lost their fighting spirit.

"Hey."

Emma jumped at the sound behind her, instinctively swinging the muzzle of her rifle. She lowered her weapon when she saw the young man on his knees, his Captain America T-shirt streaked with blood and drywall dust. Just feet away lay the corpse of Christian Gardener, a silver pipe lodged in his chest.

"Henry? Henry Orr?"

45

"Yeah. I'm Henry."

Emma nodded with relief.

Outside, the wind picked up, blowing through the tractor-sized hole, sweeping up white dust and bits of pink insulation as it swirled over their heads. Emma took up a kneeling firing position between Henry and the hole in the building, ready to stop anyone from entering. Looking down her sights, she saw that, for the moment, the danger had ebbed. Pickup trucks were beginning to roll across the dry-grass war zone. Most of the men outside had put down their rifles to care for the wounded, gently hoisting them into truck beds. But some still held their guns, their eyes vigilant, scanning the sky for attackers.

"My friends? Are they okay?" asked Henry.

Emma spotted a man and a teenage boy treading carefully toward the building, their weapons up. They resembled each other. A father and a son walking together across the grass, looking nervous. Probably neither wanting to disappoint the other.

"Not another step!" yelled Emma. "I will end anyone that comes in here."

"Who are you?" the man shouted.

"I'm the last thing you're gonna see if you come closer. I'm serious. I don't want to see anyone else hurt."

"You don't belong here."

"Neither did the people Christian Gardener imprisoned. Now, move back. And tell the others—I don't want anyone else hurt. We've all lost people today. It needs to end."

273

The father said something to his son. They turned and walked toward the cracked window of a blue truck and spoke to the men inside.

"My friends?"

Emma turned her head to Henry. "Are you hurt?"

"Please. I want to know about Lily. Is she okay?"

Emma looked back to the men on the grass. There were ten or more looking at the building, but keeping their distance. "Give me one second, Henry," she said, pressing her comms bud. "I've got Henry. But we're not getting out anytime soon. What's our status?"

Gunny answered. "Folger and the two hostages didn't make it."

"How's Buck?"

"Ribs took the brunt of the fall. Definitely broken. Possibly a collapsed lung. He's stable."

"Hess? How are you holding up?"

"Okay. I called it in. Cavalry is on their way. Sit tight."

"Copy. Gunny, we need victim status. You got anyone named Lily?"

"Hold." Gunny was talking to someone. "What's your name, son?... I've got Bingo up here with me. ... And ma'am?... Lily. ... Yes, Lily is an affirmative."

"Status on last?"

"She fell out of the chopper with Buck. Popped her shoulder out. She's in pain. No major damage."

"Copy."

Emma turned and looked at Henry, her brother's eyes searching hers.

"Good news about Bingo and Lily. They're on the roof. She's a little worse for wear, but nothing to worry about—"

"Thank God," Henry said, exhaling. He looked at Emma. "Ivan and Francee?"

Emma shook her head. "I'm sorry. They didn't make it."

He lowered his head and nodded.

"Henry, you sure you're not hurt?"

"No, I'm okay."

"You did that?" Emma said, eyeing the pipe protruding from Christian Gardener's chest.

"He had it coming."

Emma looked at him. Even with a face painted with blood and drywall dust, she could see his resemblance to Sam Noble. And to herself.

"Who are you?" he asked.

"Who am I?" Emma couldn't help but grin. "There's a long answer and a short one. For now, all you need to know is that I'm with the FBI. I'm here to keep you safe."

He leaned forward, extending his arm. "Henry Orr."

She shook his hand. "Emma Noble. Pleasure to finally meet you, Henry."

Roshelle Hess was in her ear. "What's going on out there, Noble?"

"Still quiet. They're treating their wounded."

"Where do you think this is headed? Are they regrouping?"

"They lost their leaders—it depends on who steps into the void. Maybe they come in and try to finish us. Maybe they negotiate. Hard to know."

Henry Orr hobbled to a standstill, his left foot bent unnaturally, hovering above the floor.

"You want some help?" asked Emma.

"My cane's outside somewhere. I'd take a shoulder."

Emma took another cautionary glance outside. "Let's get you on the stairs."

"If you give me his rifle, I can help," Henry said, looking at the body of Christian Gardener.

"You know how to use it?"

"Not really. But I'm a quick study."

"I kinda figured you might be," Emma said.

She guided him halfway up the stairs. She retrieved Gardener's rifle, checked it, and handed it over. They sat together. It was a good, defensive position. Emma could see them coming. High ground. She looked to her right, finding it hard to believe that her brother was sitting next to her, Gardener's rifle across his knees.

"What happens now?"

"Not sure. We wait it out and see."

"How'd you find me?"

She inhaled deeply, trying to think of how best to enter the long and complicated story. Emma looked at him, waiting for his eyes to meet his. She decided on the direct approach.

"Henry, I'm your sister."

The standoff continued for hours. The injured were taken away by their compatriots. Gunny and Bingo remained in the crow's nest, helping to tend the wounds of Lily and Steven Buck. Gradually, the smoke cleared and the sun dropped below the Main House on the hill. Darkness creeped over the coal-colored building. And as the hours passed, Emma told Henry about their father. And her mother. And of prison. And of meeting Wendy Oaks.

In telling the story, she found that her anger with Sam Noble had lessened—a little. He was a flawed man. But he was honorable. And dishonorable. Loyal. And disloyal.

"I guess what I'm saying, Henry, is … he's complicated."

46

It was after midnight. Red and blue police lights flickered behind the Main House. The FBI brought an army of agents to bear. The Liberty Rangers had no fight left in them. From the top of the hill, agents pointed powerful lights, illuminating the Farm. From inside the coal-colored building, Emma watched their silhouettes spreading out, shoulder-width apart, walking in lockstep down the hill toward them. Gardener's Rangers had obeyed FBI orders and retreated into their trucks and RVs and had gotten off the Farm. The FBI team halted in front of the building. A bald man in a tactical vest walked through the tractor-sized hole, swinging his flashlight. His beam found Emma and Henry on the stairs.

"Agent Noble?"

Emma shielded her eyes. "Yeah."

"It's Chief Byum. How you holding up?"

"Fine, sir. We've got two injured on the roof."

"We'll get them safe. And you, son? You doing okay?"

Henry nodded.

"Are you ready to get out of here, Henry?"

"Yeah," he smiled. "I'm ready."

"Well, let's get to it then. I saw a cane out there. Yours? Okay, we'll have it for you in a minute."

The extrication of Buck and Lily was time-consuming. Henry and Emma waited at the top of the hill with the ambulance. Gunny and Bingo came up first. Lily was brought up on a stretcher. Henry rushed to her side. Emma witnessed his tenderness—watched his gentle kisses landing against her cheek. Her brother was making a hell of a first impression on her.

They got Roshelle Hess out of the woods and brought her up to the Main House. Last up was Steven Buck. He was in pain, but it didn't stop him from swearing most of the way up the hill, claiming the EMTs were purposefully wheeling the gurney into every misery-filled object they could come across to inflict more pain into his broken ribs.

Emma felt the tension in her shoulders release. She looked around, remembering to be grateful.

But someone had been left unaccounted for.

No one noticed the quiet boy. They didn't see him walk across the smoke-filled field that afternoon. They didn't see him find the gun lying in the grass.

A gun that had never been fired.

The gun that Henry had stolen from the barn.

The gun that had dropped out of Lily's hand.

Beto picked it out of the grass and walked it into the woods, feeling its heft, running his soft thumb across the hard diamond pattern on the handle, sliding his finger in and out of the trigger well. He'd watched everything, sitting in pine needles under the trunk of a wide oak tree. He'd seen Christian drive into the gray building, but never saw him come out. He heard them say he was dead. But that couldn't be true because Beto knew what "dead" meant. It meant that he would never come back. Ever. And that couldn't be true. Because Beto willed it not to be true.

He put the gun on a bed of leaves and pine needles. He stared at it. He knew it was real. And he knew right from wrong. Taking the gun was wrong. Christian told him: never touch one unless he was with him. But Beto already knew about guns. Everyone had guns. And he was a big boy now. Big enough to know whose fault it was. It was the limping man's fault. Henry's fault. He hit Christian with his cane. Hurt him. Made his face so bloody. Henry was a bad person.

Beto watched from the woods. He watched all afternoon, waiting for Christian to glide out of the gray building, resurrected. But, as night fell, doubt creeped into the boy that, maybe, Christian *was* dead. He scooched, unseen, to the edge of the tree line to get a look at the helmeted strangers walking down the hill. He watched them take the people out of the gray building. And he saw them drag Christian out and leave his body on the grass.

He waited until the strangers went back up the hill.

No one noticed the quiet boy walk out of the woods and sit by the corpse of Christian Gardener. No one saw him bring his lips to the dead man's ear, trying to say something that might bring him back. But the silent boy had never uttered even a single word.

Beto didn't have any life-giving words. Christian wasn't coming back. Ever. He rested his cheek against the dead man's chest, smelling the lingering cigar smoke on his shirt. And, for a long while, the silent boy wept for his father. When he was done crying, he kissed Christian's forehead, picked up the gun, and walked up the path, looking for Henry.

The limping man. It was his fault.

• • •

Steven Buck was gone—triaged in the driveway and sent away in an ambulance. Roshelle was speaking to Chief Byum. Lily's arm was in a red sling. She was holding Henry's hand, whispering something to him. Bingo was sitting quietly by their side.

Emma looked over at Gunny. He was smoking a victory cigar, looking pleased with himself. A half hour ago, he told her that when they sprung Sam, he was taking all the Nobles to the Aruba Ritz-Carlton—and no one was leaving until the family sorted out all their shit. Emma turned her attention back to Chief Byum and Roshelle Hess.

She never noticed the small boy walking in the light with tears streaming down his face. Emma heard Gunny's voice. It sounded different.

"Hey buddy? How about you give that to me? Okay?"

Emma turned. Gunny wasn't where he'd been. He'd moved between Henry and a child. A child holding a gun. She shifted her weight and sprung from the balls of her feet. But it happened too fast.

"Why don't you give it to—?"

The silent boy fired.

Gunny's soft heart took Henry's bullet.

Absorbed it all.

Epilogue

There was no breeze to carry the priest's whispered prayer across the stone rows of Arlington Cemetery. Emma looked up, catching a glimmer of dappled sunlight through the leaves of the giant oak that towered over the grave of Gunnery Sergeant Thomas Barnett—a silent sentry to guard and shade his grave. She closed her eyes, lost for a moment in the privacy of her memories of the gruff Marine. Her second father.

Emma was a pallbearer, carrying the polished mahogany casket out of the hearse and across the mowed lawn to his open tomb. She sat next to her brother, waiting to accept the folded American flag from a Marine Corps major general. Emma looked around at the men and women dressed in black. Most of them were strangers, but each grieving face held more than a few Thomas Barnett stories. And those tales of Gunny, told in the presence of whiskey, cigars, and campfires, would keep him alive for a very long time.

Seven Marine honor guards in formal dress marched across the lawn, snapping their rifles in response to the call of a soldier brandishing a saber.

"Ready."

"Aim."

"Fire."

They made their twenty-one gun salute and the bugler played a somber and sorrowful "Taps."

Emma felt Henry's hand slide across her back and squeeze her shoulder. He pulled her in. She gave him a thankful smile and dropped her head to his shoulder. It was a good send-off. Uncle Gunny would have approved.

She stood to shake hands with the priest and some of Gunny's old comrades. She promised she'd join them later at the VFW Hall to raise a glass in his honor. But her mind was not on Irish whiskey, or flags, or twenty-one gun salutes.

"You think he's coming?" Henry asked, after shaking the last stranger's hand.

A black Suburban rolled slowly through the winding cemetery road and parked nearby. FBI agents got out and opened the back door. Sam Noble was dressed in a black suit, his wrists handcuffed under a jacket. The wheels of justice were slow, but they were turning in his favor. But, for now, he remained a prisoner in custody.

"There," she said.

Sam Noble stared at Gunny's headstone under the old oak. He bowed his head. His face was heavy with grief. And shame.

"You want to introduce me?" asked Henry.

"Mind giving us a minute together first?"

"Yeah. Of course."

Emma filled her lungs and raised her chin. She walked away from her brother, closing half the distance to Sam Noble before stopping. Her father looked back at the FBI agents, holding up his wrists in a plea for freedom. They agreed to uncuff him—allowed him to walk to his daughter. The confident swagger in his step was gone. He walked slowly, his head down—avoiding her gaze. His skin was pale. Dark bags hung under his eyes. He hadn't shaved for a week. The man walking to her was not the invincible Sam Noble. In front of her was a man broken open. He stopped a few steps away, staring at the grass around her feet.

"Emmaline," he said haltingly into the ground. "I don't ..." his voice wavered—words weren't coming.

"Did you love her?"

He raised his head and looked at Emma. His lip buckled.

"Did you love her? Did you love mom?"

Sam Noble nodded. The tears rolled off his cheeks.

"What about me?"

"With everything in me. You are *everything* to me, Emmaline."

Emma stared into her father's eyes, unsure of what was supposed to happen now, not completely trusting her feelings. Standing before her was a man she'd never met. A man without secrets. It was all out in the open now, glaring in the Arlington sun. Sam Noble was fallible. But more than that, he was repentent. And, at that moment, Emma Noble realized she believed in second chances. She looked over at Thomas Barnett's headstone.

"He never gave up on you."

Sam followed her eyes to his friend's grave. "I know."

"He wanted us to get our shit sorted. It was the last thing he told me. He wanted us to start again." Emma looked at her father and whispered, "I'm sure mom would want that too."

He nodded.

"So, I guess that's what we'll do. We'll figure this out … in time. But not today. Alright?"

Sam Noble closed the distance to his daughter and touched her hair. Emma reached up and gripped his forearm with two hands. He dropped his head. His shoulders quaked, tears ran off his chin, and fell against her skin.

Emma kissed his head before releasing her hold on him. "Dry your eyes. You need to meet your son. You don't want him thinking his old man's a big pussy, right?"

He let out a sad chuckle, then wiped his face with the back of his big hand.

"Henry's a good kid. You should be proud to have a son like that. Make yourself worthy of him." Emma turned and waved her brother over. "I owe you a breakfast, Dad. I'll call soon."

Emma walked halfway up the sloping hill past rows and rows of white Vermont marble headstones. She looked back to see Henry Orr limp to meet his father. She couldn't hear what they were saying, but it wasn't long before Sam Noble reached out and shook Henry's hand. Her father looked up the hill. Emma nodded, flashing him a quick smile before turning and going on her way.

She pulled out of Arlington National Cemetery and within minutes she was mired in Beltway traffic. She scrolled through her text messages. There was one from Vice President Kimberly Hancock's personal number. Emma recalled Director O'Toole's words after taking her gun and her FBI badge:

282

It may not be with the Bureau, Emma. But from the calls I've been receiving, I don't think you're done serving just yet.

She ignored the text. Whatever the VP had in store for her, it could wait.

Emma looked around at the cars parked with her on the highway. She tilted the rearview mirror to see into the vehicle behind her. A ten-year-old girl was laughing in the passenger seat—bobbing her head, seat-dancing next to her father.

She connected her playlist, and turned up the volume, tapping her fingers against the wheel. She allowed the music to transport her back to the kitchen of her childhood—seeing her shoes shuffling across the linoleum. Her arms like a locomotive, churning with the beat. Inviting Emma to join the dance.

Emma Noble smiled, not bothering to wipe the tears off her cheek. She lifted her eyes toward heaven.

Mamma Mia, here I go again.

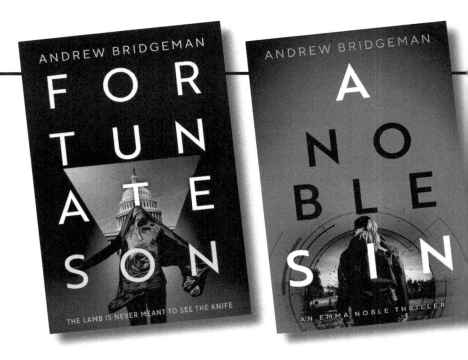

Subscribe to the Briefing newsletter and stay updated on Emma Noble's next adventure, learn about free giveaways, book signings, and other thrilling content.

Join the author on your favorite feeds:
Facebook,   Instagram   and TikTok.

About the Author

Andrew Bridgeman has nearly as many twists in his own story as there are in his novel. A former rugby player, jazz singer, salesman, and entrepreneur, he finds inspiration in the characters he's crashed into along the way. Mr. Bridgeman studied creative writing at Dickinson College and earned his MBA from Washington University in Saint Louis. After decades in the St. Louis area, he now lives in New Hampshire with his wife, Kathy. He enjoys hiking in the mountains near his home, playing guitar, and exploring the US in an Airstream RV. This is Andrew Bridgeman's second novel.

www.ingramcontent.com/pod-product-compliance
Lightning Source LLC
Chambersburg PA
CBHW032339050825
30687CB00005B/186